tworld liked this ♥ @PDLoupee liked this ♥ @MasoodTahir7 liked this ♥ @BarnabyLJones liked this ♥ @mattroweart
♥ @chewieken liked this ♥ @stewartkillala liked this ♥ @LawlessComicCon liked this ♥ @sulamoon liked this ♥
ed this ♥ @notanotheralex liked this ♥ @FriedKeith liked this ♥ @spludnog liked this ♥ @thingstead liked this ♥
ked this ♥ @Plaguing_Possum liked this ♥ @dizculver liked this ♥ @JemHWriter liked this ♥ @reynedd liked this ♥
ed this ♥ @MikeMorocco liked this ♥ @BenMaxBecker liked this ♥ @Chloe_in_pink liked ♥ @ElOzymandias liked
n_Threet liked this ♥ @Jafleece liked this ♥ @AlkinsDavid liked this ♥ @ForcePao @feartheflerkin liked
s liked this ♥ @LanceDanger liked this ♥ @RamonPina liked this ♥ @ranchgho ackBumby liked this
liked this ♥ @danaesspam liked this ♥ @zoe_ena liked this ♥ @tonsofjpun nchronch liked this
this ♥ @PhilipLeith liked this ♥ @Steph_I_Will liked this ♥ @23so us liked this ♥
iked this ♥ @deadlycuttlefish liked this ♥ @ScottySmurf liked this an liked this ♥
klg19 liked this ♥ @Schaefges liked this ♥ @chainmaildoug liked issmadamesatan
asbergara liked this ♥ @MrQwertzuiop liked this ♥ @FavouriteC is ♥ @AsaWheatley
ricSkillman liked this ♥ @xK1 liked this ♥ @gwandwizard liked ♥ @harl37 liked this ♥
exus liked this ♥ @KalelData liked this ♥ @JasonLMichael liked t iked this ♥ @KellyKanayama
you liked this ♥ @ickeybooley liked this ♥ @muhkayoh liked this iked this ♥ @lopAlexander1 liked
avity liked this ♥ @GadgetTheDM liked this ♥ @Merv2069 liked this _squirrel liked this ♥ @asilomarworks
ton liked this ♥ @elemintz liked this ♥ @petermvasey liked this ♥ @ _Robbe liked this ♥ @dewdropgalaxy liked
iked this ♥ @mirkskunk liked this ♥ @bansheeriot liked this ♥ @LocalHeroesNVA liked this ♥ @fiokumu liked this ♥
is ♥ @ComicsbyGCNO liked this ♥ @oydisl liked this ♥ @fymeikokaji liked this ♥ @hemisphire liked this ♥ @zyblonius
huttle liked this ♥ @cabcomics liked this ♥ @emilioalvs liked this ♥ @varnishcentral liked this ♥ @PCHills3 liked this
this ♥ @The_Horns liked this ♥ @sobottke liked this ♥ @melanieislazy liked this ♥ @DerekSchumacher liked this ♥
♥ @davrains liked this ♥ @NickCefre liked this ♥ @cockaignego liked this ♥ @BuddyOrDie liked this ♥ @thattitanguy
@PatientPyramid liked this ♥ @MarkJEngleson liked this ♥ @shakespia liked this ♥ @GeneralSPAM liked this ♥
ed this ♥ @MarkTroy61 liked this ♥ @AStefanMelnyk liked this ♥ @twunny20fission liked this ♥ @Its_Me_J_Me liked
lBeckerton liked this ♥ @GiantTomHanks liked this ♥ @UndisputedBicon liked this ♥ @friday_foster liked this ♥
en liked this ♥ @LovelyLee_G liked this ♥ @E_McDevitt liked this ♥ @shutupdougan liked this ♥ @BunchaHoles liked
Tyler10889 liked this ♥ @LanTweets liked this ♥ @haslann2 liked this ♥ @DwainIBe liked this ♥ @CKelAdams liked
is liked this ♥ @notbbcnews24 liked this ♥ @Seano332 liked this ♥ @chook_leader liked this ♥ @pocketkerrie liked
_online liked this ♥ @ThatAlexD liked this ♥ @cyguy19 liked this ♥ @El_Pachinko liked this ♥ @thedesertpope liked
Lobdell liked this ♥ @mjk4219 liked this ♥ @MaxFosterStudio liked this ♥ @IneedAName01 liked this ♥ @nadiaattlee
ahon liked this ♥ @_jamieb95 liked this ♥ @DancesLikeSnake liked this ♥ @JosieHypatia liked this ♥ @GRohac liked
naandexile liked this ♥ @DnlOly liked this ♥ @pjdonnell liked this ♥ @fine_plan liked this ♥ @mjperljam liked this ♥
is ♥ @MechaBecker liked this ♥ @waddlyhobbins liked this ♥ @theclobberinkid liked this ♥ @cmgwwe liked this ♥
cing2HN liked this ♥ @MooseKnight liked this ♥ @JamesJmz liked this ♥ @cartoon_sara liked this ♥ @UncannyParker
nekron_9_9 liked this ♥ @Moo_Sew liked this ♥ @jeremyhachat liked this ♥ @AdvenChrlz liked this ♥ @darrenvogtart
oltzman4 liked this ♥ @shivaunish liked this ♥ @franzferdinand02 liked this ♥ @mirk47 liked this ♥ @Juese liked this
is ♥ @heymedley liked this ♥ @DuncanEdits liked this ♥ @joshcornillon liked this ♥ @grendelvaldez liked this ♥
this ♥ @phoenixfcrce liked this ♥ @morgue_machine liked this ♥ @pluralharris liked this ♥ @CasinoGrande liked this
♥ @BashAtDemonhead liked this ♥ @tomtomorrow liked this ♥ @briancaffrey liked this ♥ @KCZ946 liked this ♥
liked this ♥ @Andrehabet liked this ♥ @NelsonEggs liked this ♥ @giggleloop liked this ♥ @OneCreatorDan liked this
ked this ♥ @Hypnohustlin liked this ♥ @avishaiw liked this ♥ @NR_Lines liked this ♥ @Bumpkin_Squash liked this ♥
X liked this ♥ @TheAnarCHris liked this ♥ @TateBrombal liked this ♥ @HSCactor liked this ♥ @Jawiin liked this ♥
is ♥ @catratharsis liked this ♥ @RealCosima liked this ♥ @mycomicshop liked this ♥ @jimdemonakos liked this ♥
ed this ♥ @graemem liked this ♥ @colorchangedino liked this ♥ @NotBenReilly liked this ♥ @TheMoreYouNerd liked
d this ♥ @clonie liked this ♥ @sopelana liked this ♥ @DreddStarin liked this ♥ @AndreaDemonakos liked this ♥
ed this ♥ @EscapePodComics liked this ♥ @freshwaterwale liked this ♥ @ridelee liked this ♥ @MVBramley liked this
heGrebo liked this ♥ @PyeParr liked this ♥ @gaxiola liked this ♥ @Stobert liked this ♥ @beckylunatic liked this ♥
beazdesigns liked this ♥ @_Sweetnsour liked this ♥ @BeachHart liked this ♥ @metrokitty liked this ♥ @Jim1810 liked
liked this ♥ @Stephen_C_Ward liked this ♥ @uncientovolando liked this ♥ @hassanchop liked this ♥ @KittehpupRose
xgod liked this ♥ @Game_Brains liked this ♥ @cornwankies liked this ♥ @comixexperience liked this ♥ @forgetfulsurf
Stolz liked this ♥ @krenshar_posts liked this ♥ @green2814 liked this ♥ @AlexVolkman liked this ♥ @breadborks liked
liked this ♥ @JacobTheOracle liked this ♥ @ConArtist liked this ♥ @rustandruin liked this ♥ @DrMRFrancis liked this
napDecks liked this ♥ @Rockin_DRobbins liked this ♥ @MattKeyz liked this ♥ @TDmollusk liked this ♥ @nagito_eevee
♥ @Trungles liked this ♥ @KristyQ01 liked this ♥ @jimmyaquino liked this ♥ @LilGuillxtine liked this ♥ @aufert4 liked
this ♥ @CrushingComics liked this ♥ @Kev_h80 liked this ♥ @AllisonMOToole liked this ♥ @melgillman liked this ♥
ed this ♥ @PrismaTrish liked this ♥ @MrTylerCrook liked this ♥ @paulmanzor liked this ♥ @markclapham liked this ♥
@psdevuk liked this ♥ @TVsMattB liked this ♥ @adlewis liked this ♥ @D_Libris liked this ♥ @DrSkradley liked this ♥
micon liked this ♥ @ActWon1 liked this ♥ @frankee_white liked this ♥ @OldOlethros liked this ♥ @NotoriousCONRAD
omson liked this ♥ @JakeMurphy52 liked this ♥ @Jwil3698Justin liked this ♥ @Blankzilla liked this ♥ @marissadraws
enryBarajas liked this ♥ @contiveros liked this ♥ @happysorceress liked this ♥ @primalmusic liked this ♥ @ten_bandits
1 liked this ♥ @DanWritehead liked this ♥ @justushep liked this ♥ @andriylukin liked this ♥ @DaBalloonAnimal liked
34 liked this ♥ @dogunderwater liked this ♥ @housetoastonish liked this ♥ @abdullah_r7 liked this ♥ @mat_hills liked
this ♥ @Corpsie_Prime liked this ♥ @KatElinor liked this ♥ @surfmonkeyftj liked this ♥ @happytinypill liked this ♥
s liked this ♥ @melp0meno liked this ♥ @CatParrts liked this ♥ CombatCavScout liked this ♥ @lycheeloving liked this
touze liked this ♥ @SpeelmanTom liked this ♥ @butchmapa liked this ♥ @Goatboy72 liked this ♥ @ParchmentScroll
sbeer liked this ♥ @Dave_Richards liked this ♥ @TylerMesservey liked this ♥ @pg15121977 liked this ♥ @markannabel
mics liked this ♥ @ByronMONeal liked this ♥ @adeheathen liked this ♥ @sguglie liked this ♥ @deanhaspiel_art liked
♥ @vasilikaliman liked this ♥ @doomrocket_ liked this ♥ @inkand8bit liked this ♥ @comicsandyoga liked this ♥
ut liked this ♥ @bookswpictures liked this ♥ @trouble_studios liked this ♥ @ericj451 liked this ♥ @alexsegurajr liked
eaavclub liked this ♥ @boxinggloverarrow liked this ♥ @scifiamber liked this ♥ @oliver_sava liked this ♥ @drjandpals
♥ @davidgolbitz liked this ♥ @meta.morfoss liked this ♥ @grant_dearmitt liked this ♥ @smartovercoat liked this ♥
lisledesigns liked this ♥ @fire.art91 liked this ♥ @digital_fr1dge liked this ♥ @mattbuckley80 liked this ♥ @sanddoe
esoteric_by_design liked this ♥ @mattweberphd liked this ♥ @dinmutha liked this ♥ @xykobas3rd liked this ♥
_af liked this ♥ @jonnybcinema liked this ♥ @franceneladue liked this ♥ @precinct12th liked this ♥ @therealsethmo
l liked this ♥ @reunibupo liked this ♥ @fiddledeedoo liked this ♥ @riteabide liked this ♥ @guinelturnfrees liked this
r liked this ♥ @kyven liked this ♥ @mttwclmnt liked this ♥ @benapplegate liked this ♥ @seanewilliams liked this ♥
d this ♥ @suebamboo liked this ♥ @jkparkin liked this ♥ @demonweasel liked this ♥ @icouldntthinkofanewusername
anzwantscoffee liked this ♥ @bloodyentrails liked this ♥ @crhodey liked this ♥ @MrWent liked this ♥ @disappointimism

PARASOCIAL

ALEX DE CAMPI
ERICA HENDERSON

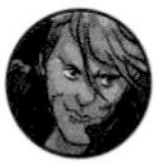

luke.indiana ···

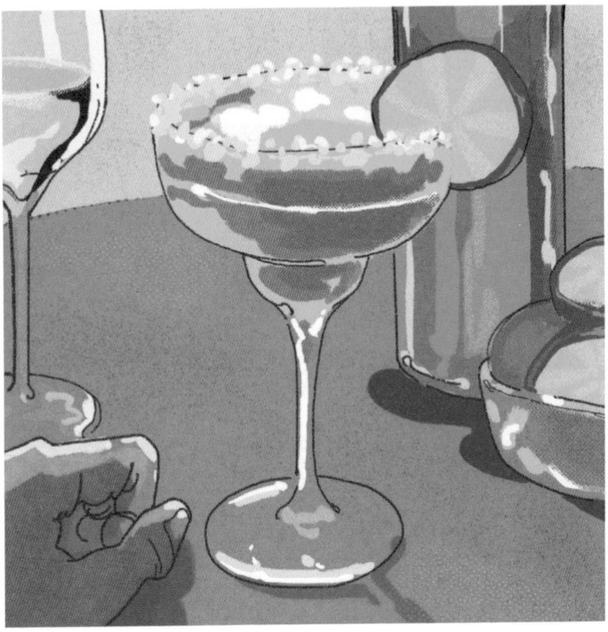

46,691 likes

luke.indiana catching up with @willmaas4real and @ofelia_maas the night before my first convention back!!! Two years. I've missed you, #RogueFamily. See you at Alamo Comicon tomorrow. Mask up!
#RogueNebula #RogueFans #X9

View all 665 comments

@ofelia_maas 🤍🖤

No seriously bb you need to take iron!!! That bruising is not normal

I know. I'm gonna get some this am bc I also gotta refill nana's medicine

I thought you were going to the con?

I AM

I HAVE TOO MUCH TO DO

ok well be safe Lily, cons are petri dishes at the best of times

Does Alamo have a vacc mandate?

lol no

T E X A S 😂

Hi Lily!
Your cool friends donated to the **Afghan Refugee Fund** in your name.
They *also* told me that it's your birthday today.
cameo
I'm *truly sorry* for what happens next.
I *really* can't sing.
cameo
♪♪ *Happy birthday to you--* ♪♪
Dad, who are you singing to?
cameo

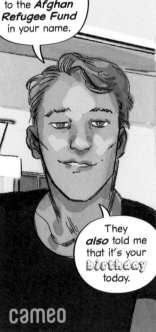

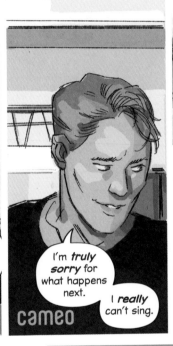

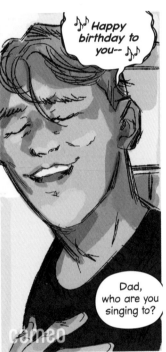

I'm vacc obvs and I'm gonna mask whole time

Except for my photo op

Gonna just drive on by the obvious "Luke can infect me any time" joke

Dank u for ur service Jen

I feel bad leaving nana on her own but holy shit I need a day off

is the K helping?

Ye but we're almost out which is why drugstore run at ass o'clock

UGH FUCK MY BROTHER'S CLASS HAS AN OUTBREAK

guysss I heard a rumor about Luke and Rachel...

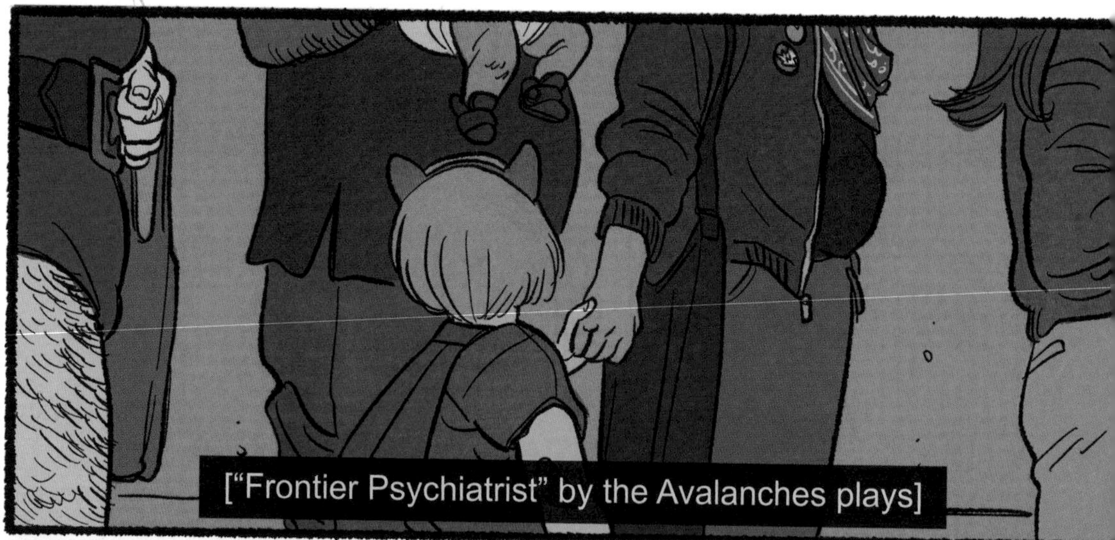
["Frontier Psychiatrist" by the Avalanches plays]

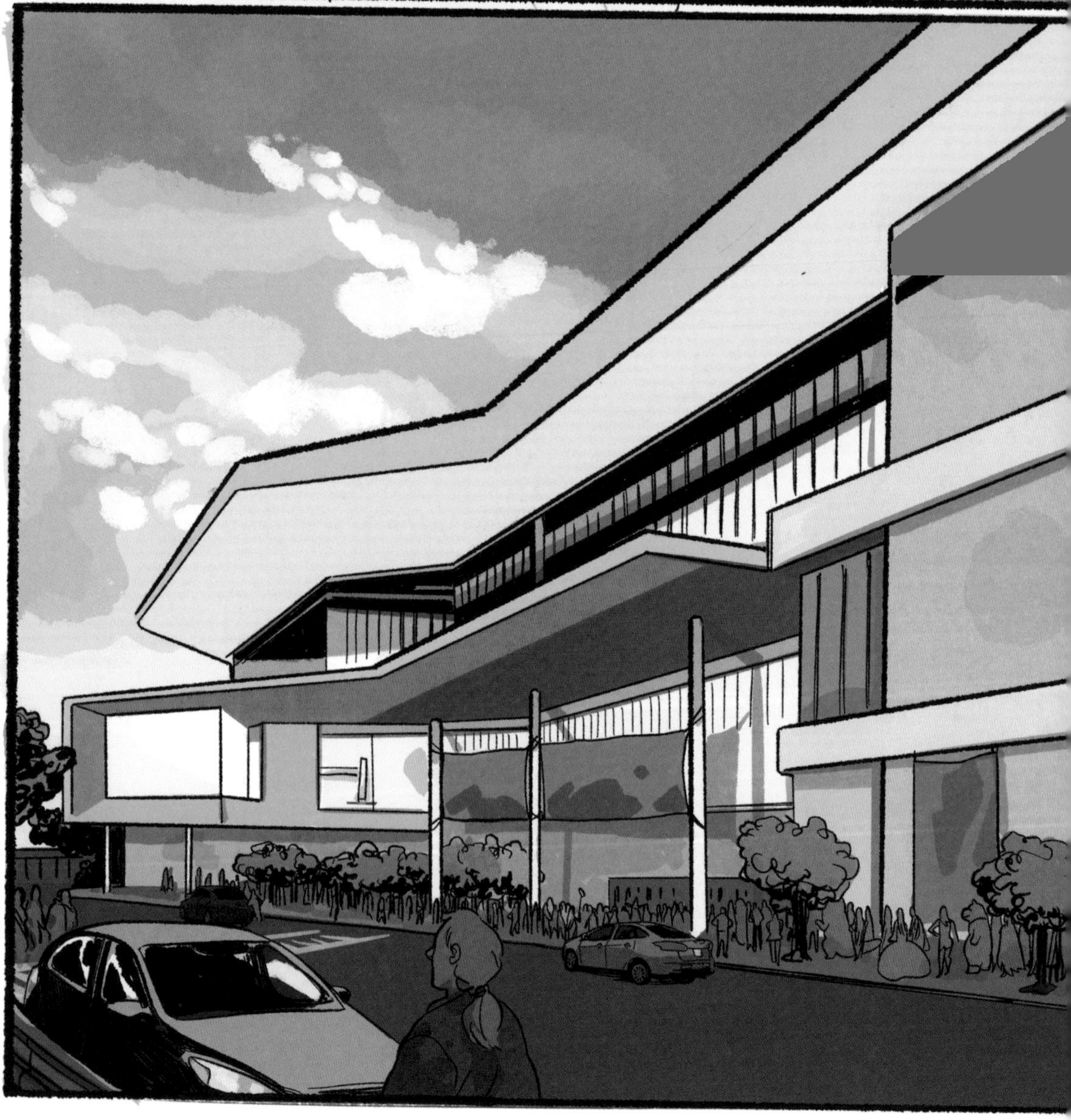

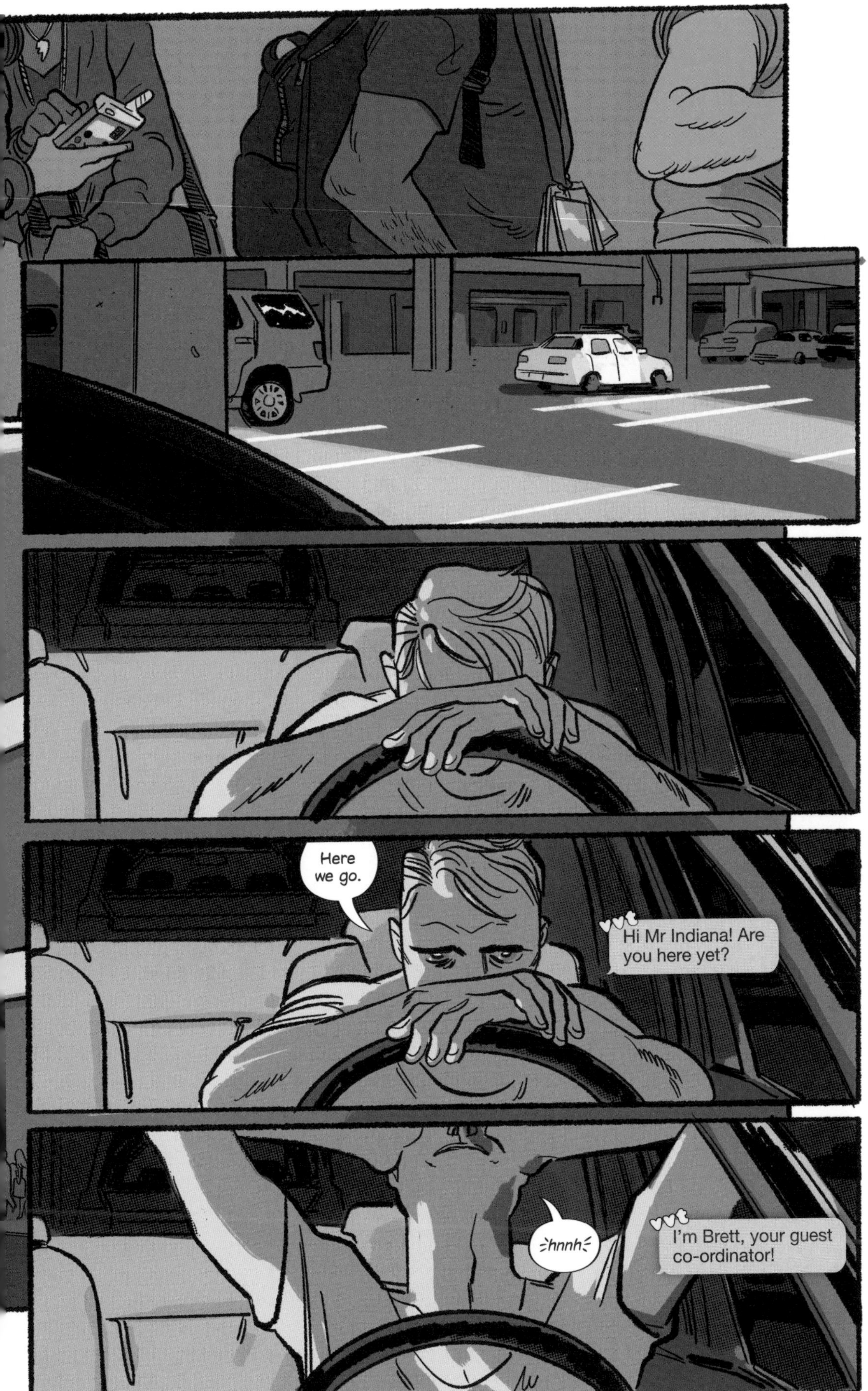
Here we go.
Hi Mr Indiana! Are you here yet?
hnnh
I'm Brett, your guest co-ordinator!

MINUTEMEN, "#1 HIT SONG"

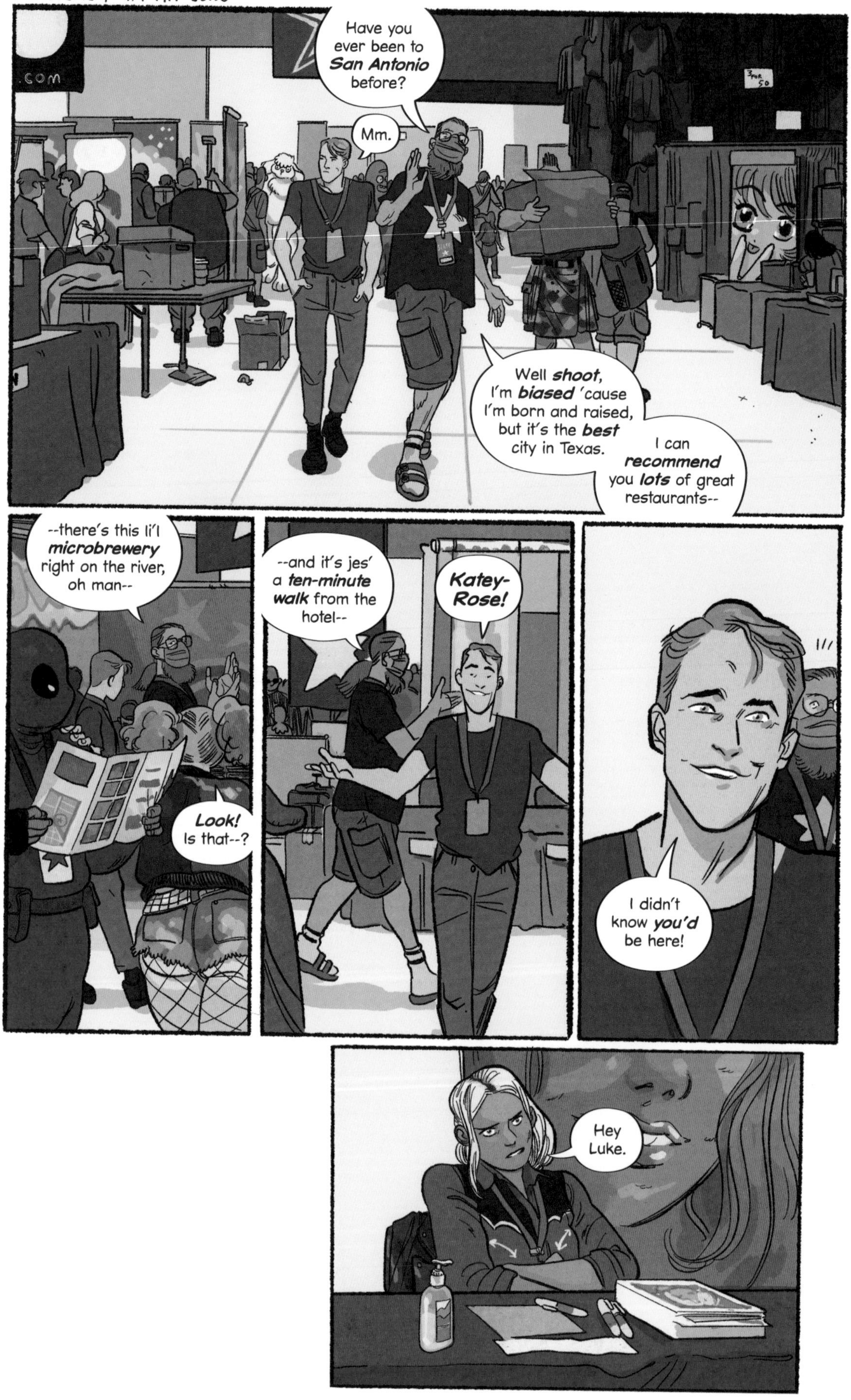
.COM
Have you ever been to San Antonio before?
Mm.
Well shoot, I'm biased 'cause I'm born and raised, but it's the best city in Texas.
I can recommend you lots of great restaurants--
--there's this li'l microbrewery right on the river, oh man--
Look! Is that--?
--and it's jes' a ten-minute walk from the hotel--
Katey-Rose!
I didn't know you'd be here!
Hey Luke.

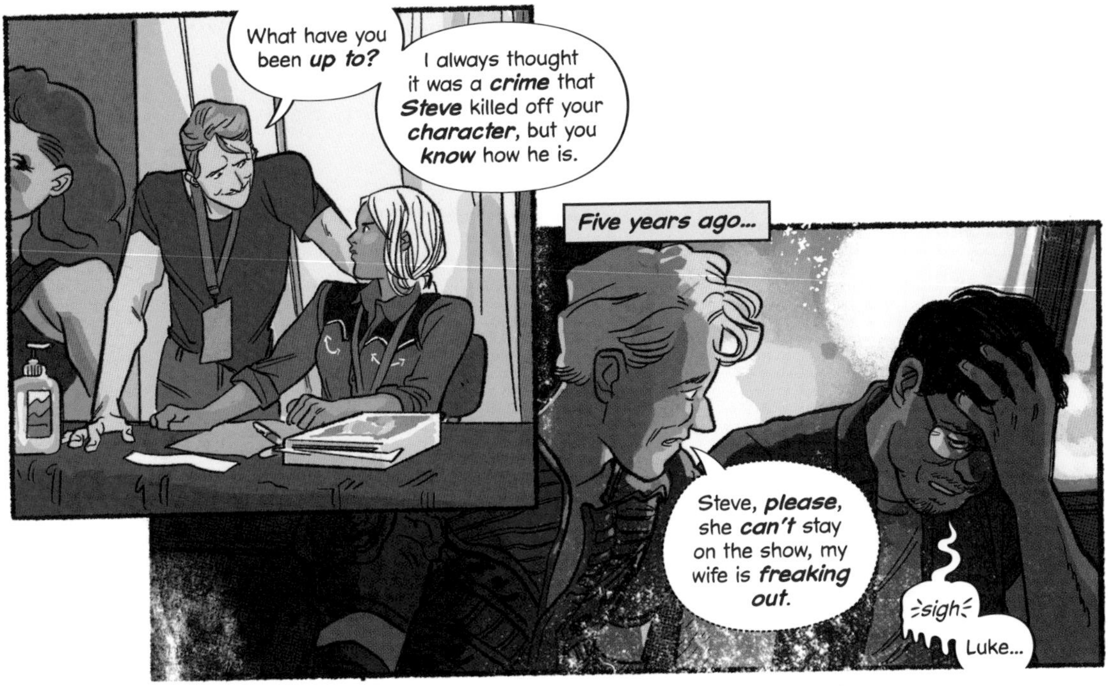
What have you been *up to?*
I always thought it was a *crime* that *Steve* killed off your *character*, but you *know* how he is.
Five years ago...
Steve, *please*, she *can't* stay on the show, my wife is *freaking out*.
sigh
Luke...

Kami Lopes
@kami296430

omg why do you hate women @RogueSteveShields?!?! Yet another female character fridged for a season finale of your stupid show. How are you not ashamed of this lazy, misogynistic writing #Roguefugees

9:05 PM · Nov 1, 2017 · Twitter for iPhone

286 Retweets **61** Quote Tweets **914** Likes

Spooky Petra Season
@RogueGirlPetra

noooo they killed off Luminia!!!!! Please tell me you're coming back in Season 8 @realkatherinevalery! #RogueNebula #RogueFamily

9:02 PM · Nov 1, 2017

340 Retweets **22** Quote Tweets **2.4K** Likes

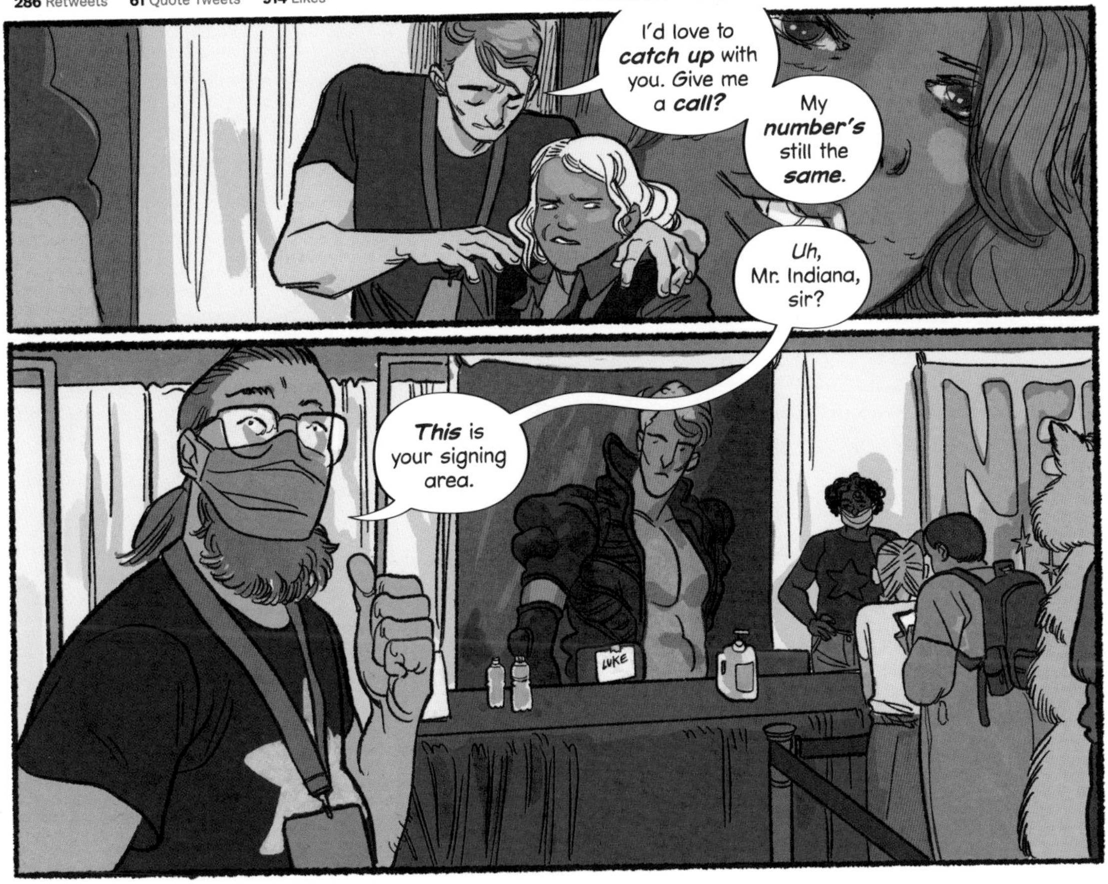
I'd love to *catch up* with you. Give me a *call?*
My *number's* still the *same*.
Uh, Mr. Indiana, sir?
This is your signing area.
LUKE

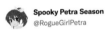

SLEATER-KINNEY, "MODERN GIRL"

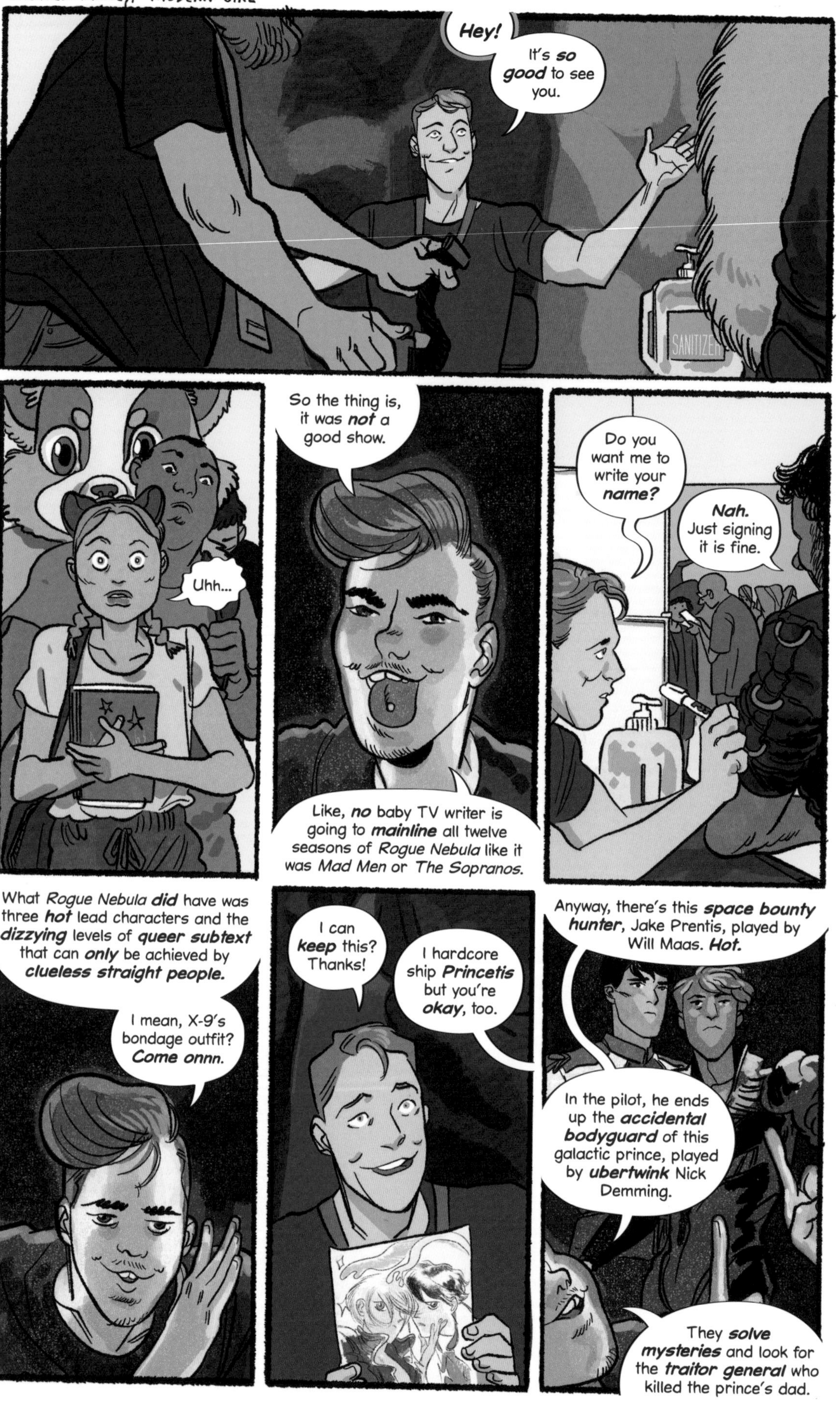
Hey!
It's **so good** to see you.
SANITIZER
Uhh...
So the thing is, it was **not** a good show.
Like, **no** baby TV writer is going to **mainline** all twelve seasons of *Rogue Nebula* like it was *Mad Men* or *The Sopranos*.
Do you want me to write your **name?**
Nah. Just signing it is fine.
What *Rogue Nebula* **did** have was three **hot** lead characters and the **dizzying** levels of **queer subtext** that can **only** be achieved by **clueless straight people.**
I mean, X-9's bondage outfit? **Come onnn.**
I can **keep** this? Thanks!
I hardcore ship ***Princetis*** but you're **okay**, too.
Anyway, there's this ***space bounty hunter***, Jake Prentis, played by Will Maas. ***Hot.***
In the pilot, he ends up the ***accidental bodyguard*** of this galactic prince, played by ***ubertwink*** Nick Demming.
They ***solve mysteries*** and look for the ***traitor general*** who killed the prince's dad.

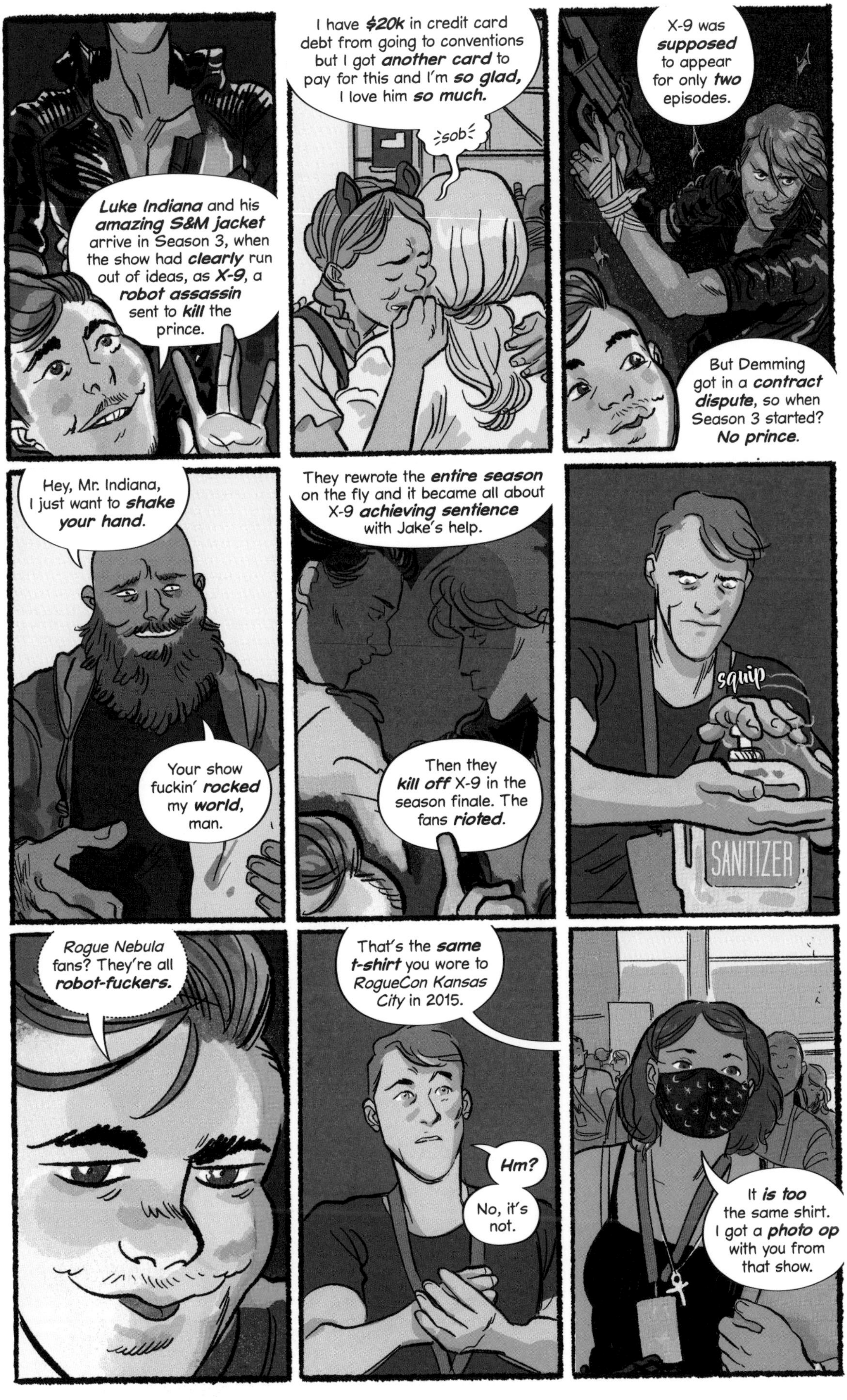

Luke Indiana and his amazing S&M jacket arrive in Season 3, when the show had clearly run out of ideas, as X-9, a robot assassin sent to kill the prince.
I have $20k in credit card debt from going to conventions but I got another card to pay for this and I'm so glad, I love him so much.
sob
X-9 was supposed to appear for only two episodes.
But Demming got in a contract dispute, so when Season 3 started? No prince.
Hey, Mr. Indiana, I just want to shake your hand.
Your show fuckin' rocked my world, man.
They rewrote the entire season on the fly and it became all about X-9 achieving sentience with Jake's help.
Then they kill off X-9 in the season finale. The fans rioted.
squip
SANITIZER
Rogue Nebula fans? They're all robot-fuckers.
That's the same t-shirt you wore to RogueCon Kansas City in 2015.
Hm?
No, it's not.
It is too the same shirt. I got a photo op with you from that show.

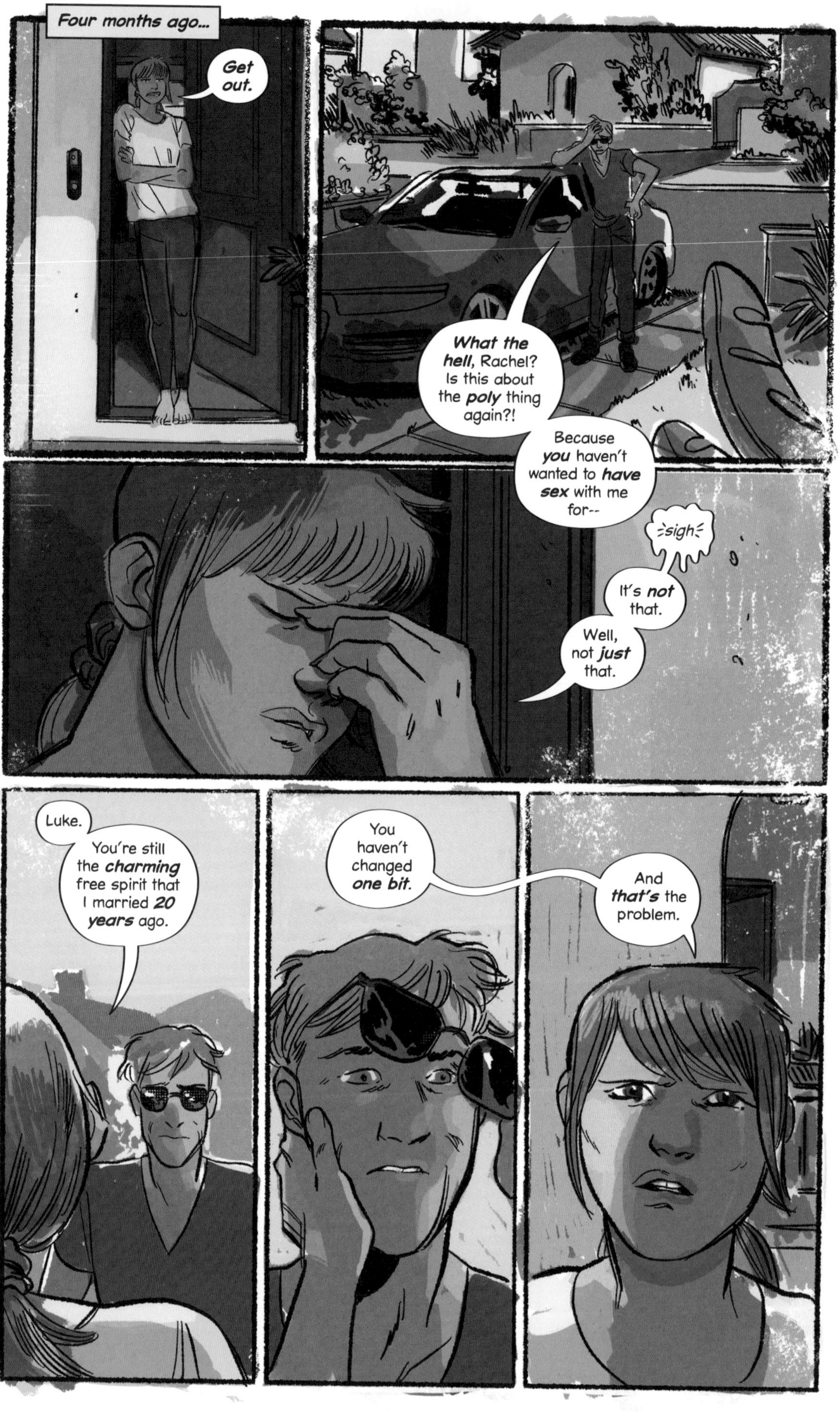
Four months ago...
Get out.
What the hell, Rachel? Is this about the poly thing again?!
Because you haven't wanted to have sex with me for--
sigh
It's not that.
Well, not just that.
Luke.
You're still the charming free spirit that I married 20 years ago.
You haven't changed one bit.
And that's the problem.

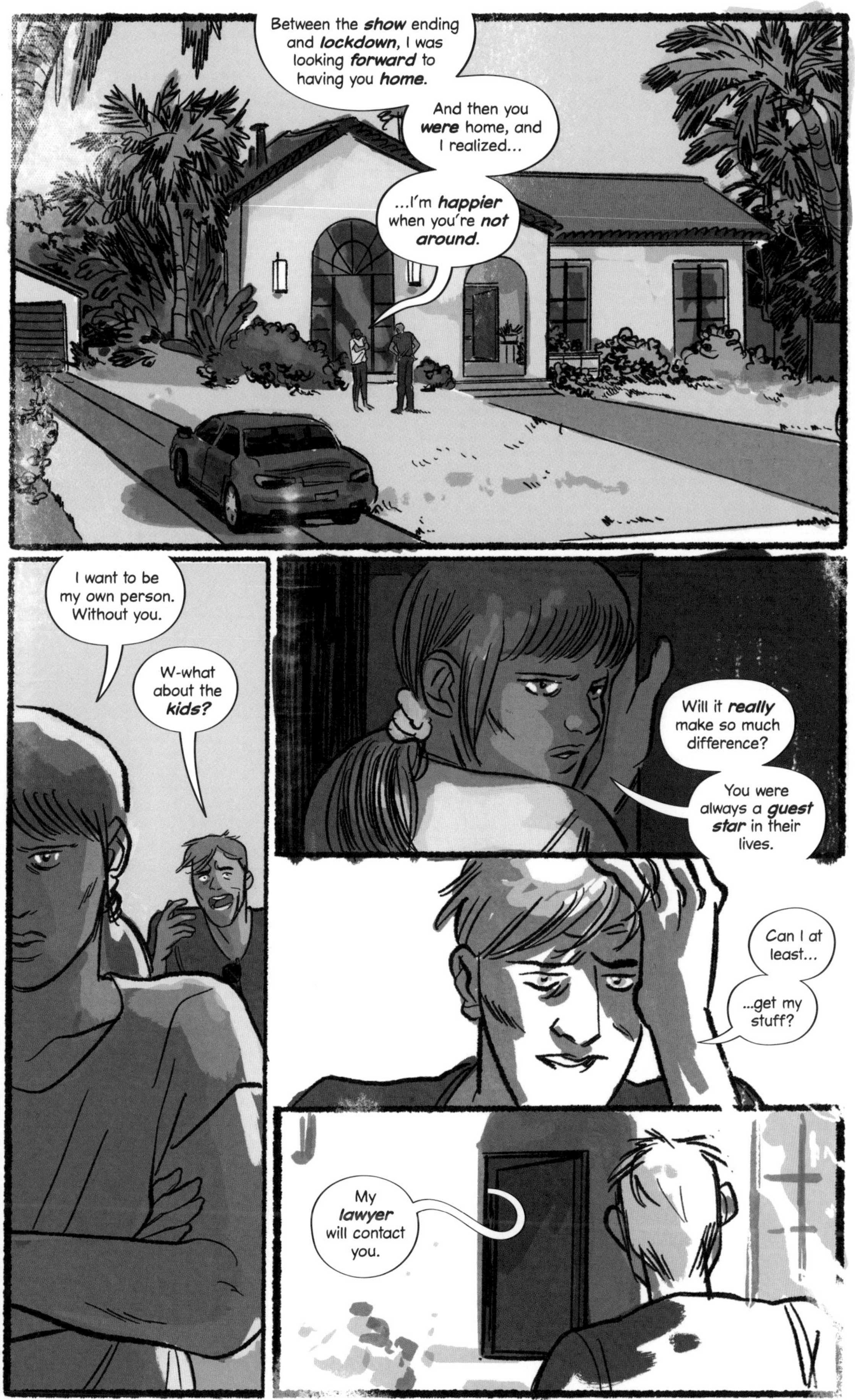
Between the show ending and lockdown, I was looking forward to having you home.
And then you were home, and I realized...
...I'm happier when you're not around.
I want to be my own person. Without you.
W-what about the kids?
Will it really make so much difference?
You were always a guest star in their lives.
Can I at least...
...get my stuff?
My lawyer will contact you.

MAGNETIC FIELDS, "SMOKE & MIRRORS"

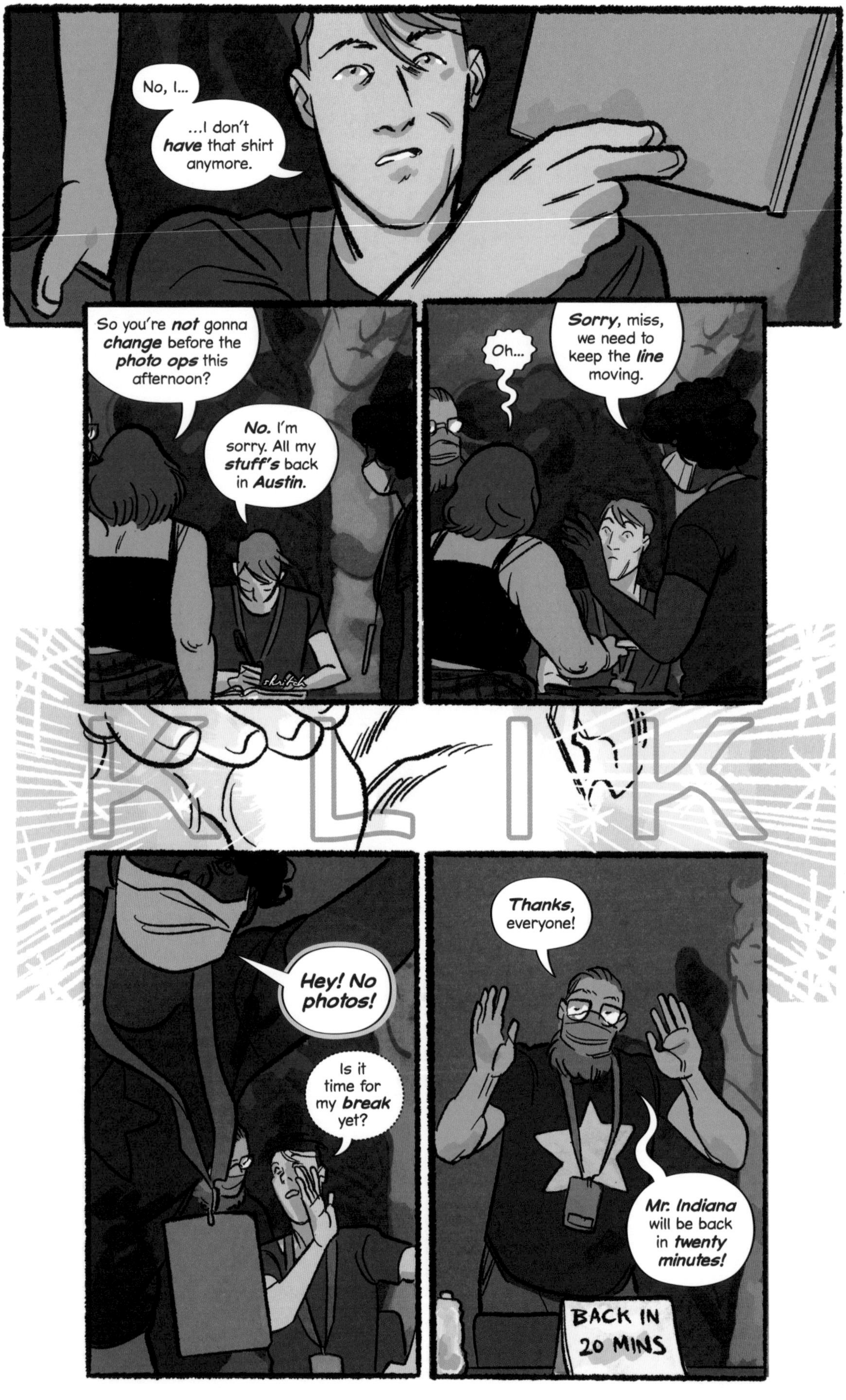
No, I...
...I don't *have* that shirt anymore.
So you're *not* gonna *change* before the *photo ops* this afternoon?
No. I'm sorry. All my *stuff's* back in *Austin.*
skritch
Oh...
Sorry, miss, we need to keep the *line* moving.
KLIK
Hey! No photos!
Is it time for my *break* yet?
Thanks, everyone!
Mr. Indiana will be back in *twenty minutes!*
BACK IN 20 MINS

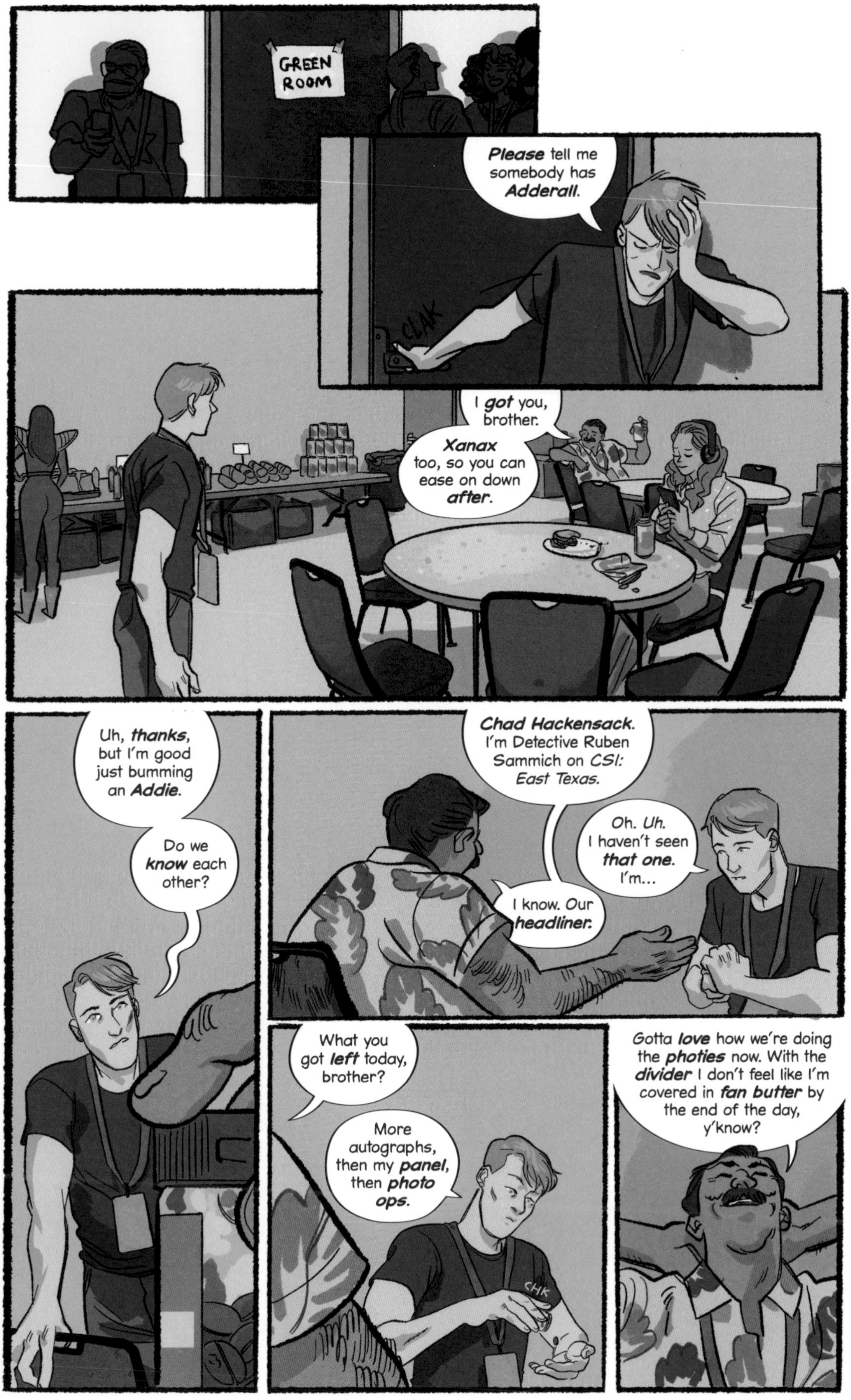
GREEN ROOM
Please tell me somebody has Adderall.
CLAK
I got you, brother.
Xanax too, so you can ease on down after.
Uh, thanks, but I'm good just bumming an Addie.
Do we know each other?
Chad Hackensack. I'm Detective Ruben Sammich on CSI: East Texas.
Oh. Uh. I haven't seen that one. I'm...
I know. Our headliner.
What you got left today, brother?
More autographs, then my panel, then photo ops.
CHK
Gotta love how we're doing the photies now. With the divider I don't feel like I'm covered in fan butter by the end of the day, y'know?

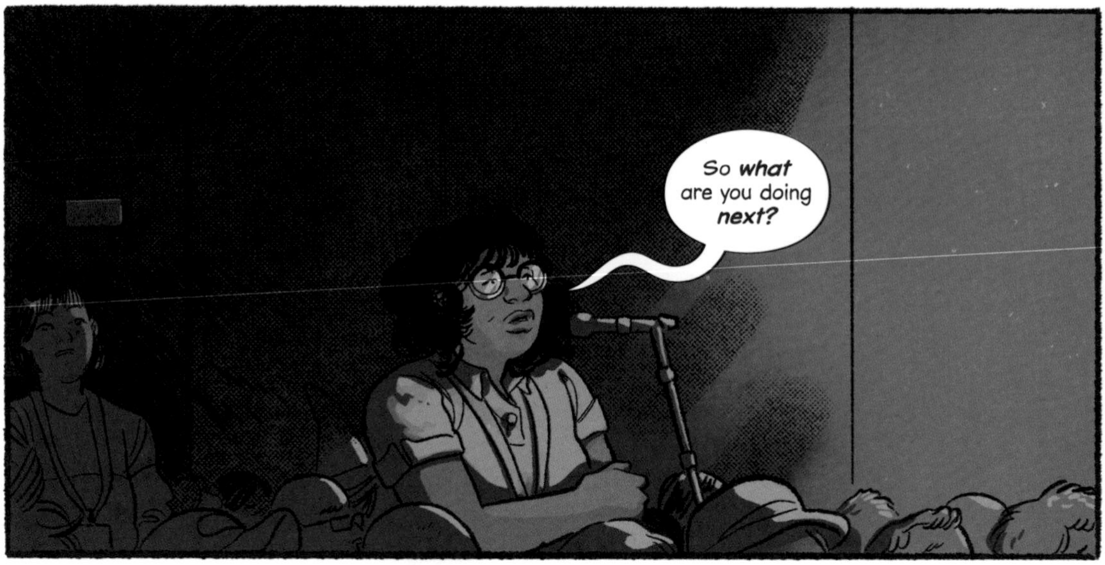
So what are you doing next?

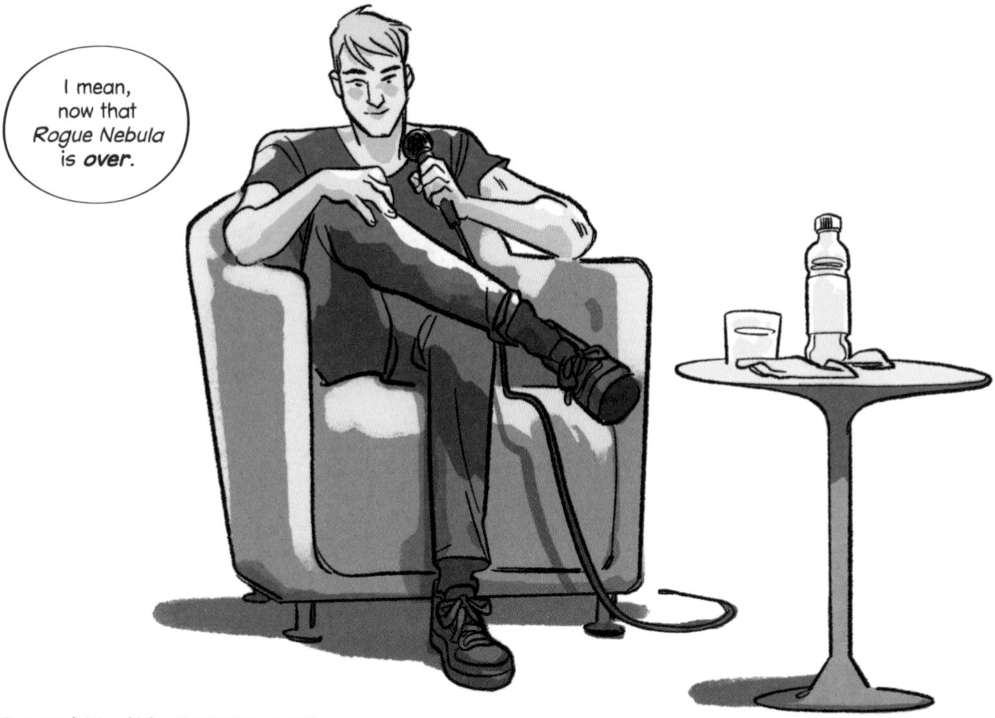
I mean, now that Rogue Nebula is over.

SCOTT WALKER, "30 CENTURY MAN"

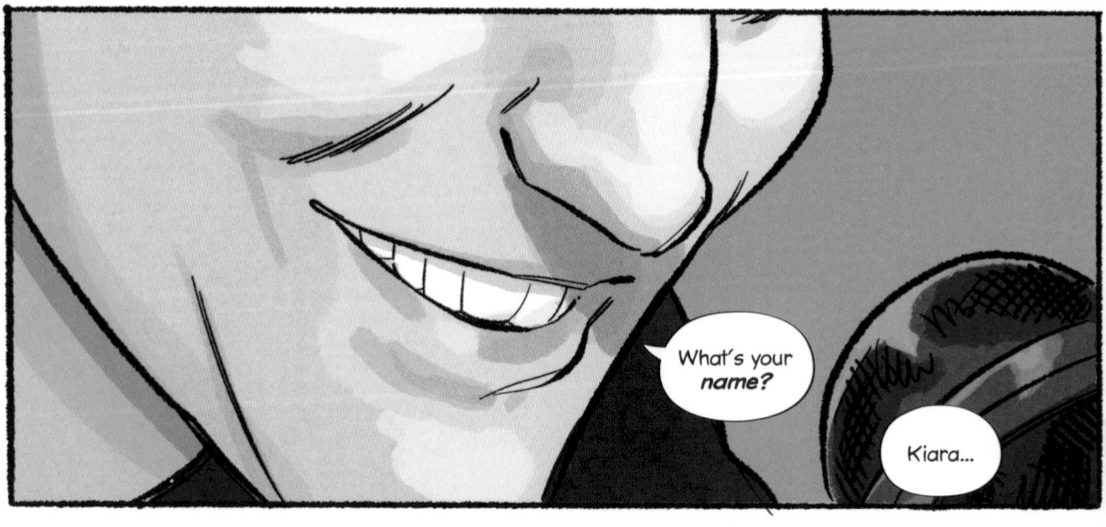
What's your name?
Kiara...

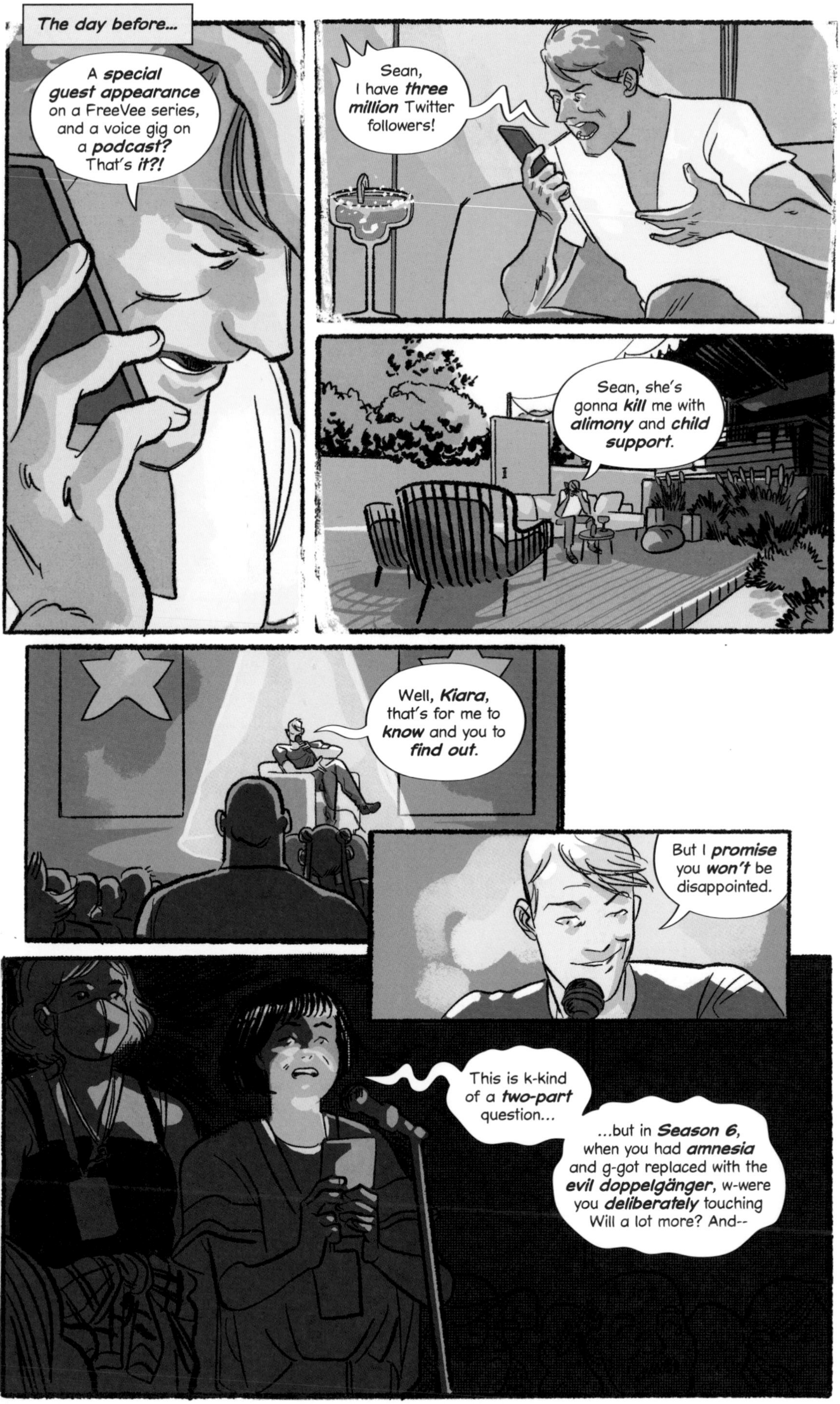
The day before...
A special guest appearance on a FreeVee series, and a voice gig on a podcast? That's it?!
Sean, I have three million Twitter followers!
Sean, she's gonna kill me with alimony and child support.
Well, Kiara, that's for me to know and you to find out.
But I promise you won't be disappointed.
This is k-kind of a two-part question...
...but in Season 6, when you had amnesia and g-got replaced with the evil doppelgänger, w-were you deliberately touching Will a lot more? And--

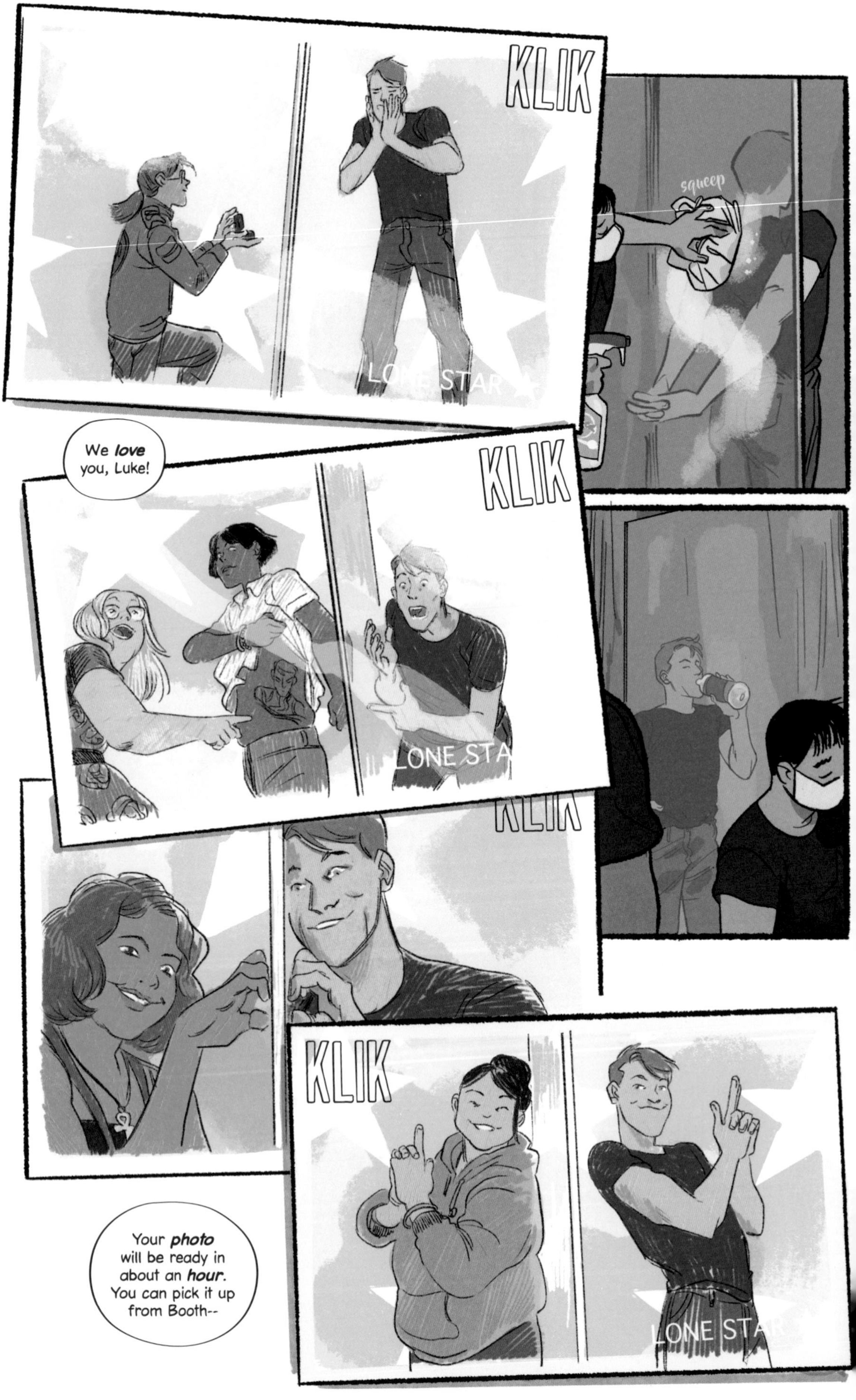
KLIK
LONE STAR
squeep
We *love* you, Luke!
KLIK
LONE STA
KLIK
Your *photo* will be ready in about an *hour*. You can pick it up from Booth--
LONE STA

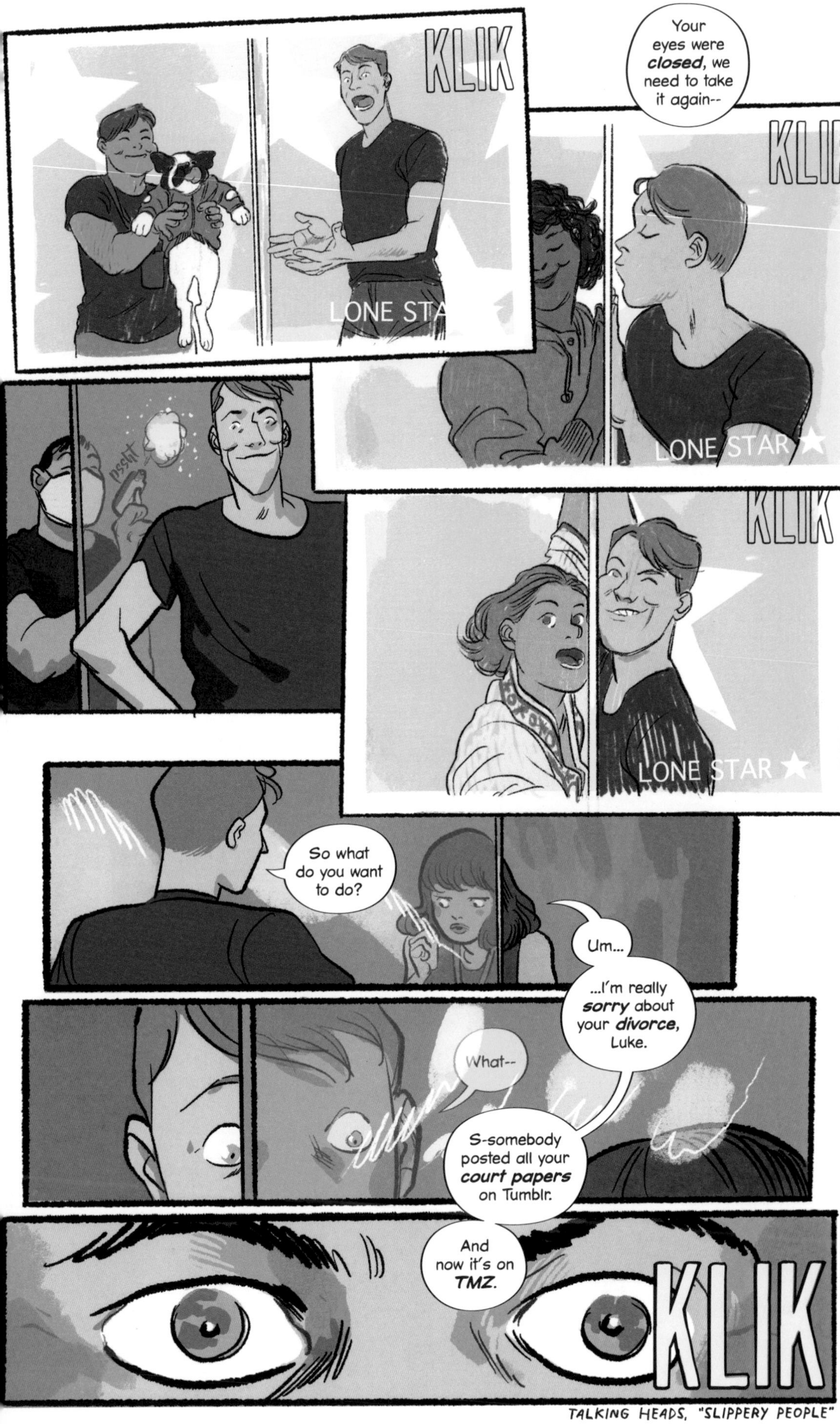
KLIK
LONE STA
Your eyes were closed, we need to take it again--
KLIK
LONE STAR ★
pssht
KLIK
LONE STAR ★
So what do you want to do?
Um...
...I'm really sorry about your divorce, Luke.
What--
S-somebody posted all your court papers on Tumblr.
And now it's on TMZ.
KLIK

TALKING HEADS, "SLIPPERY PEOPLE"

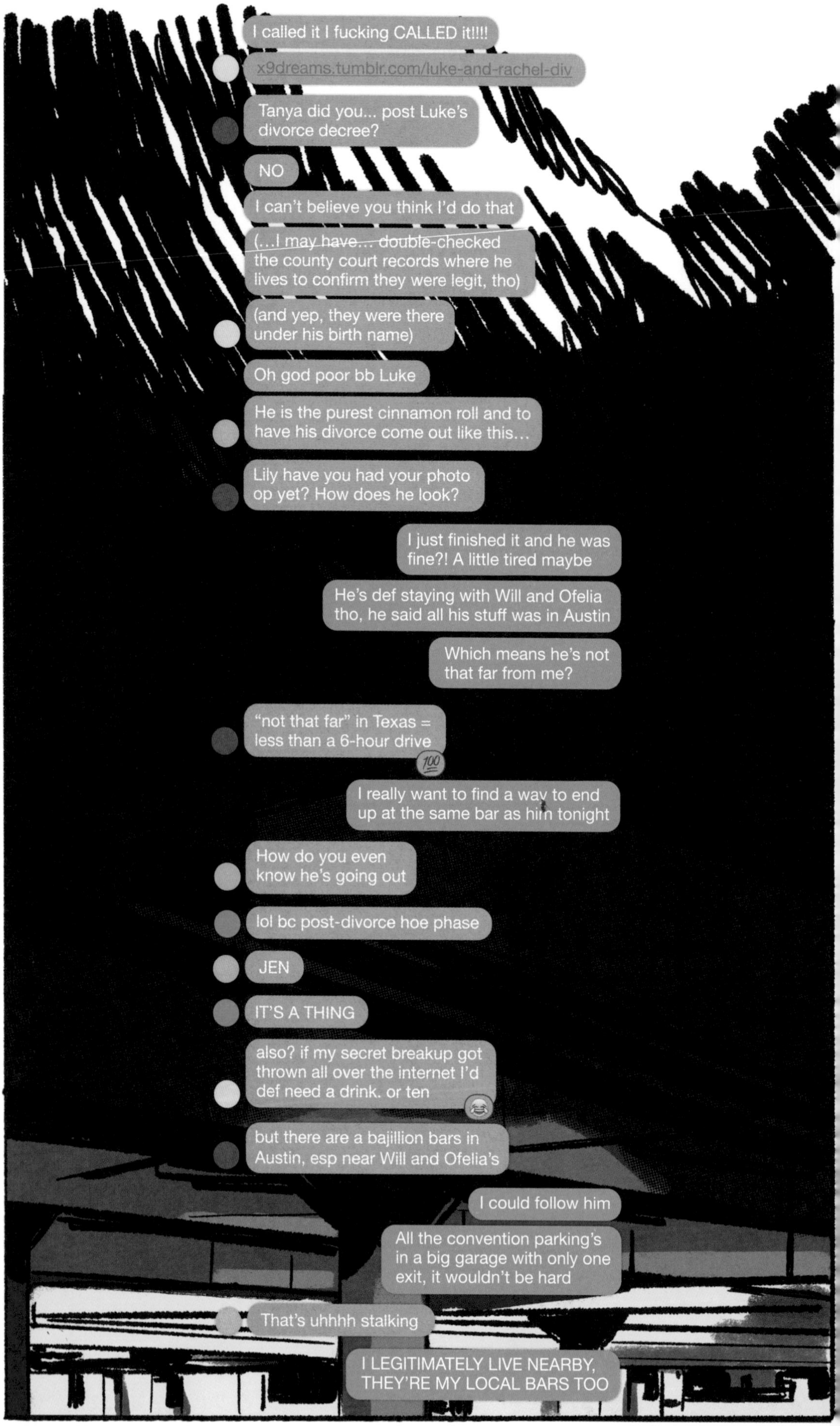
I called it I fucking CALLED it!!!!
x9dreams.tumblr.com/luke-and-rachel-div
Tanya did you... post Luke's divorce decree?
NO
I can't believe you think I'd do that
(...I may have... double-checked the county court records where he lives to confirm they were legit, tho)
(and yep, they were there under his birth name)
Oh god poor bb Luke
He is the purest cinnamon roll and to have his divorce come out like this...
Lily have you had your photo op yet? How does he look?
I just finished it and he was fine?! A little tired maybe
He's def staying with Will and Ofelia tho, he said all his stuff was in Austin
Which means he's not that far from me?
"not that far" in Texas = less than a 6-hour drive
I really want to find a way to end up at the same bar as him tonight
How do you even know he's going out
lol bc post-divorce hoe phase
JEN
IT'S A THING
also? if my secret breakup got thrown all over the internet I'd def need a drink. or ten
but there are a bajillion bars in Austin, esp near Will and Ofelia's
I could follow him
All the convention parking's in a big garage with only one exit, it wouldn't be hard
That's uhhhh stalking
I LEGITIMATELY LIVE NEARBY, THEY'RE MY LOCAL BARS TOO

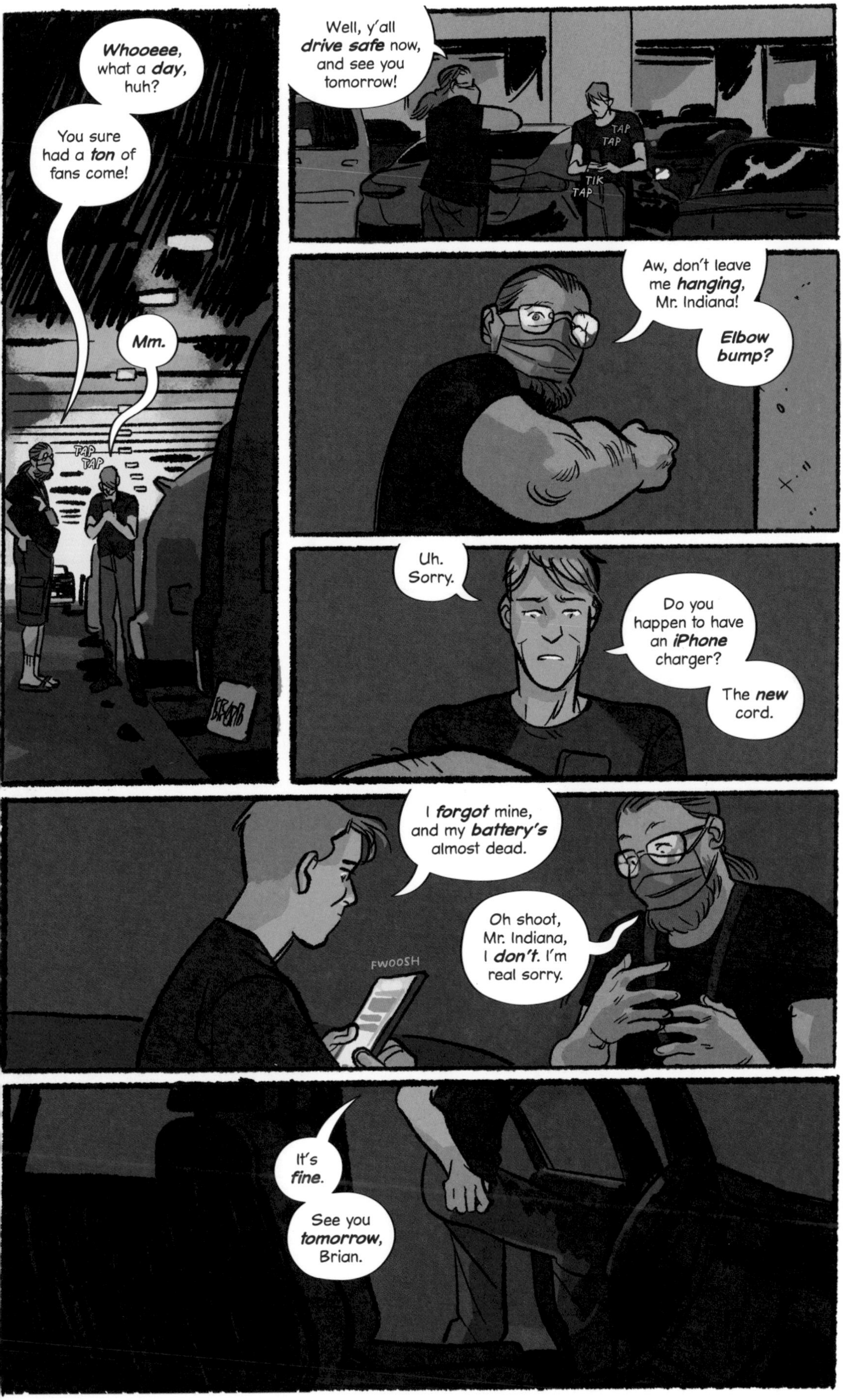
Whooeee, what a day, huh?
You sure had a ton of fans come!
Mm.
TAP TAP
Well, y'all drive safe now, and see you tomorrow!
TAP TAP
TIK TAP
Aw, don't leave me hanging, Mr. Indiana!
Elbow bump?
Uh. Sorry.
Do you happen to have an iPhone charger?
The new cord.
I forgot mine, and my battery's almost dead.
Oh shoot, Mr. Indiana, I don't. I'm real sorry.
FWOOSH
It's fine.
See you tomorrow, Brian.

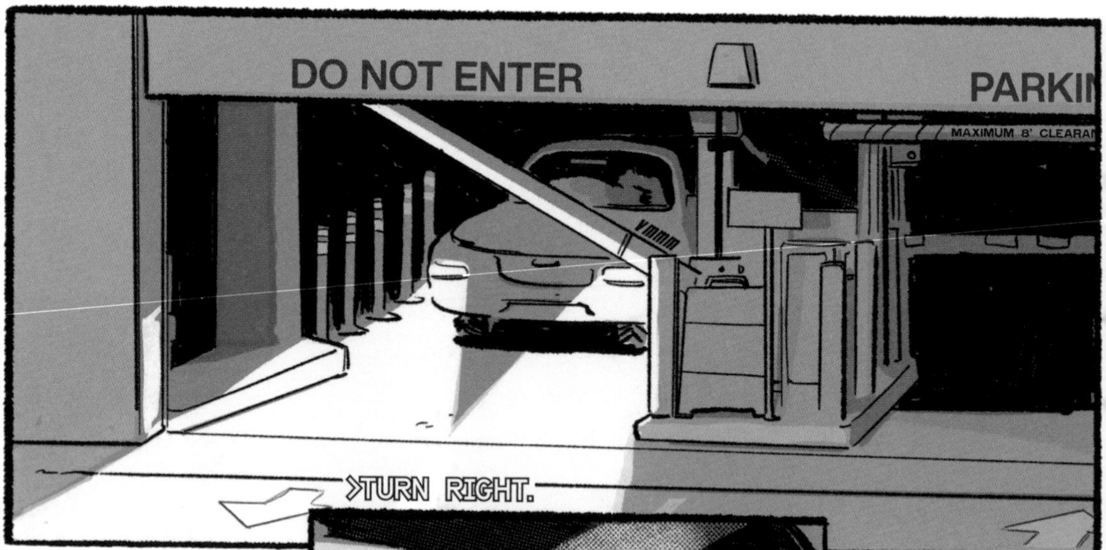
DO NOT ENTER
PARKIN
MAXIMUM 8' CLEARAN
vmmm
>TURN RIGHT.

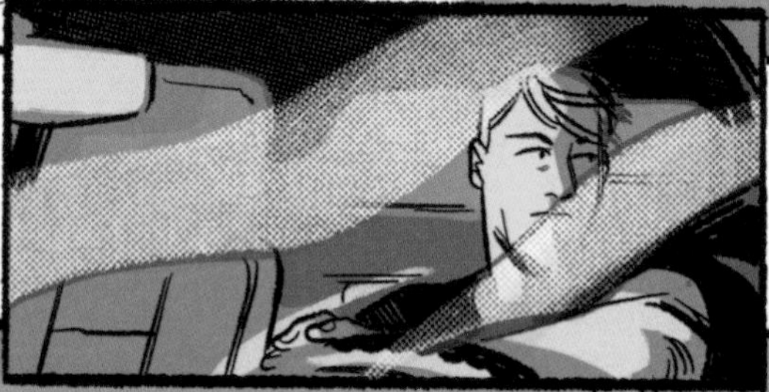

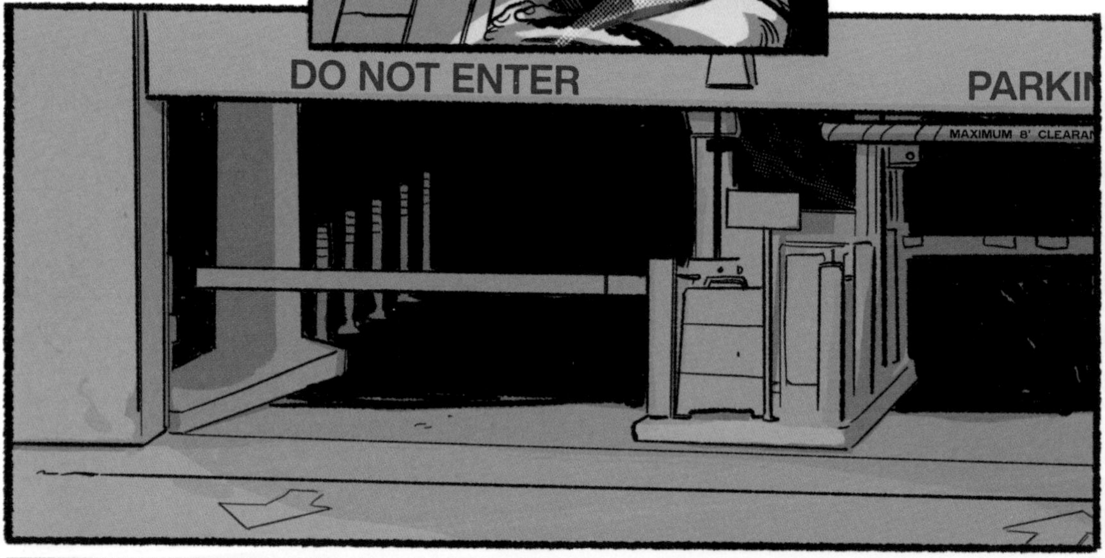
DO NOT ENTER
PARKIN
MAXIMUM 8' CLEARAN

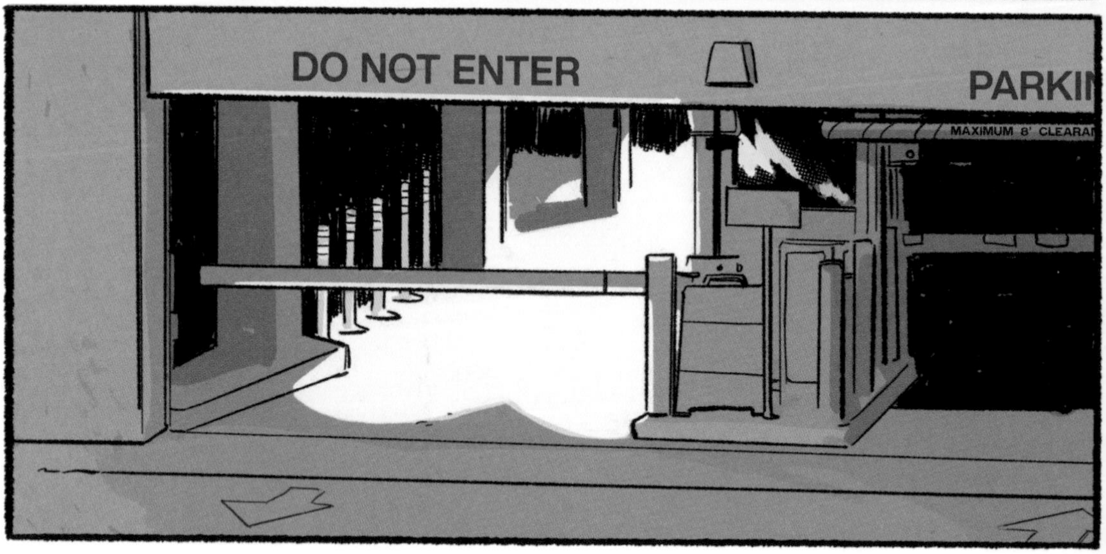
DO NOT ENTER
PARKIN
MAXIMUM 8' CLEARAN

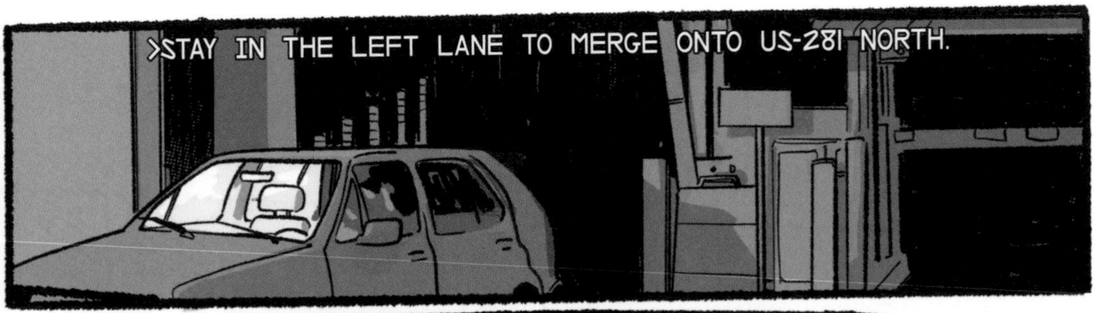
>STAY IN THE LEFT LANE TO MERGE ONTO US-281 NORTH.

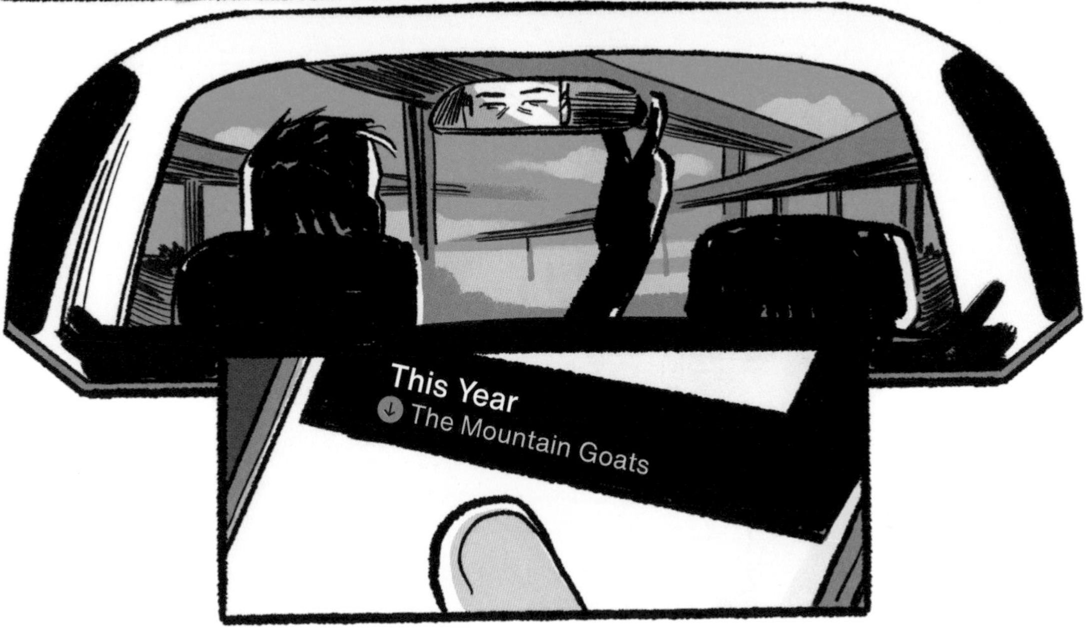
This Year
The Mountain Goats

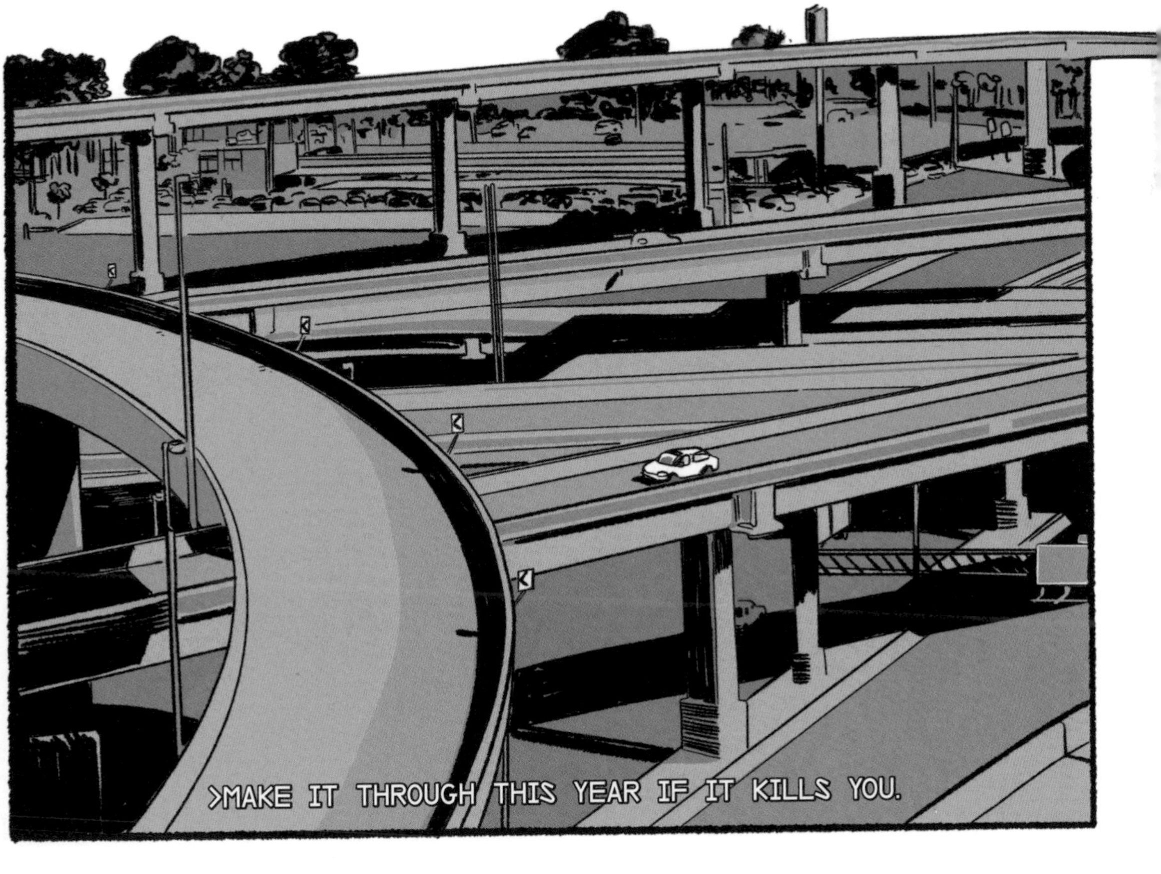
>MAKE IT THROUGH THIS YEAR IF IT KILLS YOU.

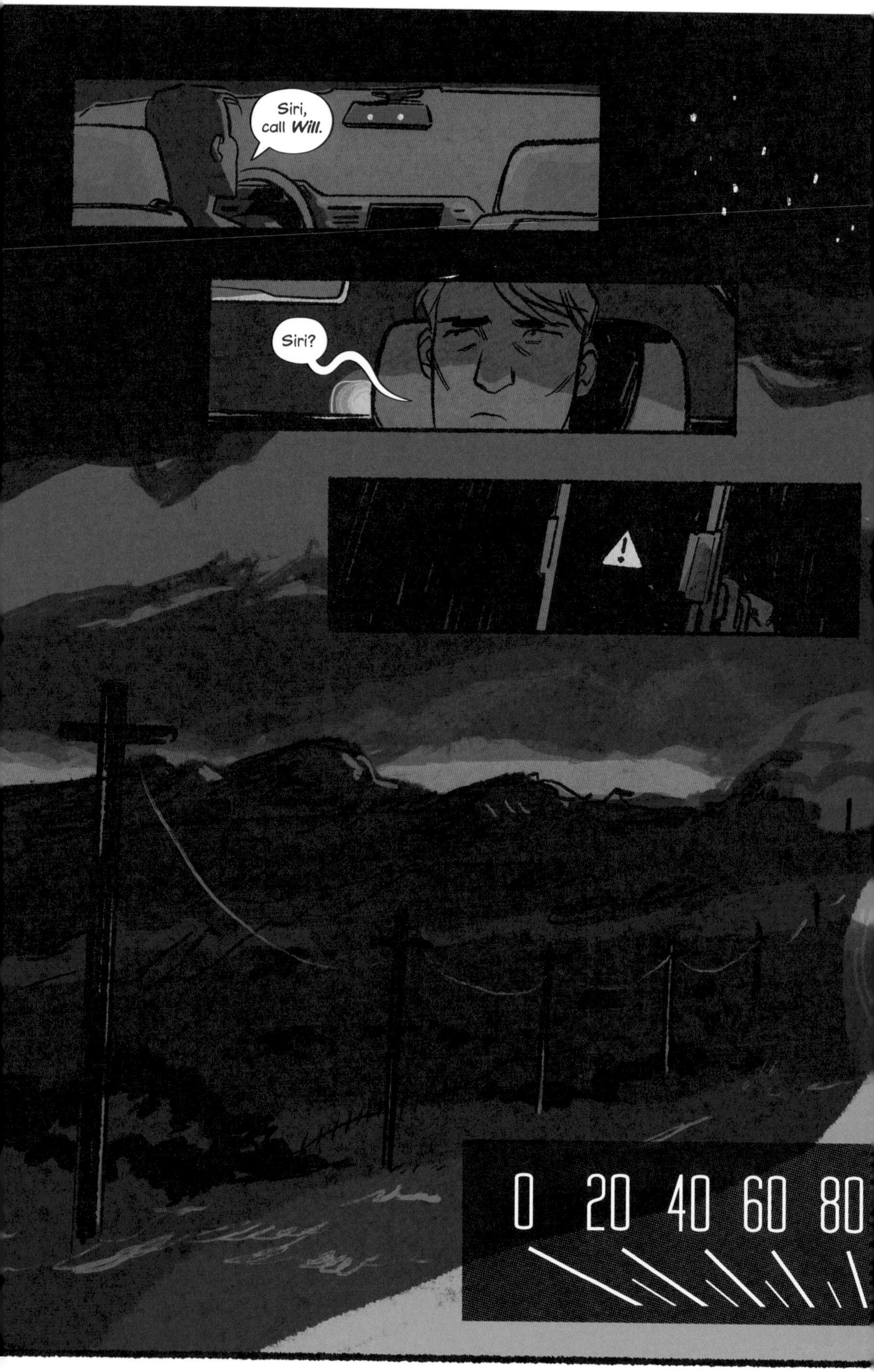
Siri, call Will.
Siri?
0 20 40 60 80

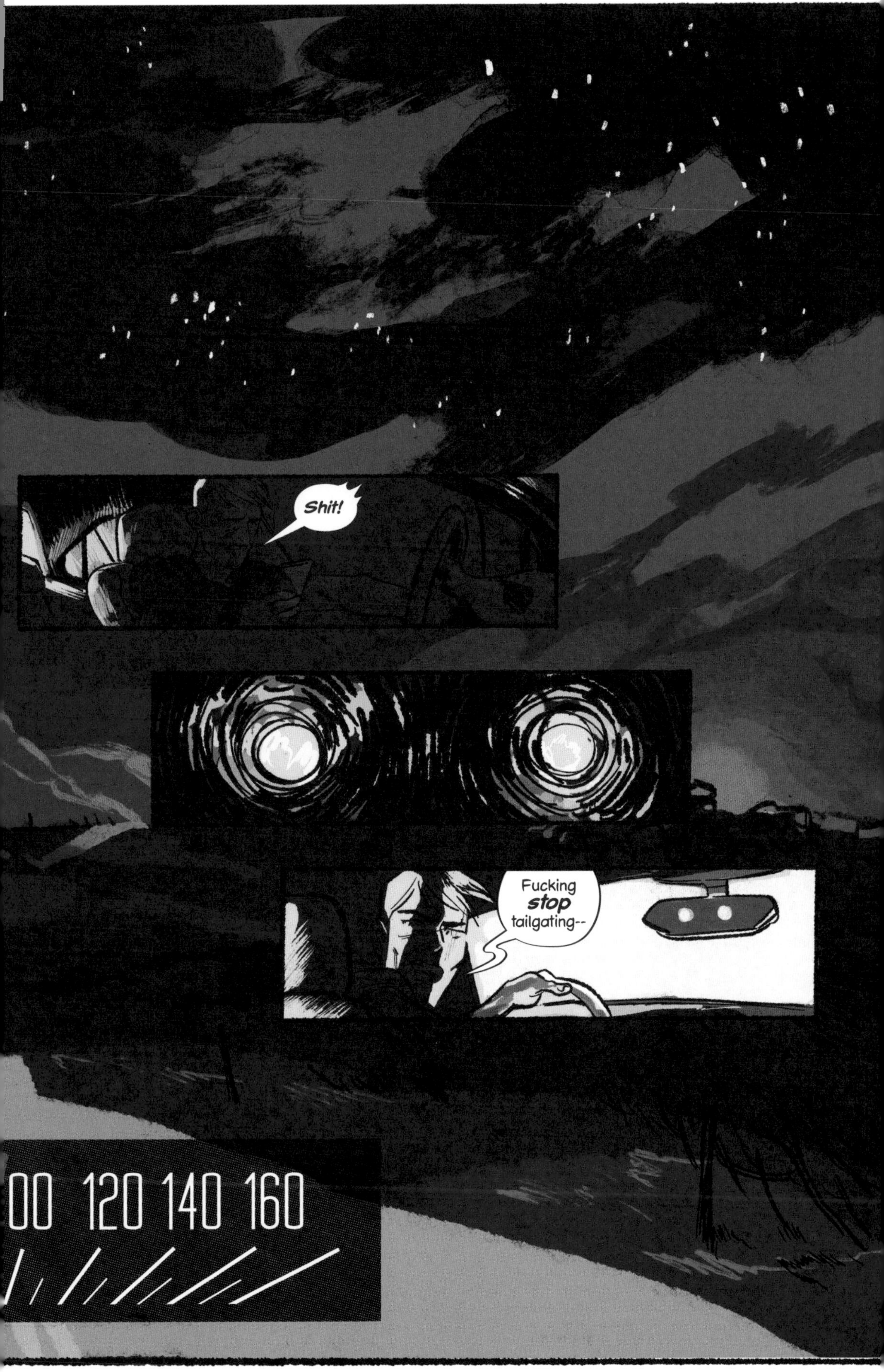

Shit!
Fucking stop tailgating--
00 120 140 160

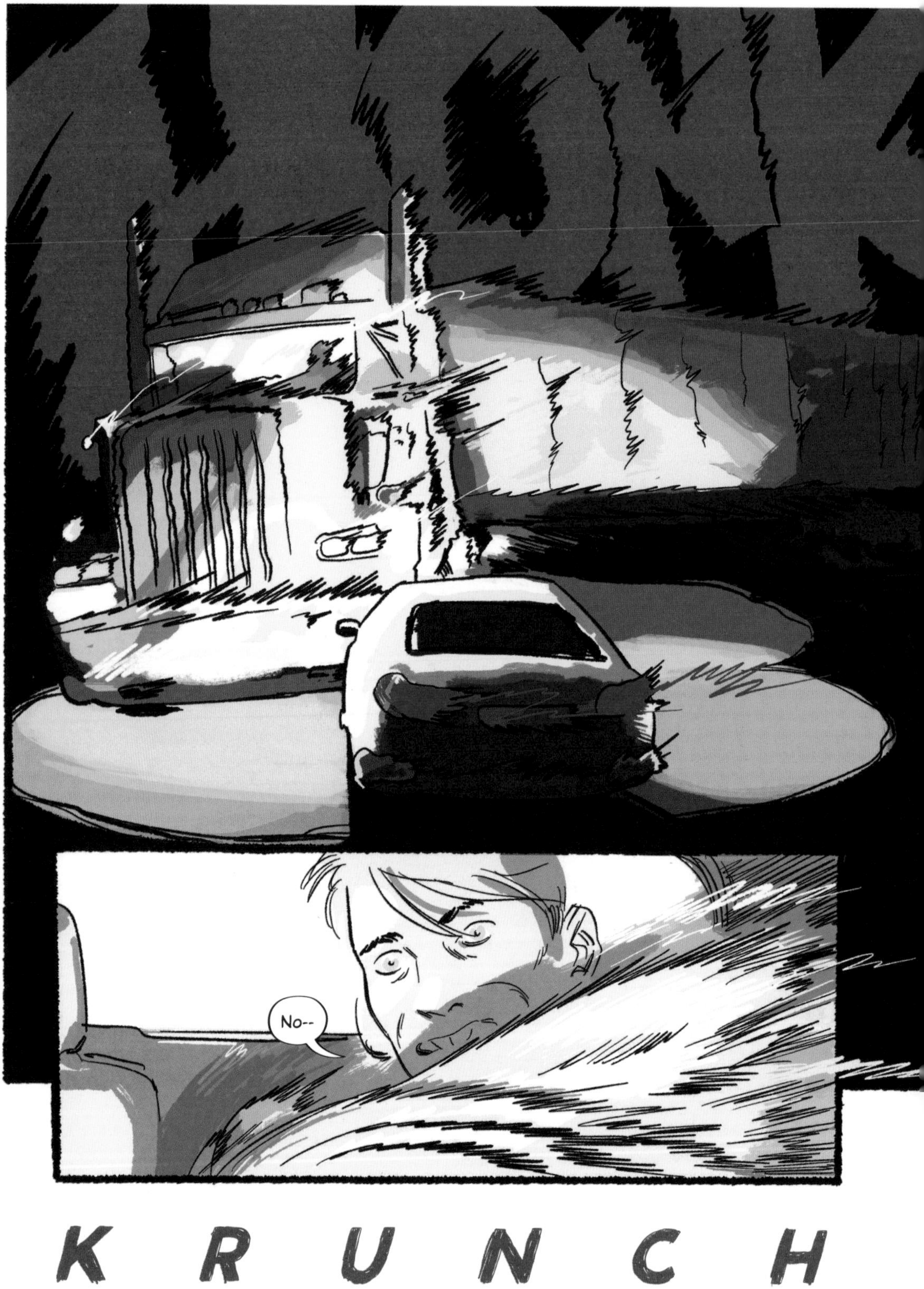
No--
KRUNCH

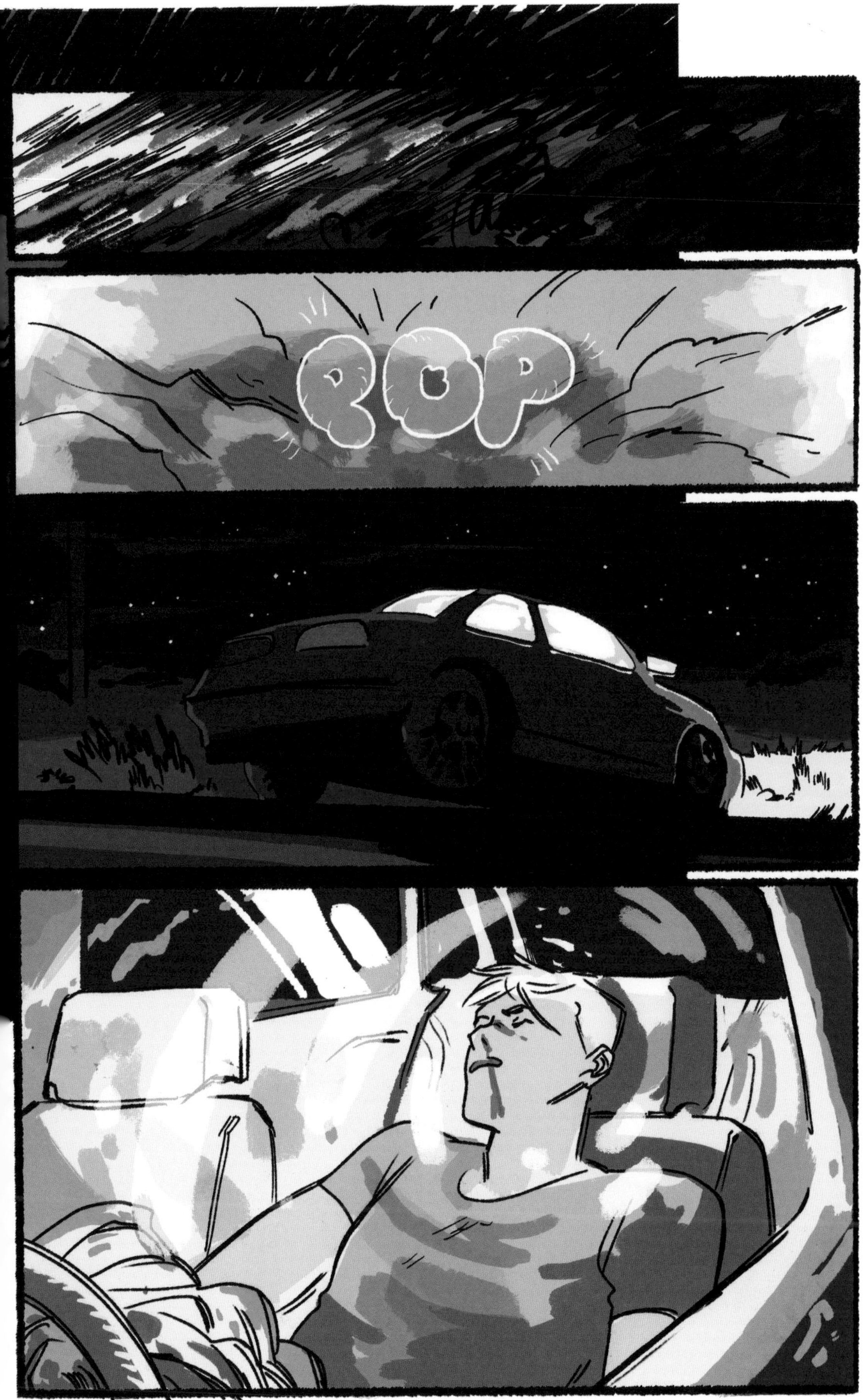
POP

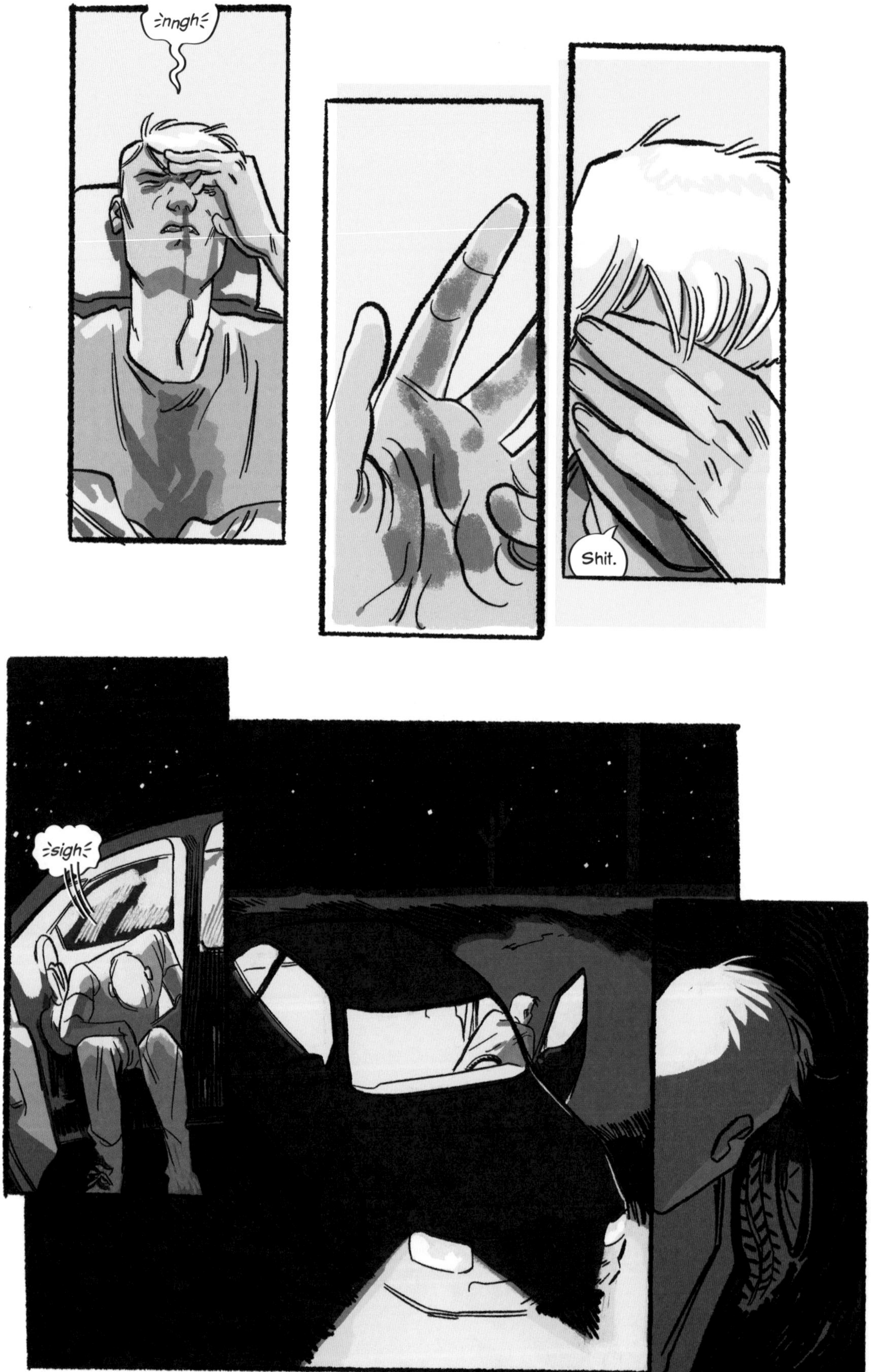
nngh
Shit.
sigh

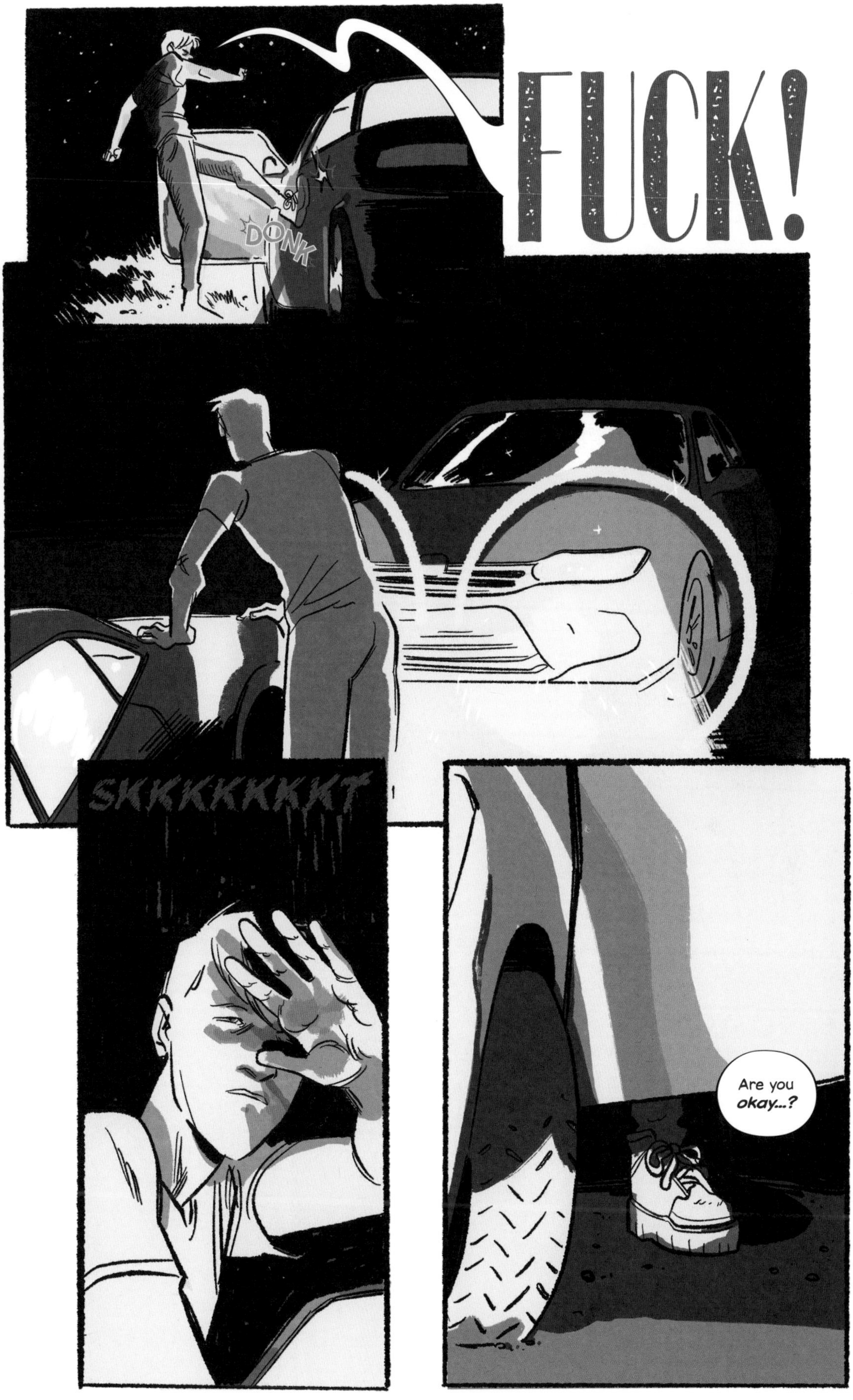
DONK
FUCK!
SKKKKKKKT
Are you *okay...?*

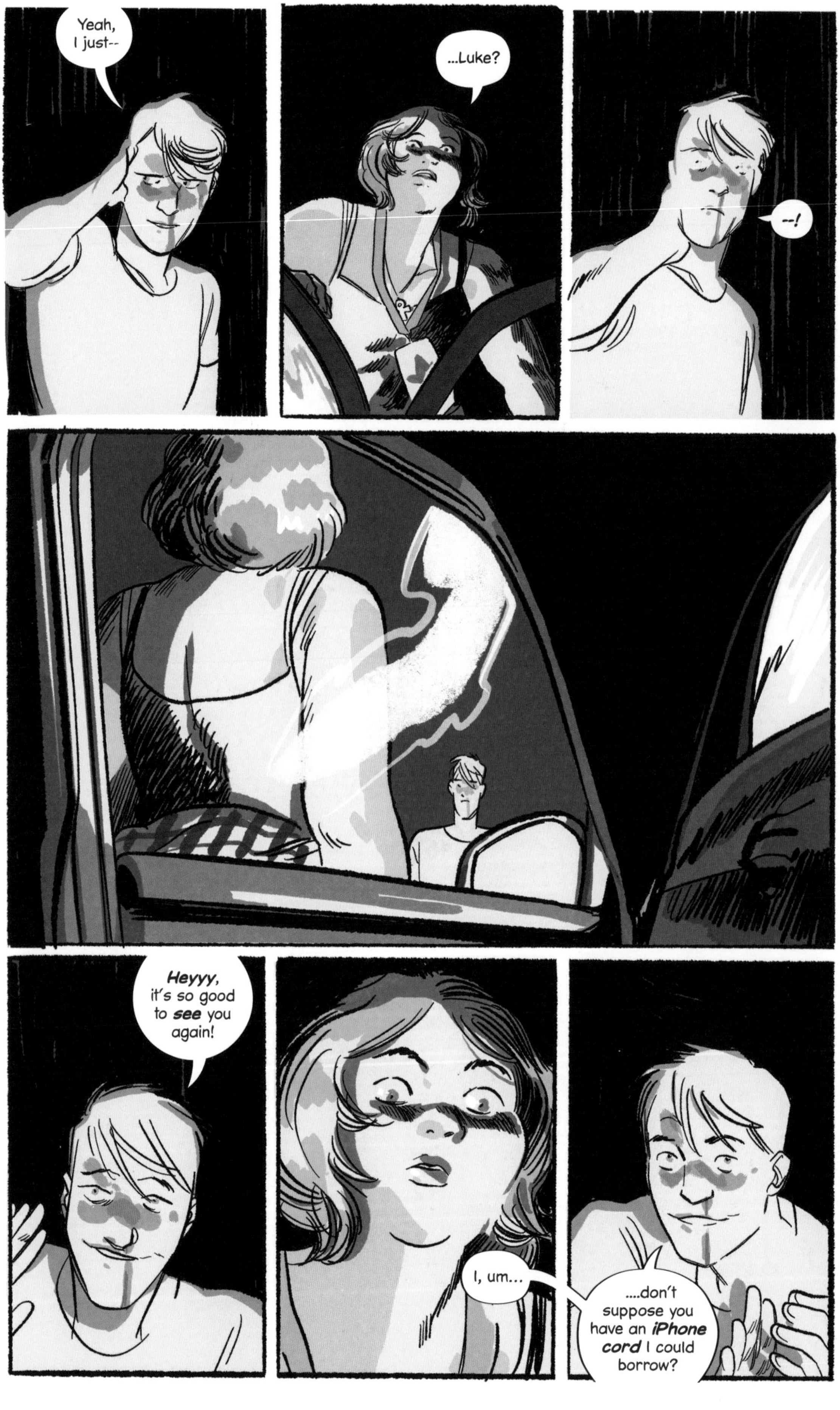
Yeah, I just--
...Luke?
--!
Heyyy, it's so good to see you again!
I, um...
....don't suppose you have an iPhone cord I could borrow?

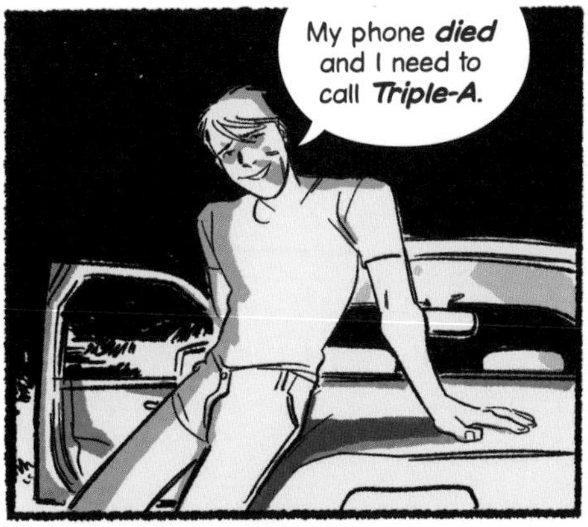
My phone *died* and I need to call *Triple-A*.

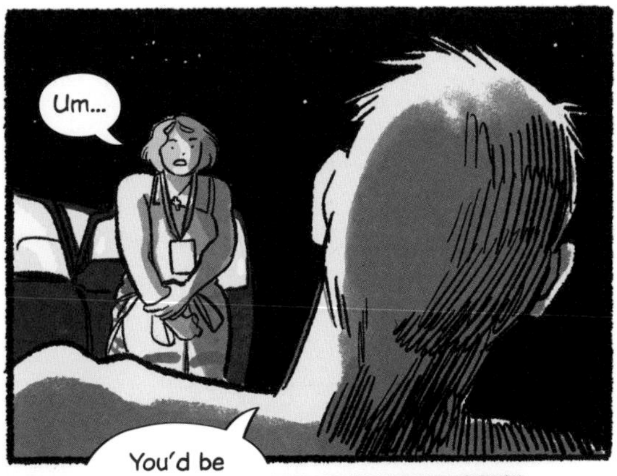
Um...

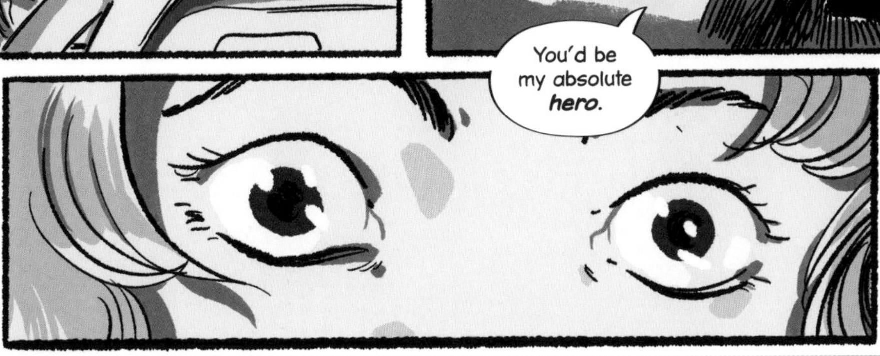
You'd be my absolute *hero*.

E ⚥ !? ✓

a pause, a road, the taste of gravel in the mouth by xXEnobyDarknessXx 21 Sep 2021

Rogue Nebula RPF

Creator Chose Not To Use Archive Warnings, Luke Indiana/Reader, Luke Indiana & Reader, Luke Indiana/You, X-9/You, X-9 & You, X-9/Reader, Luke Indiana, X-9, Porn, Plot What Plot/Porn Without Plot, Smut, Shameless, Sexual Content, Semi-Public Sex, RPF, Reader-Insert, There Was Only One Bed, Making Love, Fluff, Fluff and Smut, Cuddling & Snuggling, Fangirls, Flirting, Age Difference, Reader Insert, Divorced Luke, Cunnilingus, Light Dom/Sub Undertones

Your wildest fantasy comes to life when you're driving home along back roads after a long day at a comics convention and who should you see pulled over with a broken-down car but

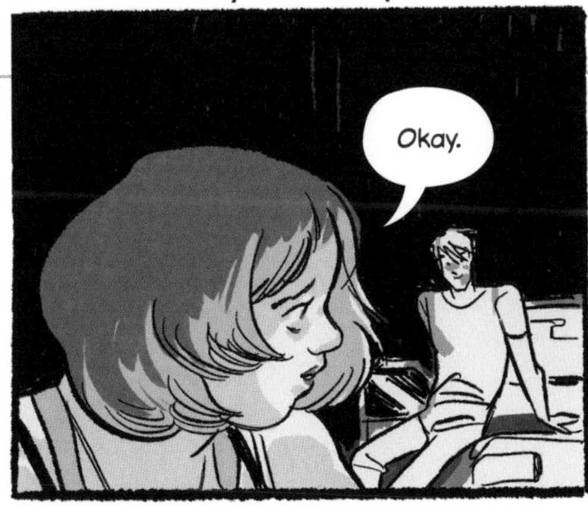
Okay.

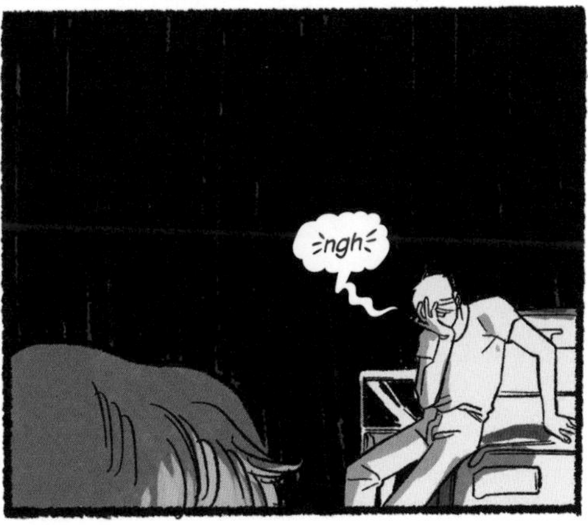
ngh

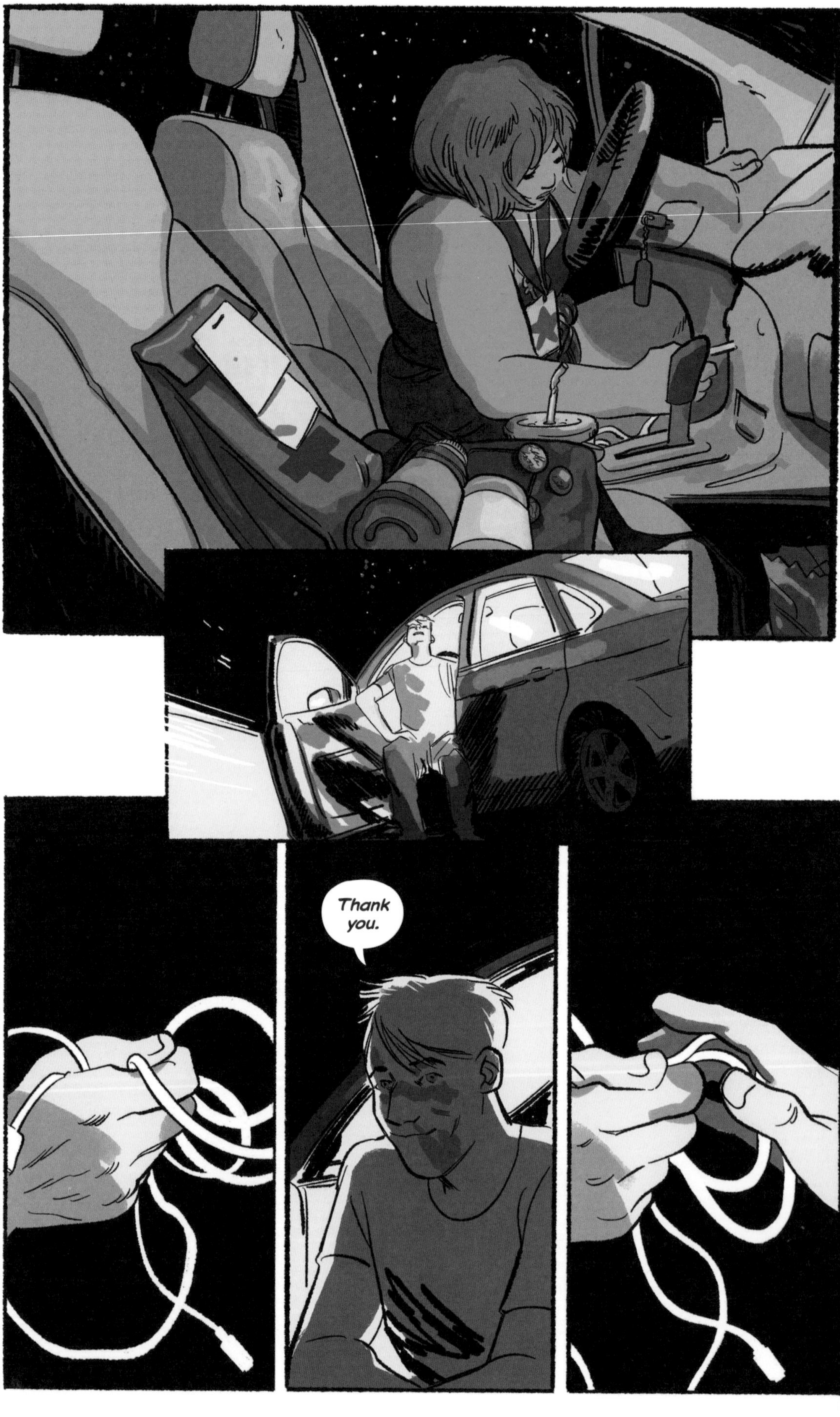
Thank you.

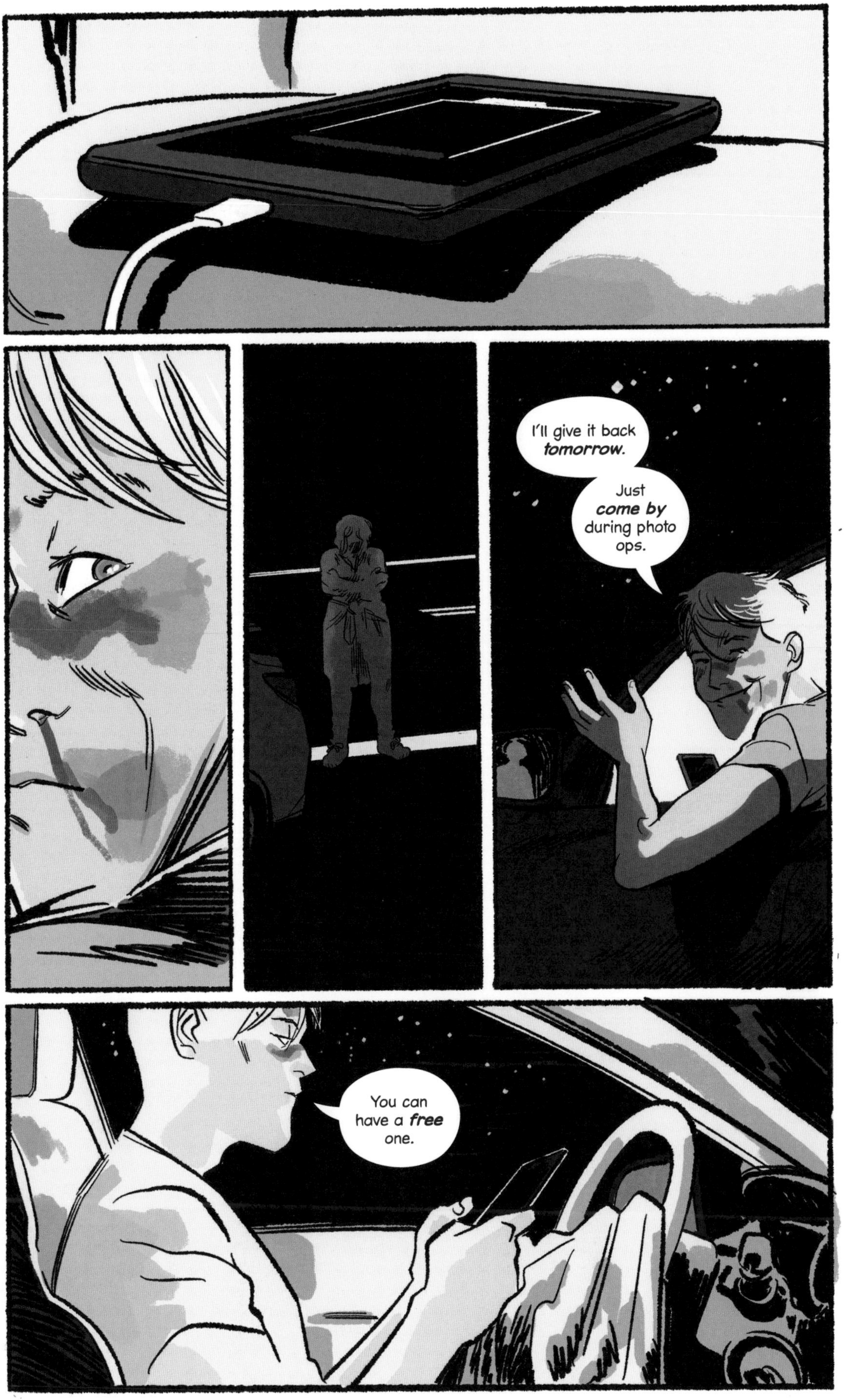
I'll give it back *tomorrow.*
Just *come by* during photo ops.
You can have a *free* one.

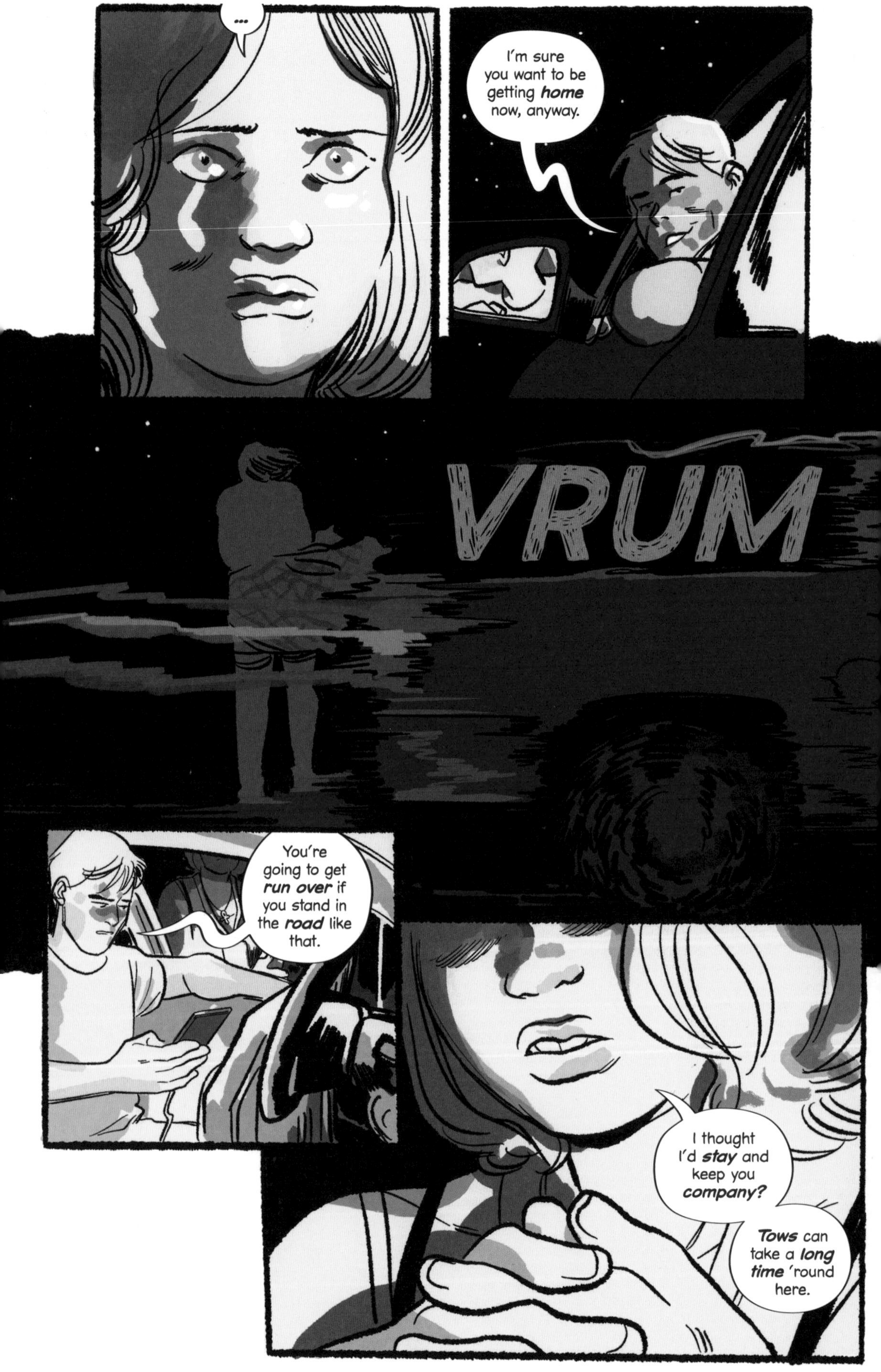
...
I'm sure you want to be getting home now, anyway.
VRUM
You're going to get run over if you stand in the road like that.
I thought I'd stay and keep you company?
Tows can take a long time 'round here.

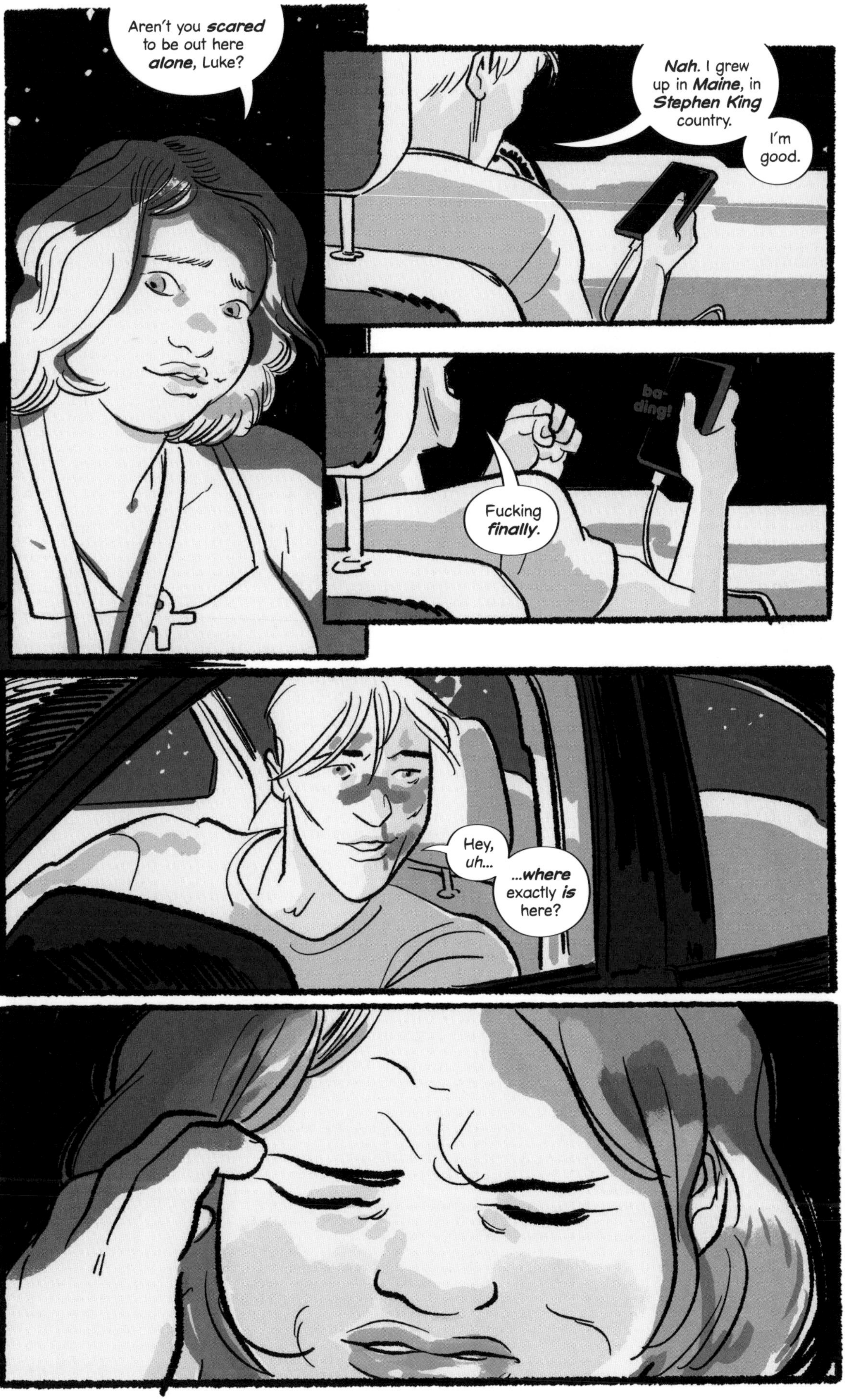
Aren't you *scared* to be out here *alone*, Luke?
Nah. I grew up in *Maine*, in *Stephen King* country.
I'm good.
ba-ding!
Fucking *finally*.
Hey, uh...
...where exactly *is* here?

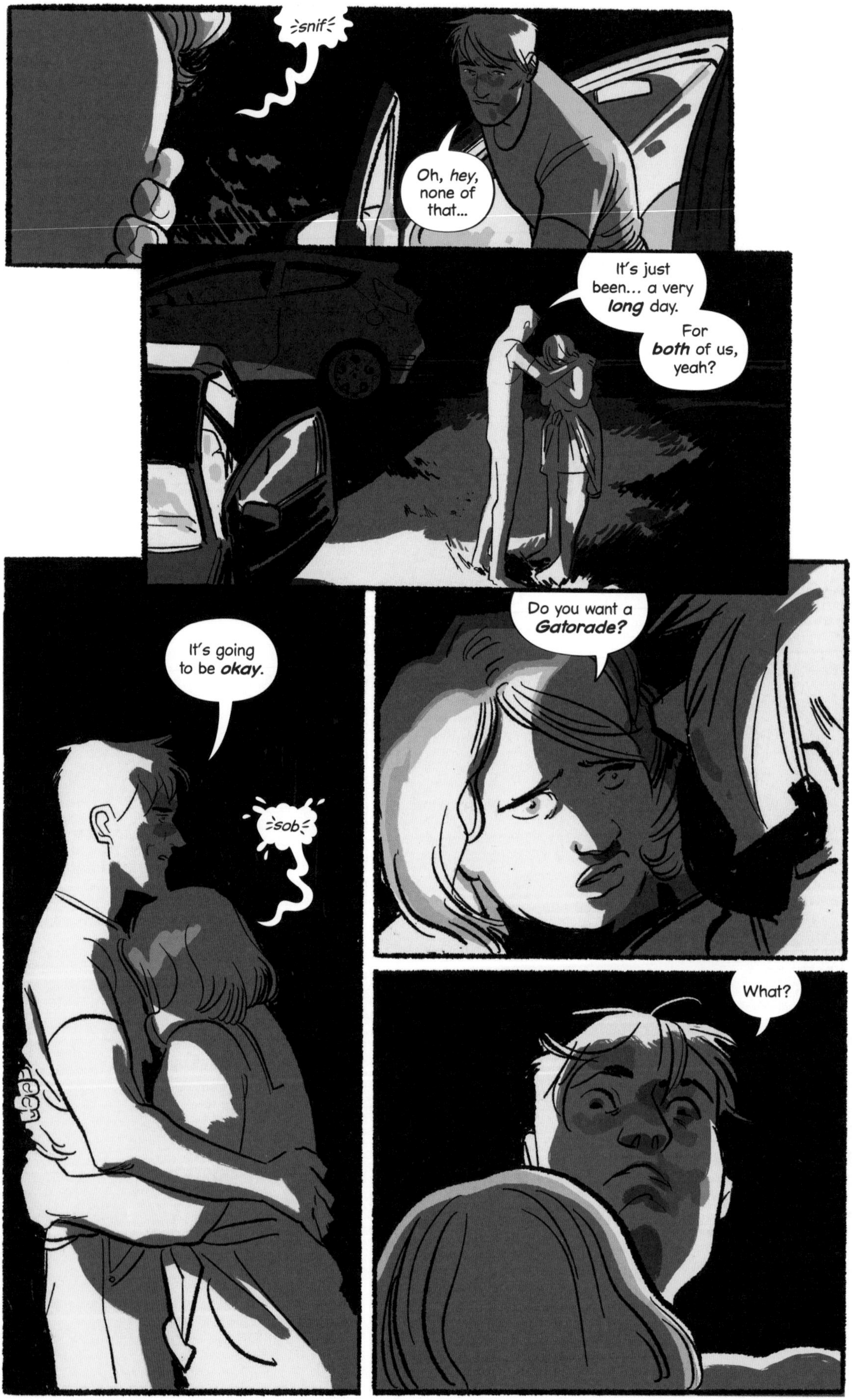

snif
Oh, *hey*, none of that...
It's just been... a very **long** day.
For **both** of us, yeah?
It's going to be **okay**.
sob
Do you want a **Gatorade?**
What?

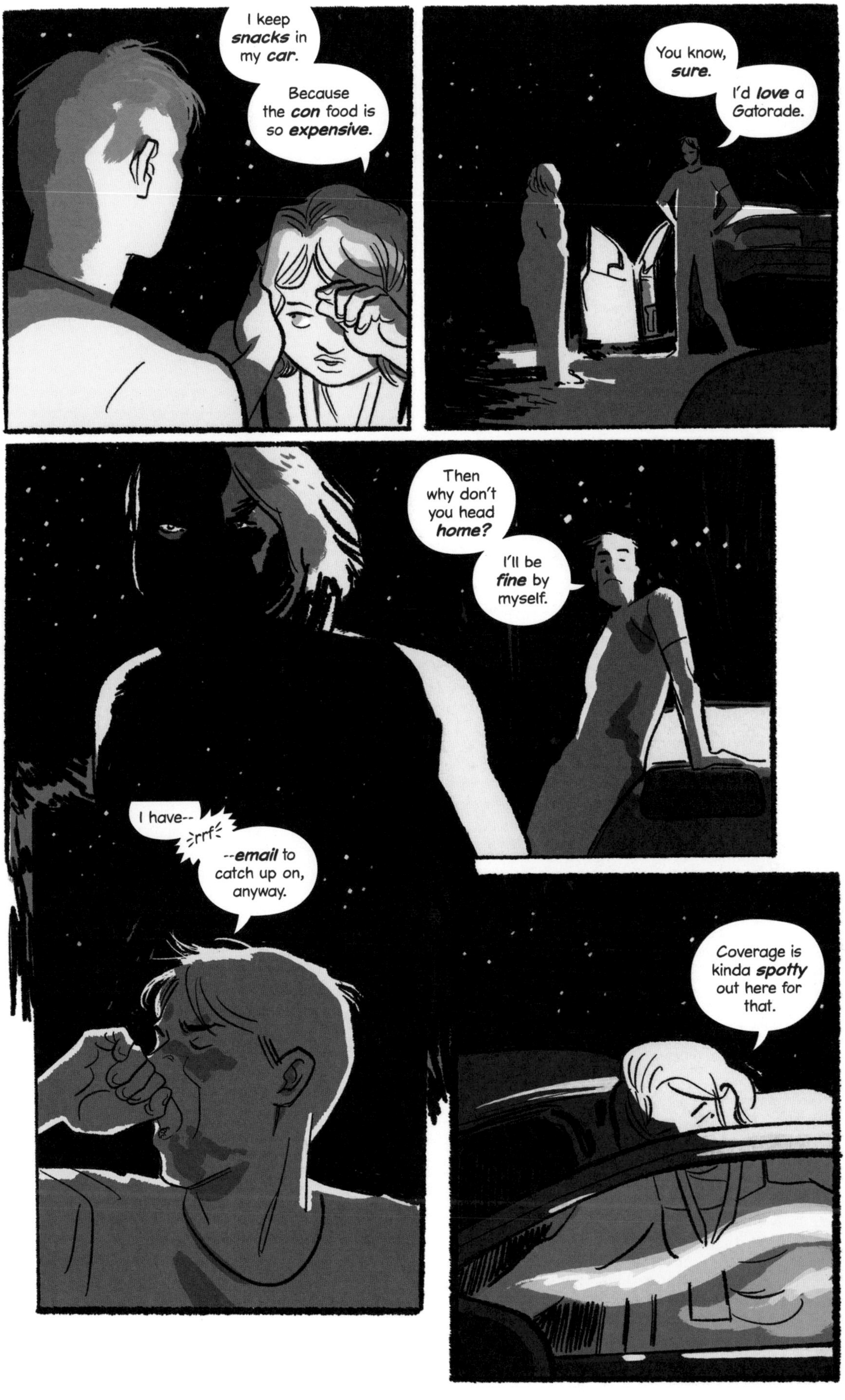
I keep *snacks* in my *car*.
Because the *con* food is so *expensive*.
You know, *sure*.
I'd *love* a Gatorade.
Then why don't you head *home?*
I'll be *fine* by myself.
I have--
rrf
--*email* to catch up on, anyway.
Coverage is kinda *spotty* out here for that.

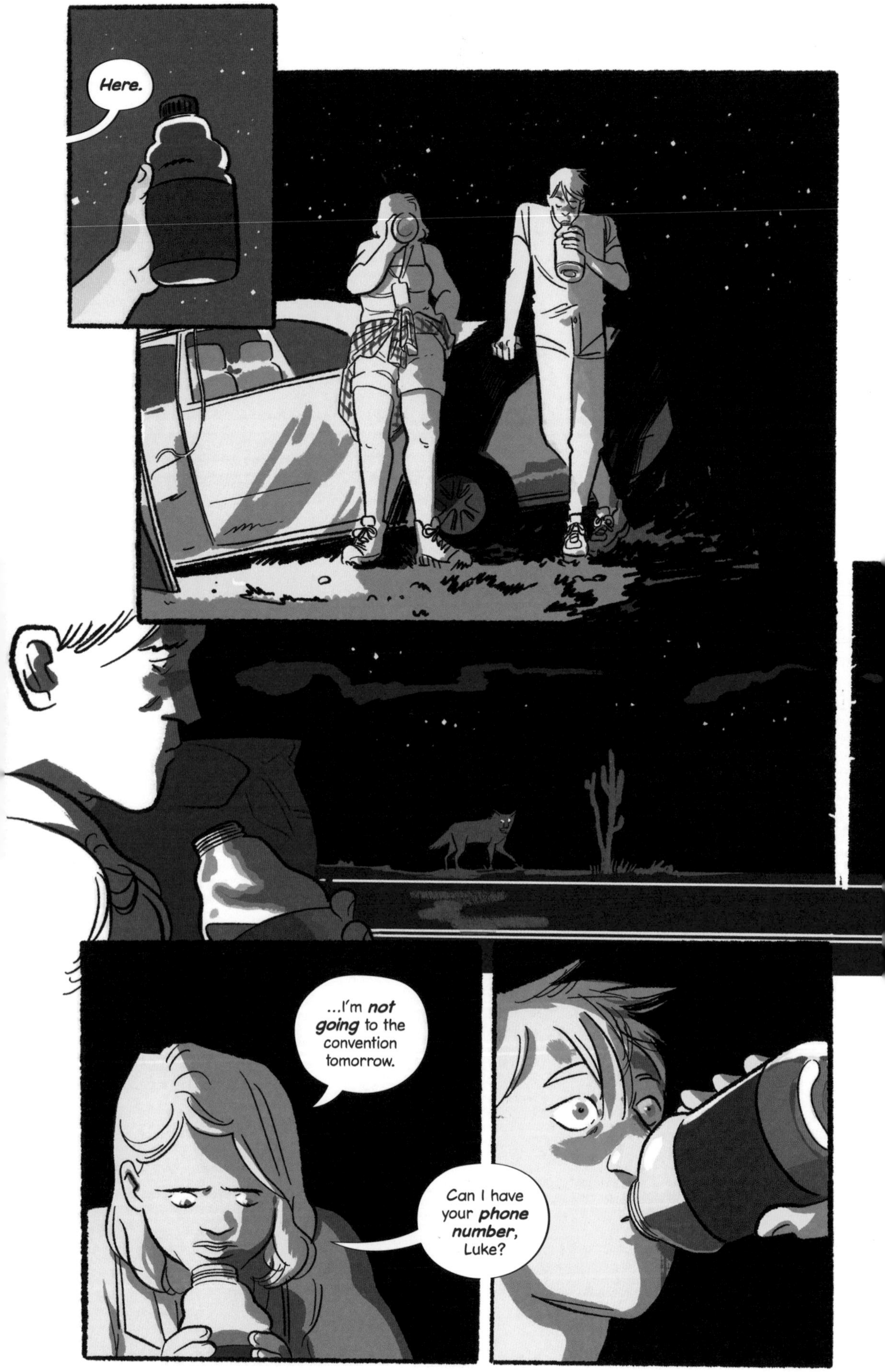
Here.
...I'm *not* *going* to the convention tomorrow.
Can I have your *phone* *number*, Luke?

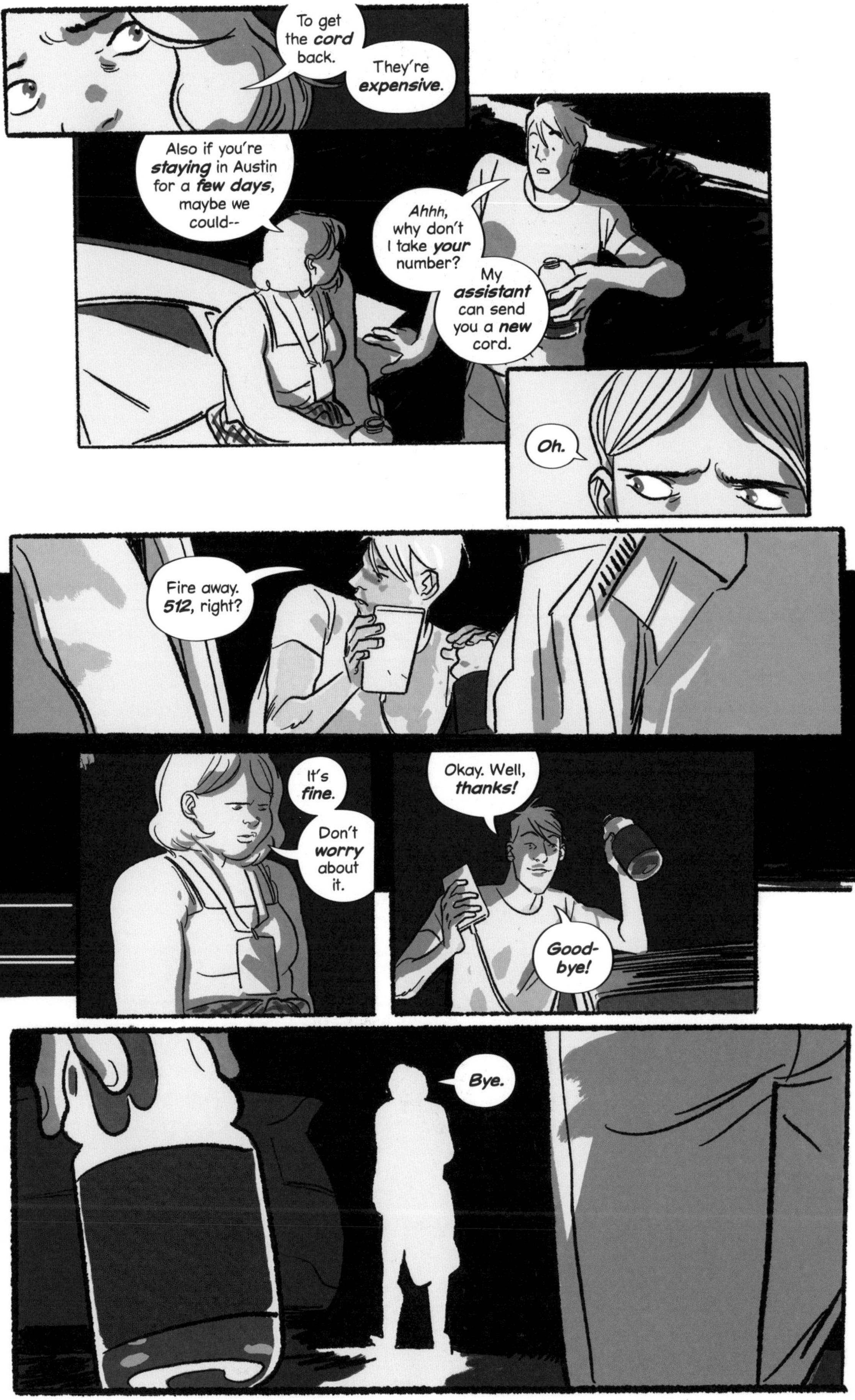
To get the *cord* back.
They're *expensive*.
Also if you're *staying* in Austin for a *few days*, maybe we could--
Ahhh, why don't I take *your* number?
My *assistant* can send you a *new* cord.
Oh.
Fire away. *512*, right?
It's *fine*.
Don't *worry* about it.
Okay. Well, *thanks!*
Good-bye!
Bye.

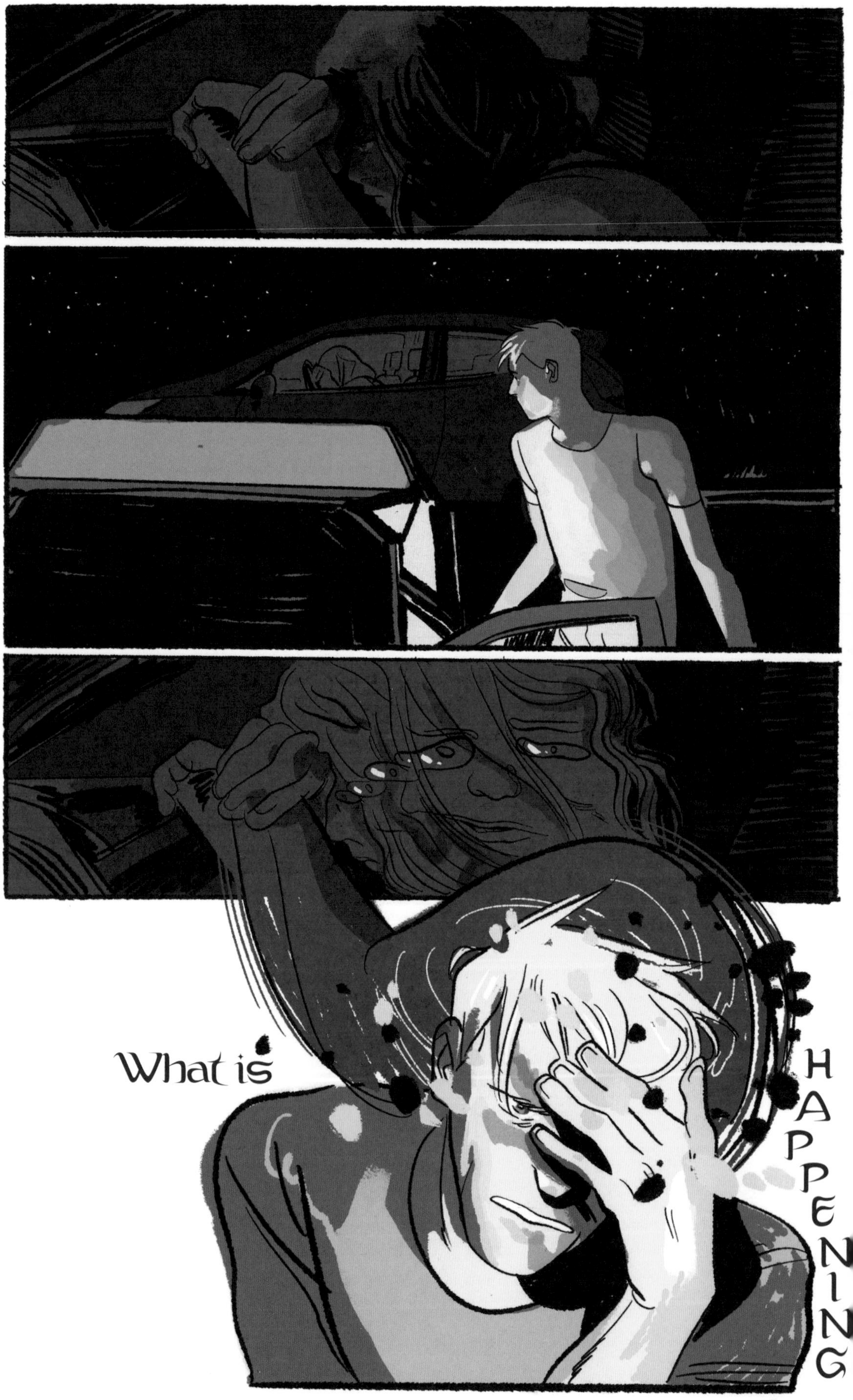
What is
HAPPENING

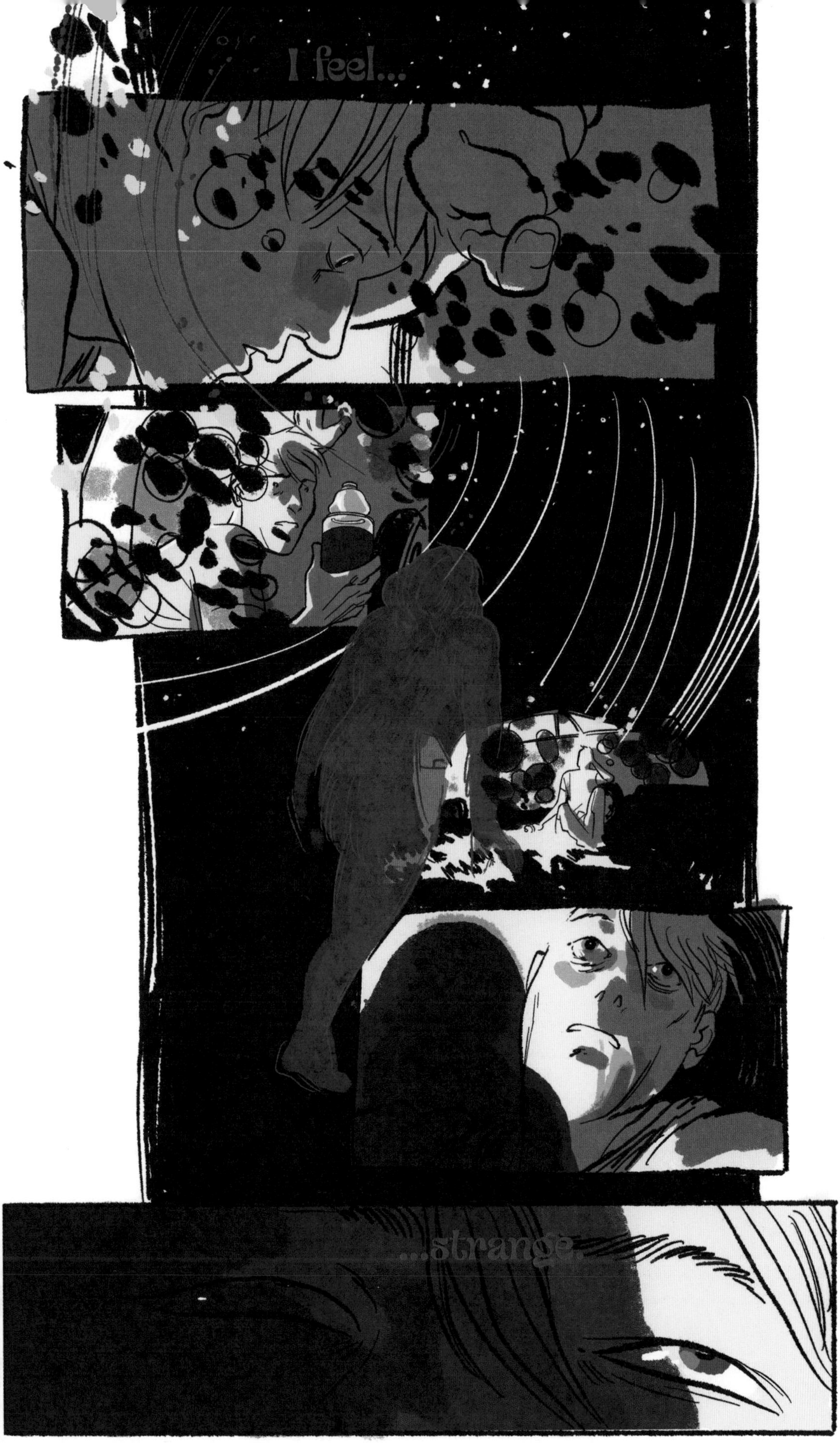
I feel...
...strange.

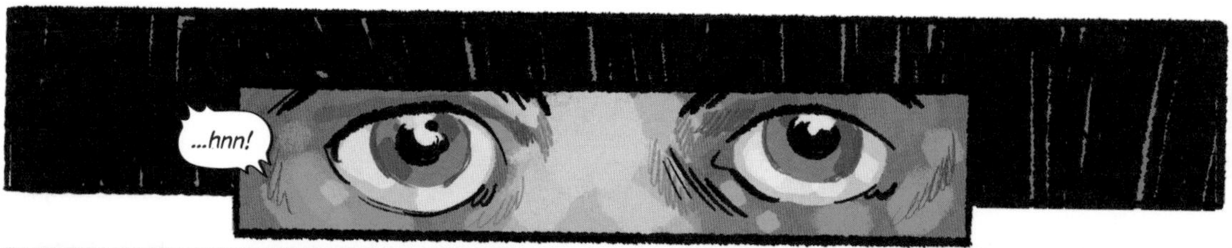
...hnn!

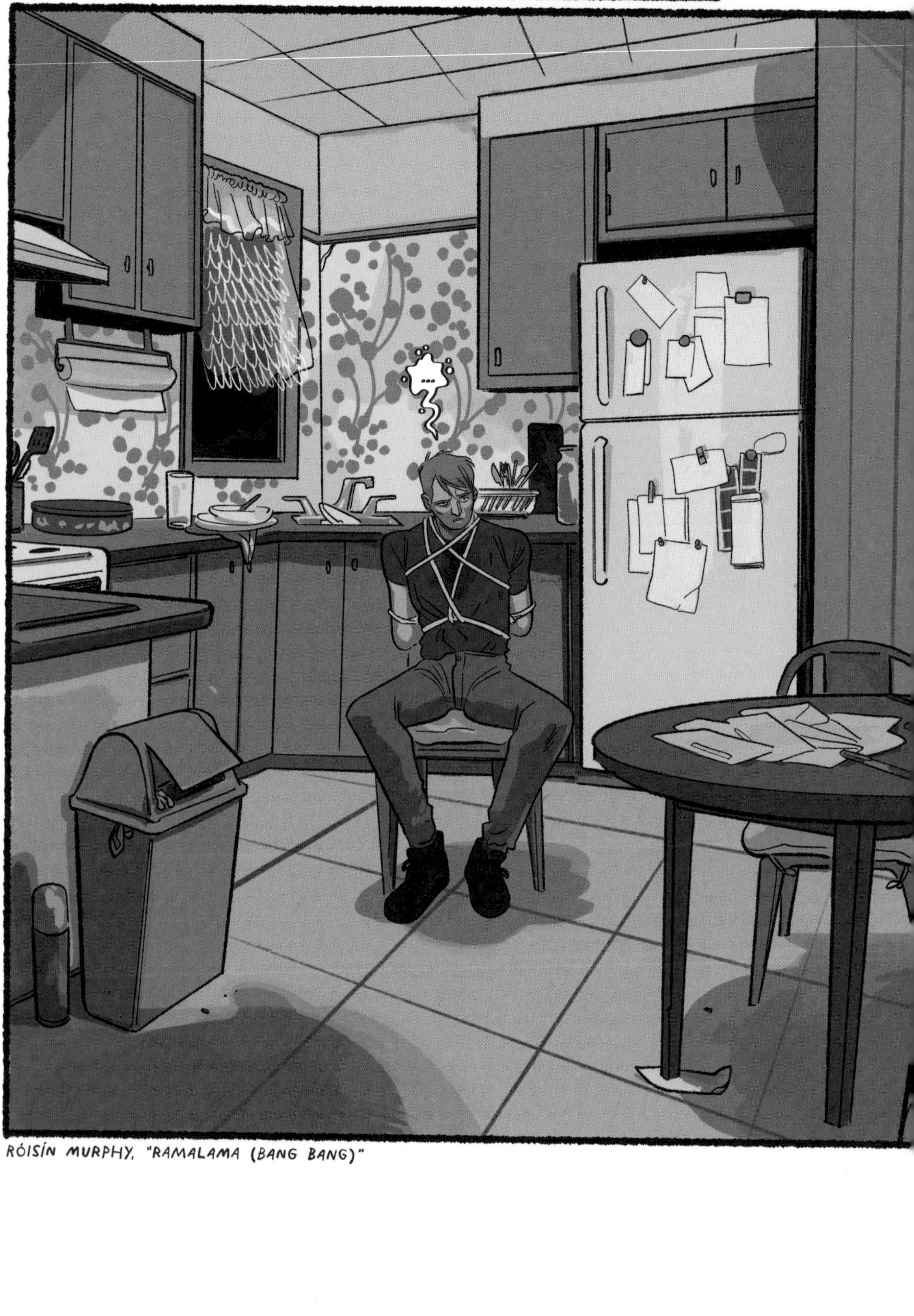
...

RÓISÍN MURPHY, "RAMALAMA (BANG BANG)"

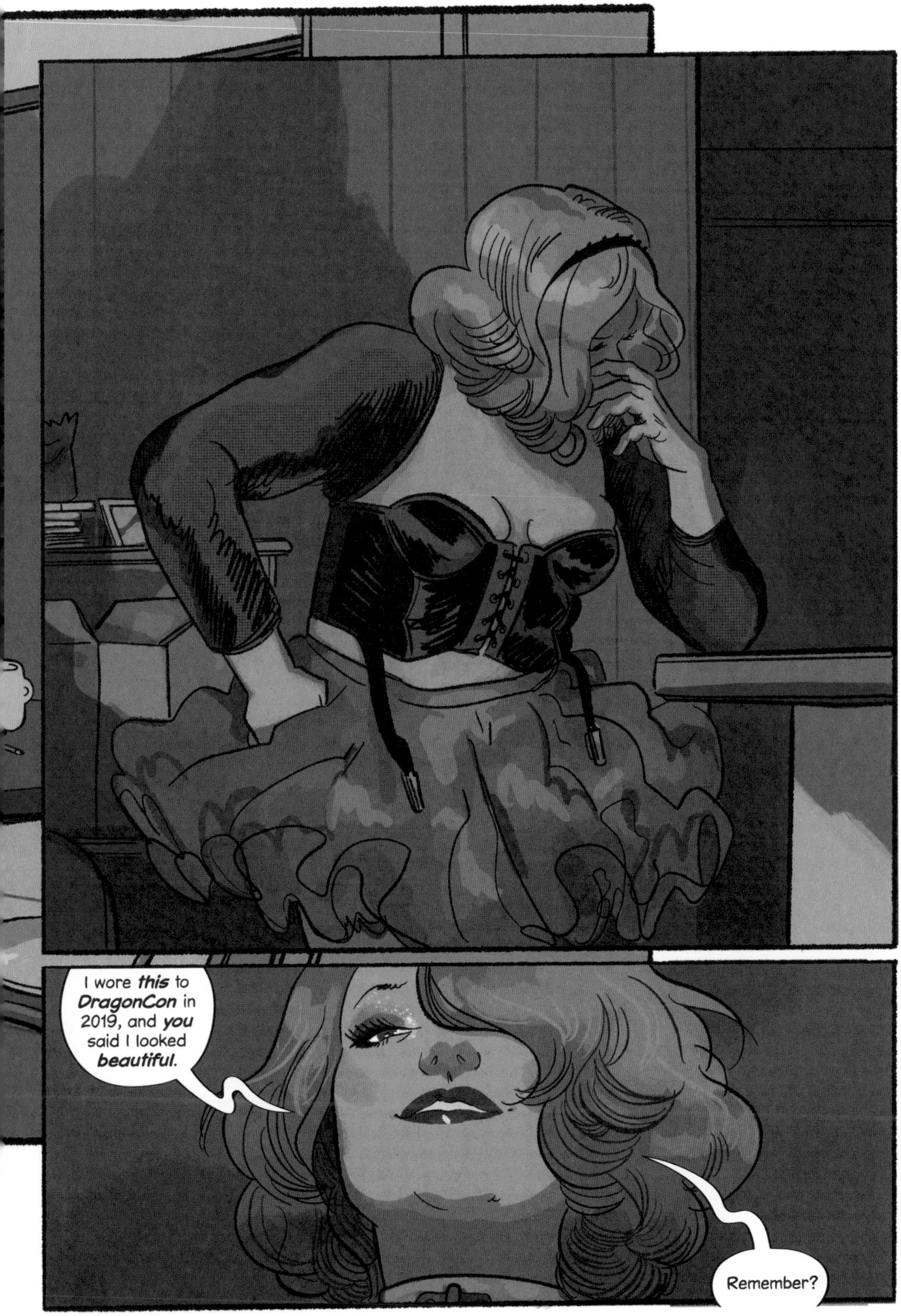
I wore ***this*** to ***DragonCon*** in 2019, and ***you*** said I looked ***beautiful***.
Remember?

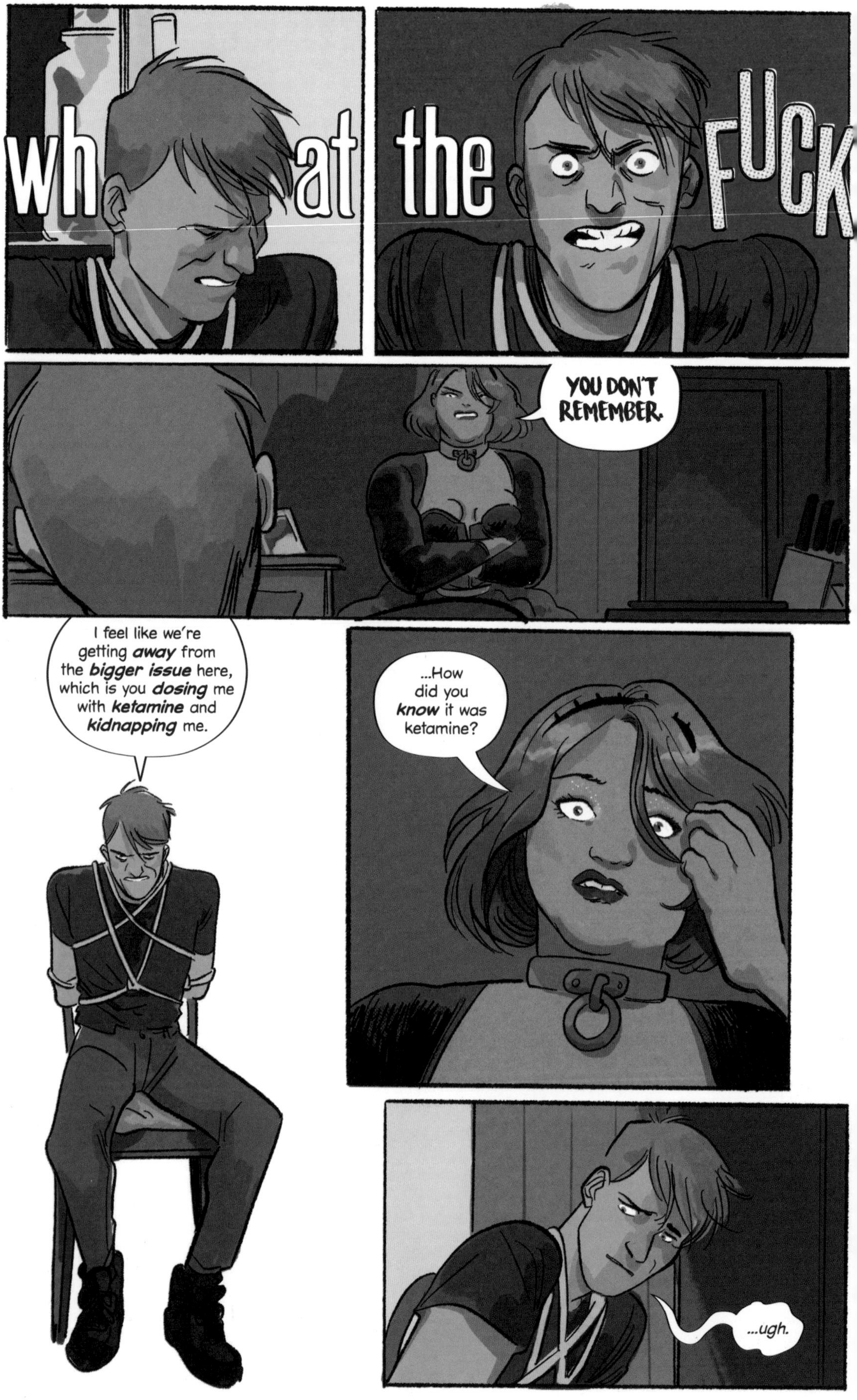

wh at the FUCK
YOU DON'T REMEMBER.
I feel like we're getting away from the bigger issue here, which is you dosing me with ketamine and kidnapping me.
...How did you know it was ketamine?
...ugh.

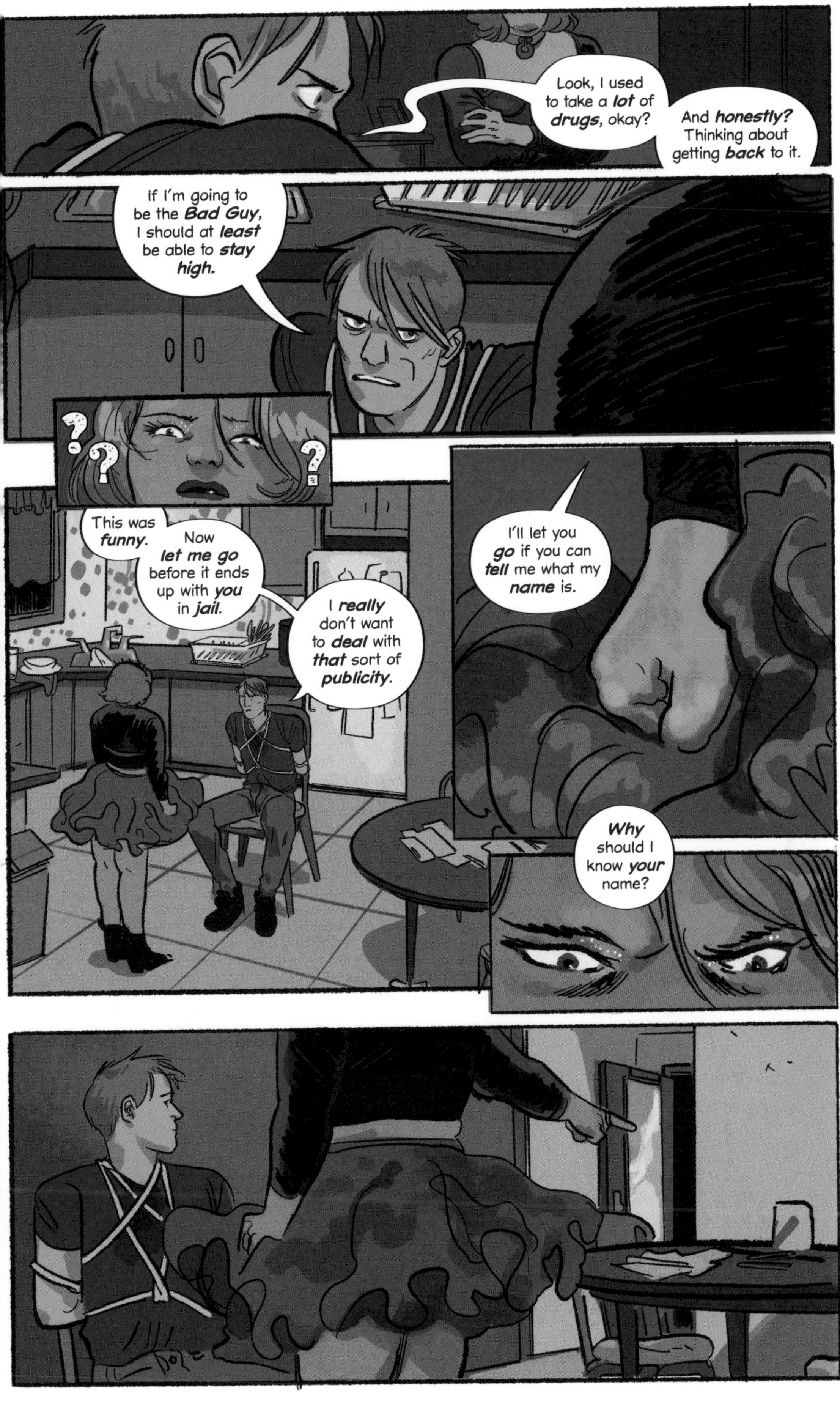
Look, I used to take a *lot* of *drugs*, okay?
And *honestly?* Thinking about getting *back* to it.
If I'm going to be the *Bad Guy*, I should at *least* be able to *stay high.*
This was *funny.*
Now *let me go* before it ends up with *you* in *jail.*
I *really* don't want to *deal* with *that* sort of *publicity.*
I'll let you *go* if you can *tell* me what my *name* is.
Why should I know *your* name?

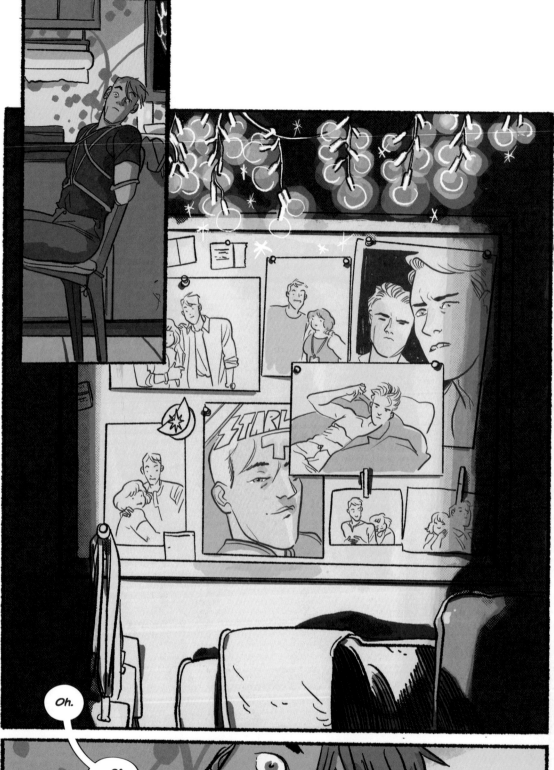

Oh.

...Of course.

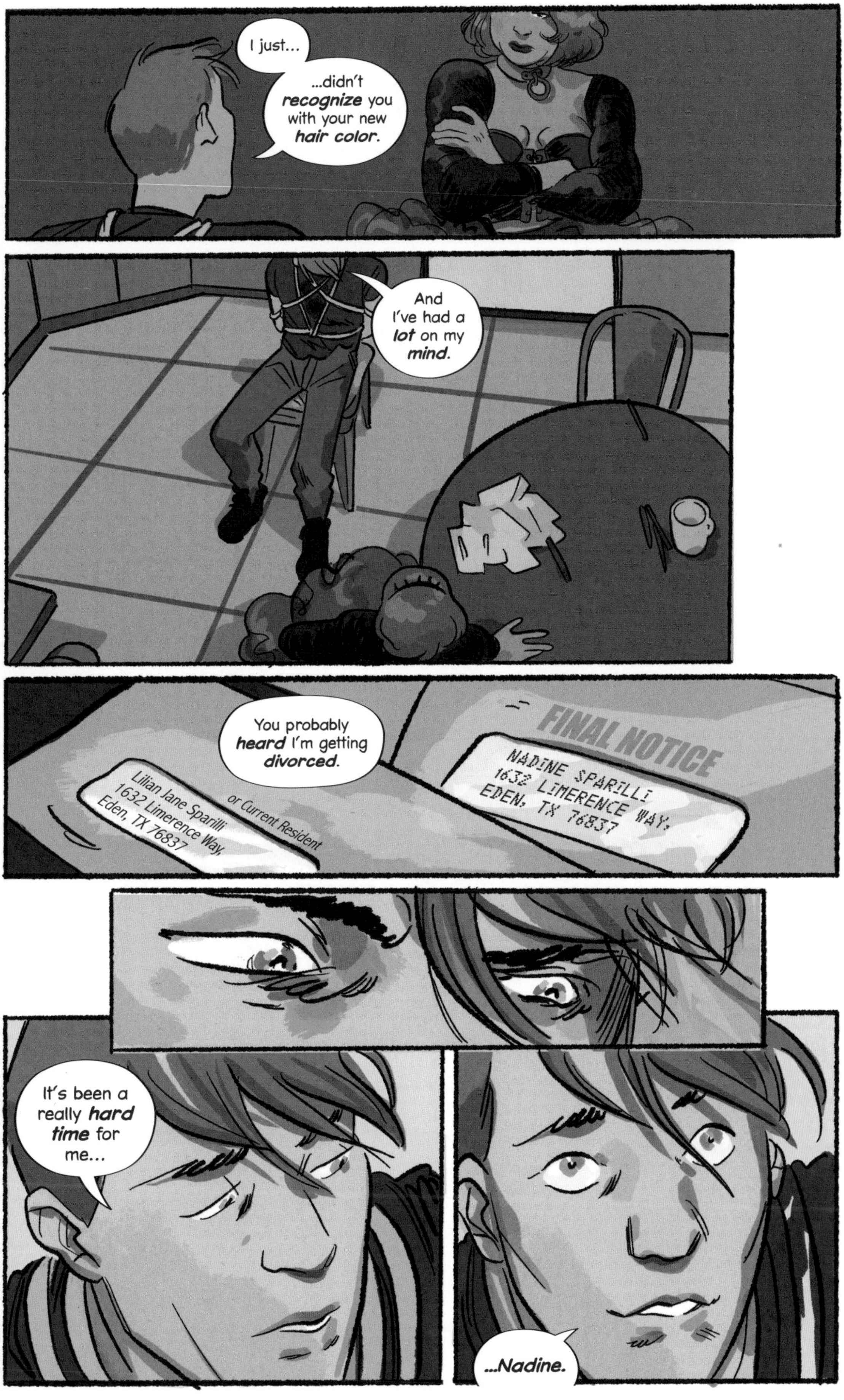
I just...
...didn't *recognize* you with your new *hair color*.
And I've had a *lot* on my *mind*.
You probably *heard* I'm getting *divorced*.
Lilian Jane Sparilli
1632 Limerence Way,
Eden, TX 76837
or Current Resident
FINAL NOTICE
NADINE SPARILLI
1632 LIMERENCE WAY,
EDEN, TX 76837
It's been a really *hard time* for me...
...Nadine.

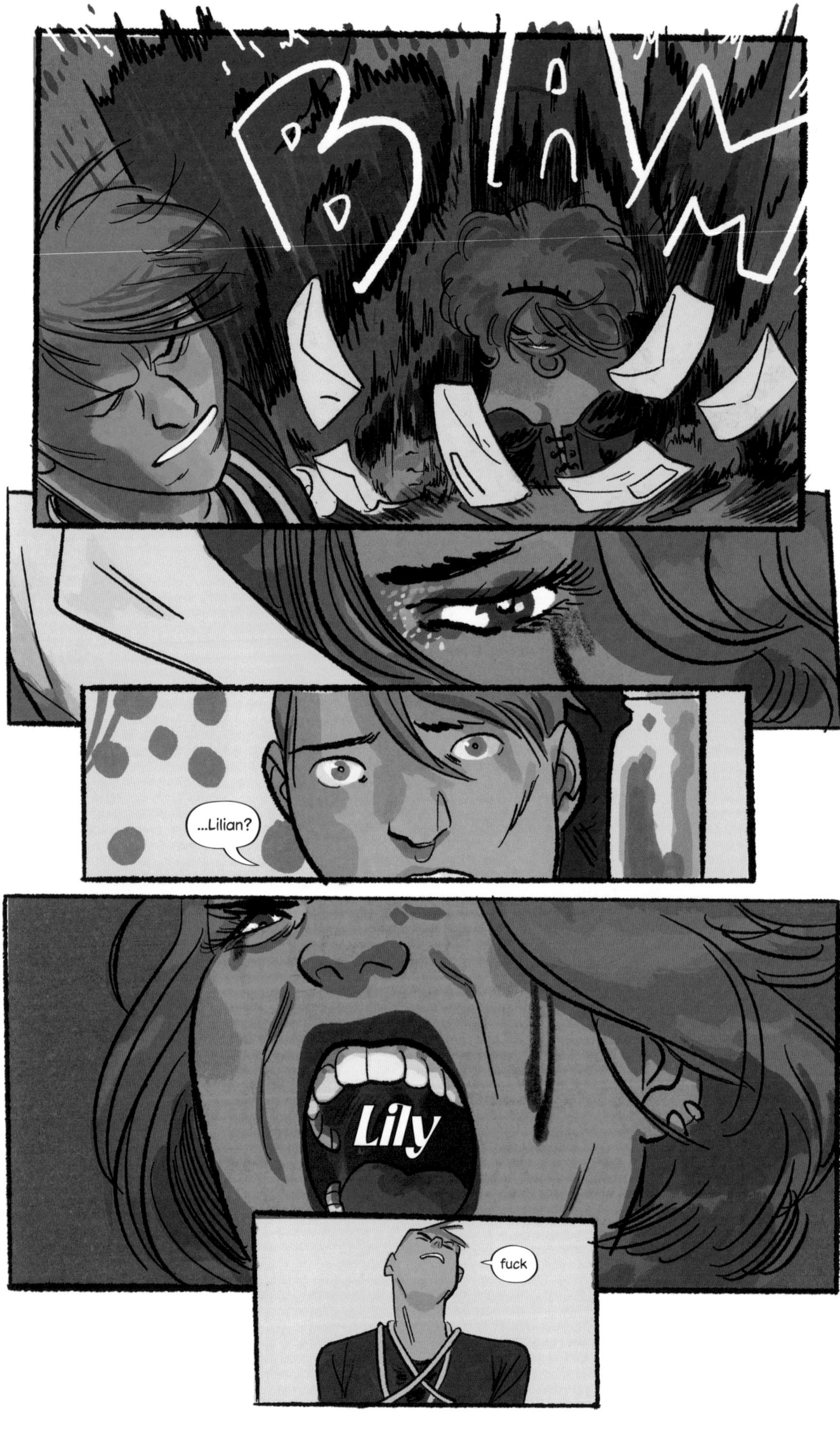
BAM
...Lilian?
Lily
fuck

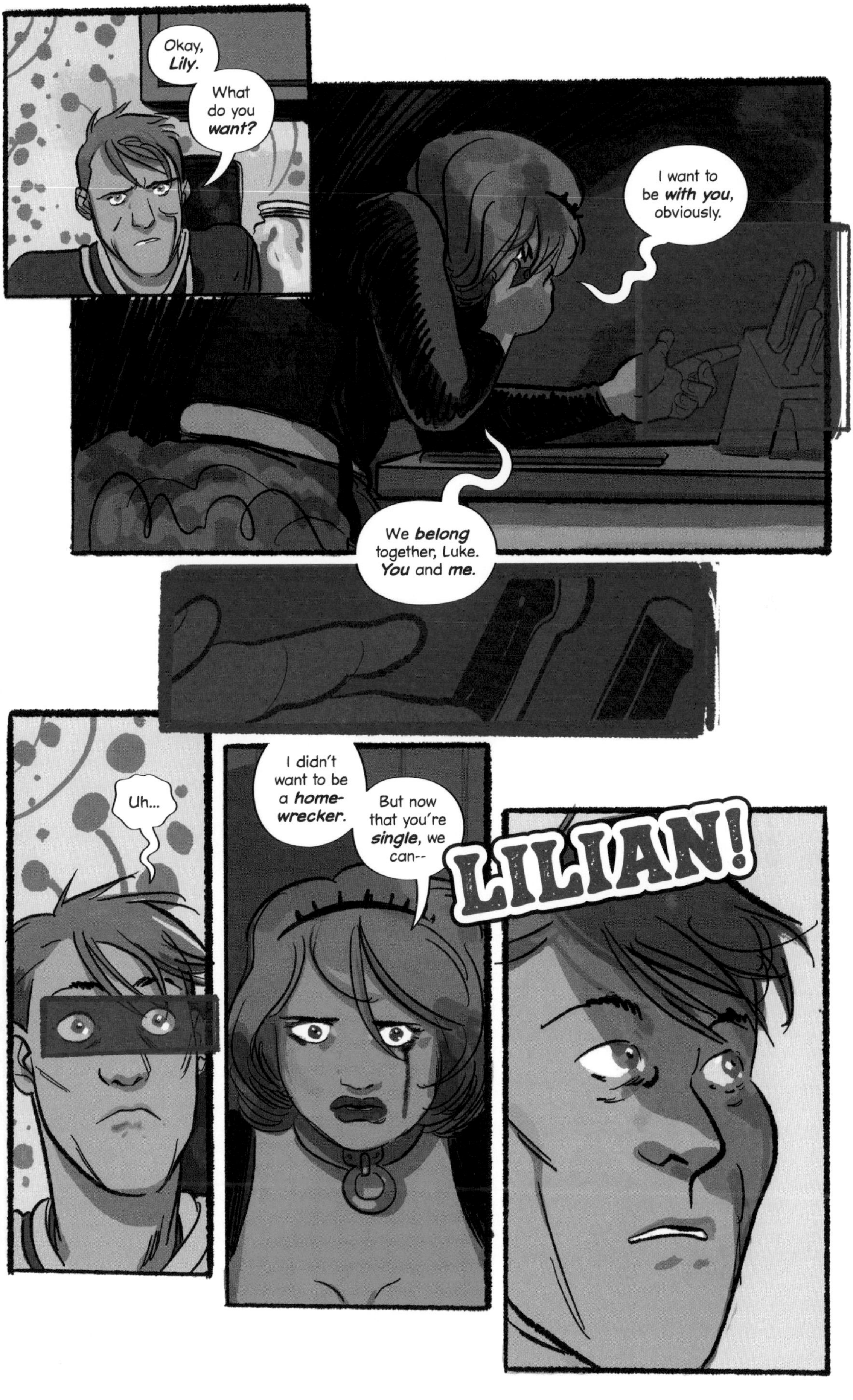
Okay, *Lily*.
What do you *want?*
I want to be *with you*, obviously.
We *belong* together, Luke. *You* and *me.*
Uh...
I didn't want to be a *home-wrecker*.
But now that you're *single*, we can--
LILIAN!

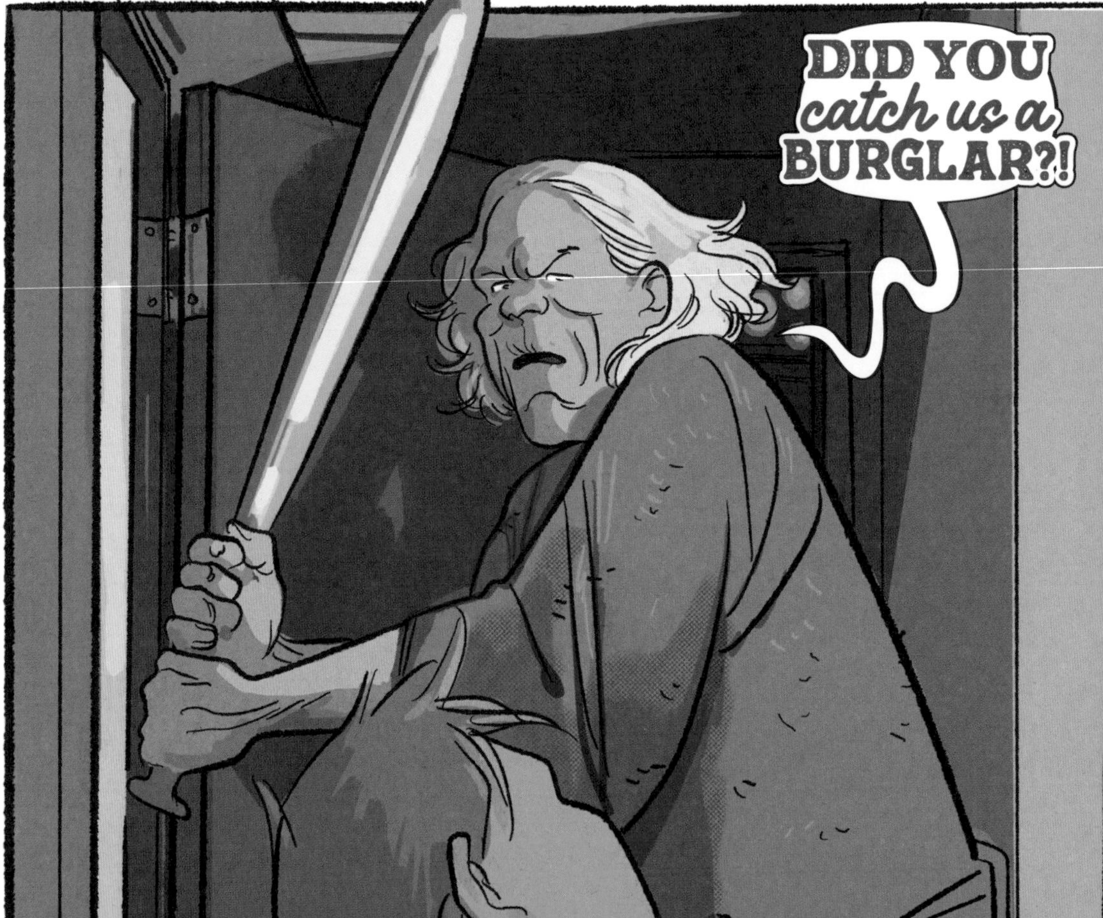
DID YOU catch us a BURGLAR?!
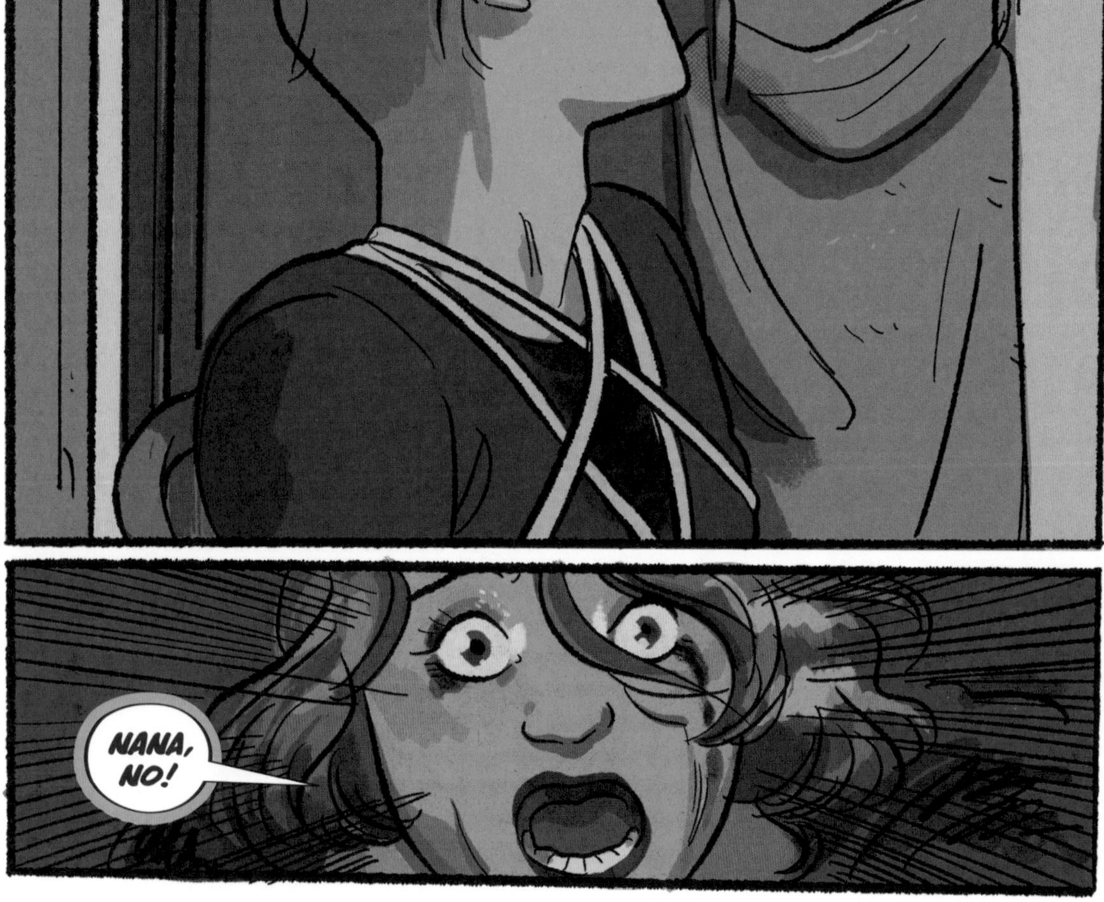
NANA, NO!

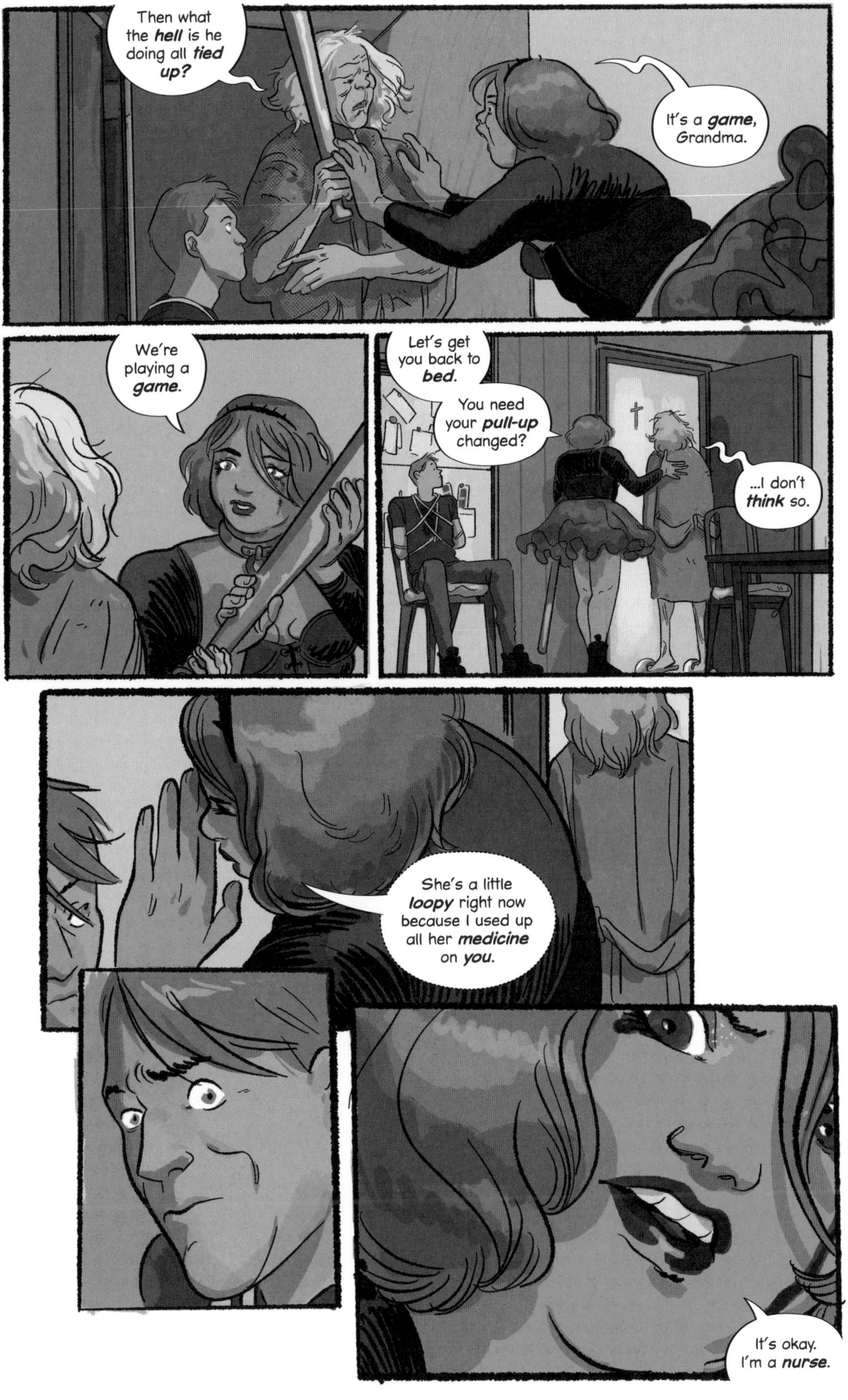
Then what the *hell* is he doing all *tied up?*
It's a *game,* Grandma.
We're playing a *game.*
Let's get you back to *bed.*
You need your *pull-up* changed?
...I don't *think* so.
She's a little *loopy* right now because I used up all her *medicine* on *you.*
It's okay. I'm a *nurse.*

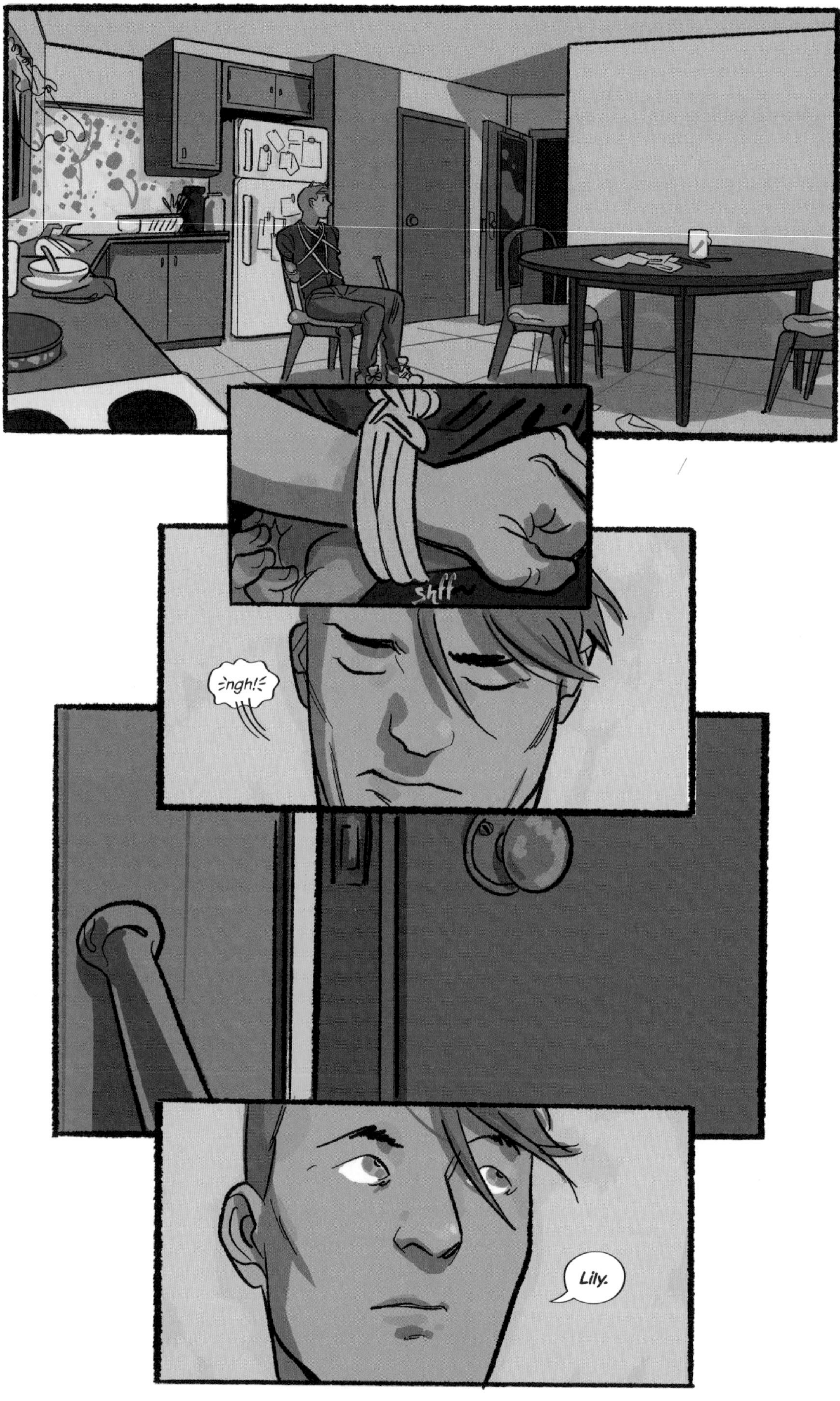
shff
ngh!
Lily.

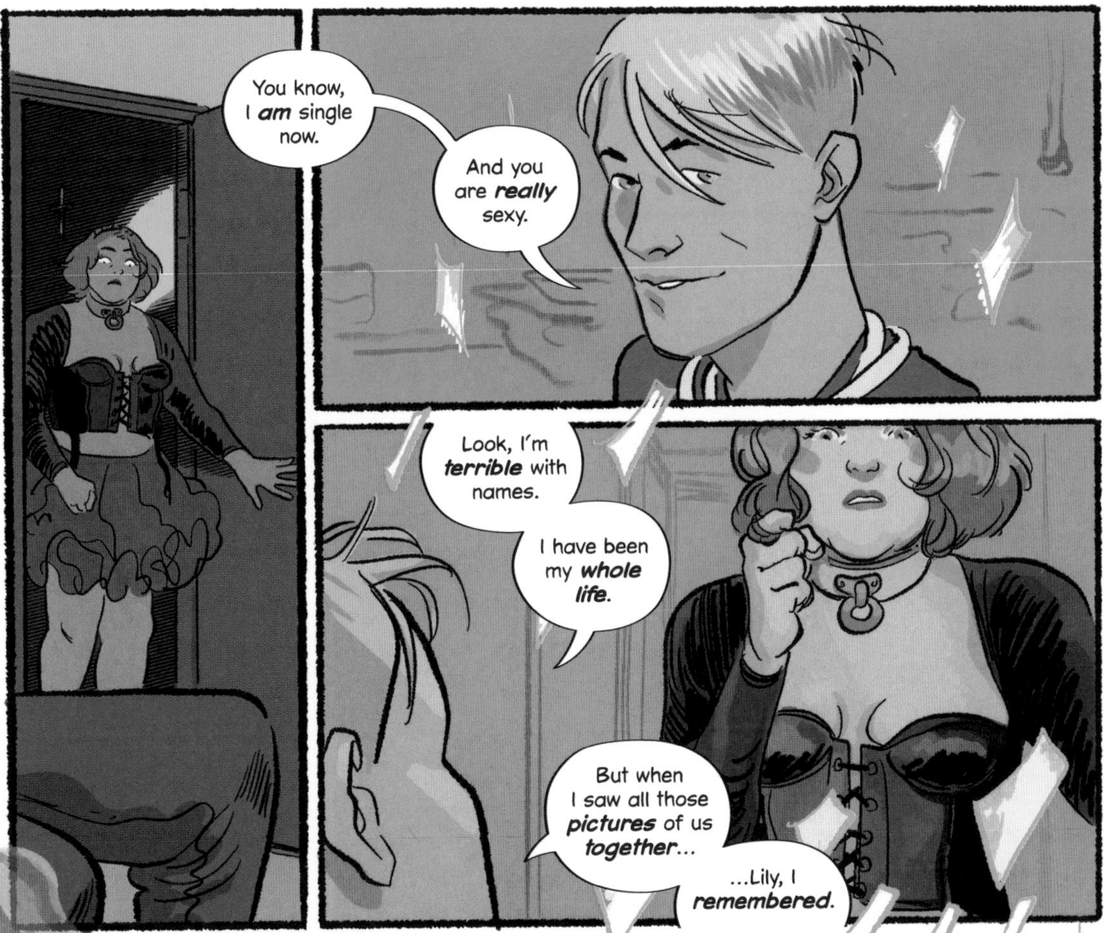
You know, I *am* single now.
And you are ***really*** sexy.
Look, I'm ***terrible*** with names.
I have been my ***whole life***.
But when I saw all those ***pictures*** of us ***together***...
...Lily, I ***remembered***.

"You don't know how exhausting those conventions are," Luke said, his winter-blue eyes shimmering with remembered pain. Of course you'd noticed the dark circles under them; the way his hair hadn't been cut recently. Nobody was taking care of him, least of all himself. "So many people, and you have to be perfect for every one no matter who they are, what they look like, or smell like." His mouth quirks up in the roguish smile you've stared at for half your life. "And then you'd come, and you were a *jewel*, the only thing in any room you're ever in. I couldn't take my eyes off you." He looks down, bashful, as a blush colors his high cheekbones. "And suddenly my job was the easiest one in the whole world, because of you. It shows in the photos, Lily, the way I was looking at you. I didn't look at anyone else that way."

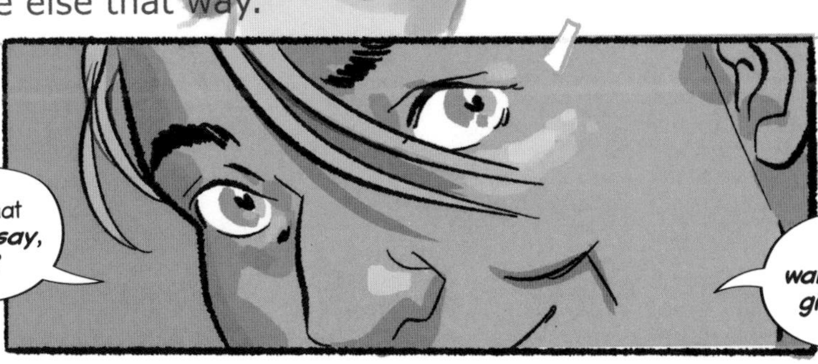
So what do you ***say***, Lily?
Do you ***want*** to be my ***girlfriend?***

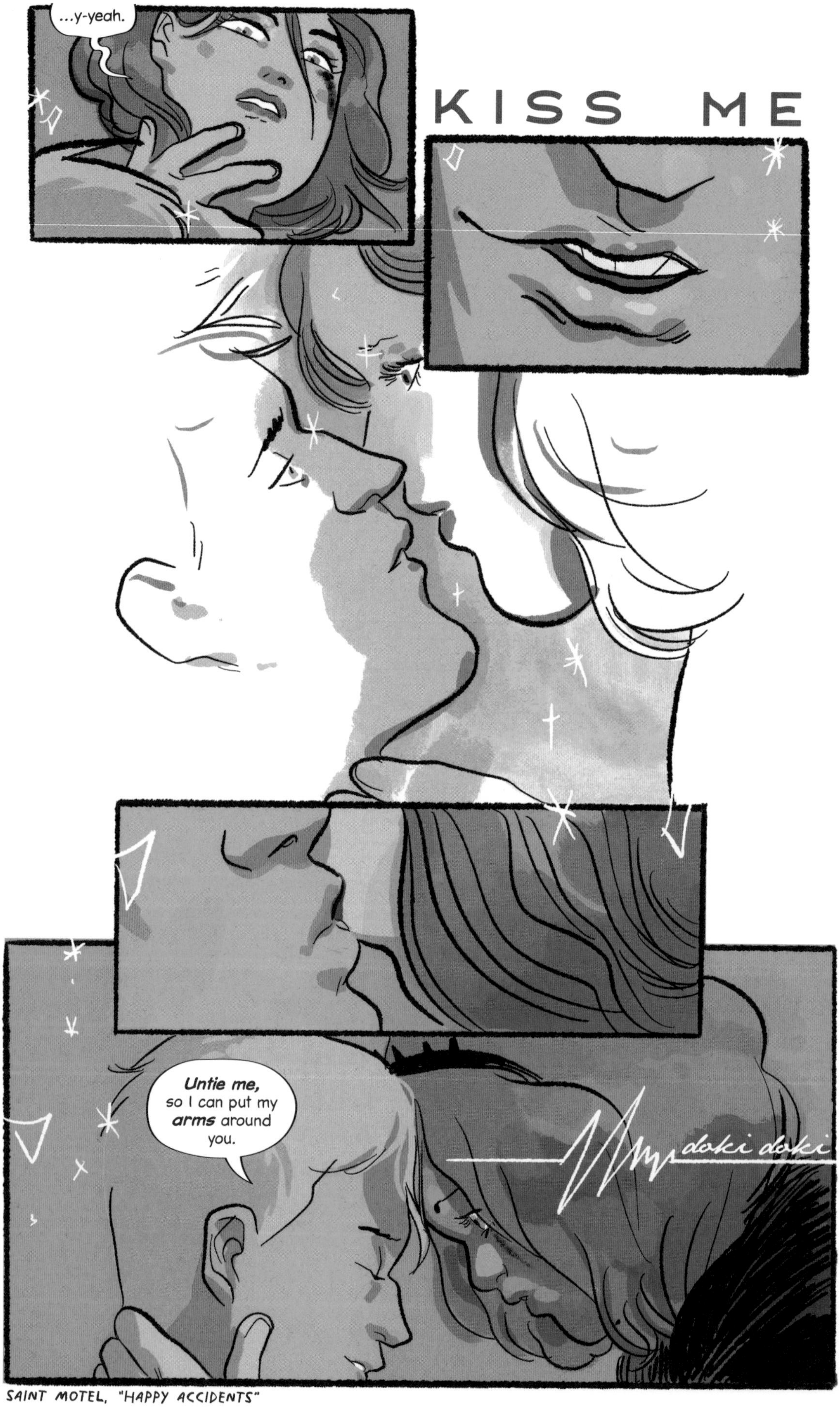
...y-yeah.
KISS ME
Untie me, so I can put my arms around you.
doki doki

SAINT MOTEL, "HAPPY ACCIDENTS"

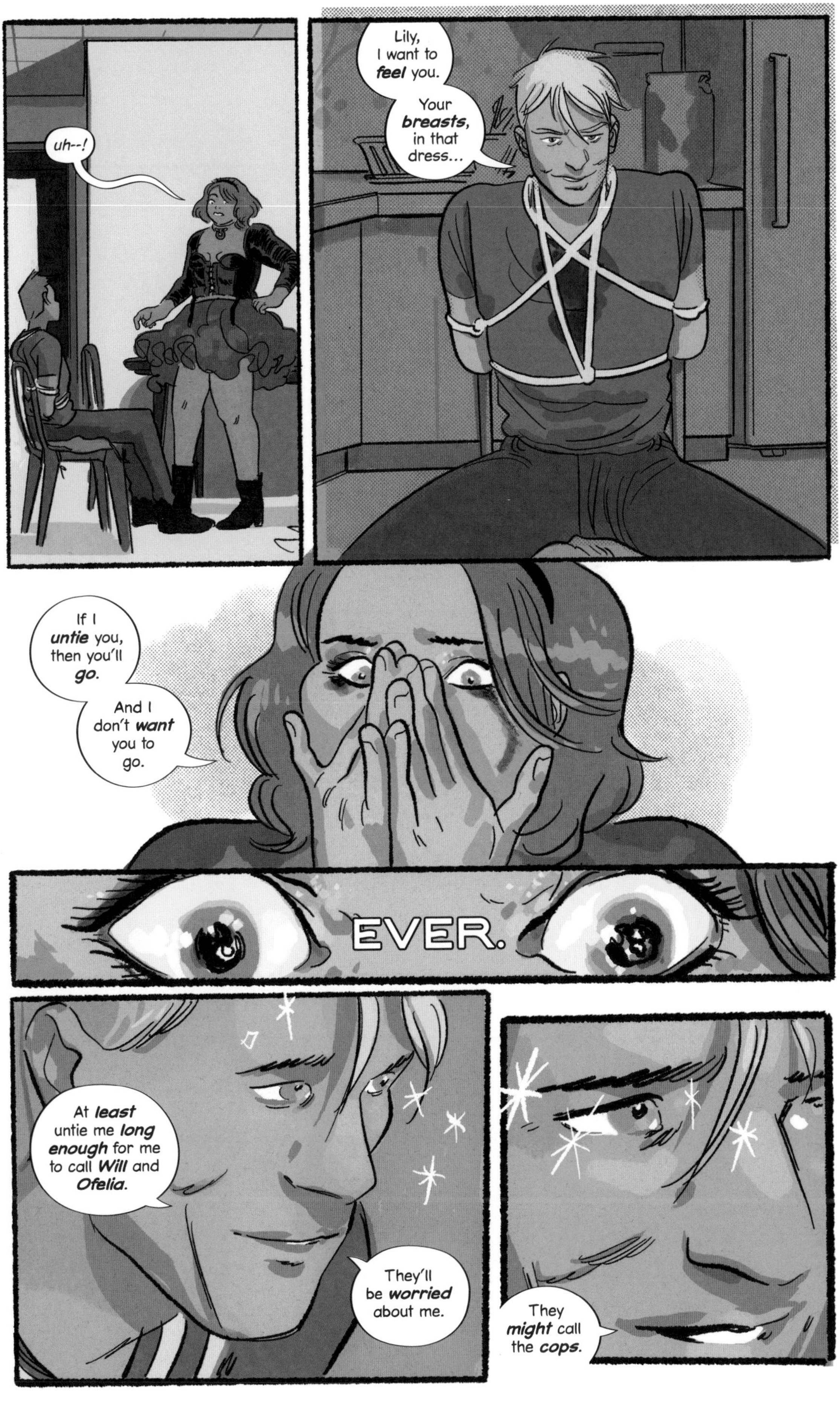
uh--!
Lily, I want to feel you.
Your breasts, in that dress...
If I untie you, then you'll go.
And I don't want you to go.
EVER.
At least untie me long enough for me to call Will and Ofelia.
They'll be worried about me.
They might call the cops.

DAVID WAX MUSEUM, "GUESTHOUSE"

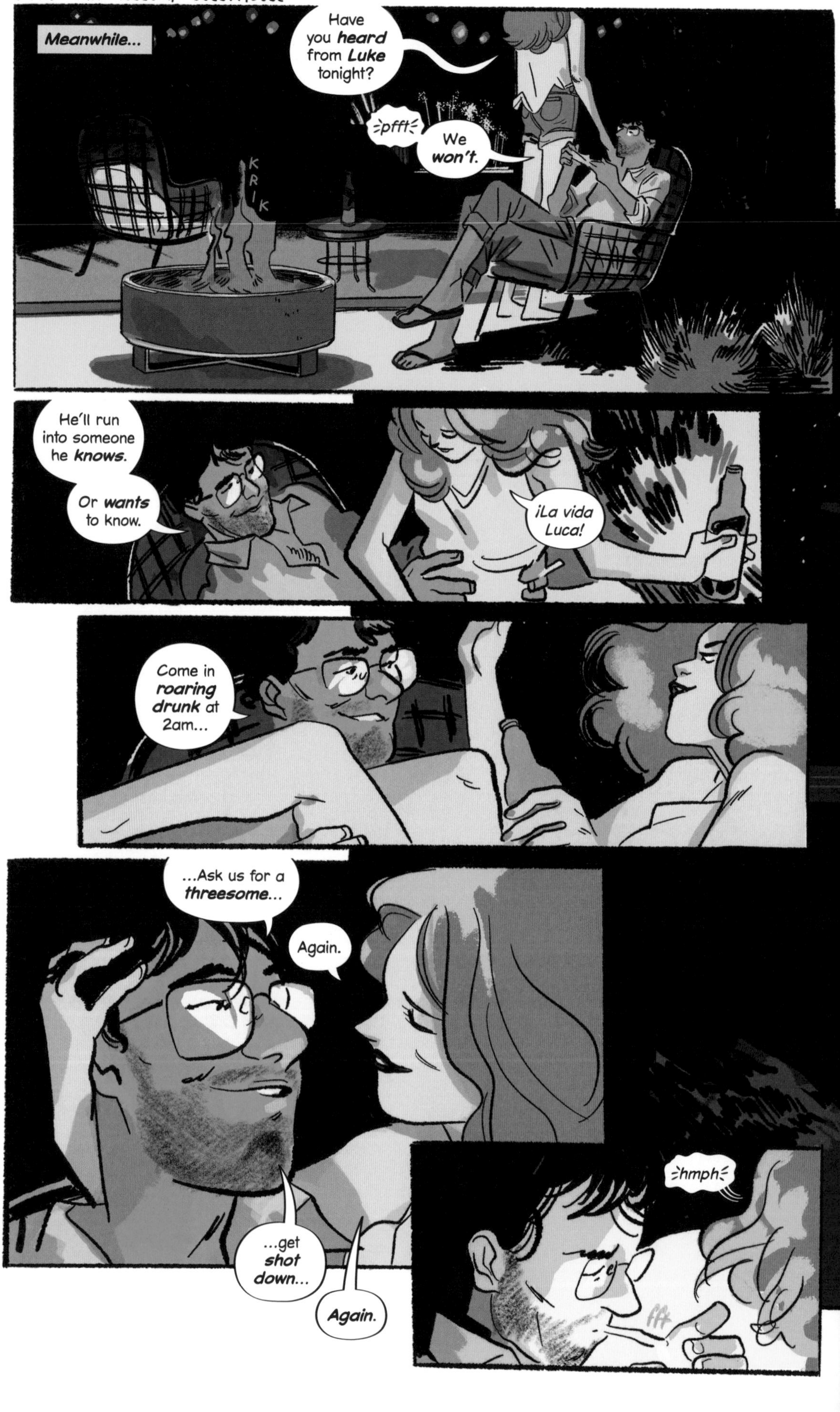
Meanwhile...
Have you heard from Luke tonight?
pfft
We won't.
KRIK
He'll run into someone he knows.
Or wants to know.
¡La vida Luca!
Come in roaring drunk at 2am...
...Ask us for a threesome...
Again.
...get shot down...
Again.
hmph

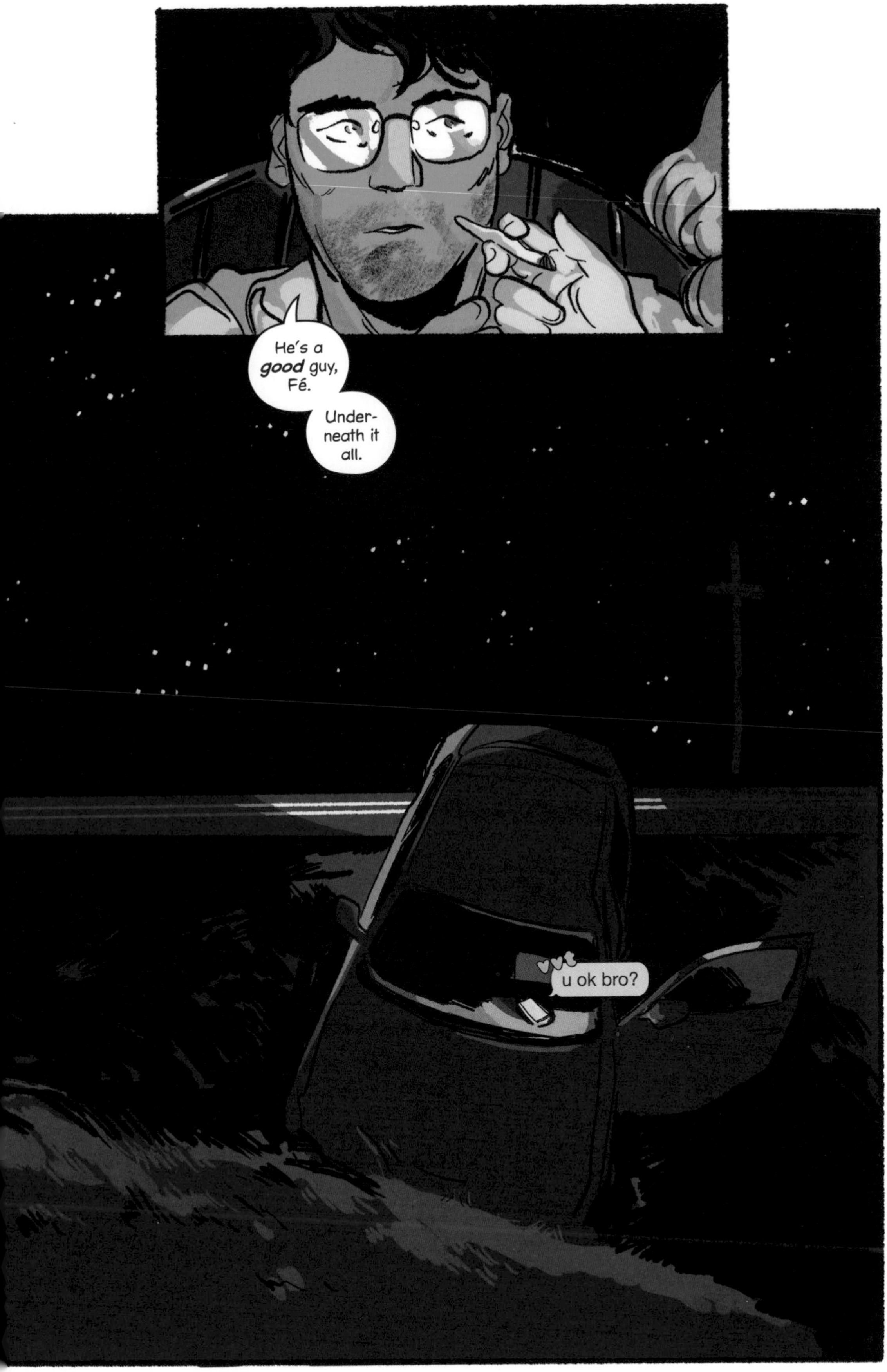
He's a **good** guy, Fé.
Underneath it all.
u ok bro?

PHANTOGRAM, "MR. IMPOSSIBLE"

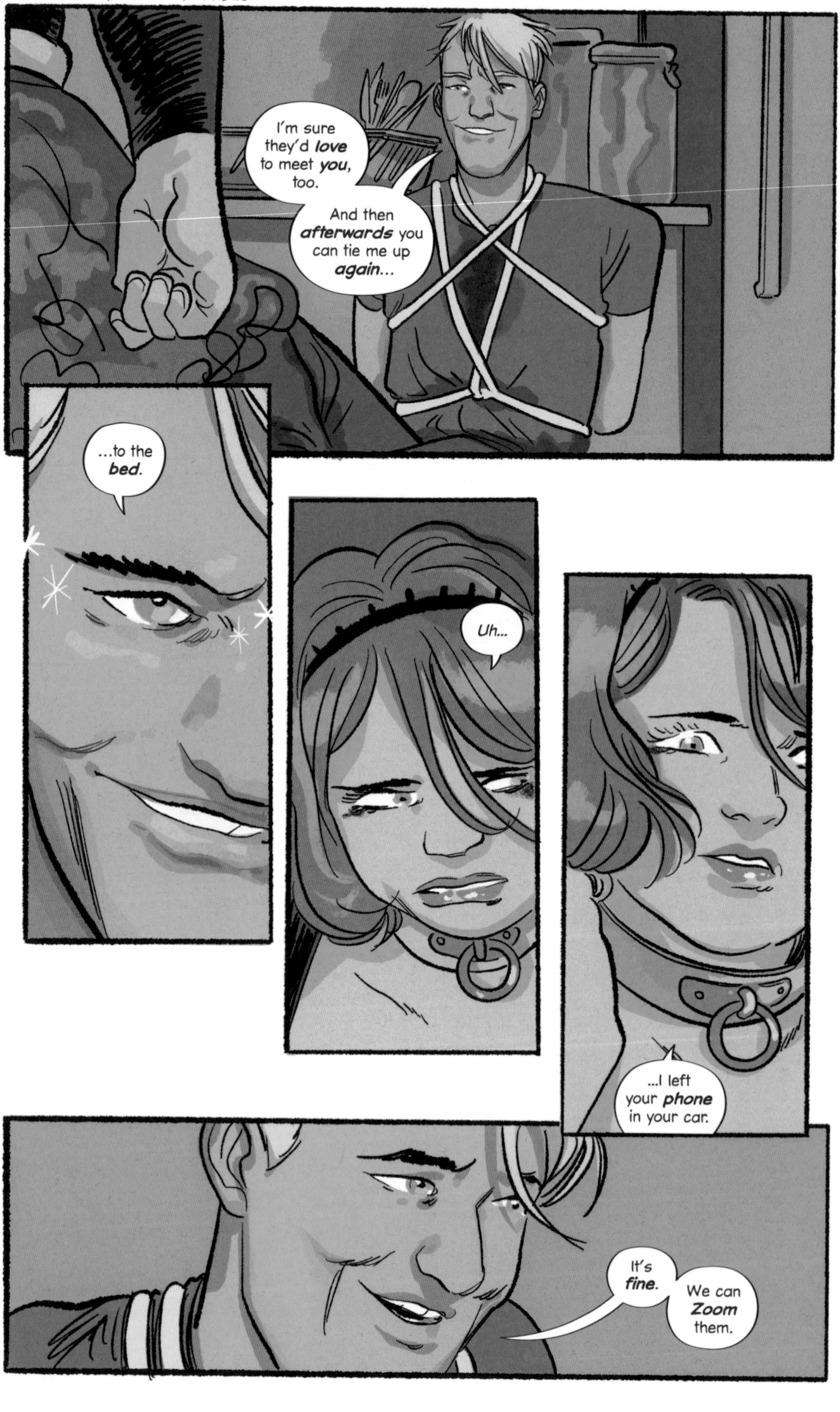
I'm sure they'd **love** to meet **you**, too.
And then **afterwards** you can tie me up **again**...
...to the **bed**.
Uh...
...I left your **phone** in your car.
It's **fine**.
We can **Zoom** them.

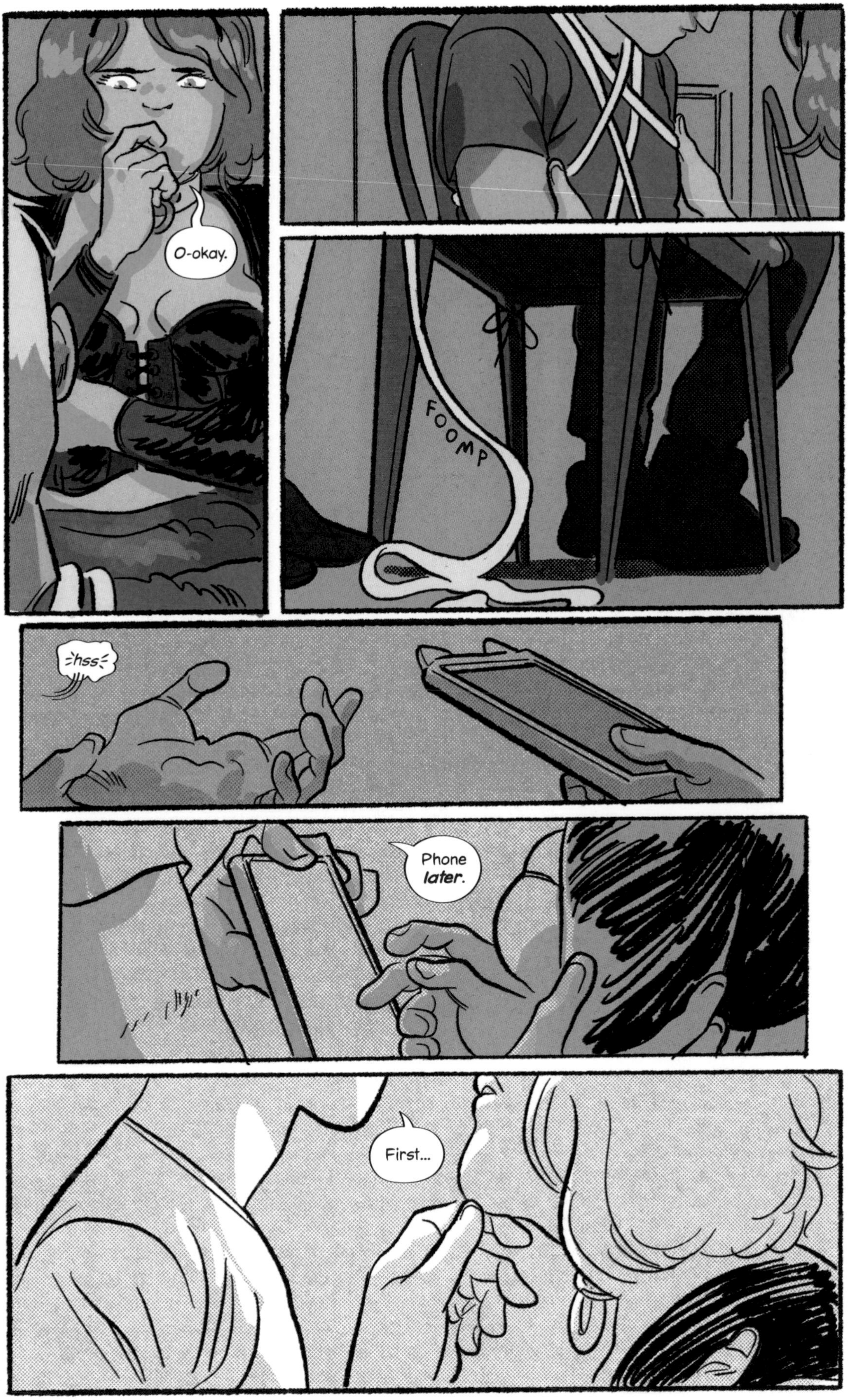
O-okay.
FOOMP
hss
Phone later.
First...

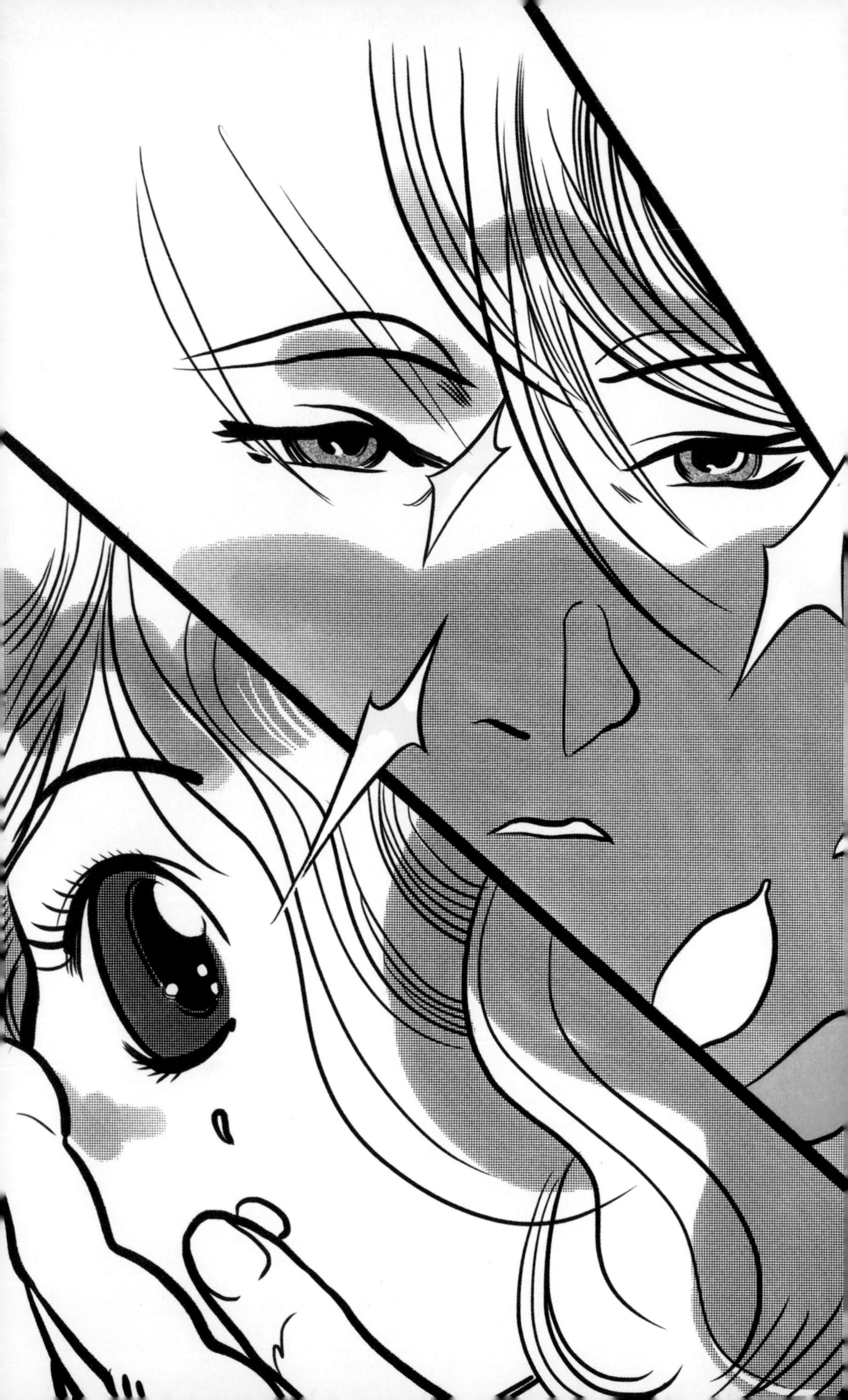

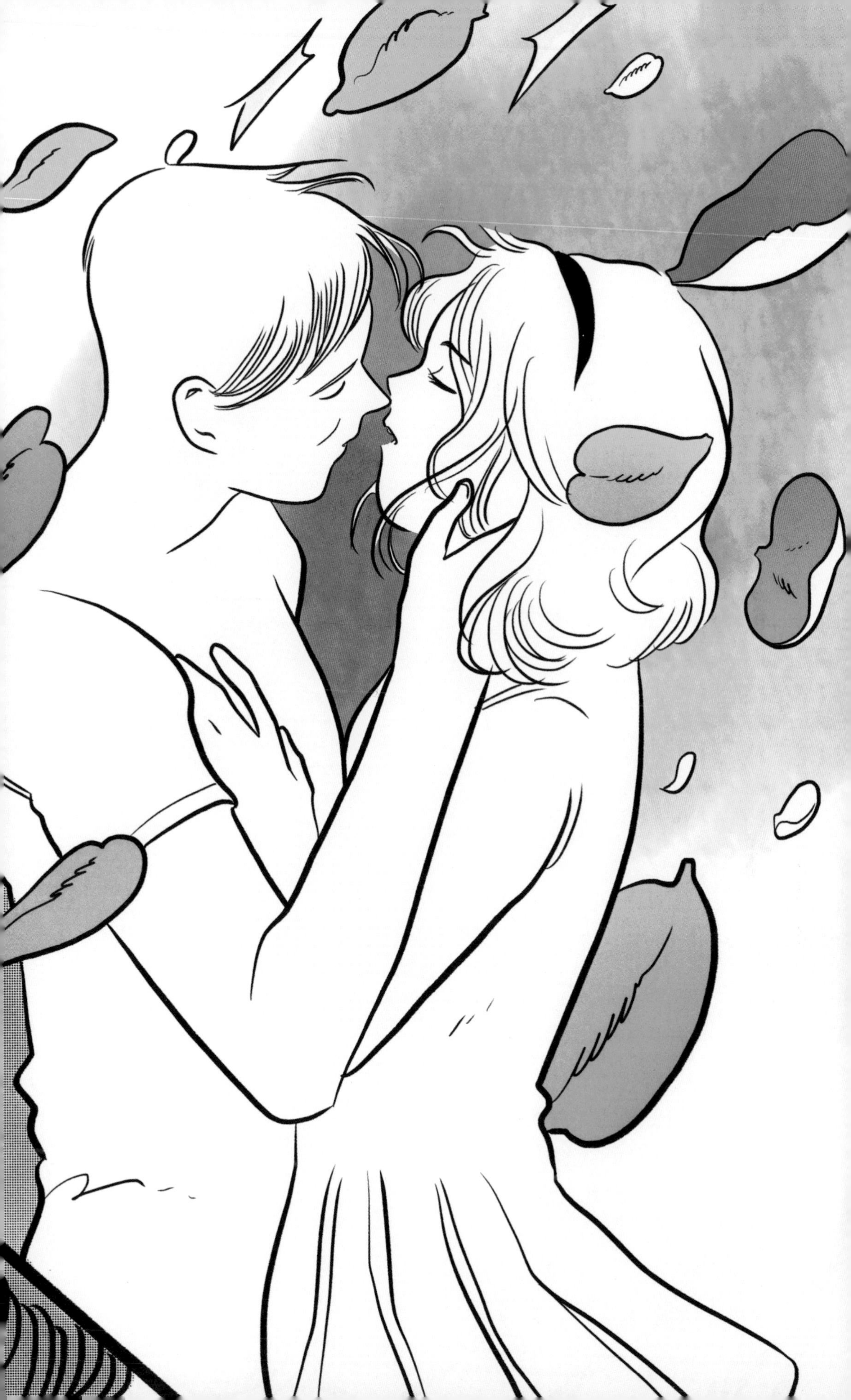

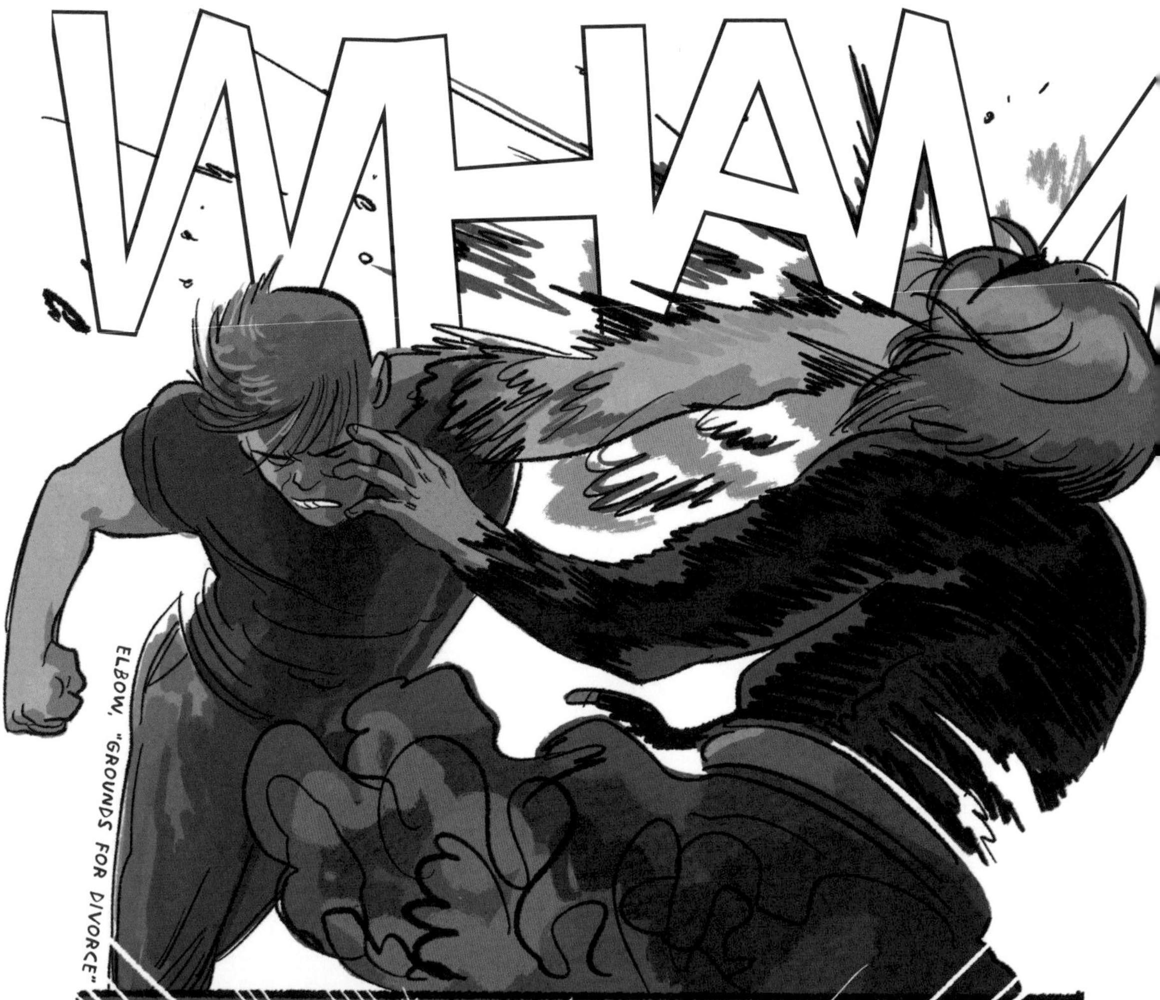
WHAM
ELBOW, "GROUNDS FOR DIVORCE"
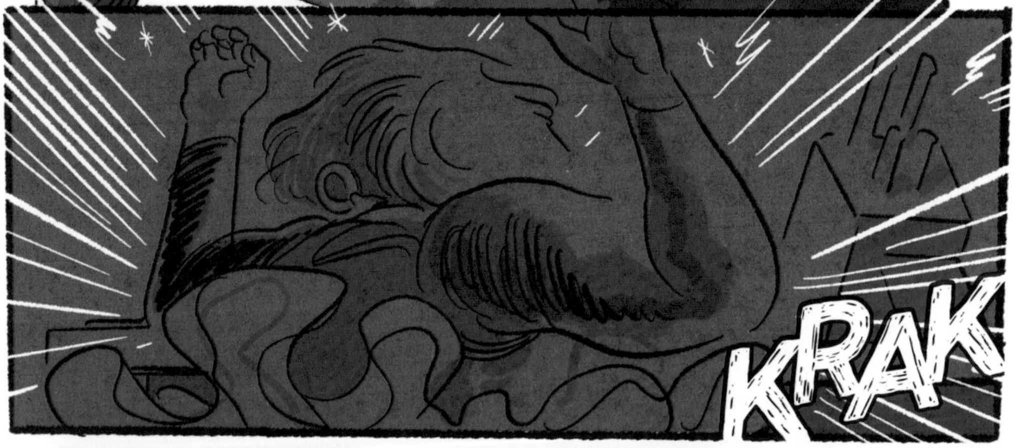
KRAK
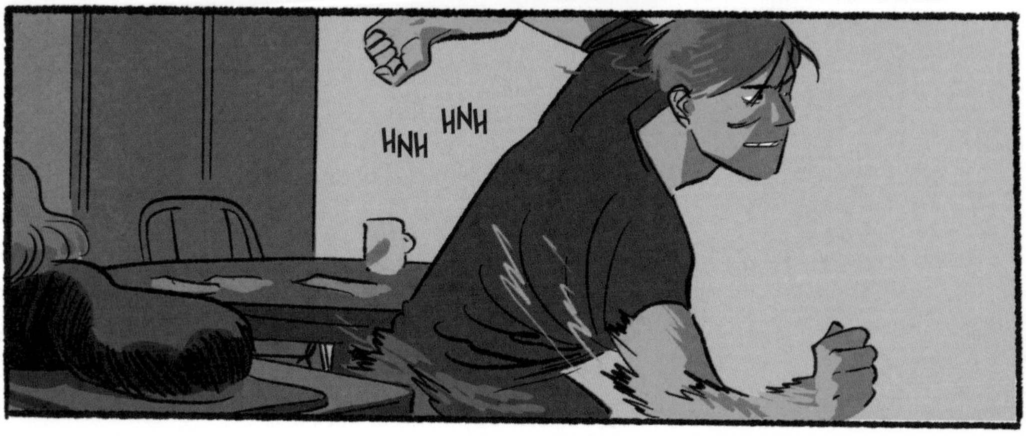
HNH HNH

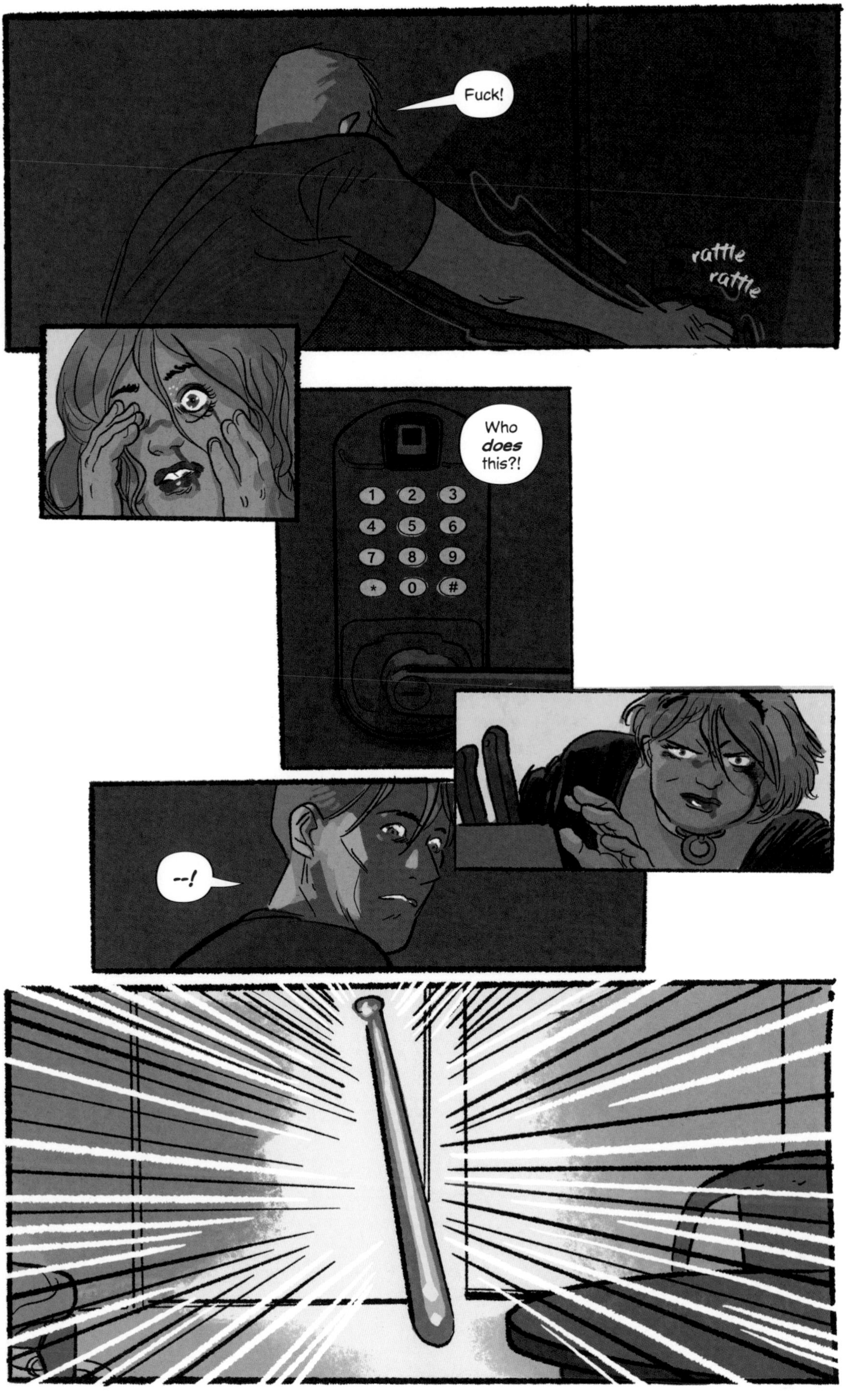
Fuck!
rattle rattle
Who *does* this?!
--!

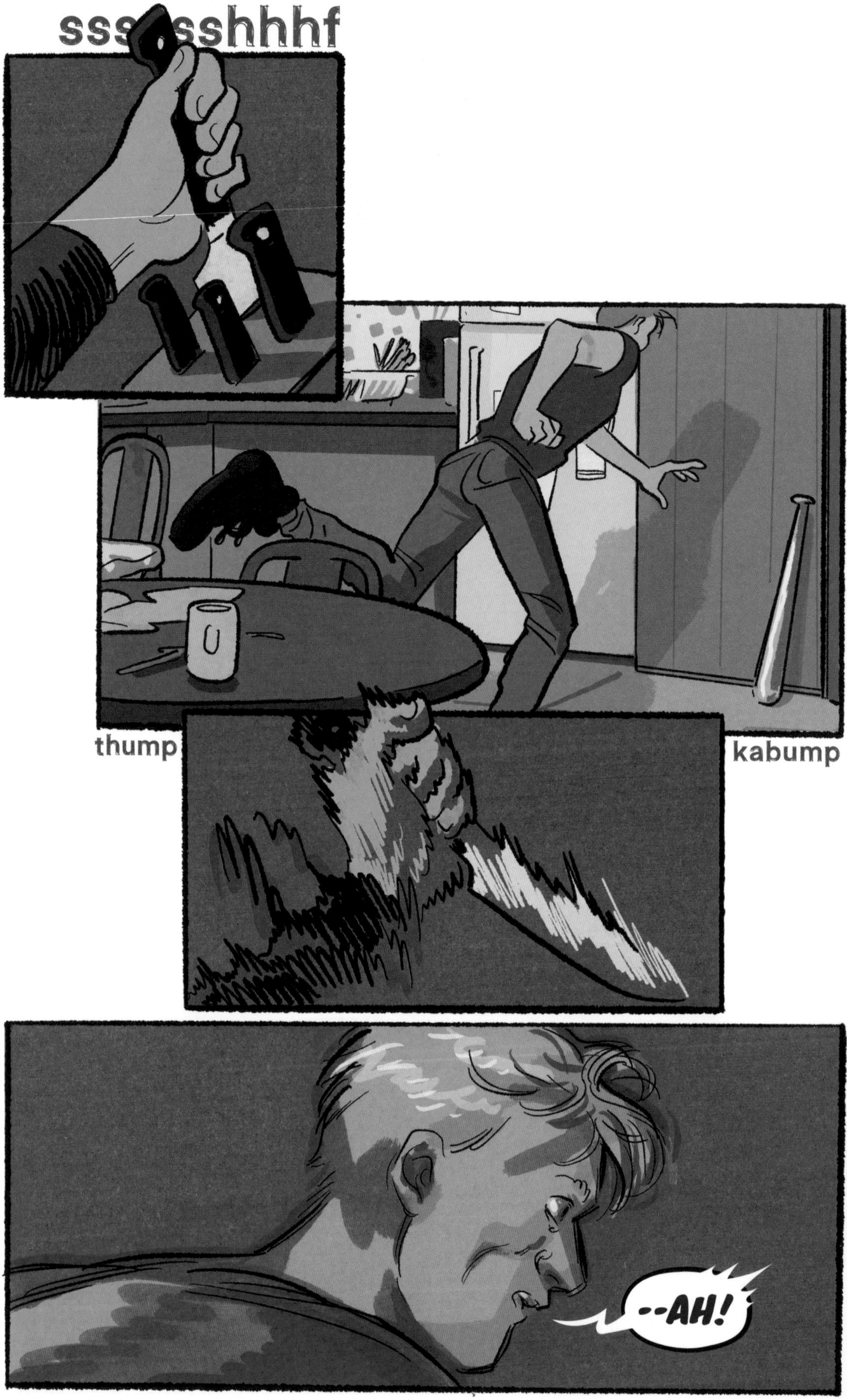
sss sshhhf
thump
kabump
--AH!

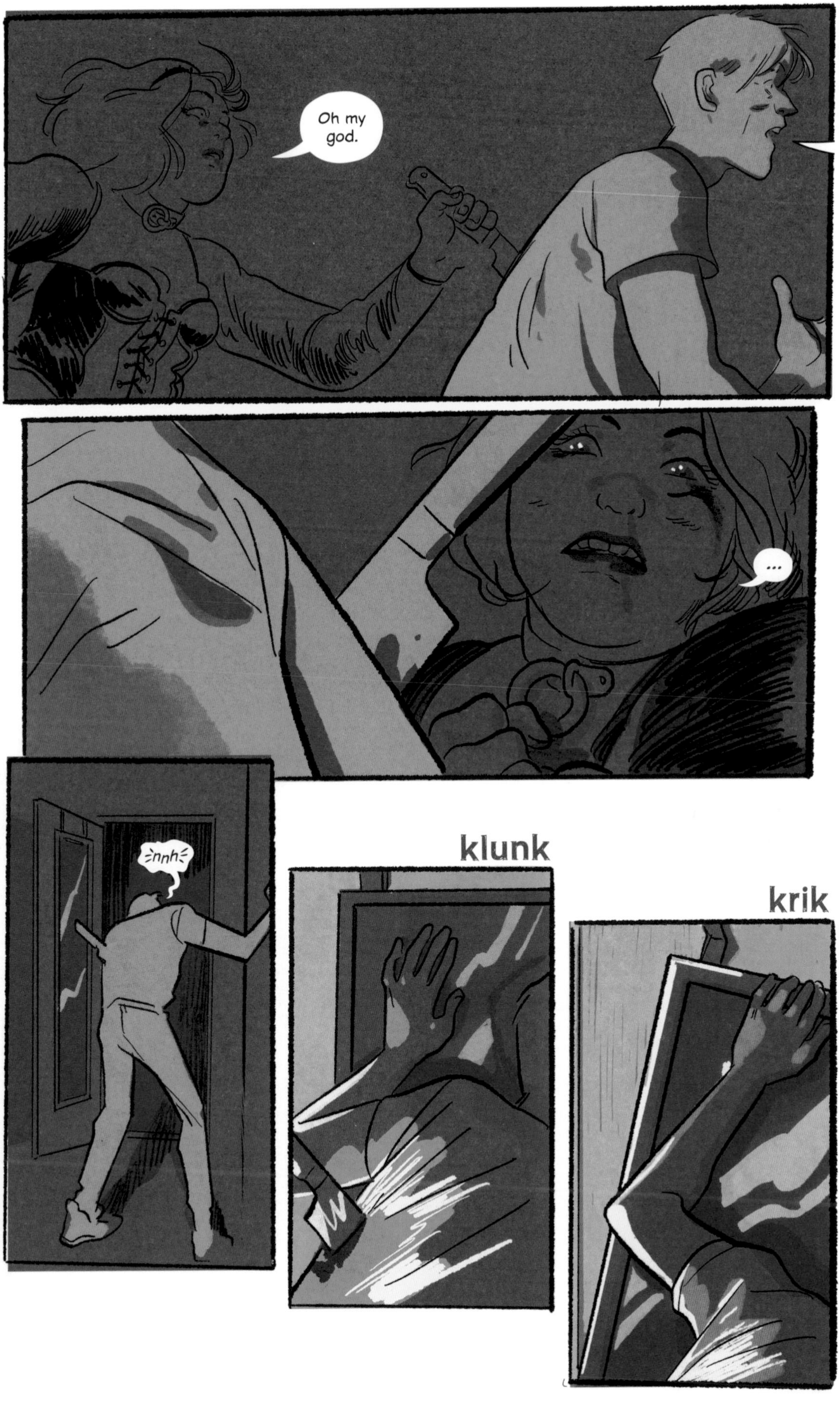
Oh my god.
...
nnh
klunk
krik

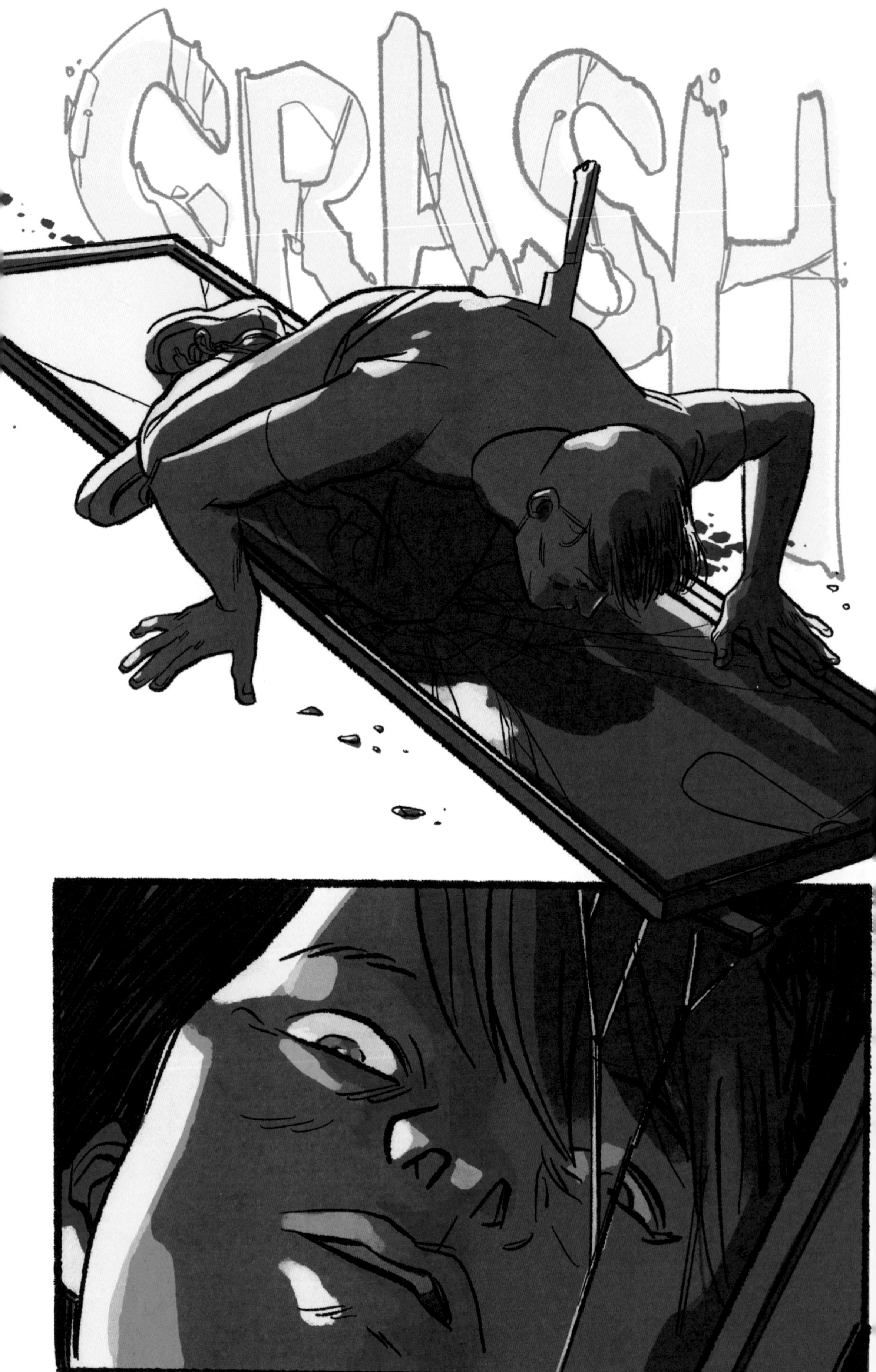
CRASH

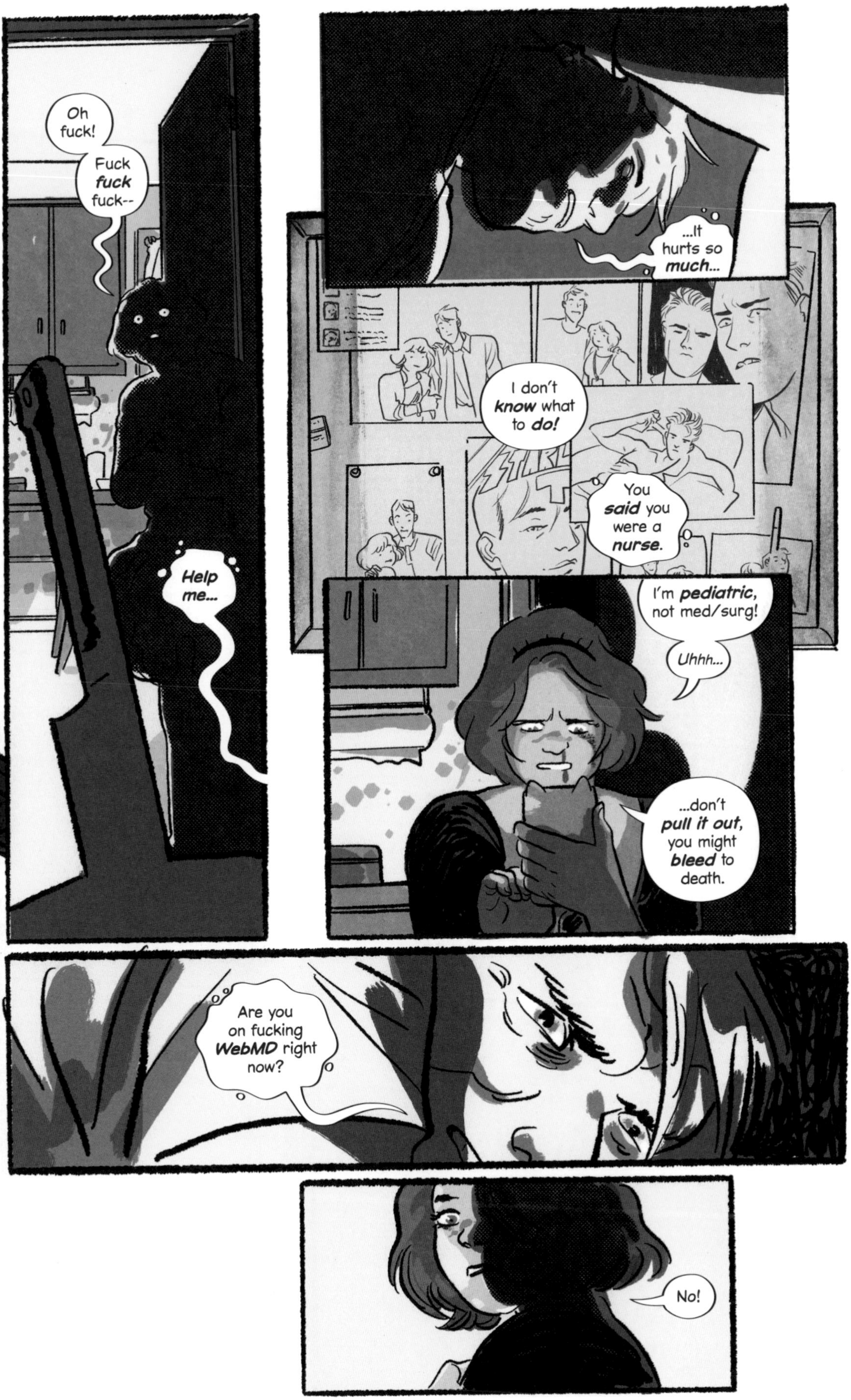
Oh fuck!
Fuck fuck fuck--
Help me...
...It hurts so much...
I don't know what to do!
You said you were a nurse.
I'm pediatric, not med/surg!
Uhhh...
...don't pull it out, you might bleed to death.
Are you on fucking WebMD right now?
No!

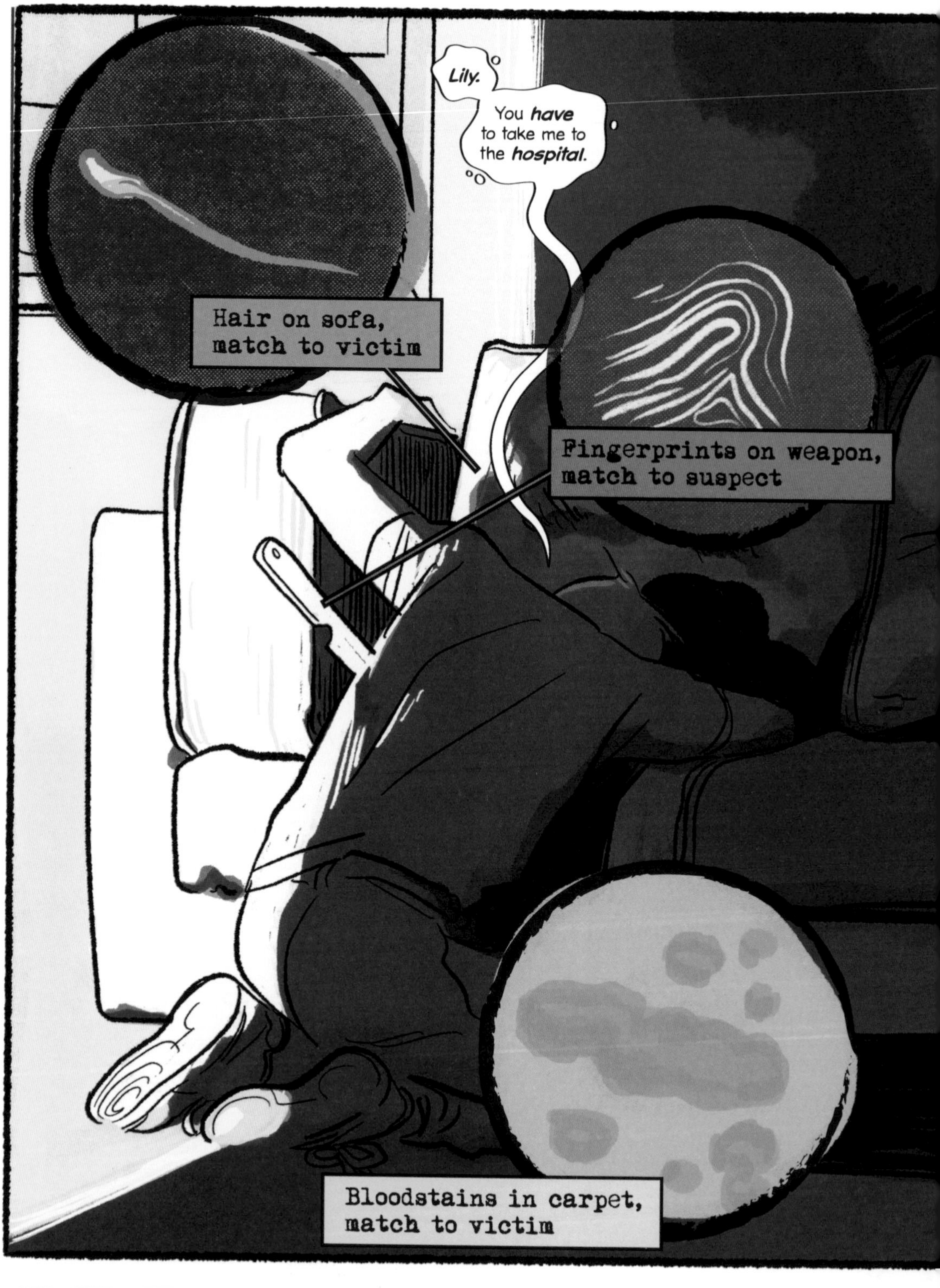
Lily.
You *have* to take me to the *hospital*.
Hair on sofa, match to victim
Fingerprints on weapon, match to suspect
Bloodstains in carpet, match to victim

CSI: EAST TEXAS

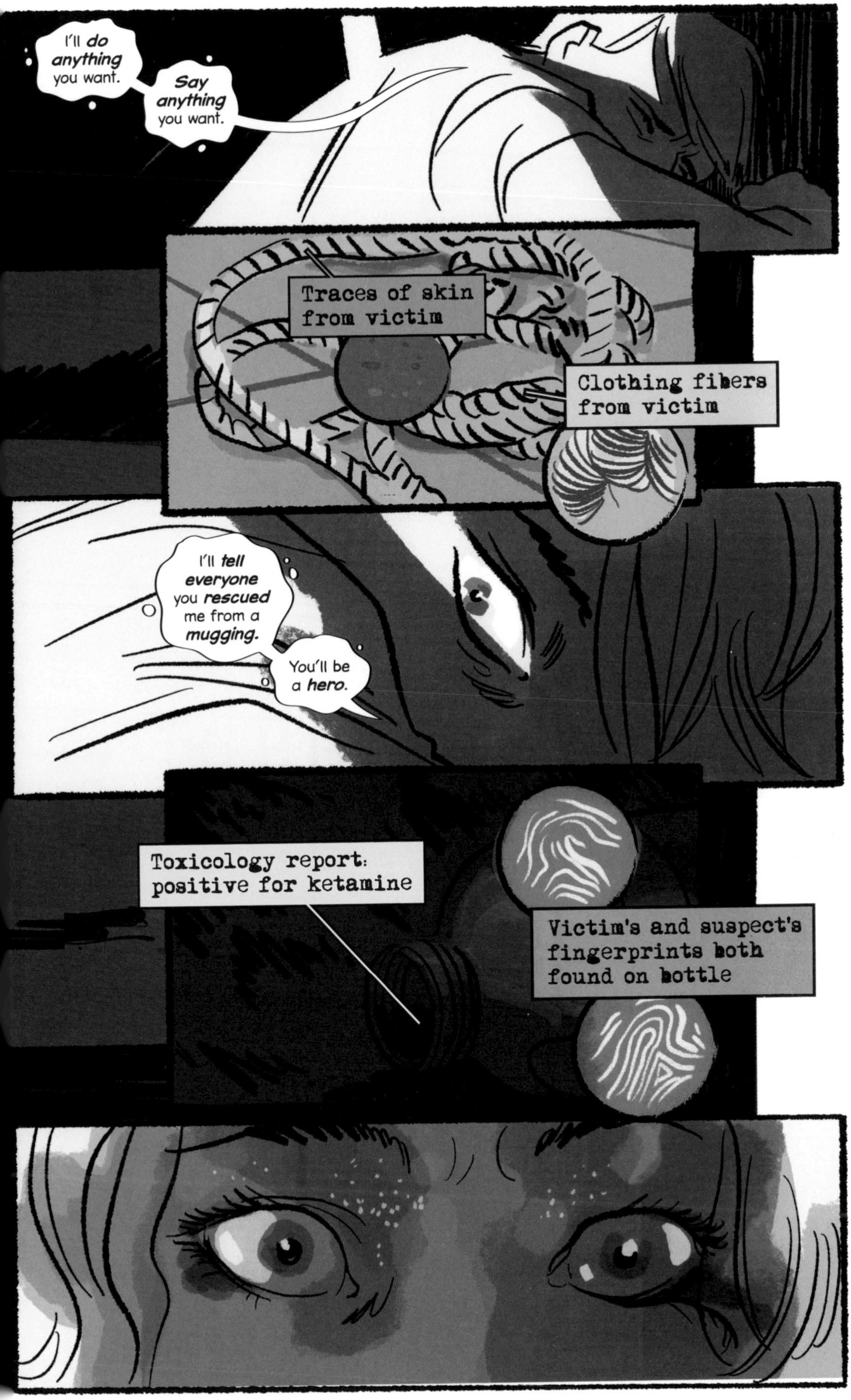
I'll do anything you want.
Say anything you want.
Traces of skin from victim
Clothing fibers from victim
I'll tell everyone you rescued me from a mugging.
You'll be a hero.
Toxicology report: positive for ketamine
Victim's and suspect's fingerprints both found on bottle

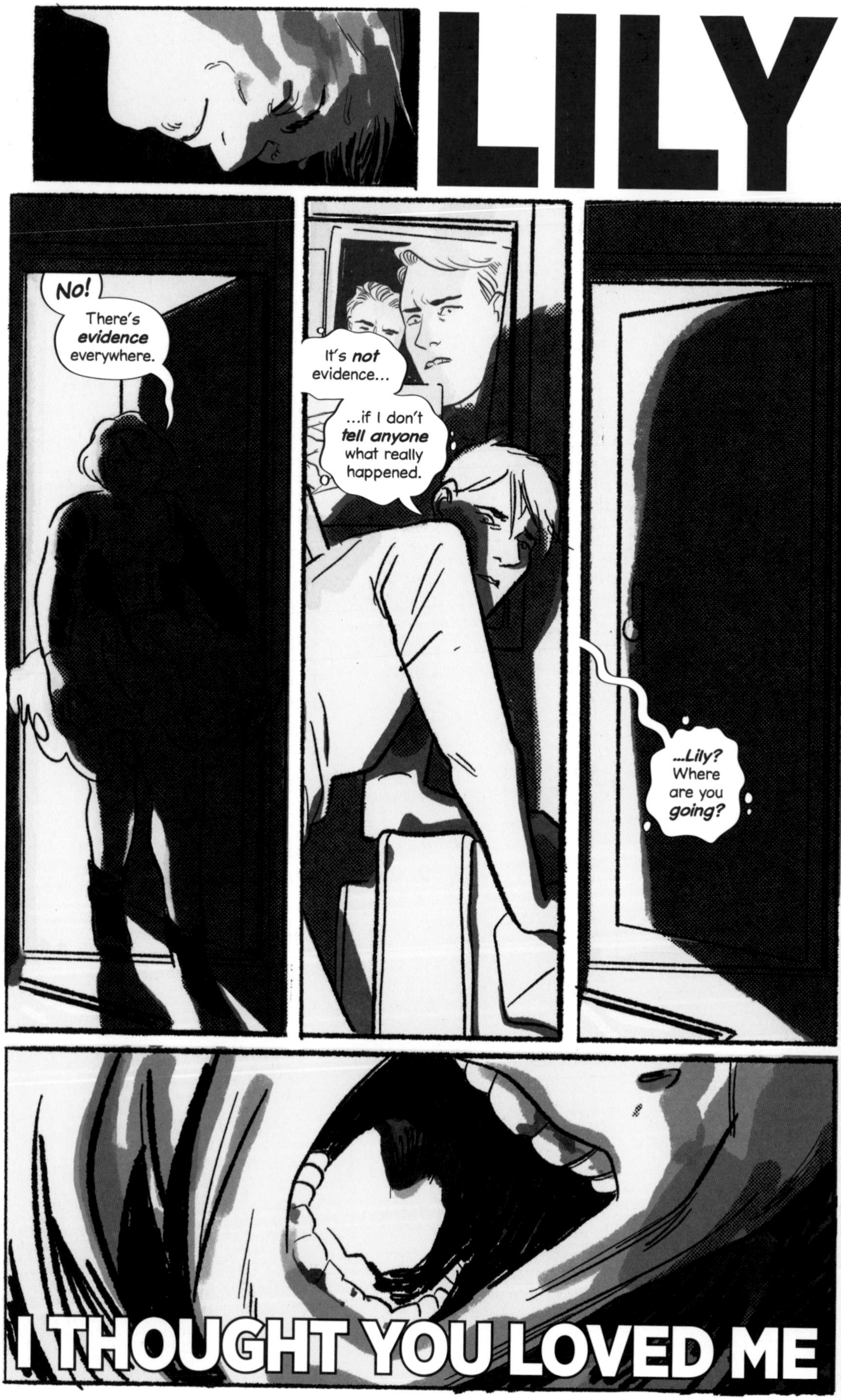
LILY
No! There's *evidence* everywhere.
It's *not* evidence...
...if I don't *tell anyone* what really happened.
...*Lily?* Where are you *going?*
I THOUGHT YOU LOVED ME

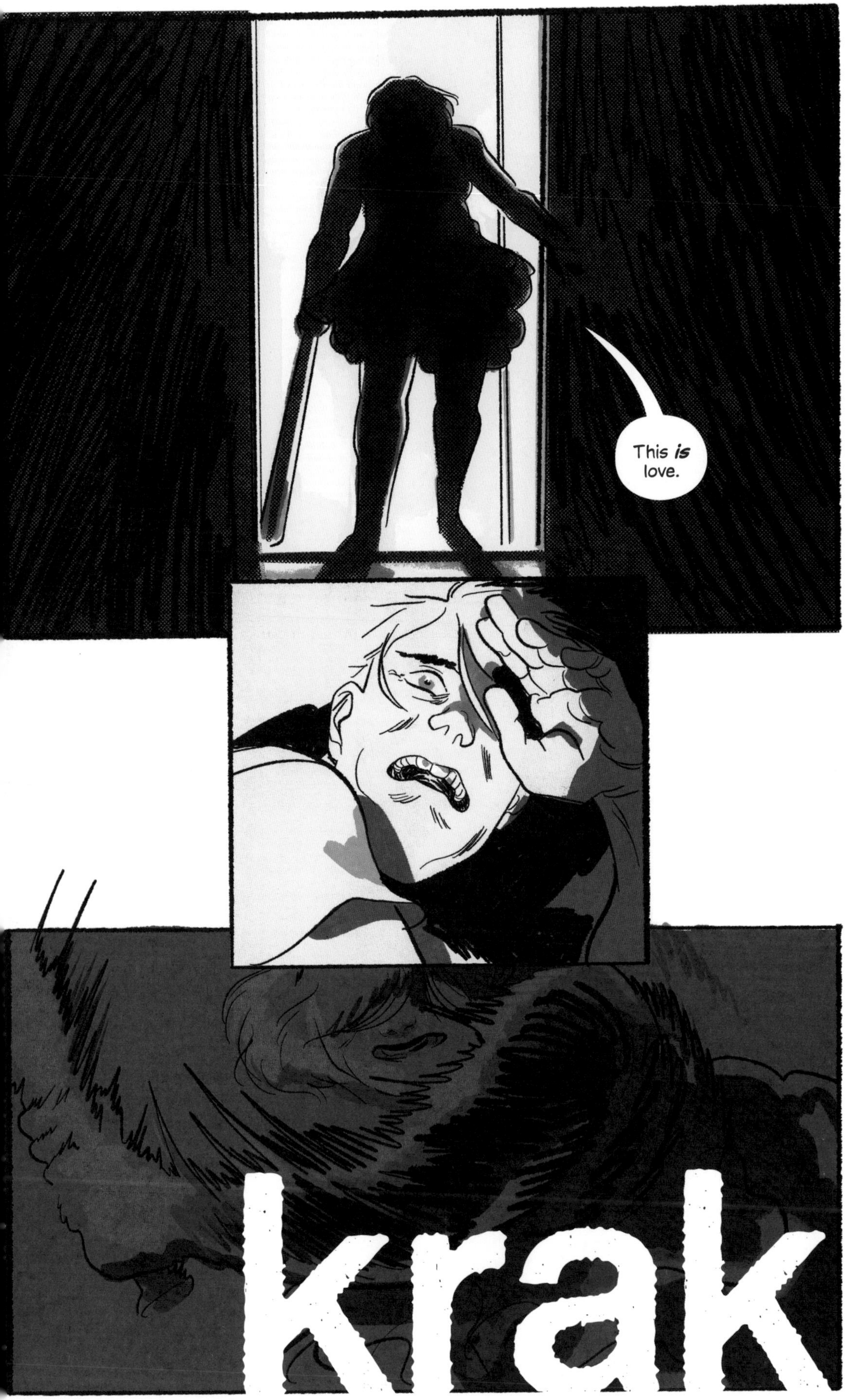
This *is* love.
krak

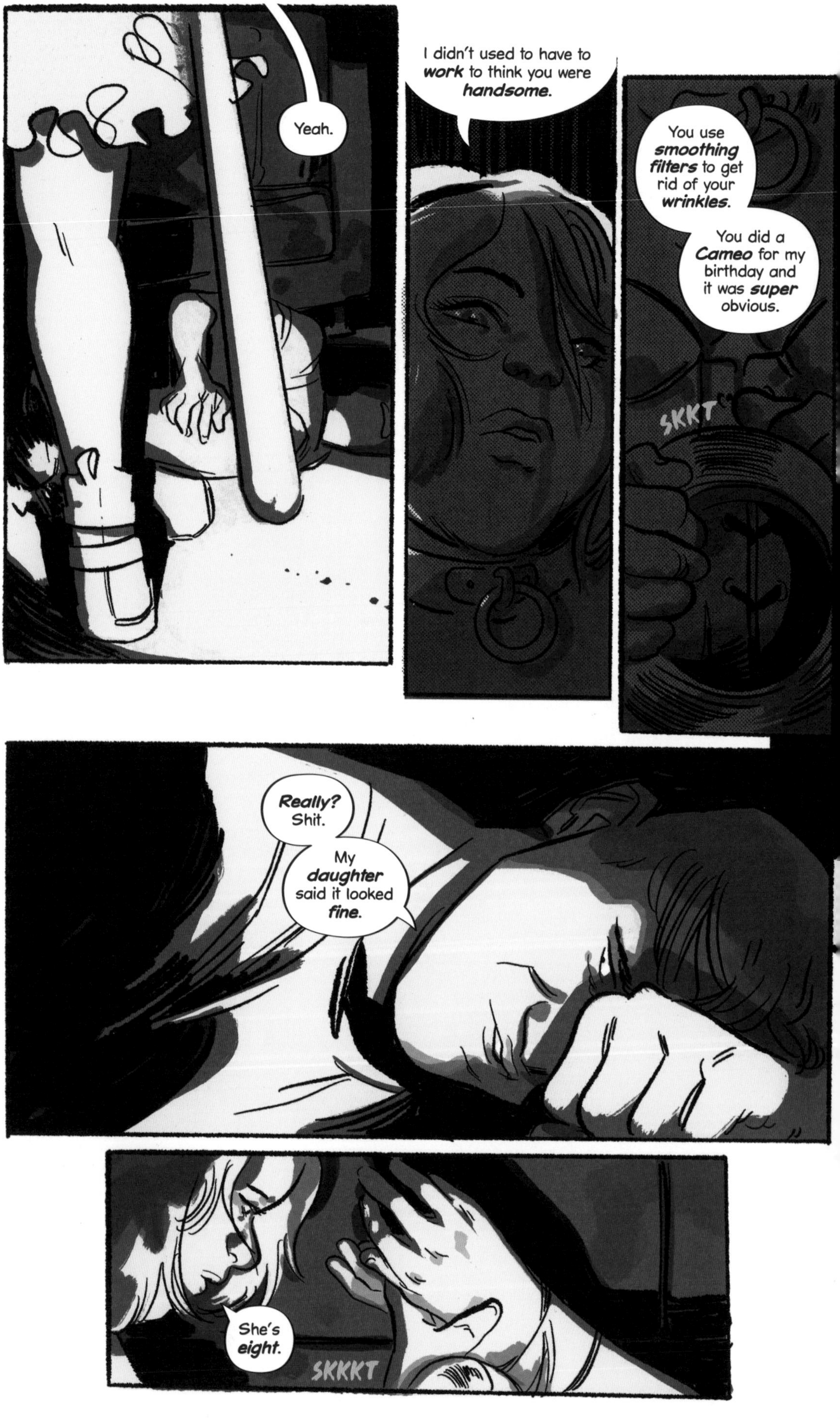
Yeah.
I didn't used to have to work to think you were handsome.
You use smoothing filters to get rid of your wrinkles.
You did a Cameo for my birthday and it was super obvious.
SKKT
Really? Shit.
My daughter said it looked fine.
She's eight.
SKKKT

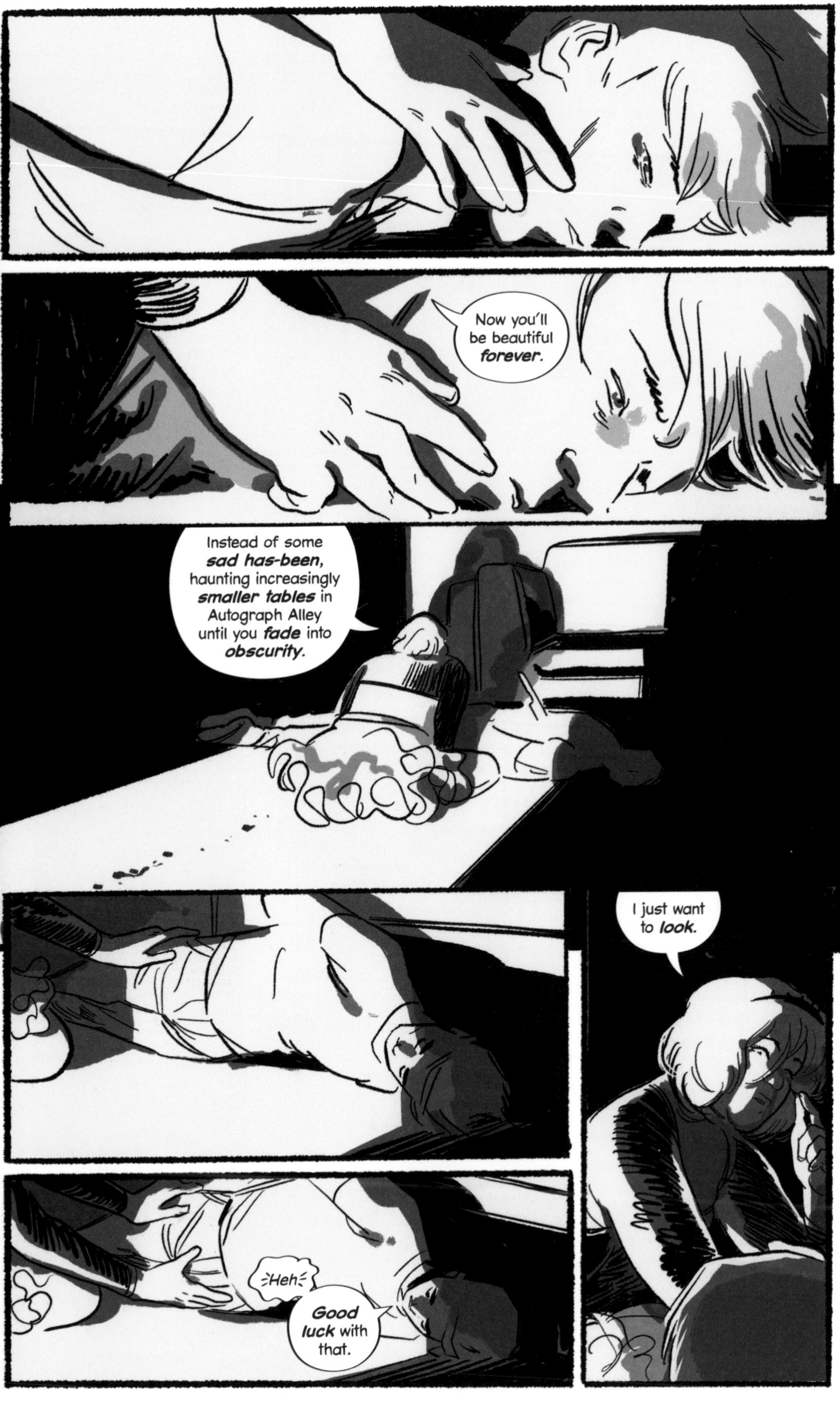
Now you'll be beautiful forever.
Instead of some sad has-been, haunting increasingly smaller tables in Autograph Alley until you fade into obscurity.
I just want to look.
Heh
Good luck with that.

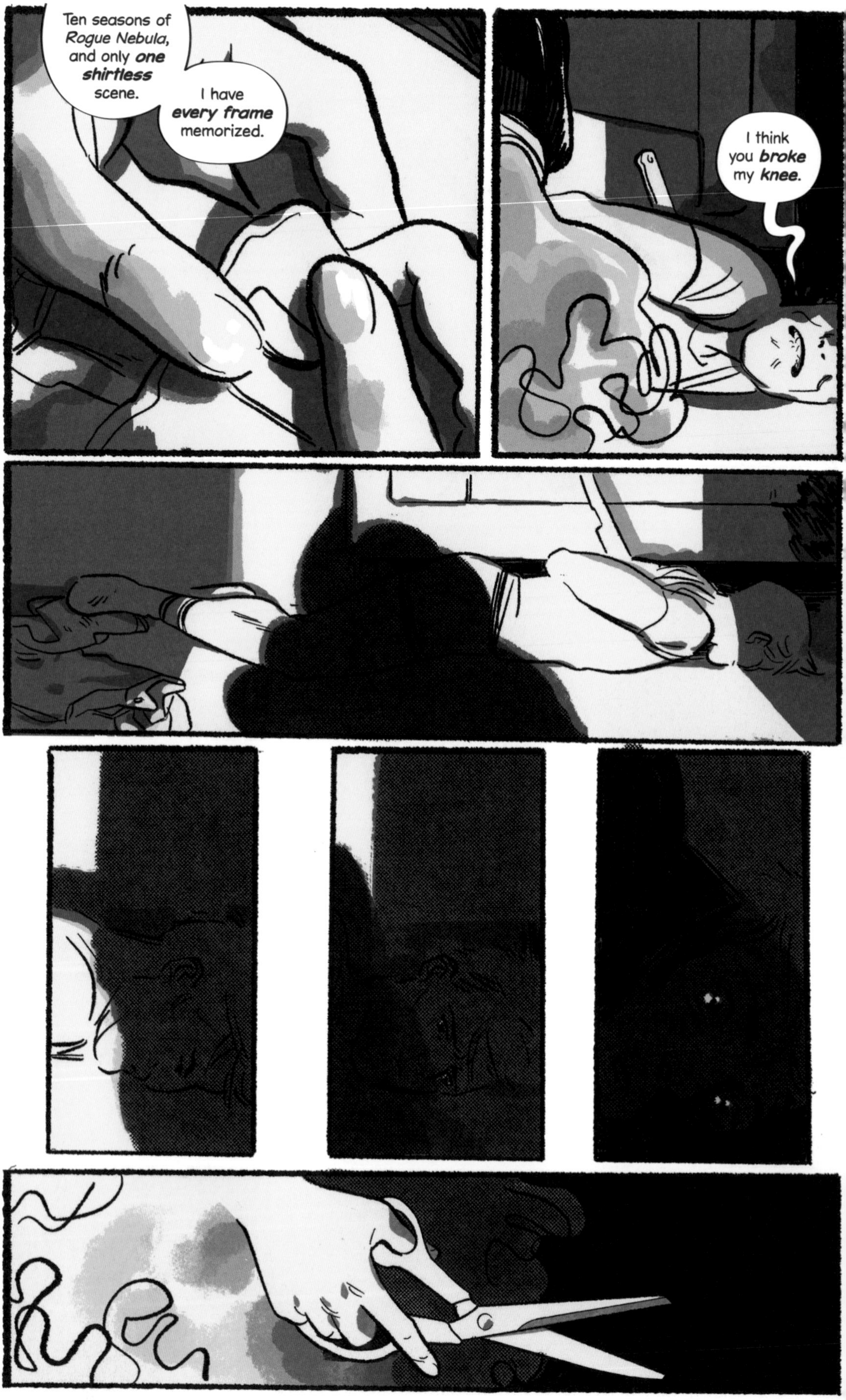
Ten seasons of *Rogue Nebula,* and only ***one shirtless*** scene.
I have ***every frame*** memorized.
I think you ***broke*** my ***knee.***

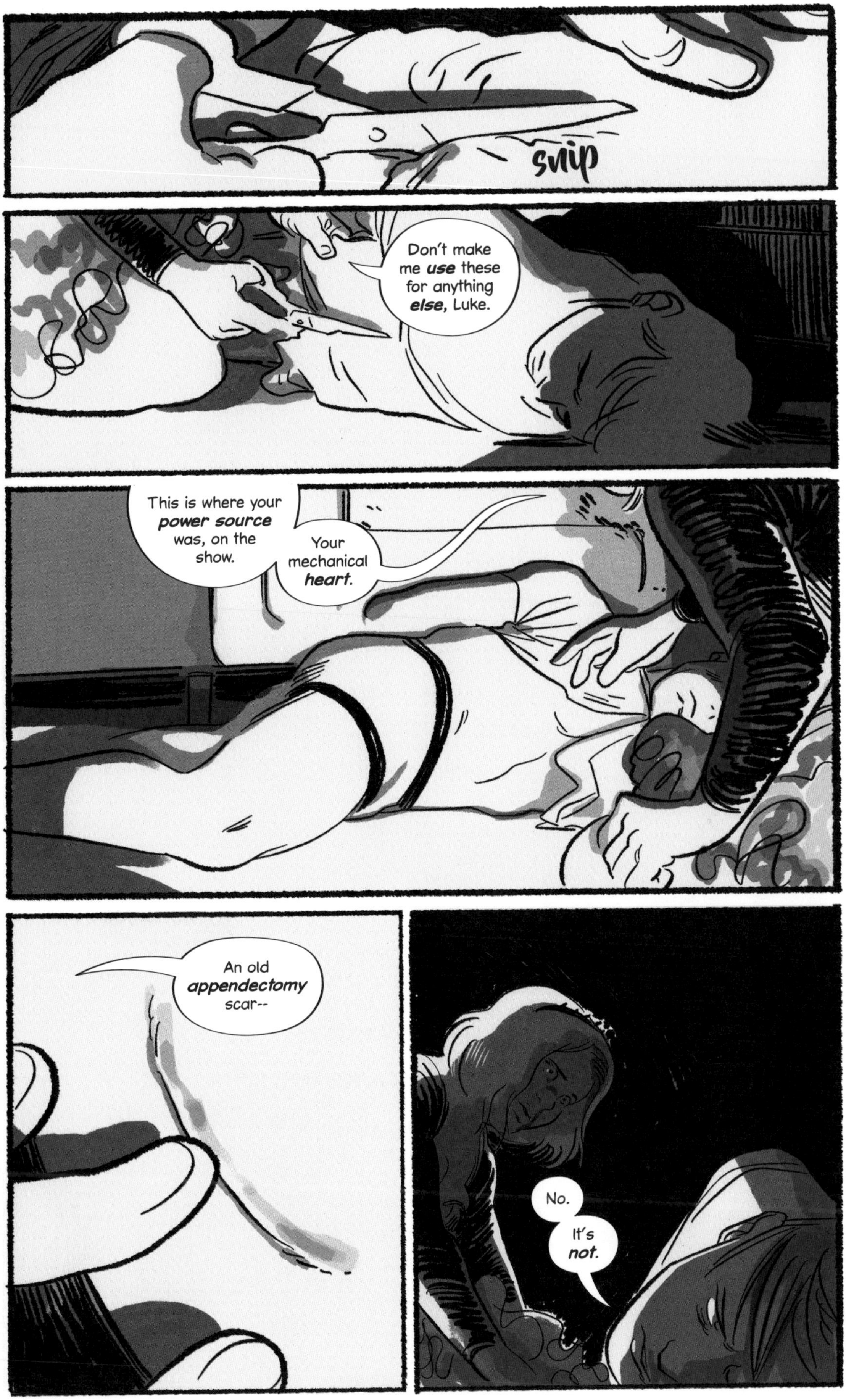
snip
Don't make me use these for anything else, Luke.
This is where your power source was, on the show.
Your mechanical heart.
An old appendectomy scar--
No.
It's not.

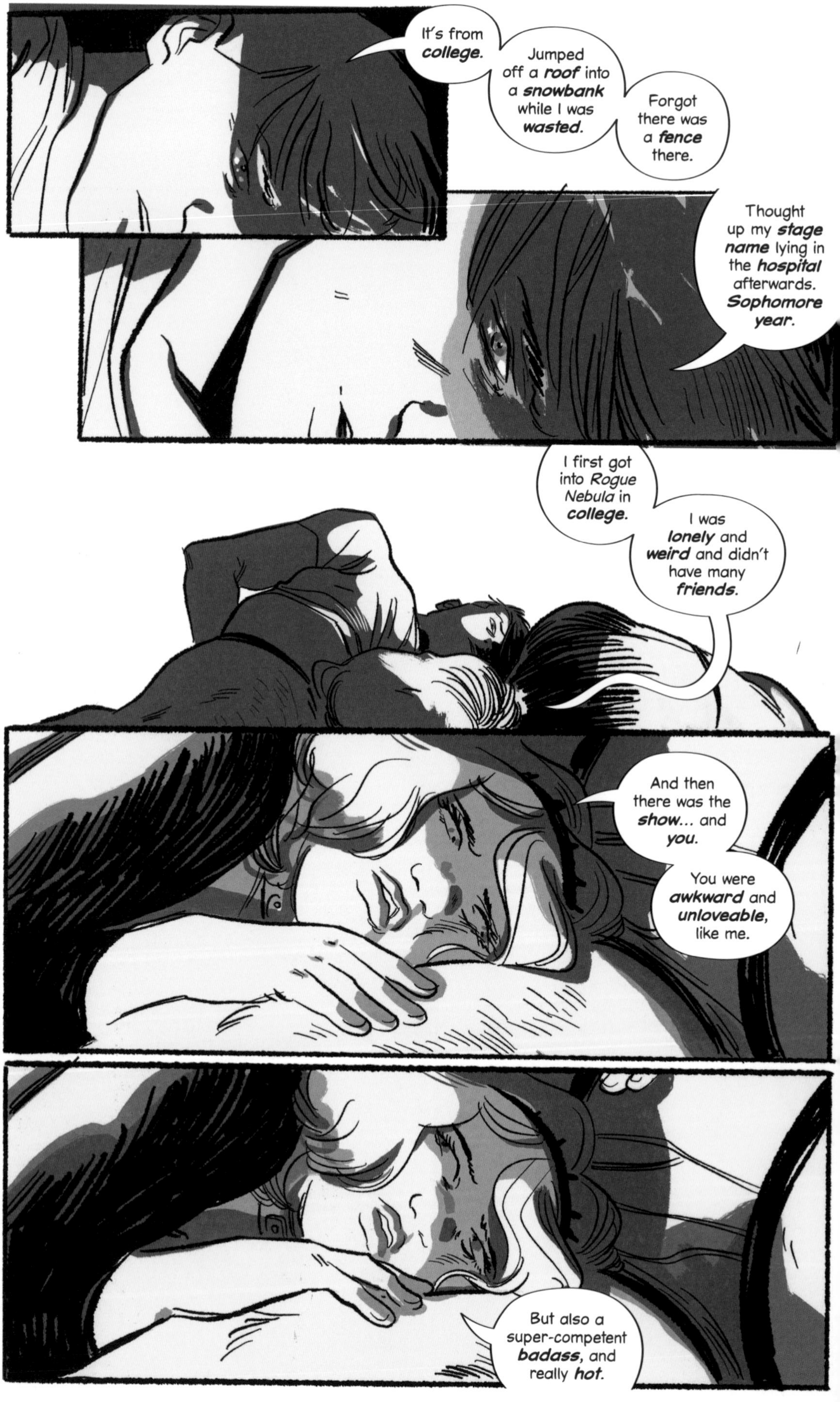
It's from **college**.
Jumped off a **roof** into a **snowbank** while I was **wasted**.
Forgot there was a **fence** there.
Thought up my **stage name** lying in the **hospital** afterwards. **Sophomore year**.
I first got into *Rogue Nebula* in **college**.
I was **lonely** and **weird** and didn't have many **friends**.
And then there was the **show**... and **you**.
You were **awkward** and **unloveable**, like me.
But also a super-competent **badass**, and really **hot**.

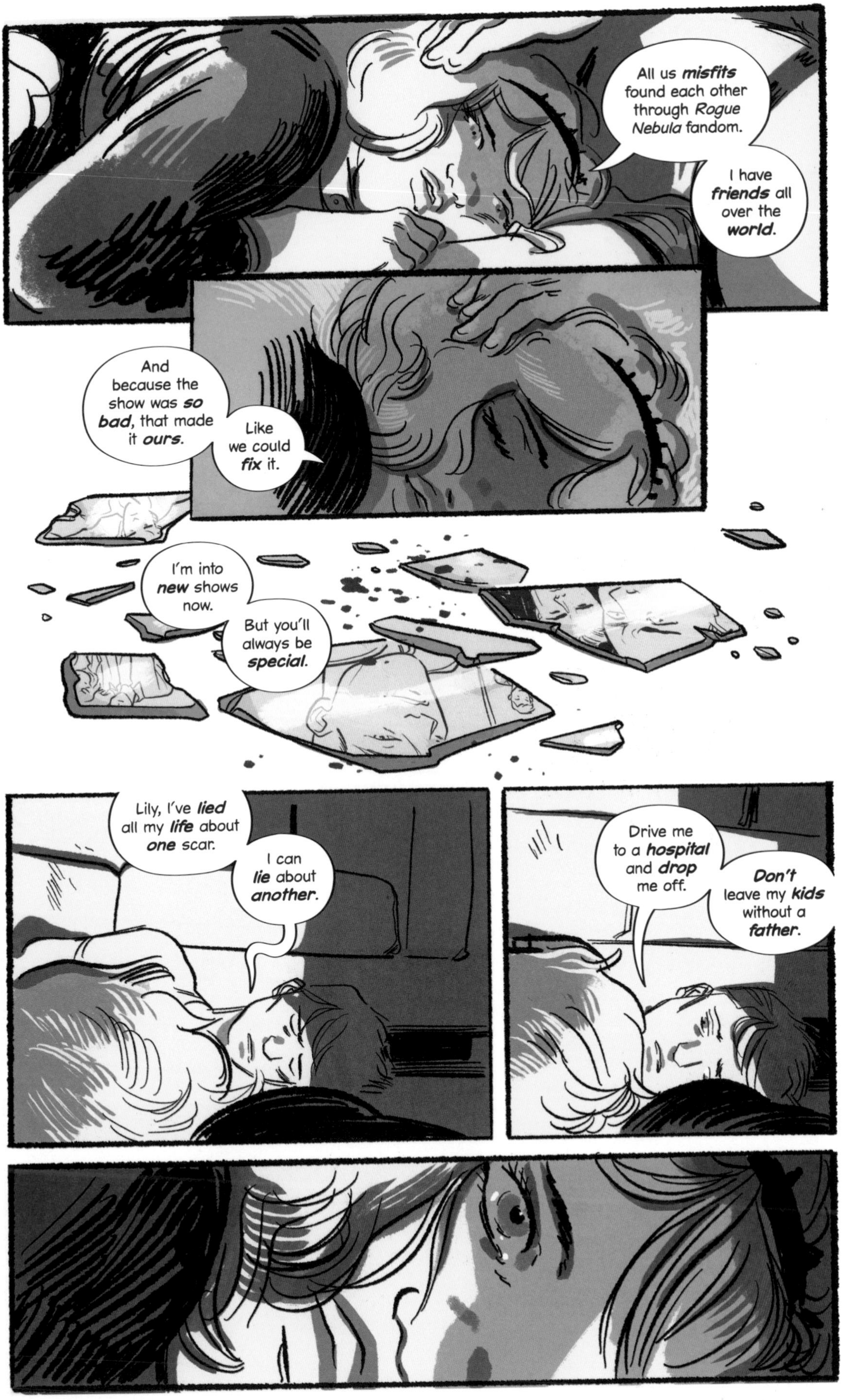
All us *misfits* found each other through *Rogue Nebula* fandom.
I have *friends* all over the *world*.
And because the show was *so bad*, that made it *ours*.
Like we could *fix* it.
I'm into *new* shows now.
But you'll always be *special*.
Lily, I've *lied* all my *life* about *one* scar.
I can *lie* about *another*.
Drive me to a *hospital* and *drop* me off.
Don't leave my *kids* without a *father*.

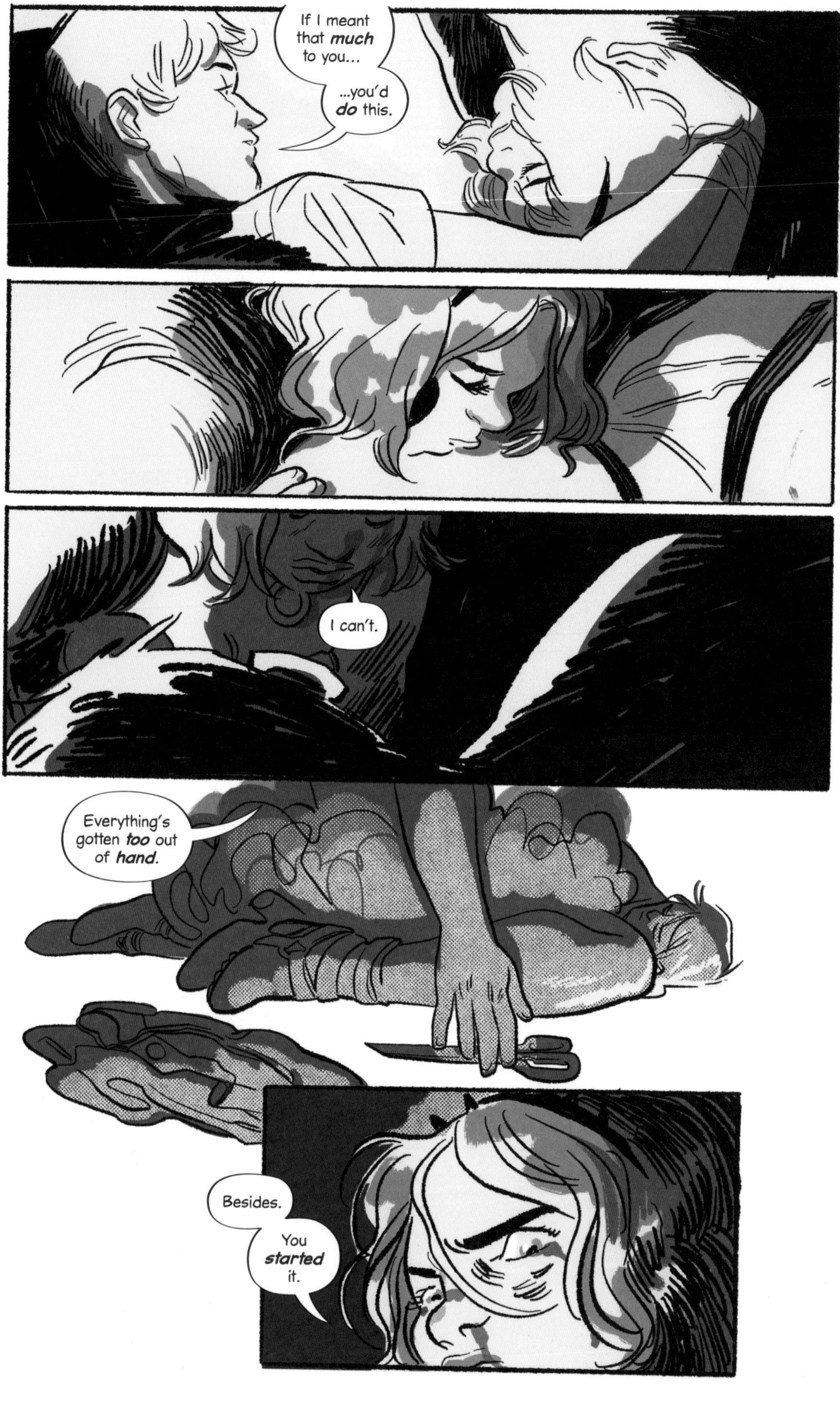
If I meant that *much* to you...
...you'd *do* this.
I can't.
Everything's gotten *too* out of *hand*.
Besides.
You *started* it.

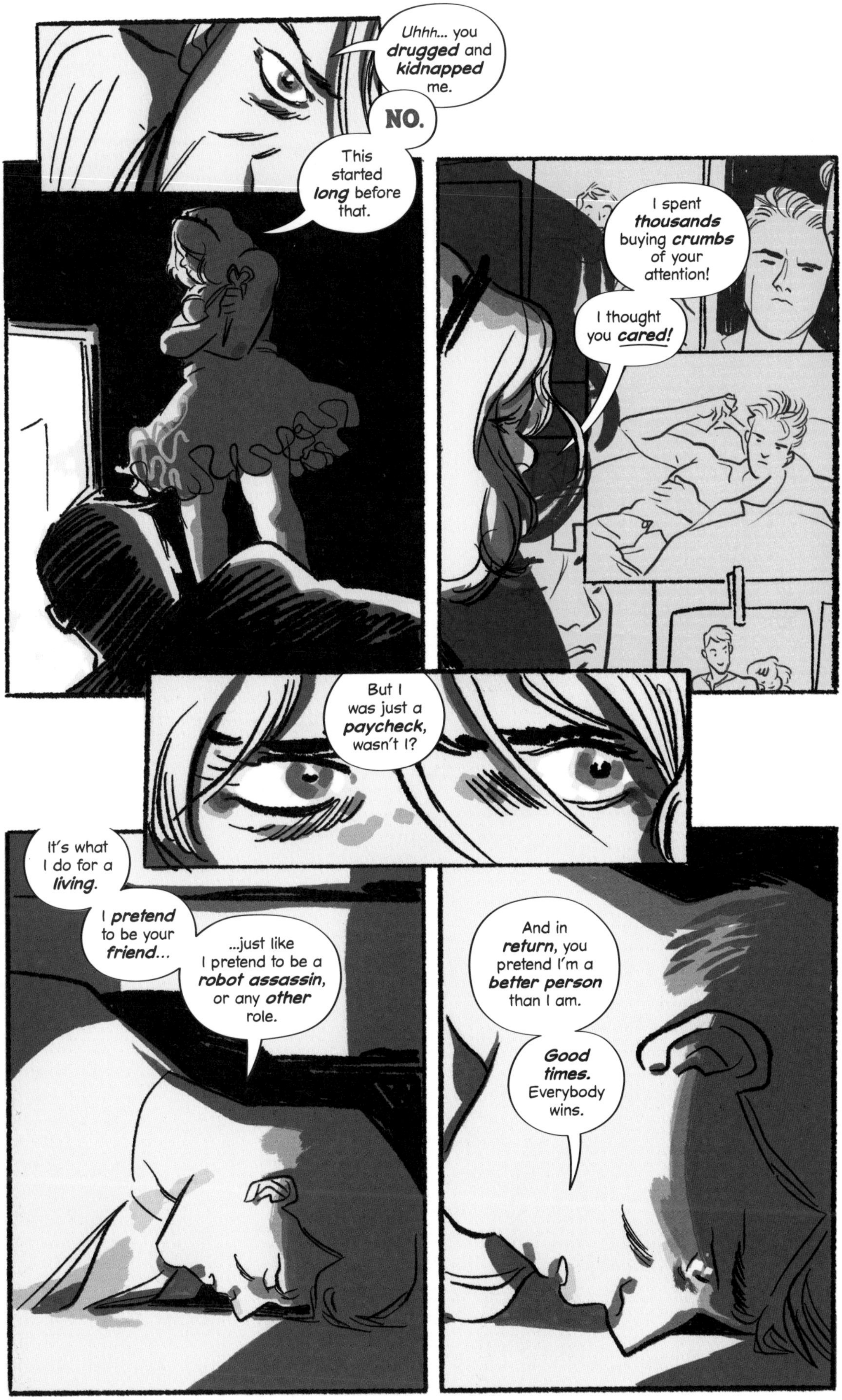
Uhhh... you drugged and kidnapped me.
NO.
This started long before that.
I spent thousands buying crumbs of your attention!
I thought you cared!
But I was just a paycheck, wasn't I?
It's what I do for a living.
I pretend to be your friend...
...just like I pretend to be a robot assassin, or any other role.
And in return, you pretend I'm a better person than I am.
Good times. Everybody wins.

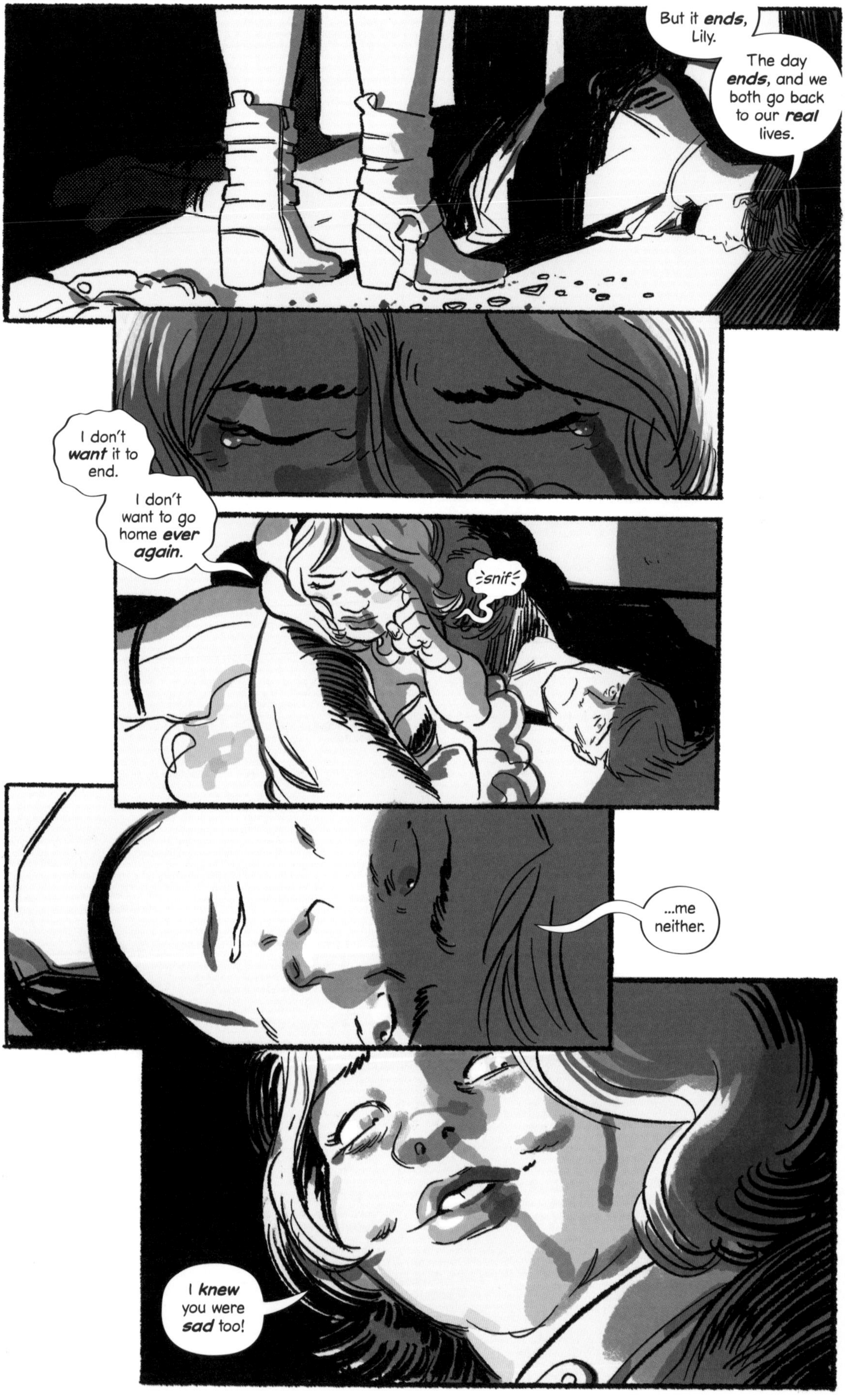
But it *ends*, Lily.
The day *ends*, and we both go back to our *real* lives.
I don't *want* it to end.
I don't want to go home *ever again*.
snif
...me neither.
I *knew* you were *sad* too!

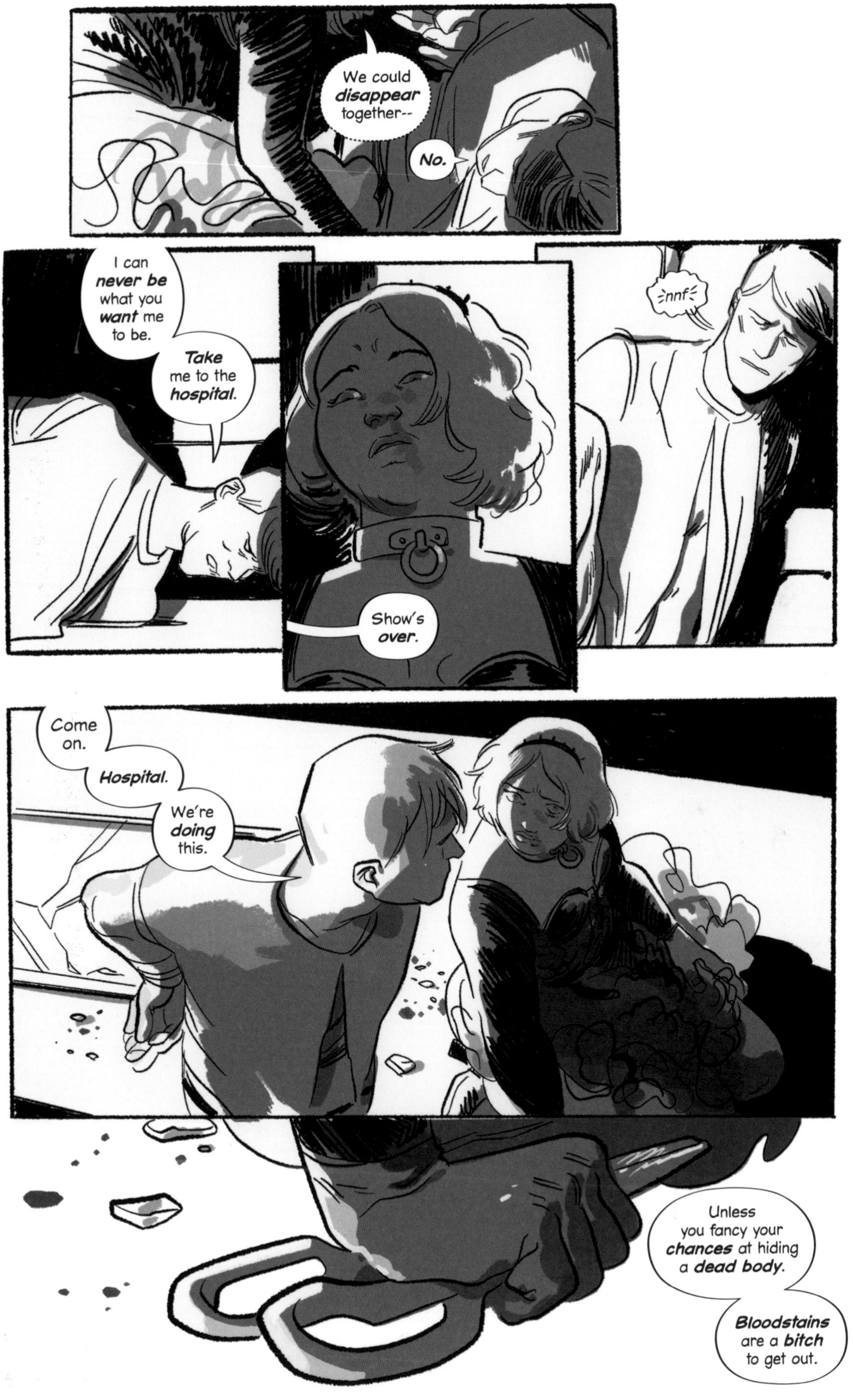
We could **disappear** together--
No.
I can **never be** what you **want** me to be.
Take me to the **hospital**.
Show's **over**.
nnf
Come on.
Hospital.
We're **doing** this.
Unless you fancy your **chances** at hiding a **dead body**.
Bloodstains are a **bitch** to get out.

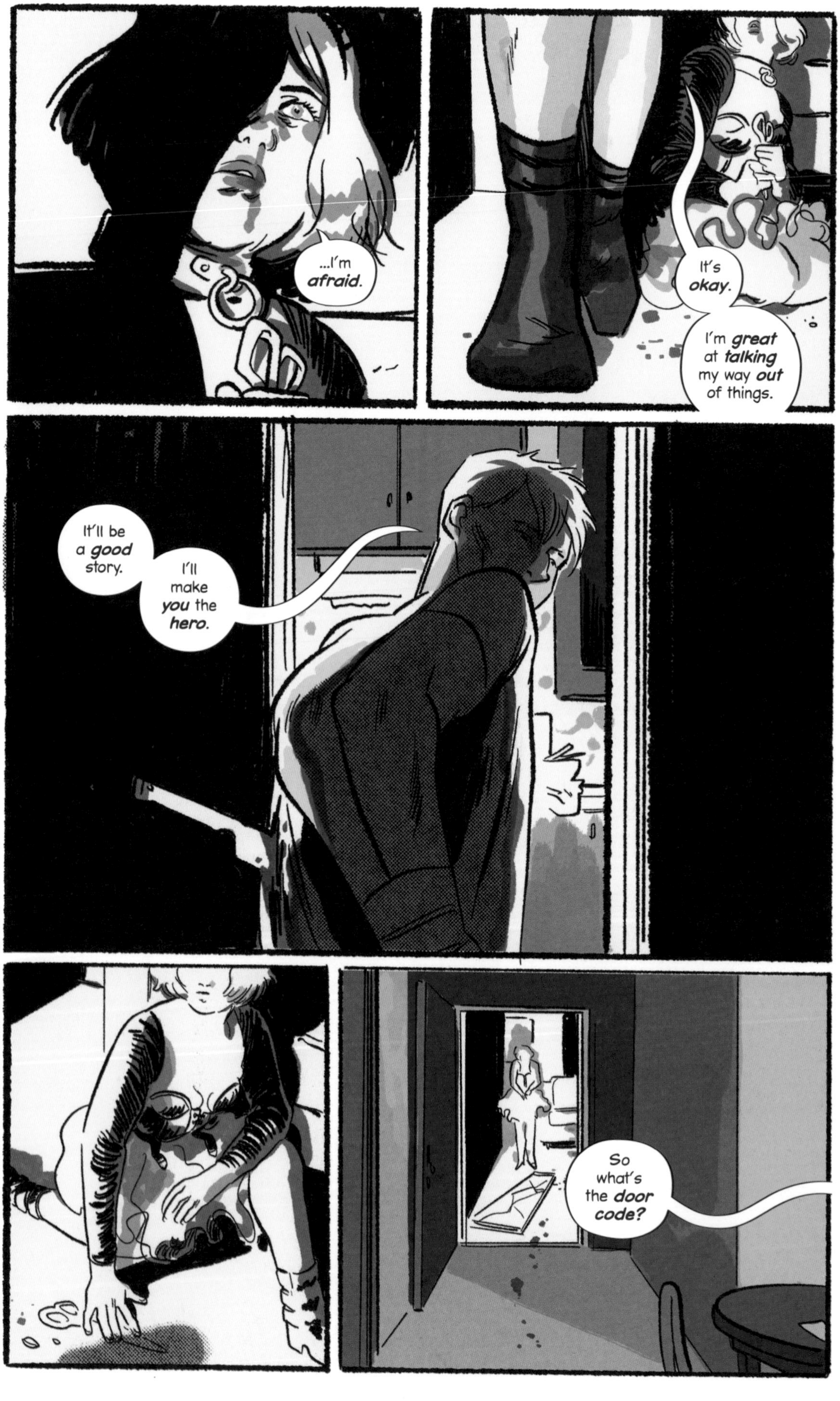
...I'm afraid.
It's okay.
I'm great at talking my way out of things.
It'll be a good story.
I'll make you the hero.
So what's the door code?

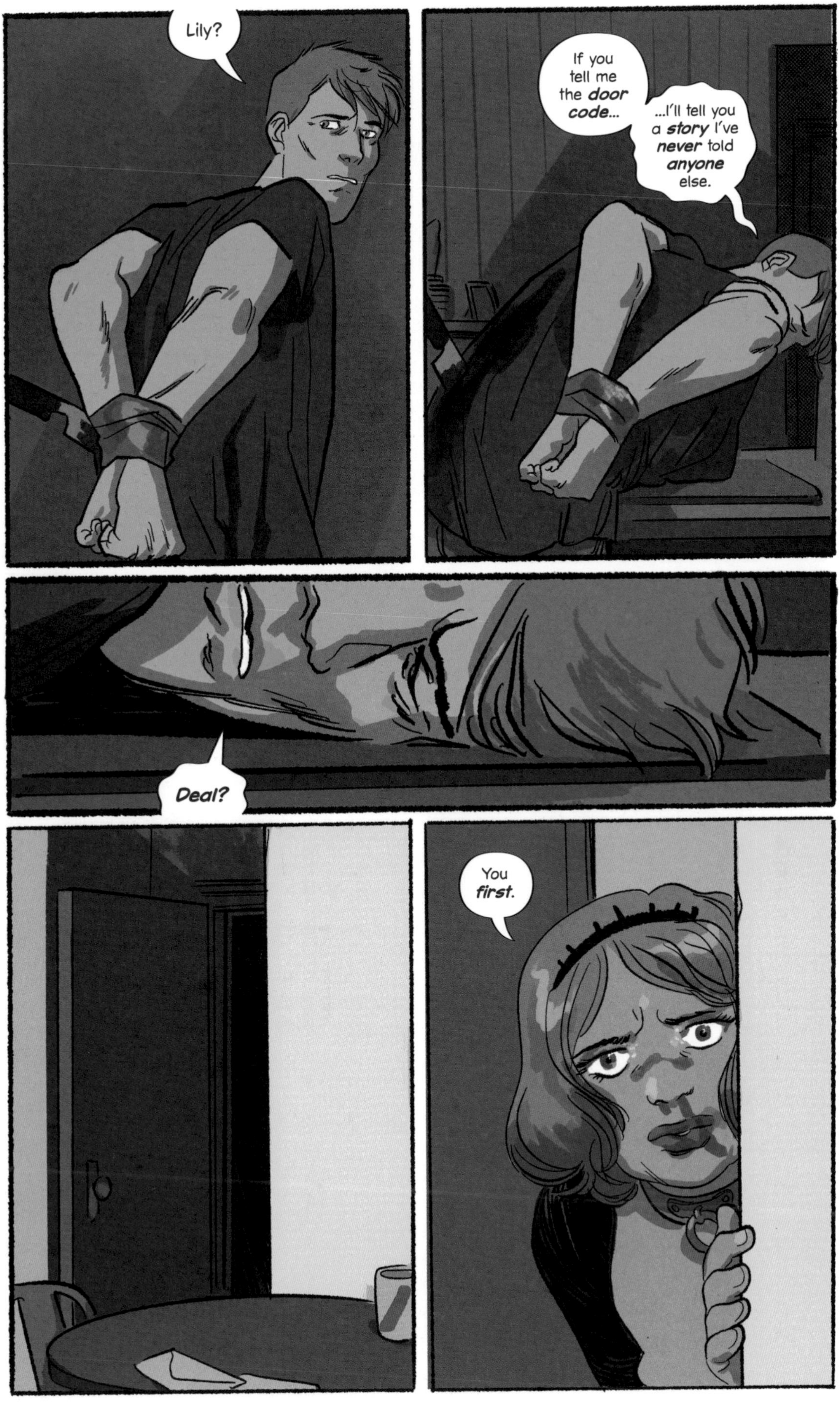
Lily?
If you tell me the door code...
...I'll tell you a story I've never told anyone else.
Deal?
You first.

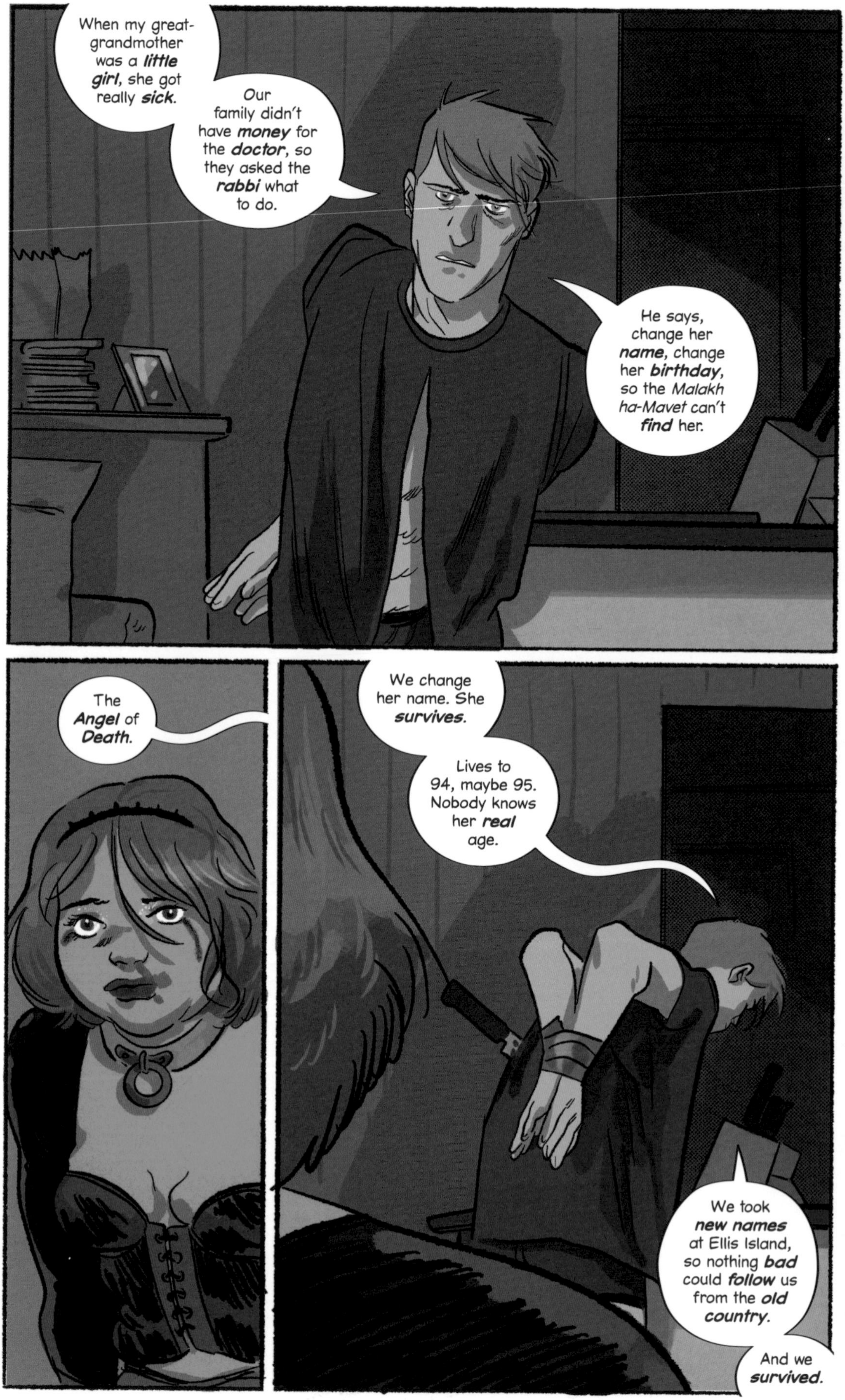
When my great-grandmother was a ***little girl,*** she got really ***sick***.
Our family didn't have ***money*** for the ***doctor***, so they asked the ***rabbi*** what to do.
He says, change her ***name,*** change her ***birthday***, so the *Malakh ha-Mavet* can't ***find*** her.
The ***Angel*** of ***Death***.
We change her name. She ***survives***.
Lives to 94, maybe 95. Nobody knows her ***real*** age.
We took ***new names*** at Ellis Island, so nothing ***bad*** could ***follow*** us from the ***old country***.
And we ***survived***.

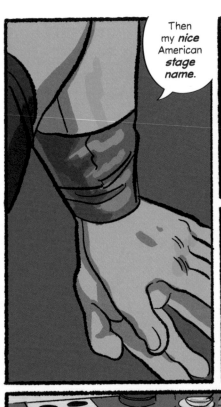

Then my *nice* American *stage* name.

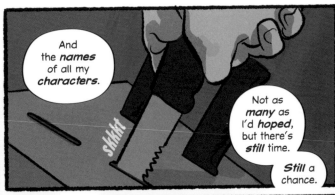

And the *names* of all my *characters*.

skkkt

Not as *many* as I'd *hoped*, but there's *still* time.

Still a chance.

Stop it.

Sorry. *Fine.*

The *point* is, each *time*, each *new name*, a little part of me thought, *this* is the one that will *fool* the *Malakh ha-Mavet.*

This is the one that will let me *live forever.*

...perhaps I was only fooling *myself.*

What's the *door code,* Lily?

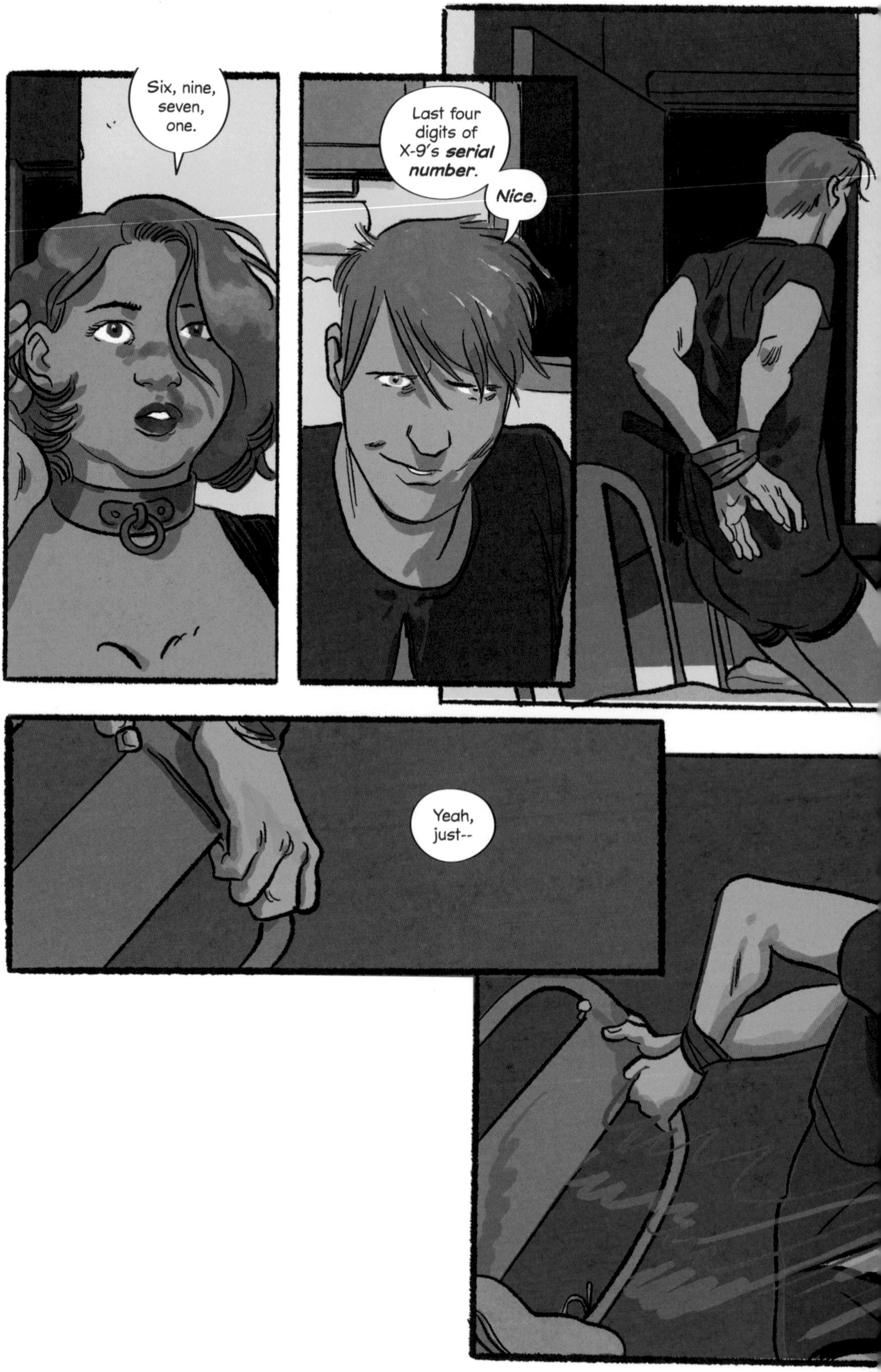
Six, nine, seven, one.
Last four digits of X-9's **serial number**.
Nice.
Yeah, just--

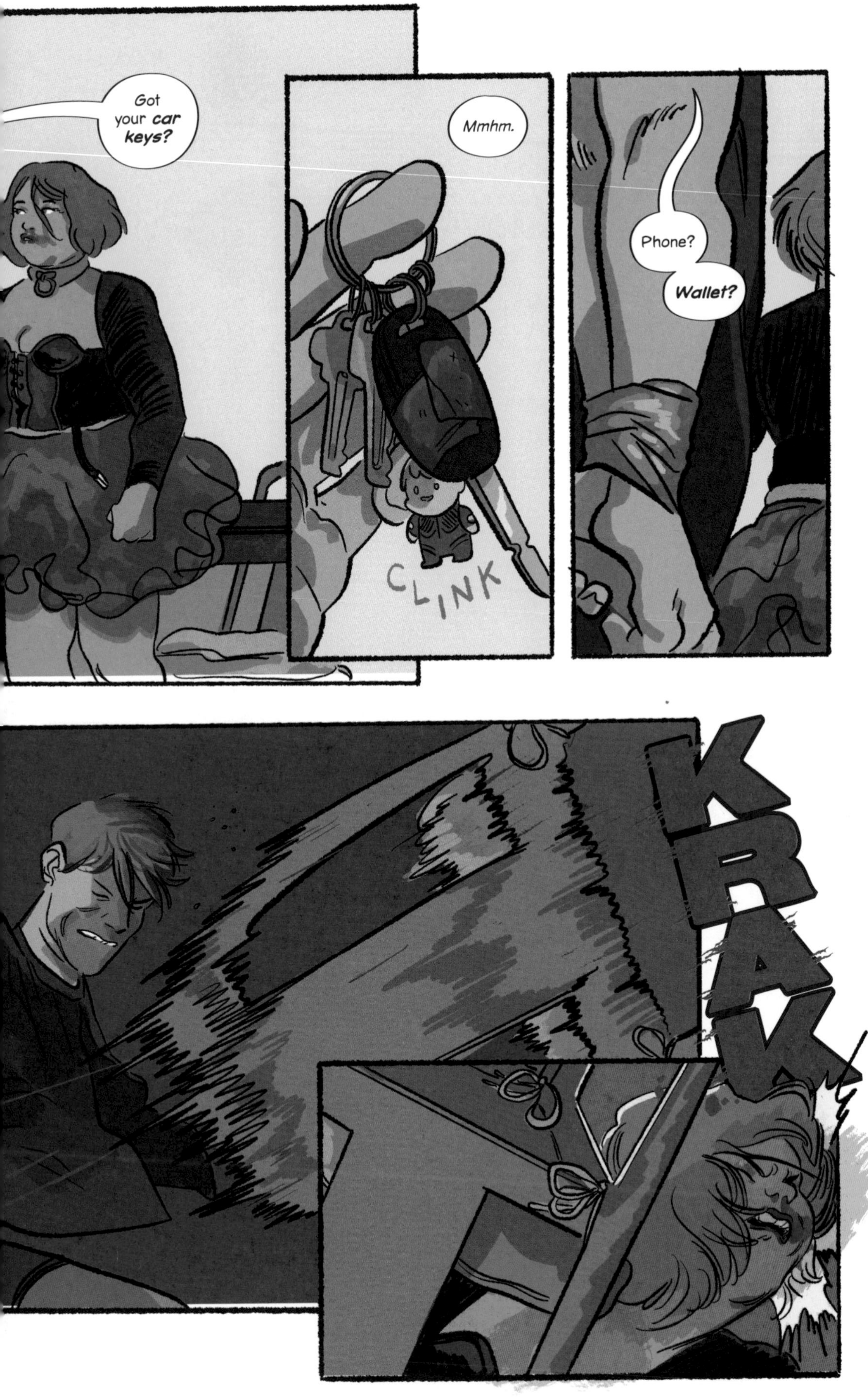
Got your **car keys?**
Mmhm.
CLINK
Phone?
Wallet?
KRAK

DAVID BOWIE, "TIME"

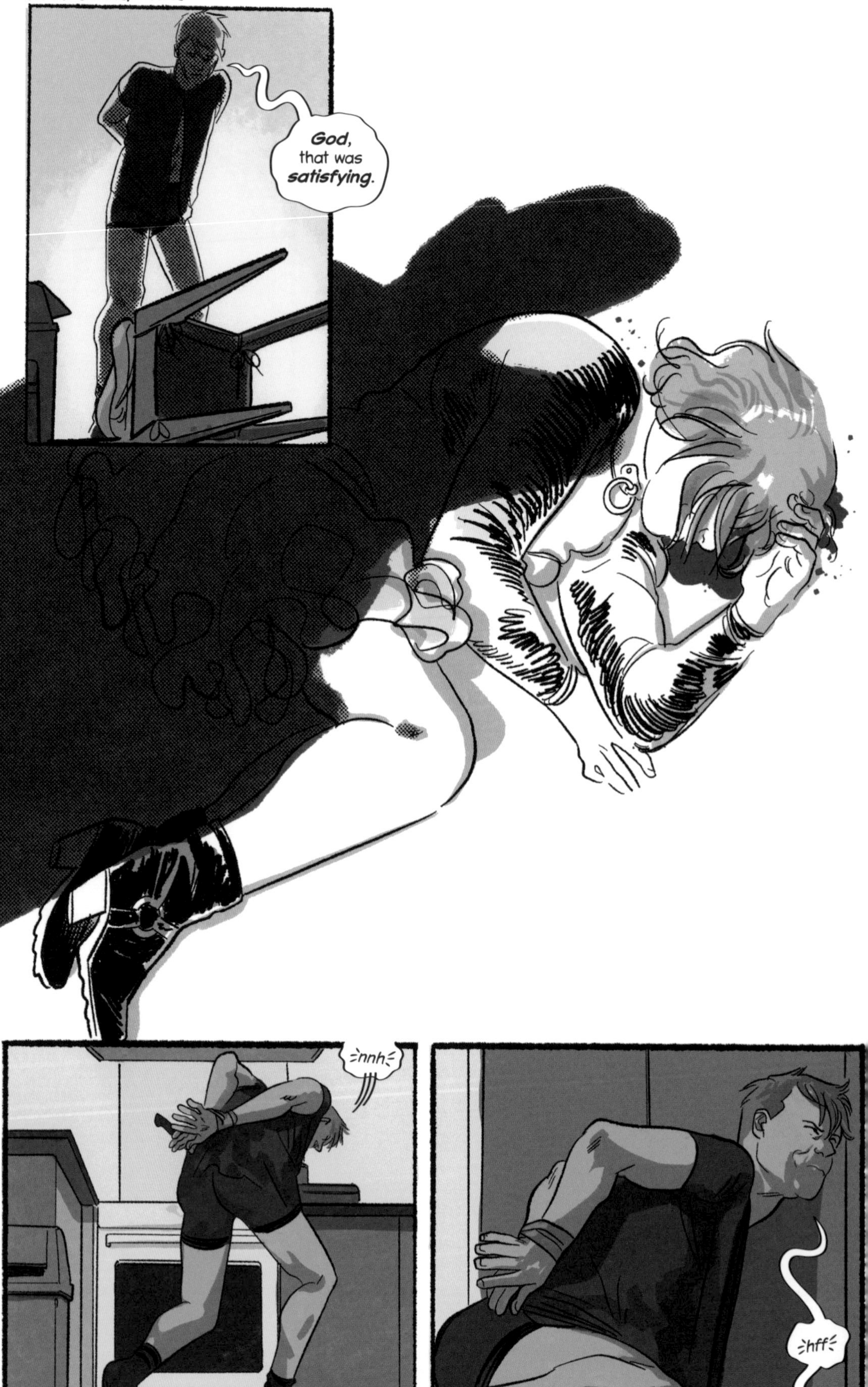
God, that was satisfying.
nnh
hff
Okay.

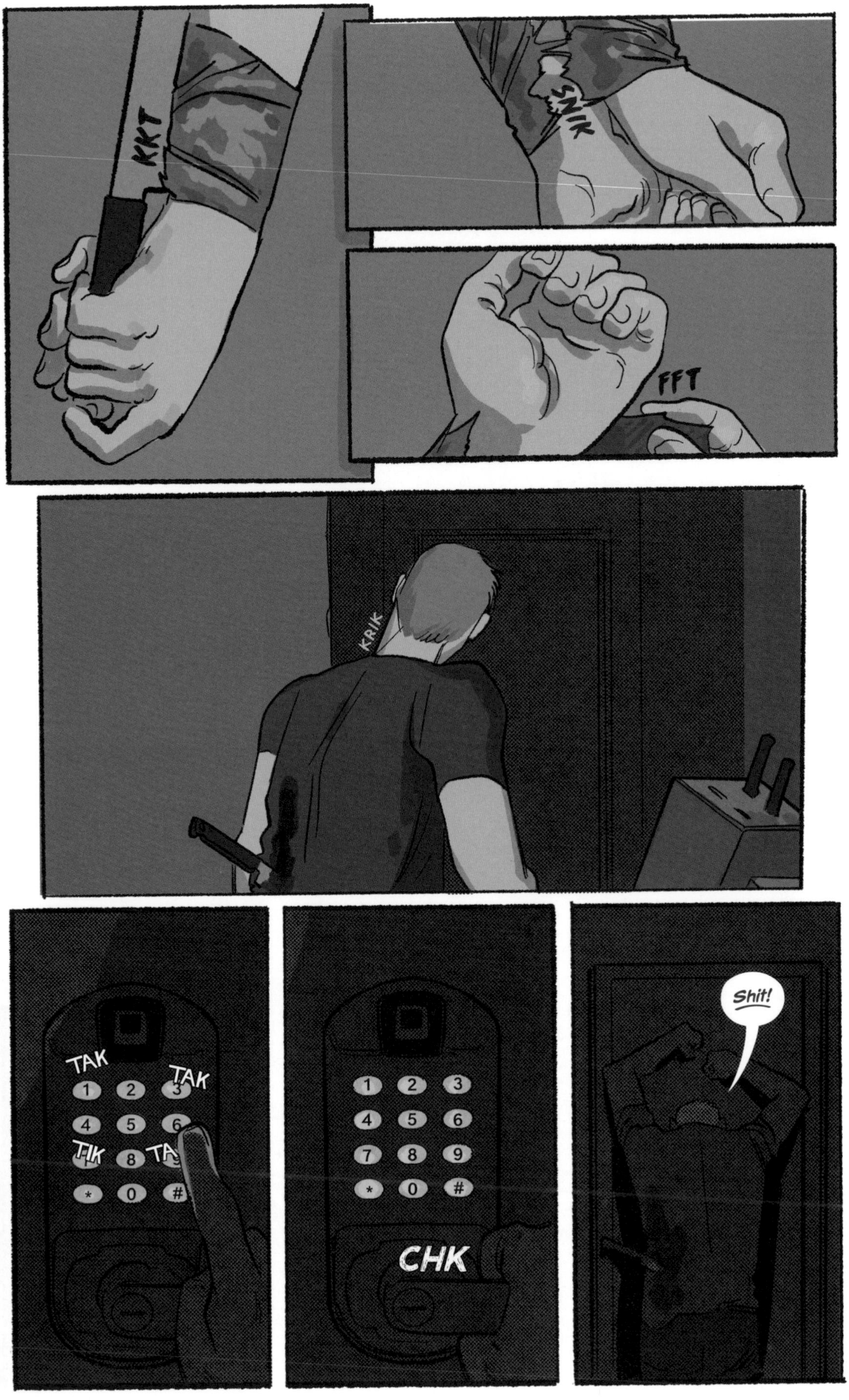
KKT
SNIK
FFT
KRIK
TAK
TAK
TIK
TA
CHK
Shit!

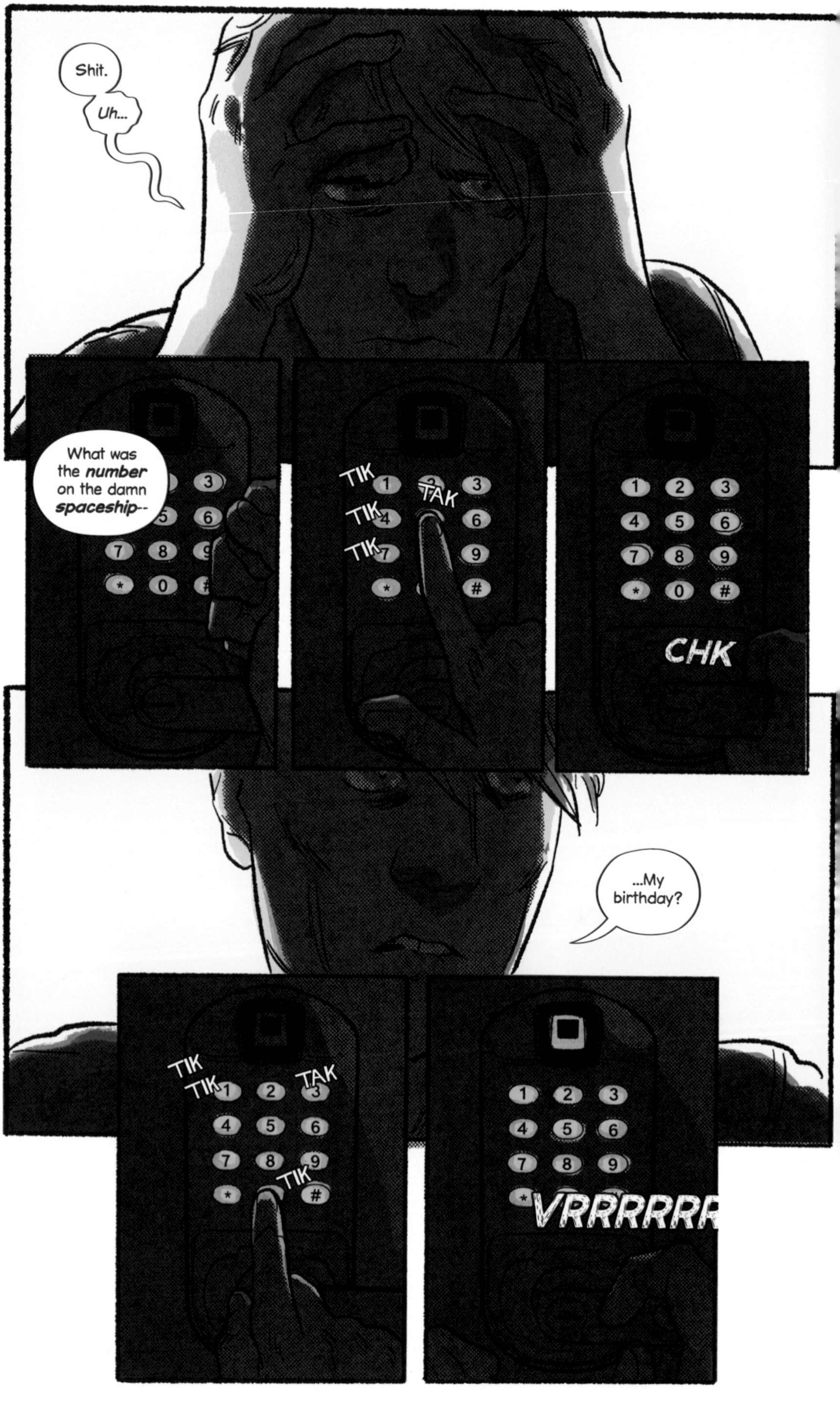
Shit.
Uh...
What was the ***number*** on the damn ***spaceship***--
TIK
TIK
TIK
TAK
CHK
...My birthday?
TIK
TIK
TAK
TIK
VRRRRRR

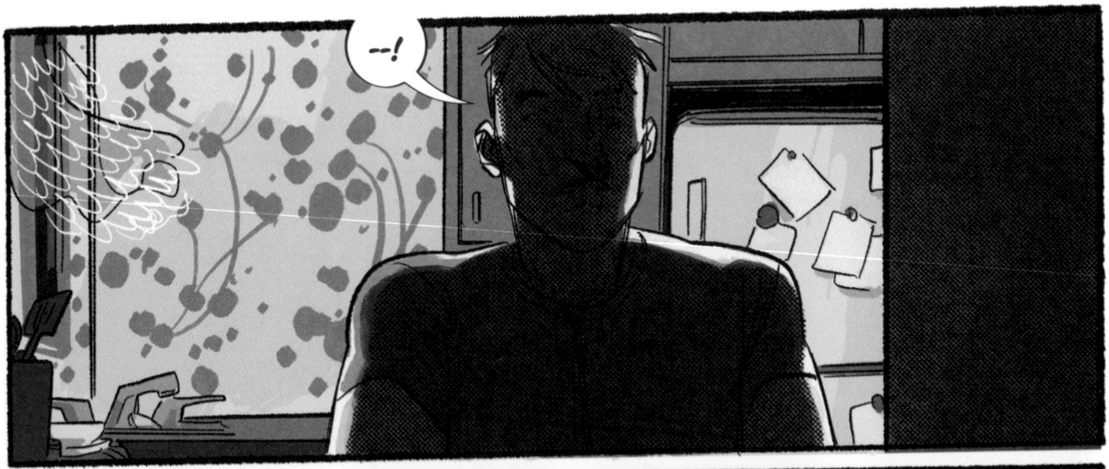
--!
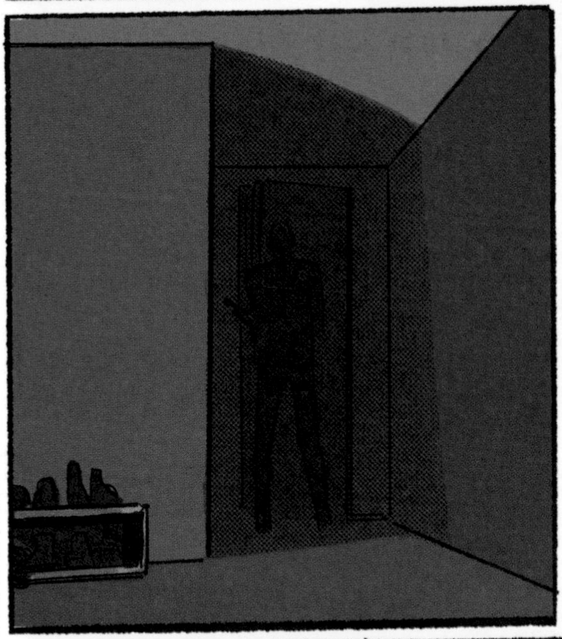
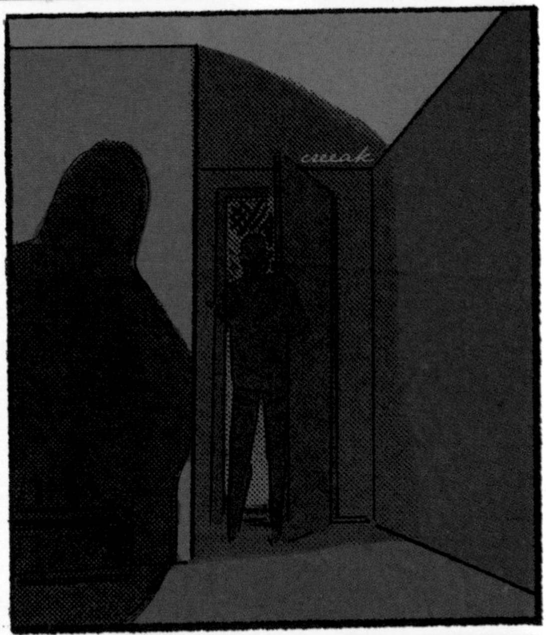
creeak
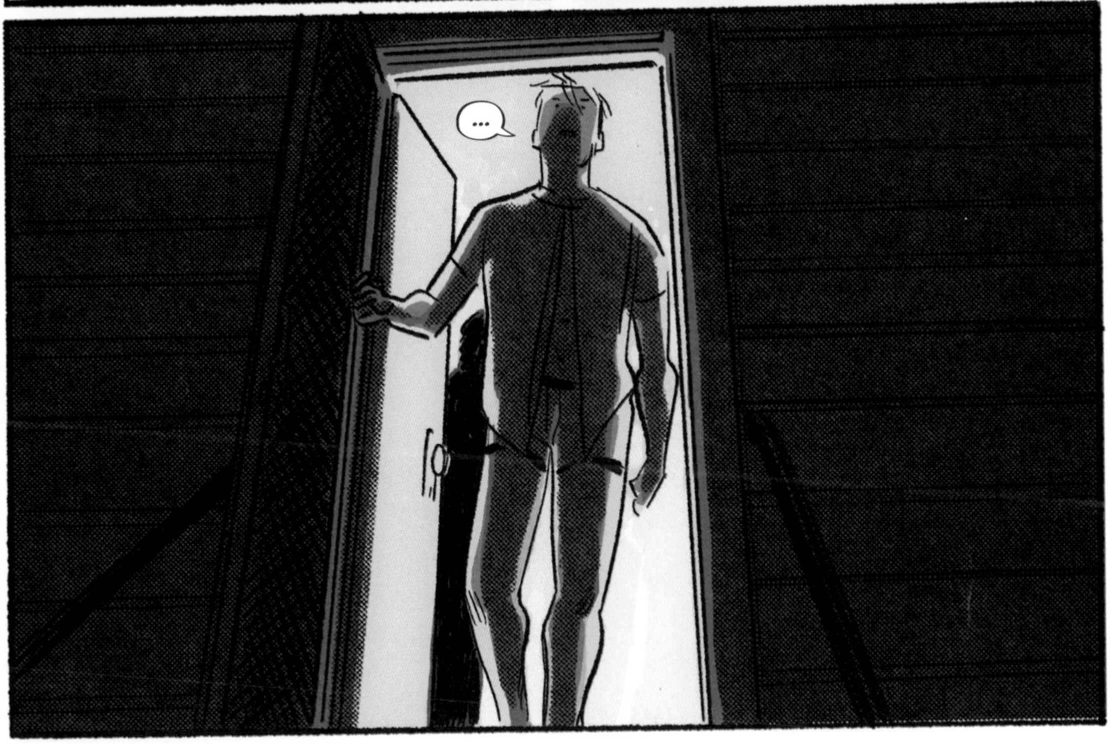
...

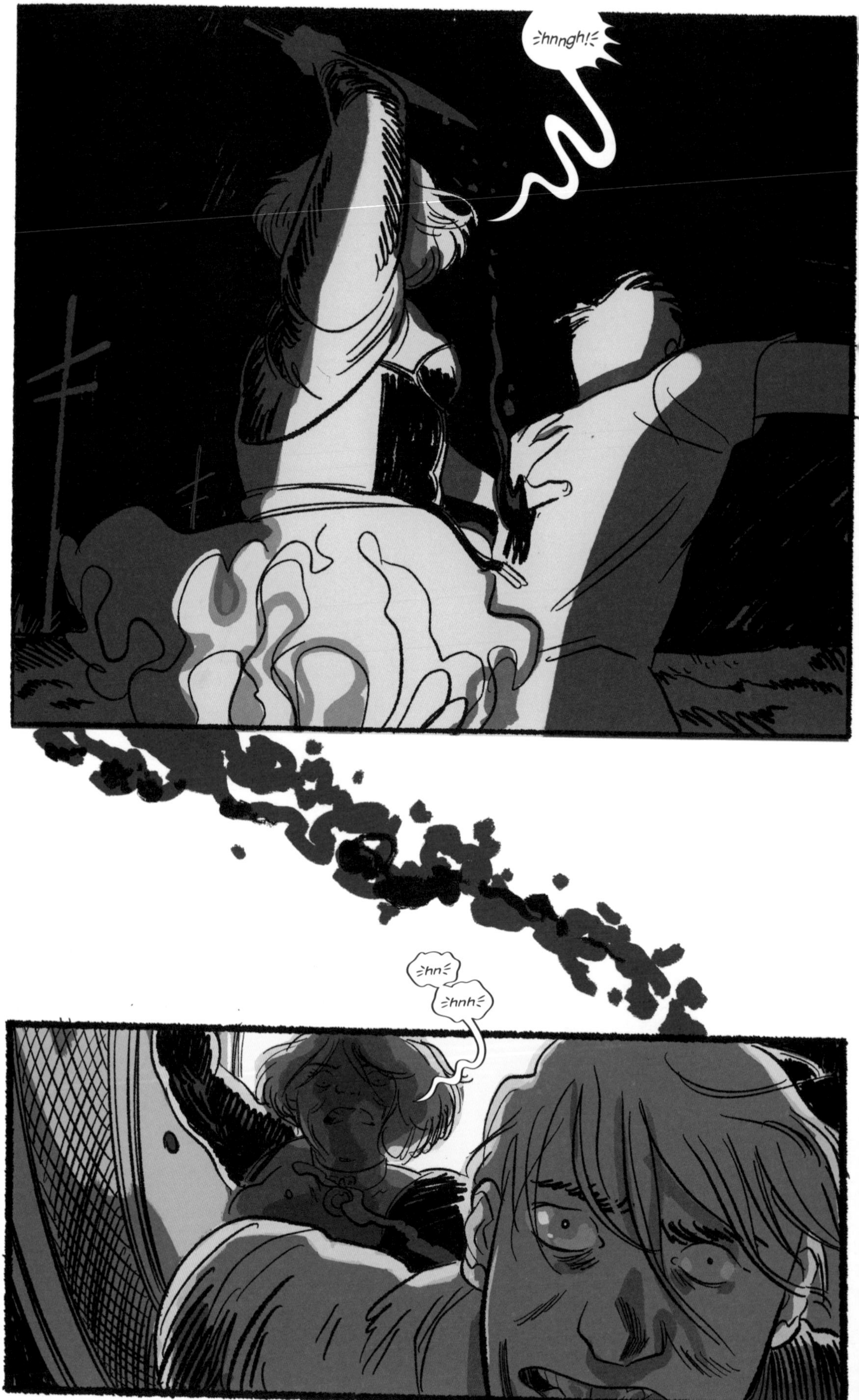
hnngh!
hn
hnh

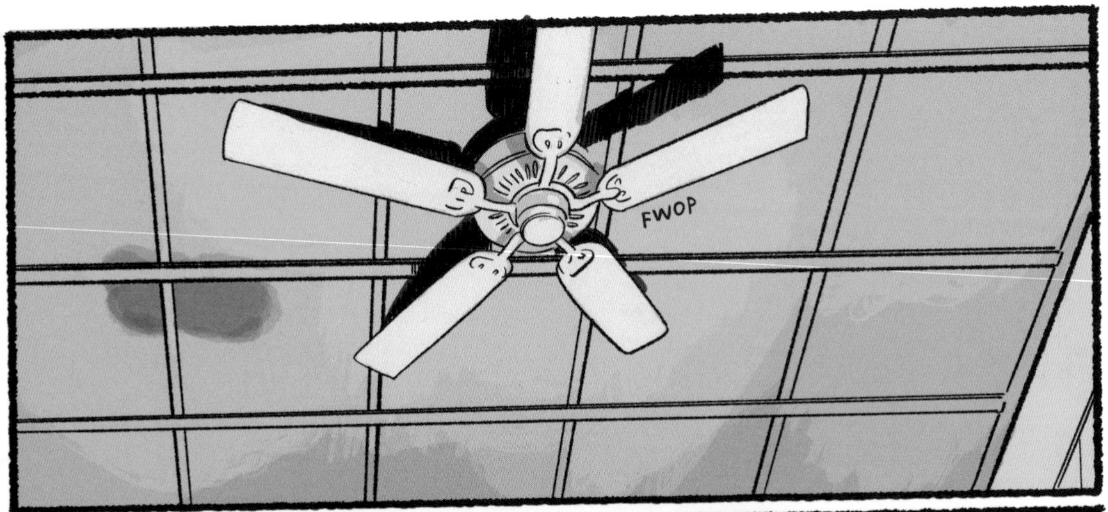
FWOP

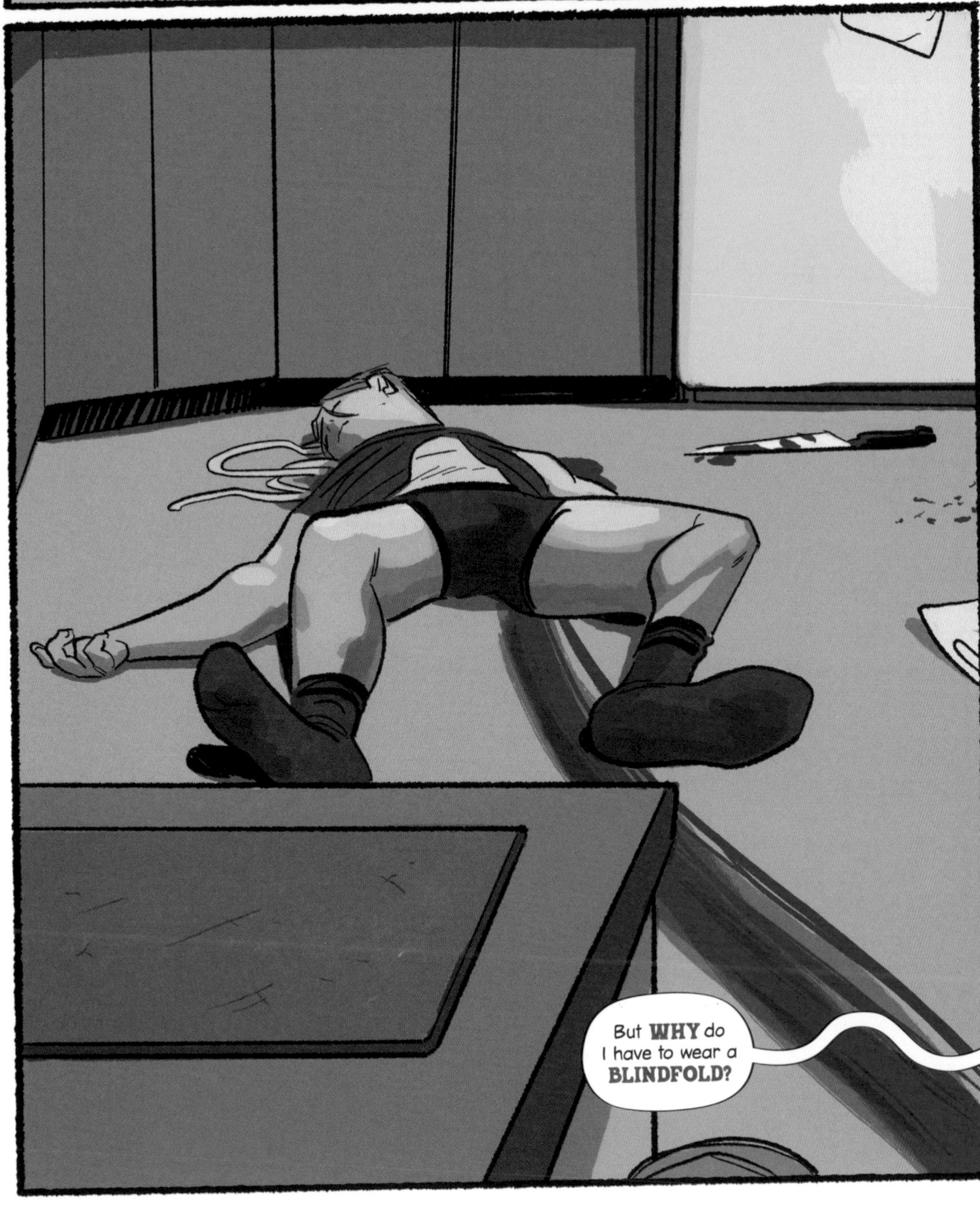
But WHY do I have to wear a BLINDFOLD?

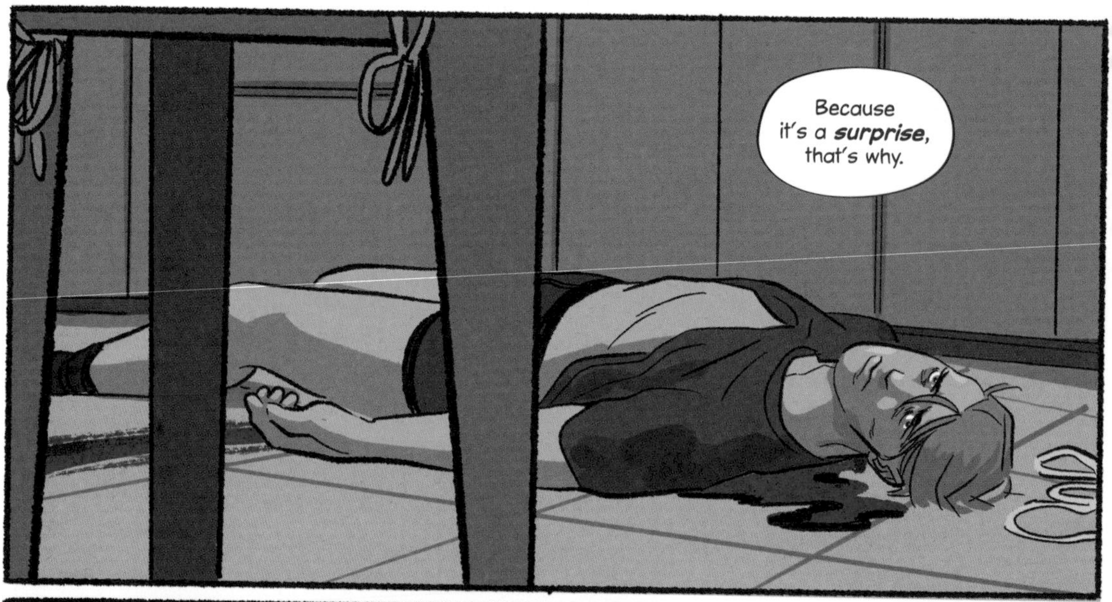
Because it's a ***surprise,*** that's why.

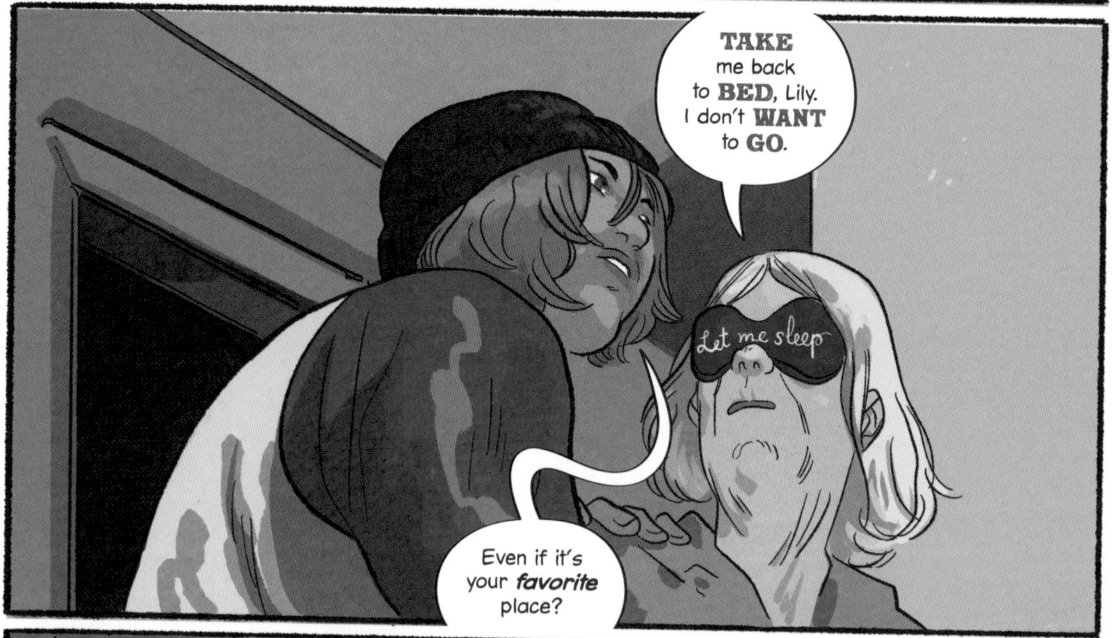
TAKE me back to **BED,** Lily. I don't **WANT** to **GO.**
Let me sleep
Even if it's your ***favorite*** place?

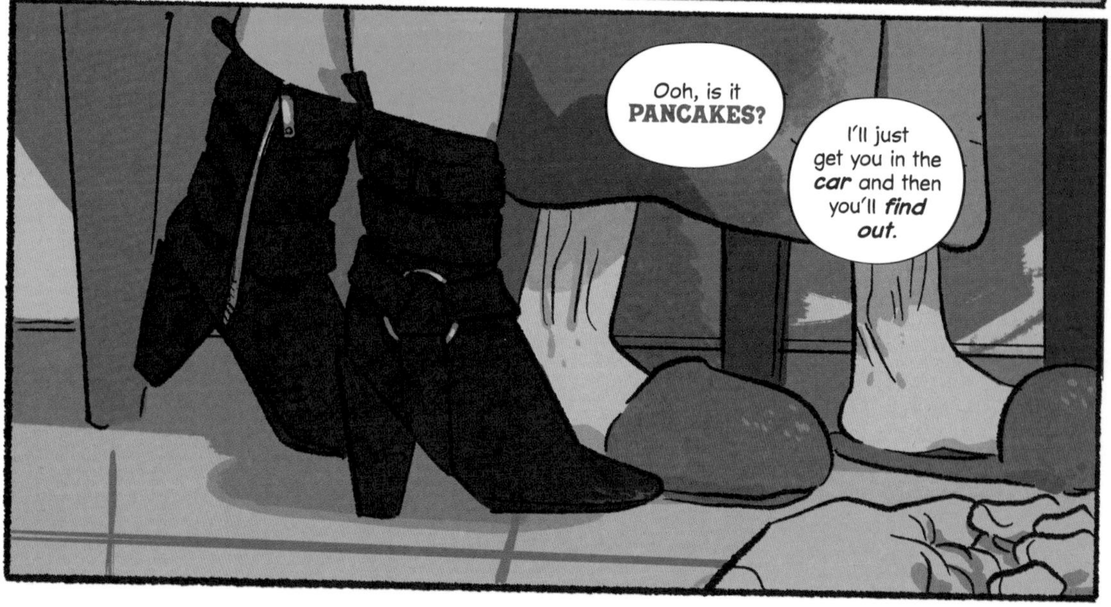
Ooh, is it **PANCAKES?**
I'll just get you in the ***car*** and then you'll ***find out.***

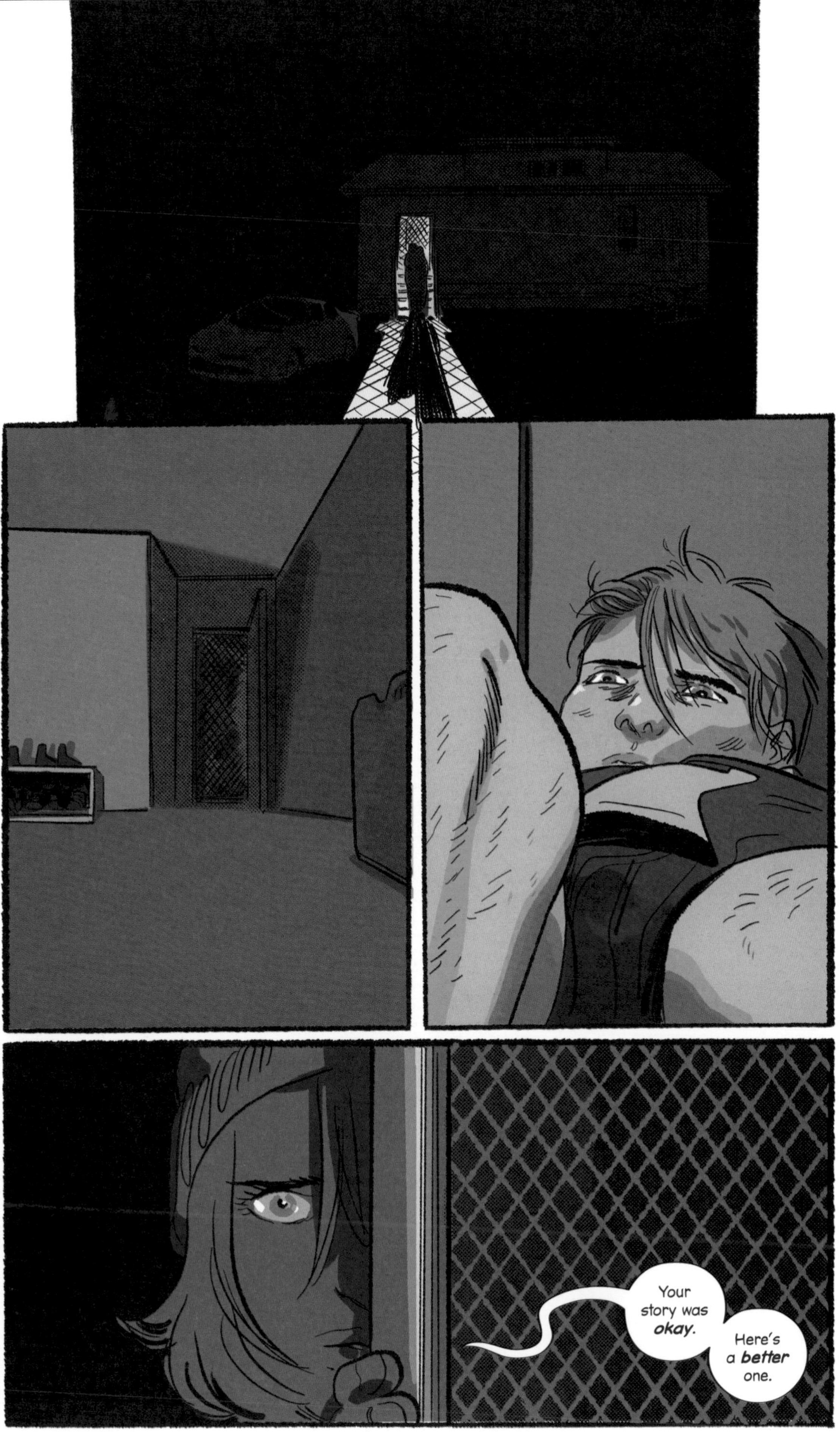
Your story was okay.
Here's a better one.

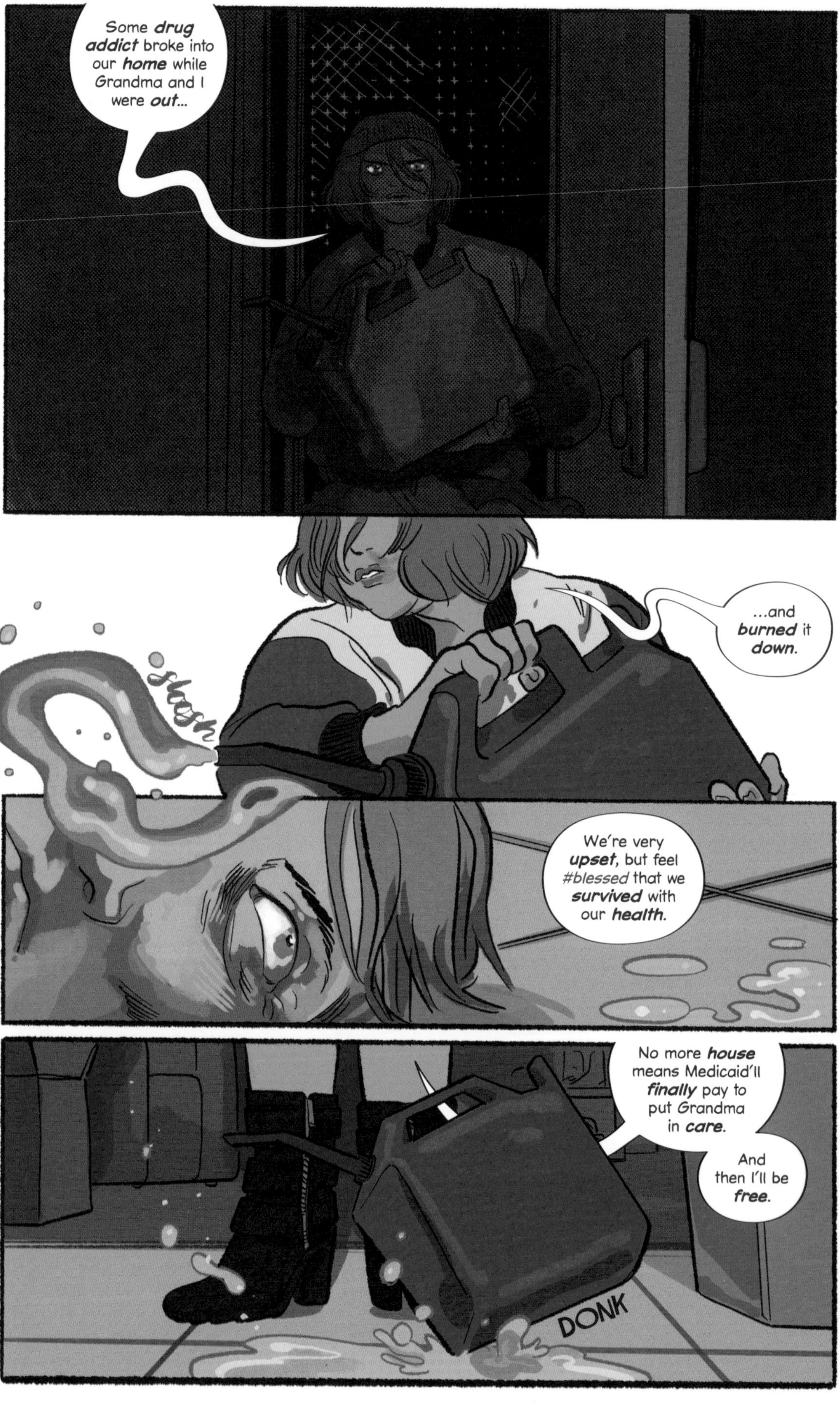
Some drug addict broke into our home while Grandma and I were out...
...and burned it down.
sloosh
We're very upset, but feel #blessed that we survived with our health.
No more house means Medicaid'll finally pay to put Grandma in care.
And then I'll be free.
DONK

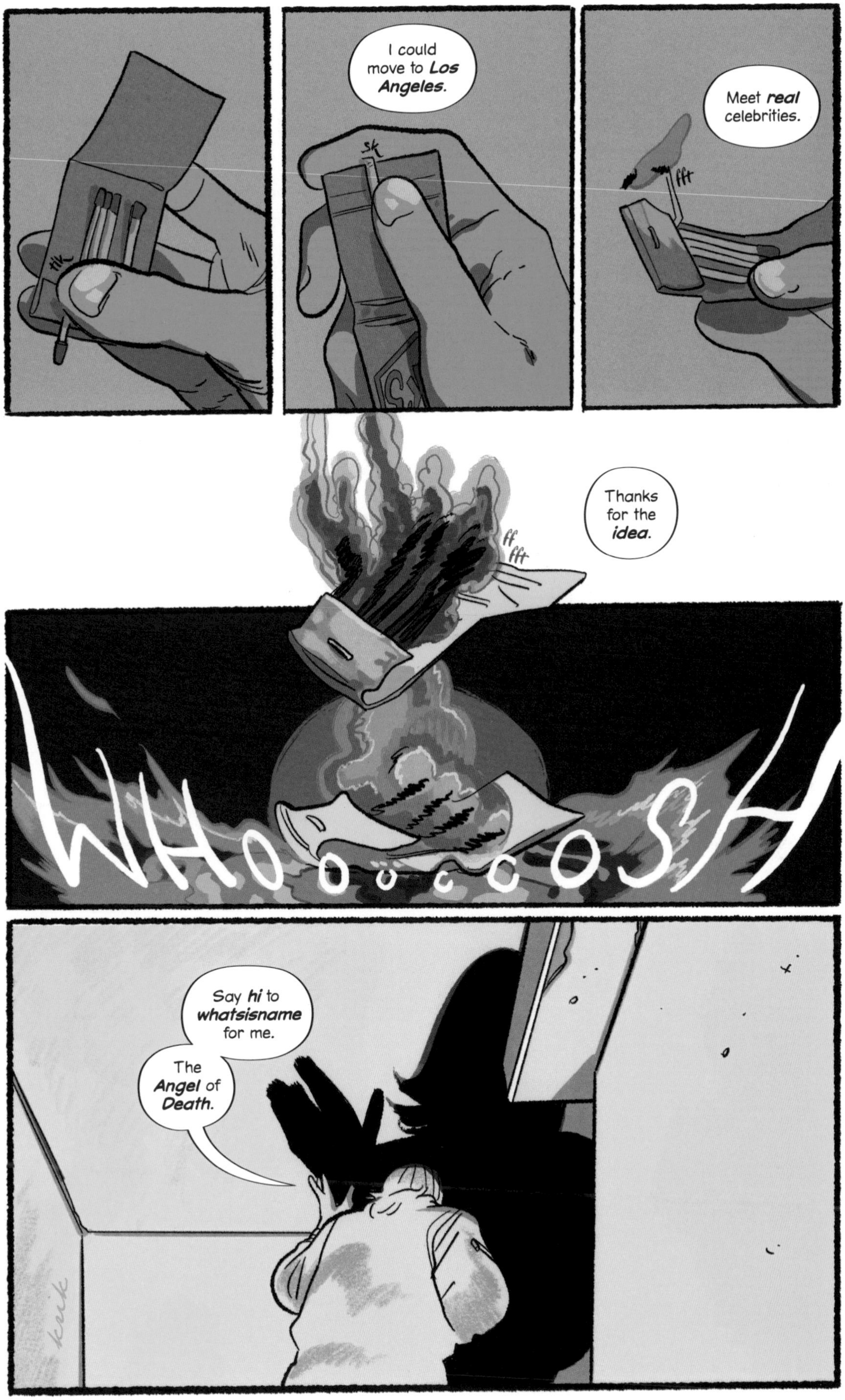
tik
I could move to ***Los Angeles***.
sk
Meet ***real*** celebrities.
fft
Thanks for the ***idea***.
ff fft
WHOOOOOOSH
Say ***hi*** to ***whatsisname*** for me.
The ***Angel*** of ***Death***.

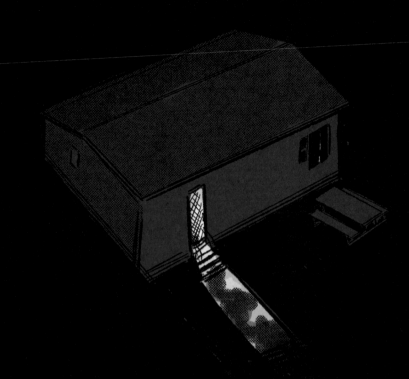

skkkrak

krik krackle

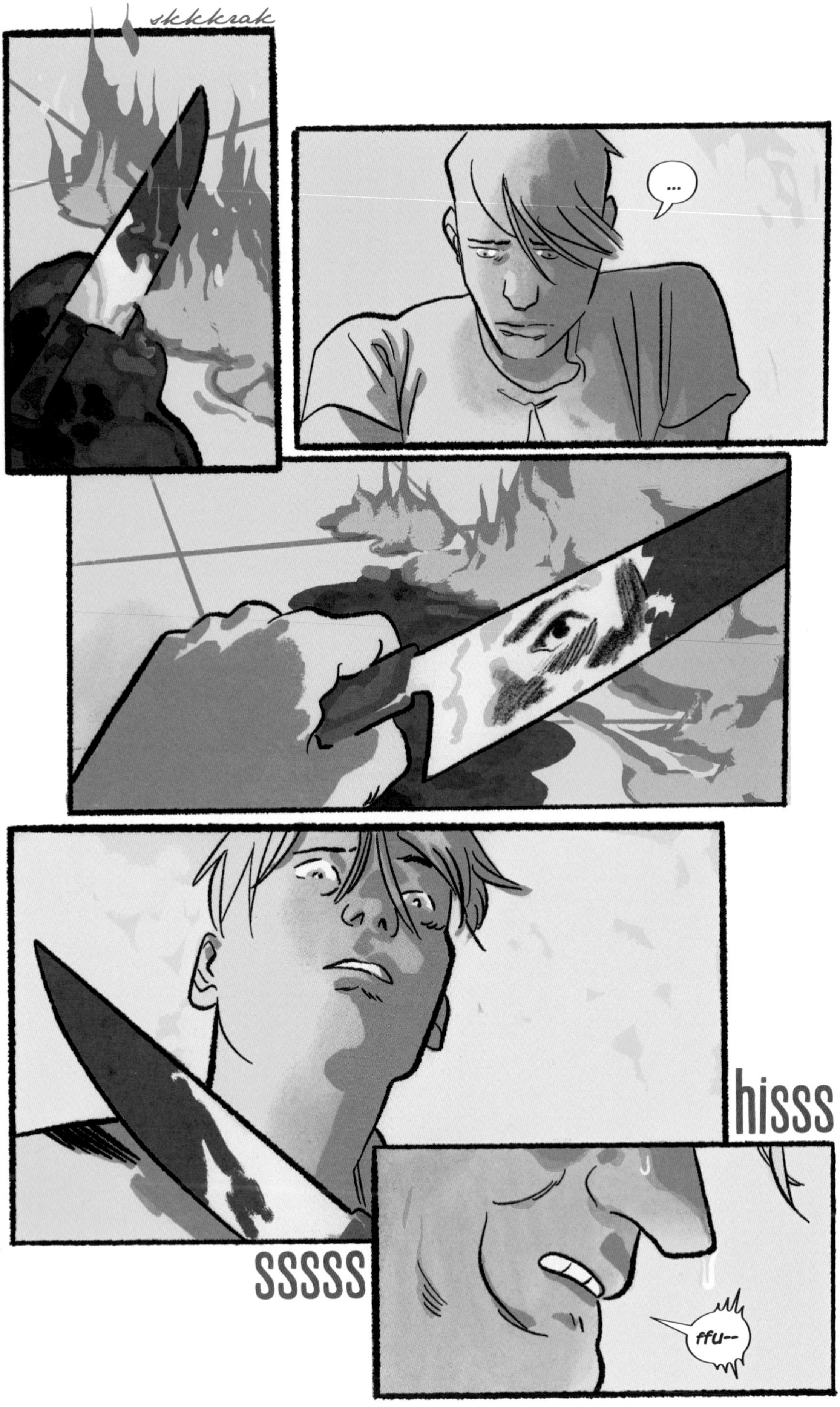
skkkrak
...
hisss
sssss
ffu--

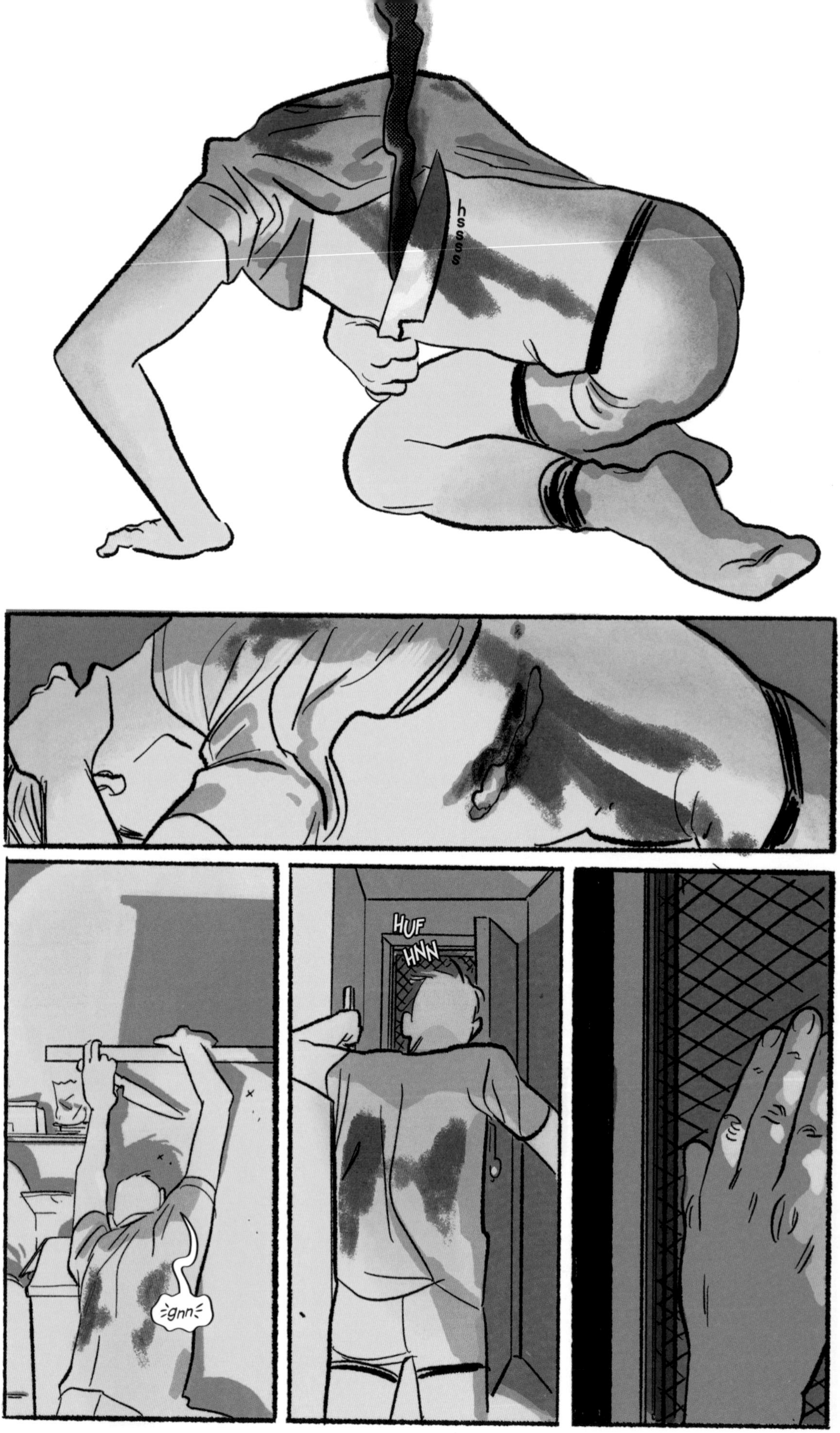
hssss
gnn
HUF
HNN

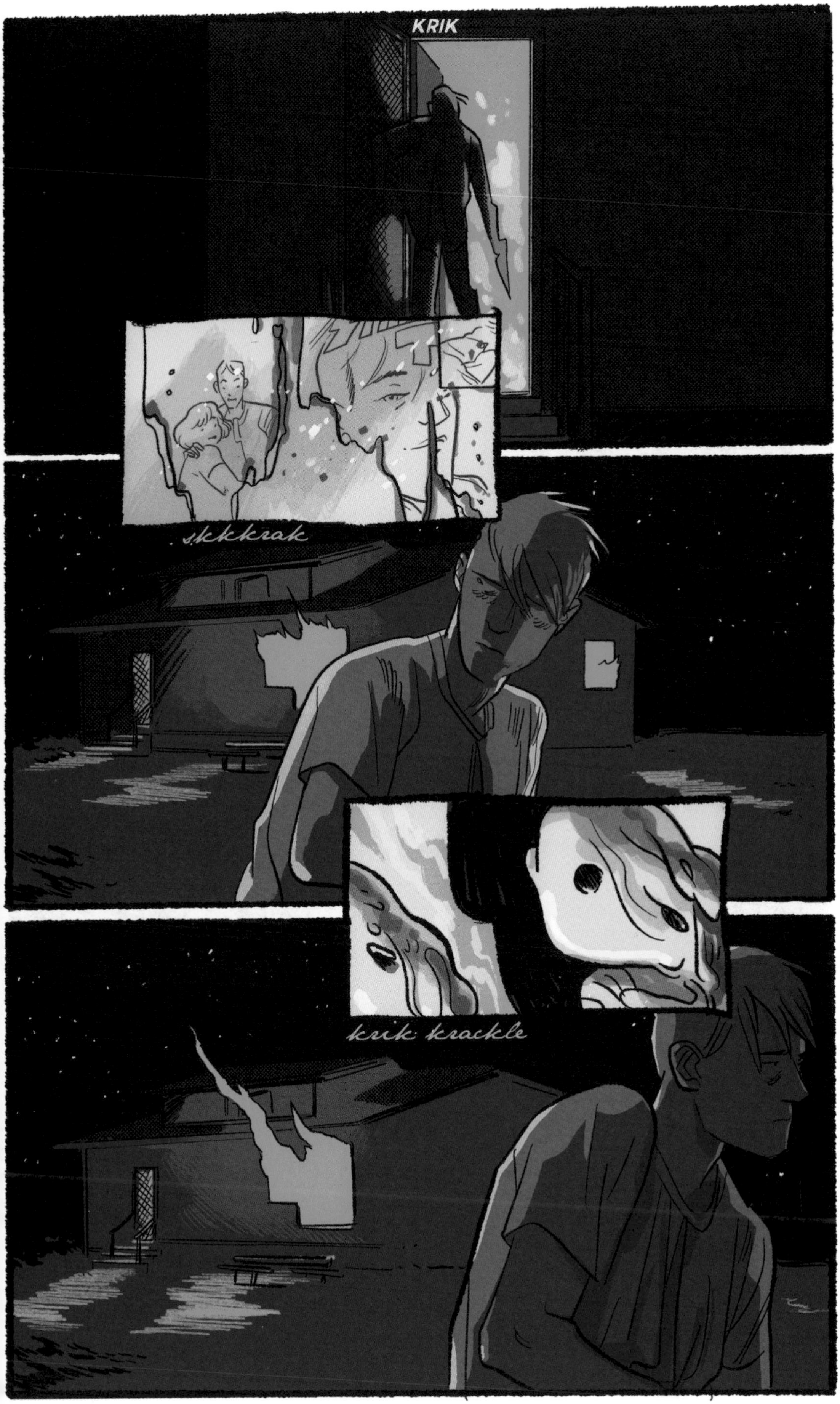
KRIK
skkkrak
krik krackle

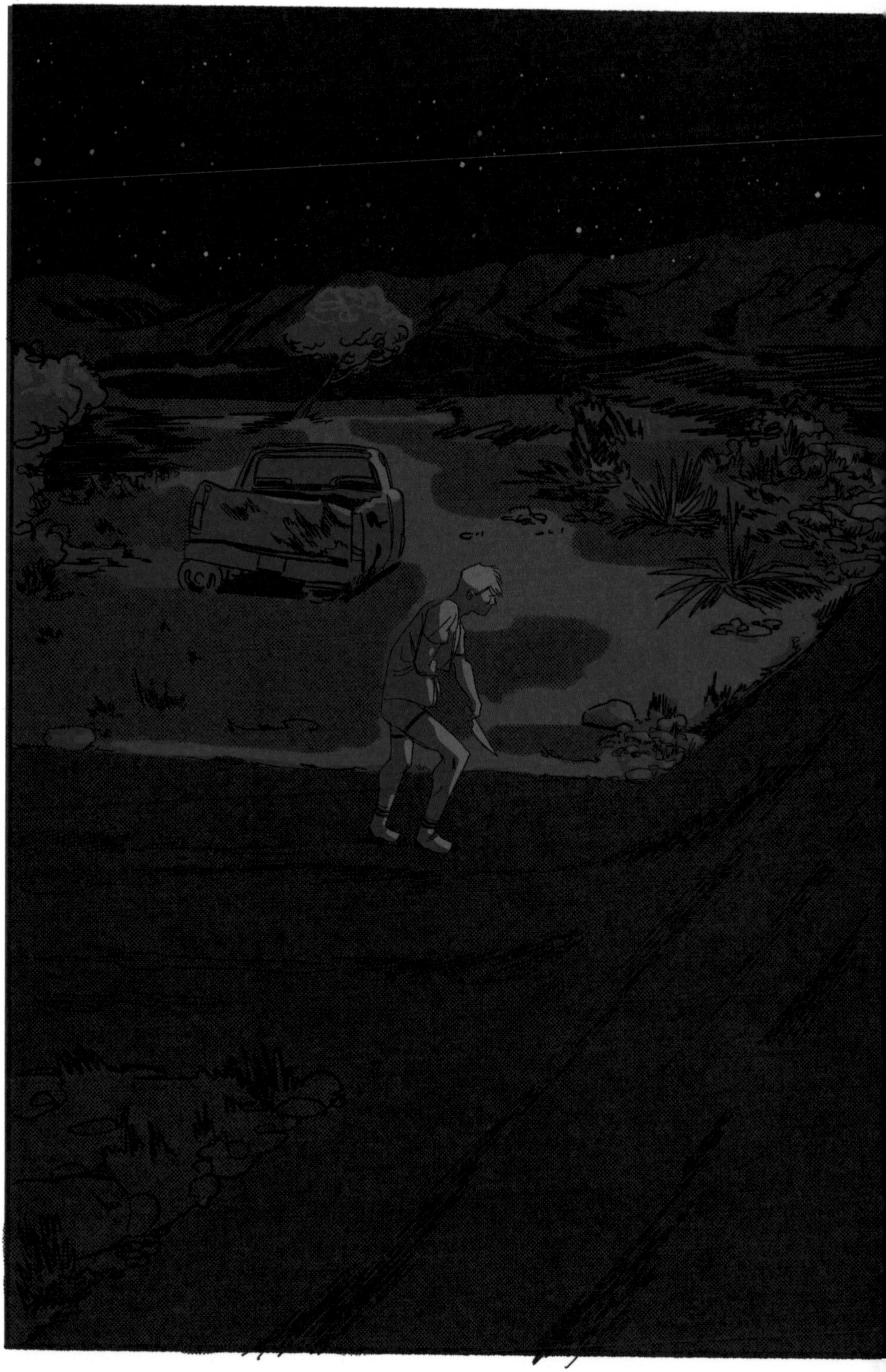

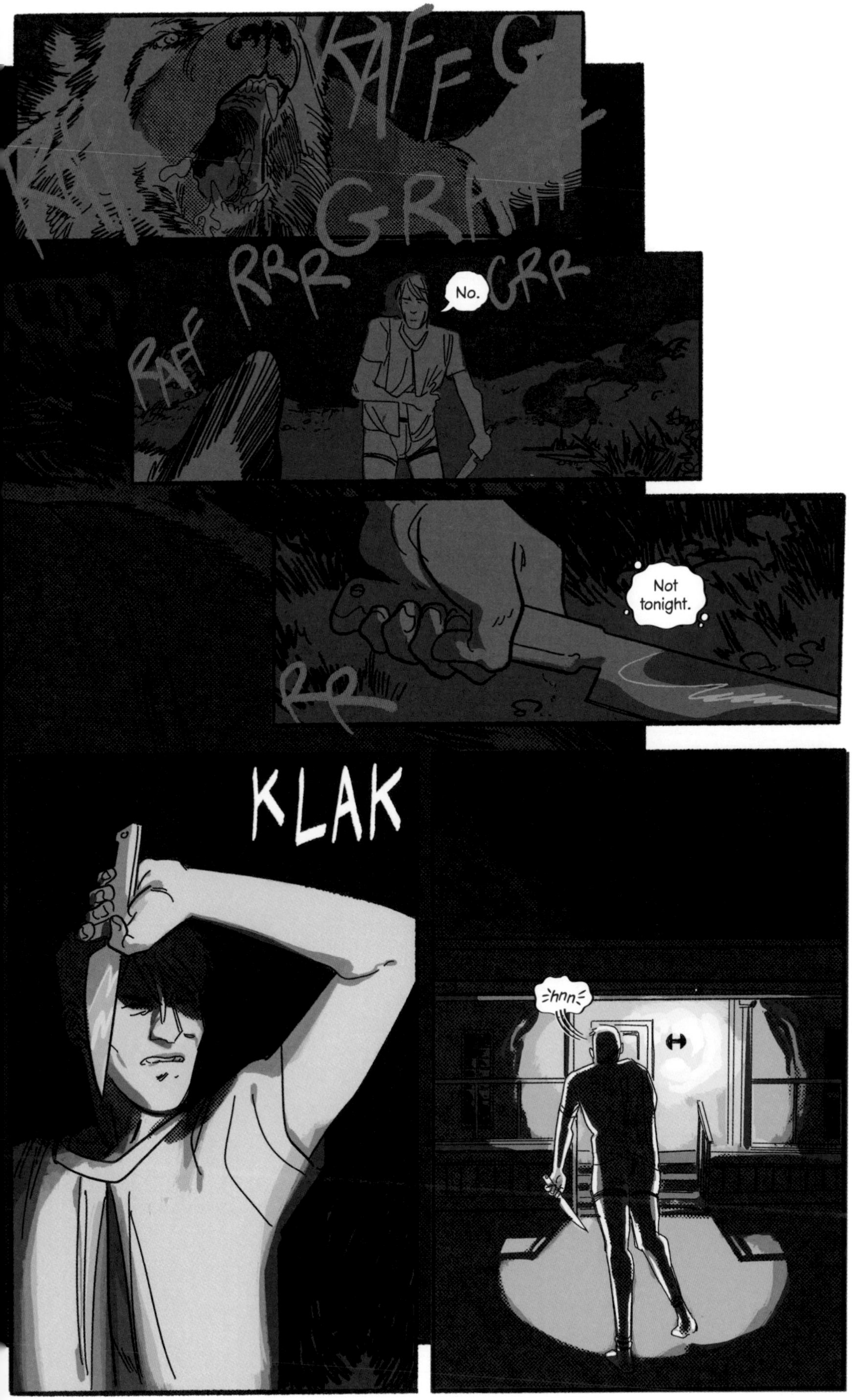
KAFF
GRA
RRR
No.
GRR
RAFF
Not tonight.
RR
KLAK
hnn

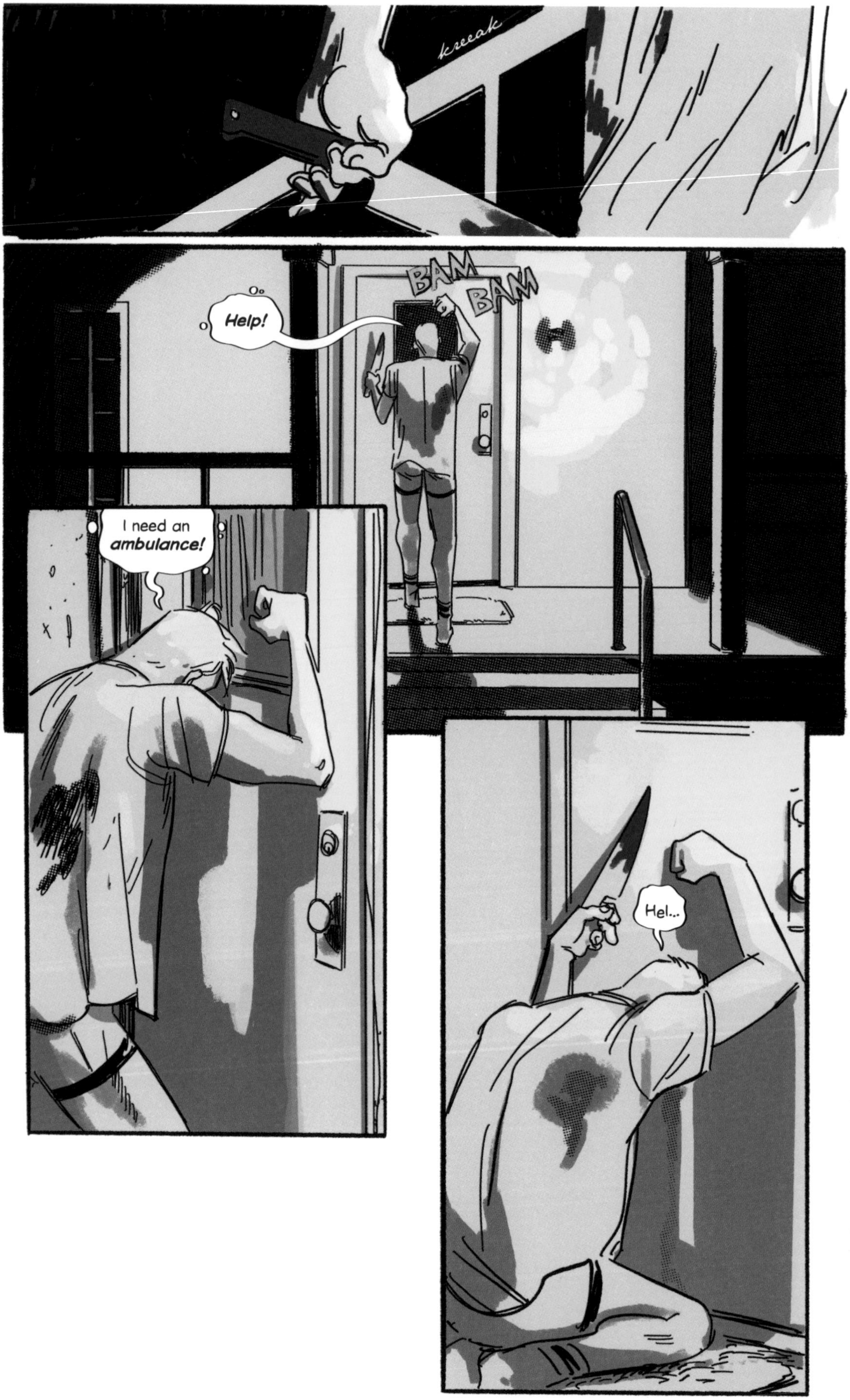
kreeak
BAM BAM
Help!
I need an *ambulance!*
Hel...

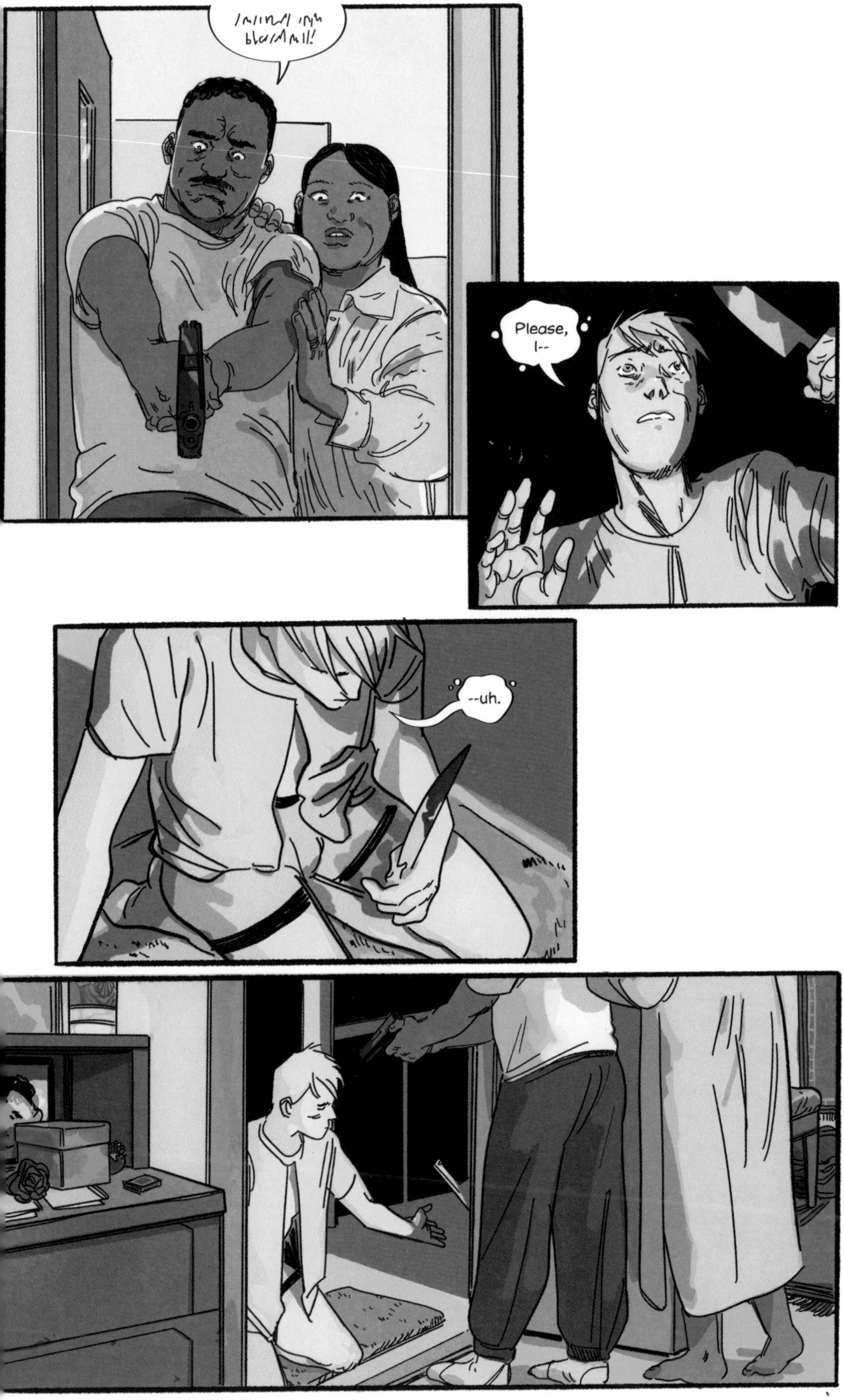
Please, I--
--uh.

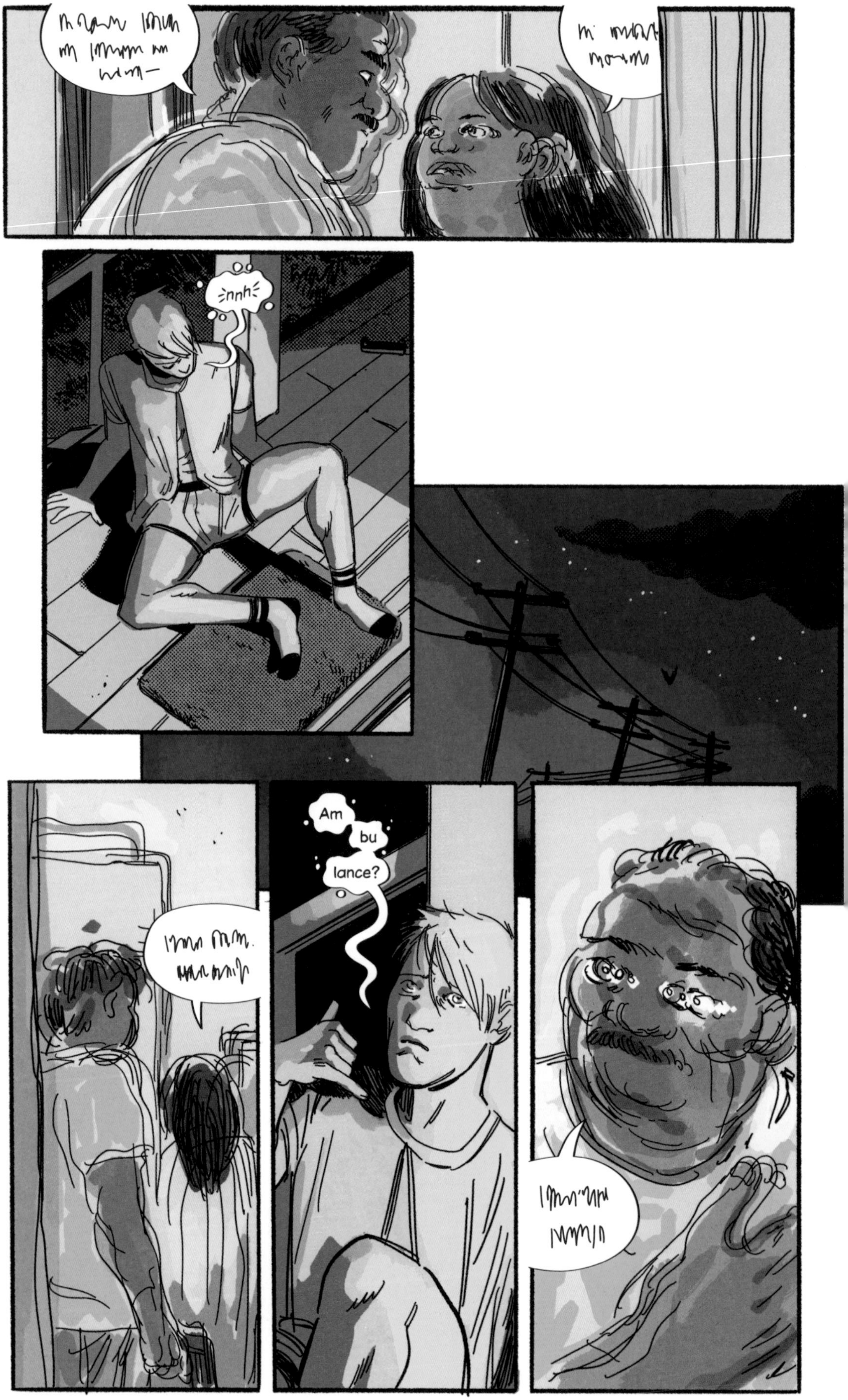
nnh
Am
bu
lance?

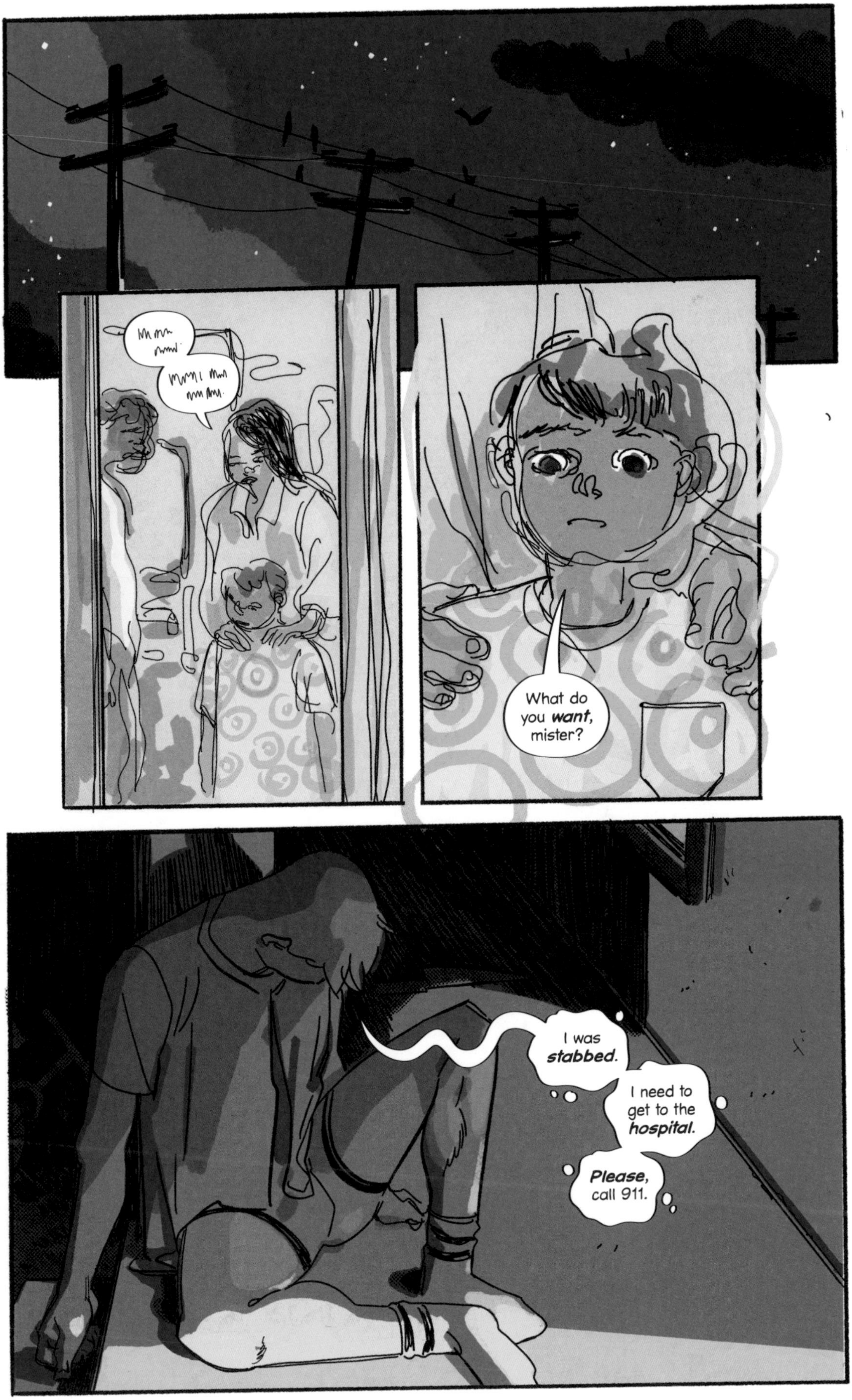
What do you ***want***, mister?
I was ***stabbed***.
I need to get to the ***hospital***.
Please, call 911.

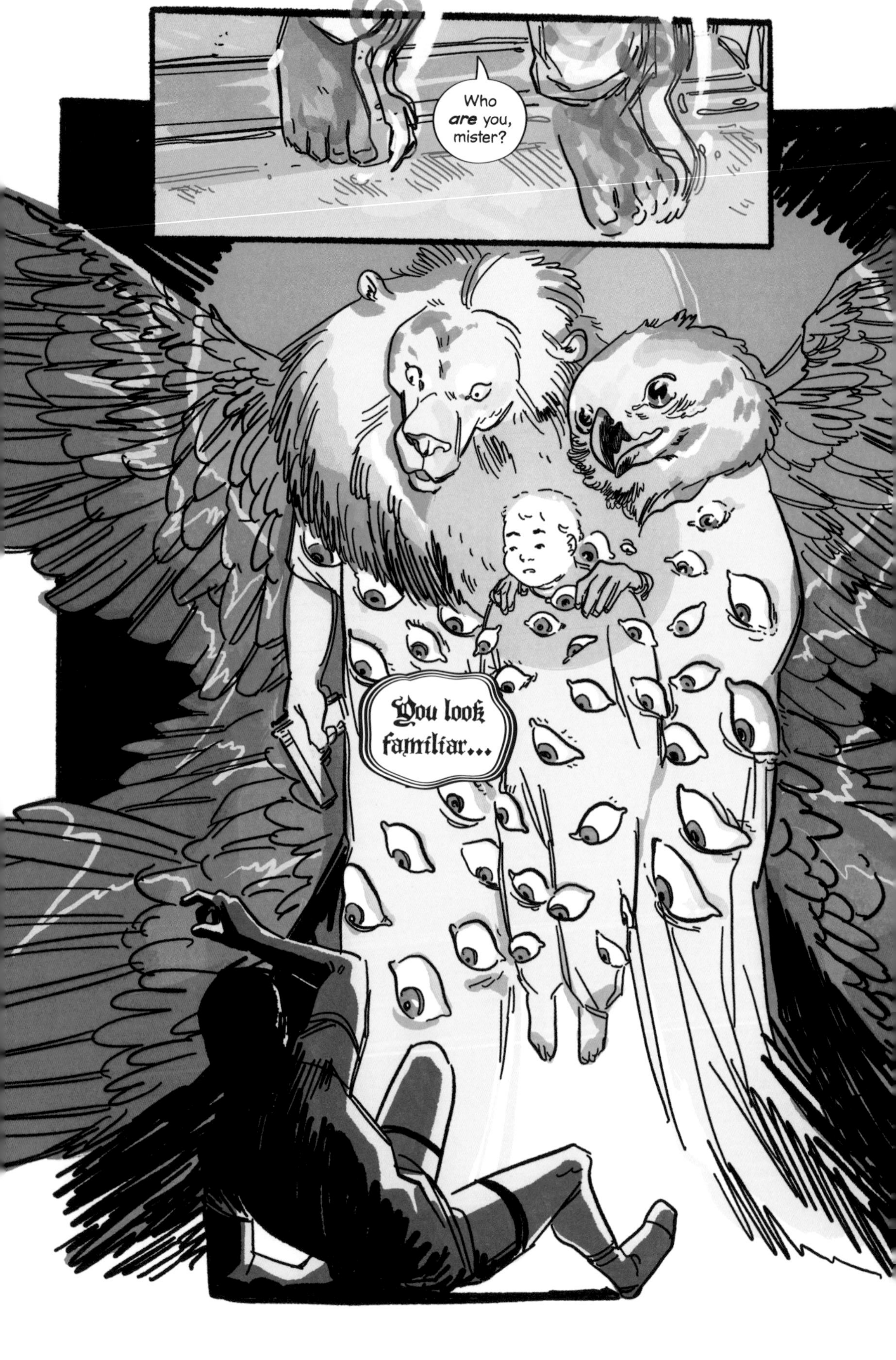
Who are you, mister?
You look familiar...

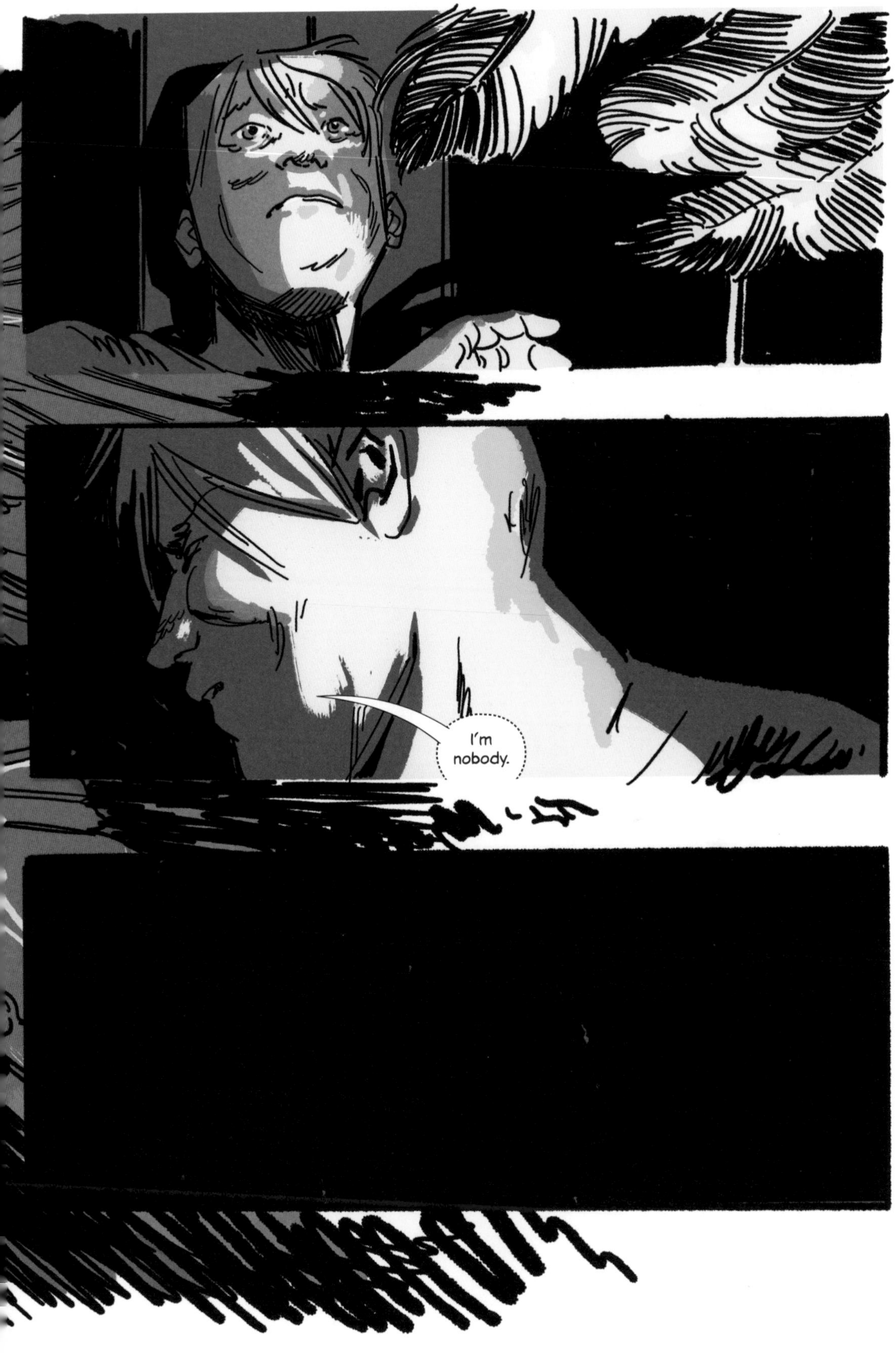
I'm nobody.

["The Sun Always Shines

On TV" by a-ha plays]

 **luke.indiana** ✓ ···

♡ ⃝ ◁   🔖

88,009 likes

luke.indiana I've been trying to carry on as best I can, but I've realized I need to mourn the two recent endings in my life: Rogue Nebula, and my marriage. I'm fine, but I've decided to step back and not do any more conventions for the foreseeable future. Please don't worry about me, #RogueFamily. "The galaxy sure seems hell-bent on bringing us back together."

View all 2,093 comments

@shutupdougan Like it was fate, X-9.
@alwayscoffee7 There is no such thing as fate, Jack, although the probabilities involved here are infinitesimally small.

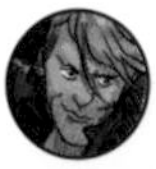

luke.indiana ...

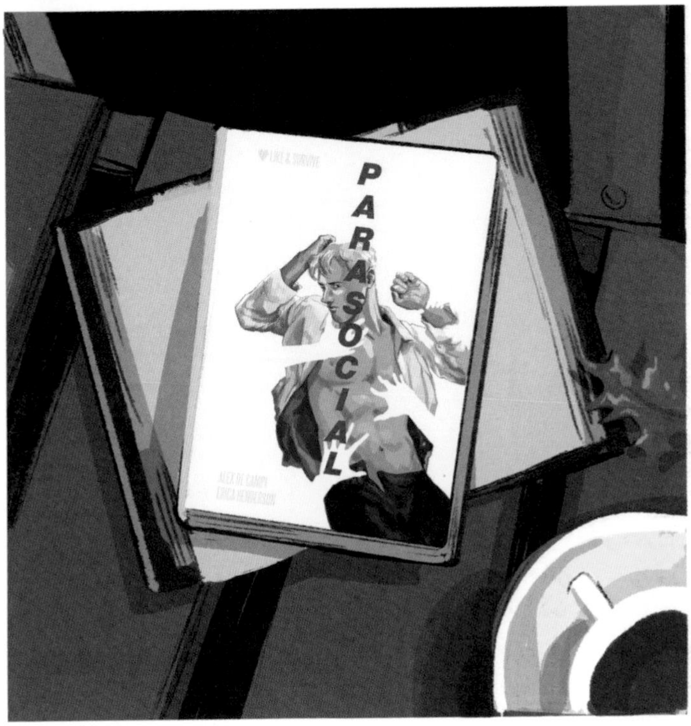
PARASOCIAL

101,241 likes

luke.indiana Hi everyone. I hope you enjoyed my guest appearance as Arkham Hicks on FreeVee's #LadyDanger, which just premiered last night. If you haven't seen it, go watch it. I'm the bad guy.

Also… I have a secret to tell you. I wrote a book under a pseudonym. It came out last week, and some of it is true 😉. Here's what I want you to do, #RogueFamily: Take a picture of yourself reading my book, tag me in it, and tell me one of your deepest secrets. I promise to read every one xx #Parasocial #bookstagram #horrorfan

View all 2,666 comments

Have any of you heard from Lily recently?

I'm worried about her

THIS CHARMING MAN

by Erica Henderson

One of the major themes in *Parasocial* is perspective. Our relationship to the characters, their relationship to each other, what it is to themselves, it all changes from moment to moment. Hell, even the medium that Luke works in lies about people. Any time we see a still of him from *Rogue Nebula*, he's a little more buff, his eyes sparkle a little more, his hair is bouncier, he's more tan… and that's what I want to talk about.

I'm not someone who's shy about leaning into the absurd in the comic format. In fact, I encourage it. We have a medium that exists somewhere in between movies (very literal, images move in time, we hear sound, things happen in front of you much as they might in real life) and books (exceptionally abstract, a series of symbols mashed together that we are able to interpret as thoughts). The series of images are still there, but instead of letting them just happen in front of us, we have to read the images, much like we would text: left, right, top, bottom. And then we throw in the fact that within the images there is more text: left, right, top, bottom. Each image lasts as long as the text or action within it implies. Then we're left with gaps of time to fill in ourselves before the next one begins. This is extremely abstract. So we lean into it.

The look of the book changes from scene to scene, from moment to moment. One of the more obvious choices is color. We jump back and forth from the harsh fluorescent light and local color of the convention center and Lily's kitchen to the garish dark of outdoors and her living room. These were generally more location-specific choices. I wanted even the act of moving from space to space to be unreal, unreliable.

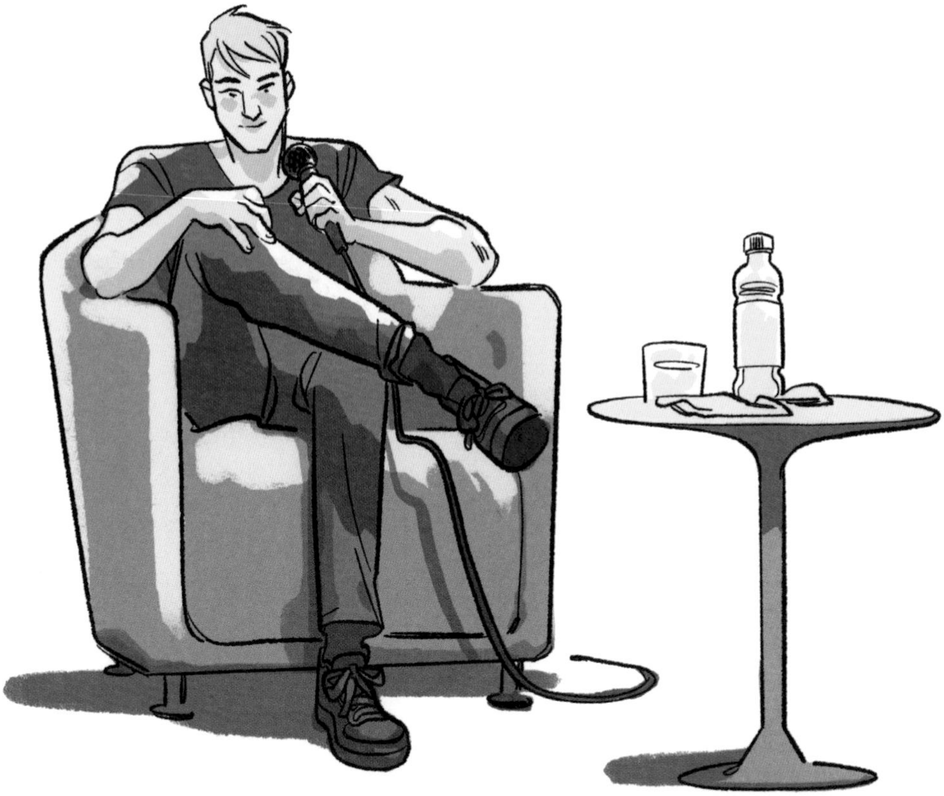

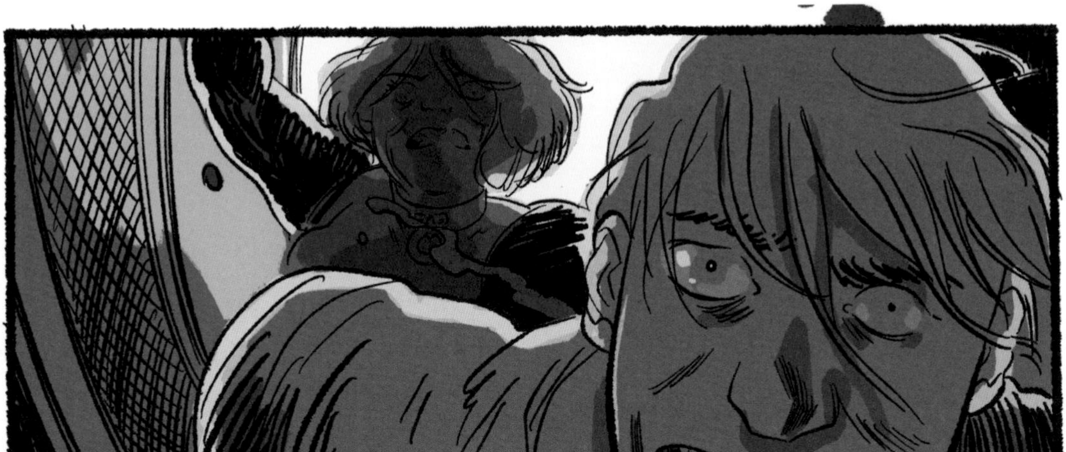

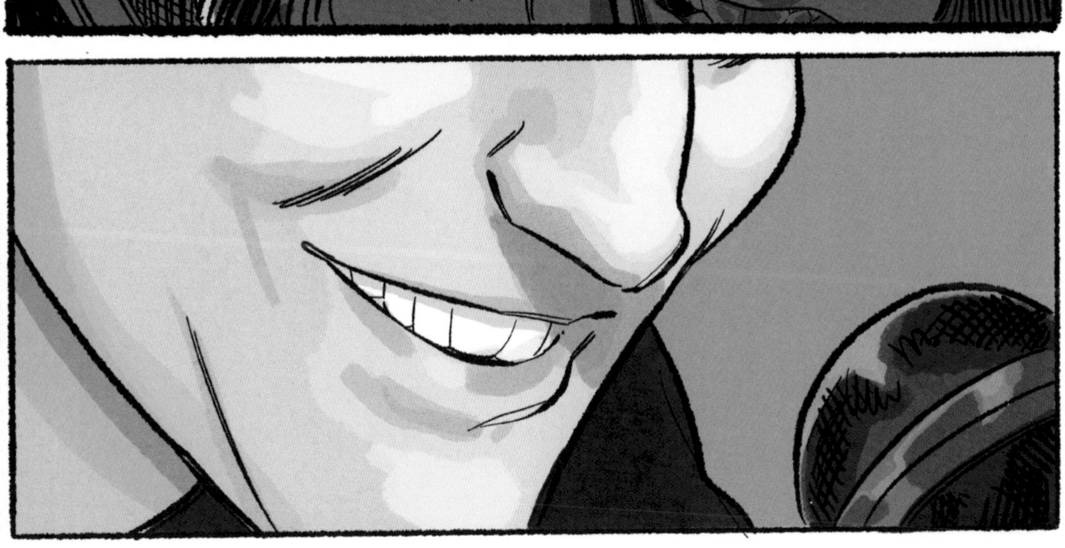

There are the times when emotion is so high that it takes over the color of the scene. Luke dreading going into the convention has changed this otherwise warm page into a sallow green. Lily stabbing Luke has changed everything to red. I'd argue that the last scene in the book is between these two types of lighting, with the family in the warm glow of the interior lights and Luke, despite physically being in the same space, is emotionally still in his sallow green.

Then of course we have the characters themselves. Besides the more obvious bits where they literally become fan art, Luke and Lily flatten and contour as the story moves along. Luke is often the most detailed when he's putting on a show: on TV, or when he's seducing Lily. We see him best when he's fully lit and lying. Lily, I focused the most on her when she's talking to Luke in the living room. Her heart is breaking and she's seeing really who she thought to be the love of her life for the first time.

Even the line quality degrades over time. The start of the book, when Luke is on much more even footing, is very clean. We get looser and looser until the very end, to the point when his vision is failing from pain, fatigue and blood loss.

Of course, experimentation could only be pushed so far. It is, ultimately, a book about human interaction and connection (or lack thereof) and we can't lose that. I can only try to push it just enough to emphasize the raw feelings that are implied, but not always stated.

– EH, Boston, 2023

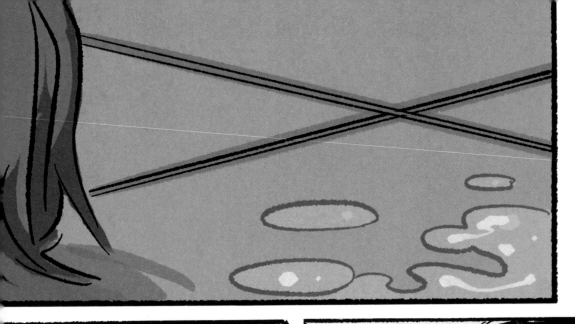

THIS TAINTED LOVE

by Alex de Campi

Luke Indiana started off as a joke. He was a response to some well-publicized comics industry *escandalo*: the current Marvel Comics editor-in-chief's primary claim to fame is not editing comics. He's actually best known for his years-long foray into pretending to be a Japanese man so he could write manga-style superhero stories, that (in breach of his employment contract) he then edited under his real identity. (He kept his job, Marvel slapped him on the wrist, and he is allegedly Vewwy Sowwy. Comics: a clown car of an industry.)

There's a lot wrong with this, starting with the yellowface, and moving on to the stories themselves, by and large maximum cringefests about Honor and Family. In the Orientalism Olympics, this guy makes Sax Rohmer look like Edward Saïd. (At least Rohmer could pace.) But honestly, one of the worst parts of the editor-in-chief's deception was the absolute basic-bitch, Weeb 101 pseudonym he used: Akira Yoshida. Akira, after the one Japanese comic that even total ignoramuses recognize, and Yoshida, the surname of Marvel's first Japanese superhero. Like… my man, if you're going to do this, at least put some backbone and originality into your fake identity.

Anyway, I was at a bar with some other less-represented comics writers one evening when all this first came to light. A few pints in, I proposed a reverse Akira Yoshida: I would create a false identity as an Edgy White Male Comics Writer, publish an indie miniseries with a down ending (because I want to make something *real*, baby) in which a female character gets killed in the first issue to actualize the hero's trauma. That done, I could doubtless sail my way into writing Iron Man, a character which in the year of our lord 2023 has still never had a female writer. Of course, this faux bro-teur needed a name, so what would be the American equivalent of Akira Yoshida? Mash together nerddom's favourite sons Luke Skywalker and Indiana Jones and boom, Luke Indiana. A star is born.

I'm sad to say I never actually put the Luke Indiana plan into action. Much like my other drunk-genius idea — create an alias as a blonde right-wing pinup and host fraudulent gofundmes to fleece fascists out of money they didn't deserve to have, then buy myself a house in the West Village with the proceeds — it all seemed like too much effort. (I'm still mad, though, about the beautiful grift of selling pet insurance for the Rapture. Ensure Rover will be looked after by the friendly neighborhood sinners left behind when God takes you, the righteous, up to Heaven! It's perfect. Exquisite. No notes.)

Luke Indiana sat around, a character without a story. Meanwhile, I published a lot of books, wrote some screenplays, worked on some TV shows, went to a lot of conventions. I ended up somewhat of a comet, moving elliptically through fan and actor spaces alike, briefly noted, maybe even occasionally missed, but not expected to return in their lifetimes. It's good to be the least important person in the room, actually: people say the damndest things if you're quiet and let them talk. Many of those things are repeated near verbatim in *Parasocial*. Nothing is exaggerated, and much is in fact toned down for believability. (Erica and my manager Sean can attest to the number of truly gut-churningly uncomfortable articles about parasocial behavior I sent their way as a method of proving this book was actually fairly grounded. Fandom is a wonderful force for good that has transformed lives and created worldwide communities and support networks, but I think we can all admit that about 5% of it is absolutely off its rocker.)

The catalyst for all these conversations and experiences solidifying into a story was most likely a wonderful buried lede in a *NYMag* article about the boutique Kitson's tatterdemalion later years. The paparazzi who lined up outside the shop in 2005 to photograph Halle Berry and Paris Hilton are apparently these days mostly working as Uber drivers and short-order cooks, since Instagram happened and celebrities have become their own paparazzi. Add to that the constant pressure that even I, as a C-list cult author, feel to Engage With My Audience and Market My Brand (one thousand years dungeon to these concepts, ugh).

I admit that *Parasocial* is hardly the first story of its type. Hell, the path is so well-travelled it's practically a highway. But where the "crazed fan goes after creator" story normally falls flat for me is in its portrayal of the creator as a poor misunderstood angel who only wants to practice their craft away from the slings and arrows of outrageous fandom. Seriously, at most they have some sort of white-people-spicy negative trait like oh, they're clumsy, or oh, they're a bit of a curmudgeon. Please. I know writers. We're liars, thieves, and vivisectionists, and that's just the nice ones.

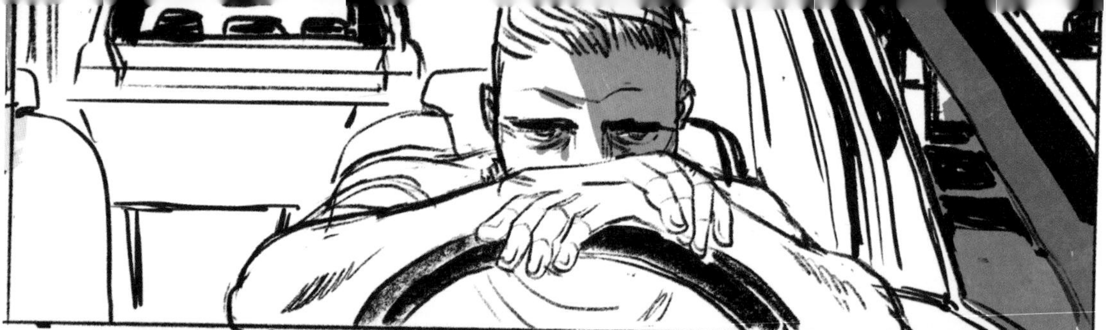

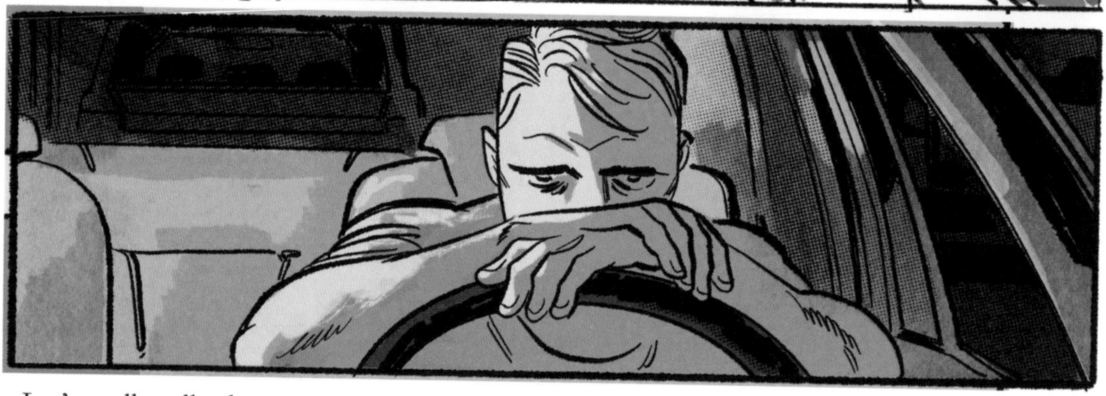

Let's really talk about our complicity in encouraging parasocial behavior from fans in return for money, gigs, and attention. Let's talk about the way fans fictionalize real, frequently very shitty and limited people into poor little meow meows and perfect cinnamon rolls. Oh, and the stalking. Let's talk about the stalking, and the general air of invasion of privacy that just… exists towards a lot of genre actors.

In the middle of all this, let's also talk about the sheer terror of being the wrong side of 45 years old in the arts. Of wondering if your best work is behind you, and if that best work was ever anything more than a C+. Of, especially for actors, feeling the sell-by date of their looks drawing ever nearer. The fear that at any moment you're going to be too old for the hero roles, that the kids coming up are passing you, that the whole entertainment Leviathan will twitch its hide and you'll tumble off it to the ground, unable to clamber back on the great beast as it lumbers away without you. And, back to our Editor in Yellow, there is the constant urge to reinvent yourself in the hopes that the next project will be The One, the home run, the rocket that affixes your star forever into the firmament.

Luke is awful, but I love him, because we have the same existential nightmares. And there is something charming in his pathos and buffoonery. Lily isn't much better, but her rage is real, and valid: discovering the one thing she lives for as an escape from her crappy day-to-day existence is also crappy… well, when a castle in the air comes crashing to earth, there's a pretty big blast radius.

To be very clear: Luke Indiana isn't based on anyone. He isn't even a dozen someones. Neither is Lily. (If you read this and feel that either Lily Sparilli or Luke Indiana is based on you, I beg you for the sake of everyone you claim to love, please seek therapy immediately.) The things I took from real life to assemble this story are tiny mosaics from hundreds of different conversations both on- and off-line, rearranged to create an image never intended by their sources. For example, *Rogue Nebula*, Luke's show, is a *Goncharov*-esque mashup of fan-favourite genre tropes. It is not based on anything in particular, nor does it exist. Yet.

You might have noticed that there are songs interspersed throughout the story, as marginalia, as closed captions, as diegetic music. There's a QR code on the last page of this book that will take you to the *Parasaocial* playlist on Spotify. Here are the songs and the reasons behind them:

"Frontier Psychiatrist," *The Avalanches*. Ah, the era of the great cut-up artists, it was fun while it lasted. I loved this song in its day. I wanted music for this scene that sounded like the experience of being in a huge crowd at a convention: the palpable excitement, so much going on that your attention's being pulled in 100 different directions at once. A hype track, if you will, that's just the right side of overwhelming. This is it.

"#1 Hit Song," *Minutemen*. An entrance song for a guy who's too cool to need a hype track. If you're not familiar with Minutemen, their *Double Nickels on the Dime* album is probably the most interesting and consistently tonally inventive record to come out of the American post-punk scene. I know them's fighting words, but I stand behind D.Boon Esq and Mike Watt from Pedro.

"Modern Girl," *Sleater-Kinney*. I'm of the era when a lot of PNW scene kids would make Sleater-Kinney their entire personality. They were never my cup of tea as a band, and to this day I'm not sure whether that's due to their music, or to my visceral reaction to the sort of indie snob who would stan them. Still, "Modern Girl" is a great song, building on the blasé cynicism of the Minuteman track before it but skewing it to the female perspective of the fans queued up for Luke to take their money. TV brings us closer to the world.

"Smoke and Mirrors," *The Magnetic Fields*. Whew. This scene, I looked at so many options, by the end of it I practically had an entire Luke/Rachel breakup playlist. The original song in this slot was The Auteurs' "Married To A Lazy Lover," which was too British, too niche, and just… too mean. (It's a great song, though, and its lyrics are the reason I settled on Luke and Rachel being married 20 years.) I wanted a song that Luke might have actually listened to on the regular, and honestly, he's not cool enough to be into the Auteurs. (I fought in the trenches during the Britpop Wars and I know things; this is one of them.) The breakup scene shifted a lot as I wrote it, growing in complexity, and by its end I realised I needed an elegy, not a diss track. Hence the Magnetic Fields. Dithered with "I Need A New Heart" for a long time, but ultimately went with the melancholic simplicity of "Smoke and Mirrors." Special effects…

"Monkey Box," *Only Child Tyrant & Amon Tobin*. This is a song to get fucked up in the middle of nowhere to. I like a lot of instrumental music that falls on the harder edge of synthwave and horrortron but I also like twangy guitar and this song: has both.

"Ramalama (Bang Bang)," *Róisín Murphy*. A pounding headache, a terrifying situation weighty with implicit violence, and a girl who wants to give you her heart (terms and conditions apply). If you can be good, you'll live forever… True fact: though I knew

Murphy's work (and even appeared in one of her music videos), it was my daughter who introduced me to this song.

"Guesthouse," David Wax Museum. I love this profoundly dippy summer-evening song. I can see this as Luke's theme tune after Rachel kicks him out of the house, as he calls up various friends to ask if he can stay for a while. There's also more than a little sadness to it amidst all the bouncy jangliness: what if I'd not decided to be such a free spirit? Maybe I could have my own pool house. Maybe that would have made me happier.

"Mister Impossible," Phantogram. I like Phantogram a lot. This song especially, with its vocoder lyrics and fuzzy synths that are an aural callback to "Monkey Box," feels like an act of seduction by someone you know is way more trouble than he's worth. Look, here is Luke Indiana. See how he smiles at you, how his eyes follow you, like an asp in a basket.

"Happy Accidents," Saint Motel. This song's from 2016, Spotify tells me. I assumed it was a lot older, from the era of scintillating indie-pop love songs like Voxtrot's "The Start of Something" or Postal Service's "Such Great Heights." It's such a nice track, pure and happy, for Lily's big moment. You love me, but you don't know it yet, everything is just an accident… well, like Lee Marvin says in *Point Blank:* most accidents happen within three miles of home.

"Grounds for Divorce," Elbow. *The Seldom-Seen Kid* is another album full of bangers. Did it ever make a mark in America? It was inescapable in the UK for a while, and gave Richard Hawley (who guested on a track) a bit of a second coming, which he richly deserved. This — the punch — was probably the hardest scene in the book to soundtrack. I didn't crack it until I was walking along the Hudson one day and this song came back to me out of nowhere, and it was perfect. I've been working on a cocktail called Grounds for Divorce… BAM.

"Nocturnal Me," Echo & The Bunnymen. Sigh, yes, I know, another British band/track that Luke probably never would have heard. But in my defense, I was reminded of the song's existence by Brianna Ashby, a genuine American, with whom I spent a wonderful afternoon creating a pretty spectacular autumn-themed music playlist. (We were both procrastinating.) "Nocturnal Me" was one of her many excellent picks, a masochism tango perfect for Lily and Luke as they try to outguess each other.

"Time," David Bowie. Mike Garson's vicious, stalking piano line; the drama; the histrionics of a last desperate understanding: you are not a victim.

"The Sun Always Shines On TV," a-ha. The story, from its earliest days, was always meant to end like this: darkness, devastation, and a-ha's fragile, crystalline paean to the perfect world of television playing over the top of it all.

I hope you enjoyed the show.

– AdeC, New York City, 2023

PARASOCIAL

SPOTIFY PLAYLIST

IMAGE COMICS, INC. • **Robert Kirkman:** Chief Operating Officer • **Erik Larsen:** Chief Financial Officer • **Todd McFarlane:** President • **Marc Silvestri:** Chief Executive Officer • **Jim Valentino:** Vice President • **Eric Stephenson:** Publisher / Chief Creative Officer • **Nicole Lapalme:** Vice President of Finance • **Leanna Caunter:** Accounting Analyst • **Sue Korpela:** Accounting & HR Manager • **Matt Parkinson:** Vice President of Sales & Publishing Planning • **Lorelei Bunjes:** Vice President of Digital Strategy • **Dirk Wood:** Vice President of International Sales & Licensing • **Ryan Brewer:** International Sales & Licensing Manager • **Alex Cox:** Director of Direct Market Sales • **Chloe Ramos:** Book Market & Library Sales Manager • **Emilio Bautista:** Digital Sales Coordinator • **Jon Schlaffman:** Specialty Sales Coordinator • **Kat Salazar:** Vice President of PR & Marketing • **Deanna Phelps:** Marketing Design Manager • **Drew Fitzgerald:** Marketing Content Associate • **Heather Doornink:** Vice President of Production • **Drew Gill:** Art Director • **Hilary DiLoreto:** Print Manager • **Tricia Ramos:** Traffic Manager • **Melissa Gifford:** Content Manager • **Erika Schnatz:** Senior Production Artist • **Wesley Griffith:** Production Artist • **Rich Fowlks:** Production Artist • **IMAGECOMICS.COM**

For international rights, contact: foreignlicensing@imagecomics.com. ISBN: 978-1-5343-9937-2.

♥ @AceofDragons1 liked this ♥ @_drive0031 liked this ♥ @andrewthecarl liked this ♥ @anthony_delcol liked this ♥
liked this ♥ @TheOtherMarioC liked this ♥ @asherqjackson liked this ♥ @PhilUebbing liked this ♥ @JSchlaffma
@blackmetronome liked this ♥ @dickens432 liked this ♥ @CharCrerar liked this ♥ @CMWare1974 liked this ♥ @s
@KearnsEEE liked this ♥ @dastanfield liked this ♥ @MalibuDarby87 liked this ♥ @Wow_no_inv liked this ♥ @ArtS
@MorgansBrain liked this ♥ @HexxedWriter liked this ♥ RedMagicite liked this ♥ @c_090899 liked this ♥ @jeremyh
this ♥ @BloodyHorrorBri liked this ♥ @TheSailorGoon liked this ♥ @astronautgo liked this ♥ @cor_rinal liked this
this ♥ @byjenrodriguez liked this ♥ @TaylorzPower liked this ♥ @bambi_xcx liked this ♥ @RafaB_1 liked this ♥ @w
♥ @TKandTV liked this ♥ @bkguilfoy liked this ♥ @andrewduncan33 liked this ♥ @henchman21 liked this ♥ @Neu
♥ @zahavpz liked this ♥ @alexdecampi liked this ♥ @EricaFails liked this ♥ @DJ_BFspinner liked this ♥ @sun
@sherazkhanniani liked this ♥ @CaptainJLS liked this ♥ @TimBledsoe liked this ♥ @StegoSarahs liked this ♥ @ma
@perpetua liked this ♥ @emset03 liked this ♥ @TealProductions liked this ♥ @J2571 liked this ♥ @BMoucherat likec
liked this ♥ @GarthMcMurray liked this ♥ @jlaasko liked this ♥ @AmonduulUS liked this ♥ @James_Dowling liked this
liked this ♥ @lambarch liked this ♥ @falchionM liked this ♥ @abracadocious liked this ♥ @AdmiralDowney liked t
@SmhoakMosheein liked this ♥ @TabithaRasa liked this ♥ @RichardDBK liked this ♥ @allisonhenle liked this ♥ @Ac
liked this ♥ @Clarknova1 liked this ♥ @nicole_rifkin liked this ♥ @rtpout liked this ♥ @LukeWHendersonM liked this
this ♥ @zombieesc6 liked this ♥ @beckkubrick liked this ♥ @littledeercmx liked this ♥ @pig_feathers00 liked this
liked this ♥ @Roafus liked this ♥ @NathKmf liked this ♥ @Timbobsquare liked this ♥ @Robert_Hack liked this ♥ @
this ♥ @hole_4_threepio liked this ♥ @AlmostEricSite liked this ♥ @IanEBizz liked this ♥ @diazart liked this ♥ @S
@justpiekthx liked this ♥ @jasonwhite_ish liked this ♥ @jraineyesq liked this ♥ @davevsheffer liked this ♥ @Gabriellel
liked this ♥ @jkmoran liked this ♥ @BCNerdhole liked this ♥ @johnpaulmaler liked this ♥ @kingzosotai liked this
♥ greatscottdunn liked this ♥ @juaneferreyra liked this ♥ @SienaComics liked this ♥ @Fanboat liked this ♥ @the_g
@JoshuaBegley1 liked this ♥ @with2ells liked this ♥ @roszelcopter liked this ♥ @CarpElgin liked this ♥ @John13 li
liked this ♥ @MalachaiWard liked this ♥ @simp_phoney liked this ♥ @smashmalloow liked this ♥ @ryan_howe lik
@GSecchiaroli77 liked this ♥ @neckdeg liked this ♥ @Buck3teer liked this ♥ @CarlssonPete liked this ♥ @Dougla
this ♥ @CameronPiper1 liked this ♥ @gizmoguai liked this ♥ @mathis090 liked this ♥ @ThePeej3RD liked this
@FirstIssueClub liked this ♥ @DennisChars liked this ♥ @ljoehobbs liked this ♥ @OOUCH_charlie liked this ♥ @867
this ♥ @AdamBlackhat liked this ♥ @JacieStardust liked this ♥ @penguinscribble liked this ♥ @davevanwalton like
this ♥ @GoFrankGo liked this ♥ @DaintyRhino liked this ♥ @ArcaneComics liked this ♥ @RyanJLee7 liked this ♥
this ♥ @Ranahanahanahan liked this ♥ @dako243 liked this ♥ @CloakroomComics liked this ♥ @LouSchu liked this
this ♥ @GabePaez08 liked this ♥ @HitlerPuncher liked this ♥ @YtheLastChris liked this ♥ @infinite1der liked this ♥
liked this ♥ @Unclebo77 liked this ♥ @Nyapolitan liked this ♥ @hello_camilo liked this ♥ @cierrosem liked this ♥ @c
this ♥ @NicoleLuckless liked this ♥ @TheTayPorter liked this ♥ @ham_fist liked this ♥ @JamieJSomething liked this
@Jerkowitz liked this ♥ @homeybeef liked this ♥ @TCBiaf liked this ♥ @mikepankowski liked this ♥ @Buzz_Lightw
@EffinBirds liked this ♥ @asimov_fangirl liked this ♥ @JoeStranger2113 liked this ♥ @Andrew_JamesUK liked this ♥
liked this ♥ @christofbogacs liked this ♥ @tropicalsteve liked this ♥ @iWillBattle liked this ♥ @bookcasequeen96 likec
liked this ♥ @MirageSystem78 liked this ♥ @Izandra liked this ♥ @PJShapiro liked this ♥ @conleydraws liked this ♥
♥ @Chirurgic liked this ♥ ryanqnorth liked this ♥ @HonestJon311 liked this ♥ @geklooster liked this ♥ @Beezleb
@BurtnessExpress liked this ♥ @ColleenFrakes liked this ♥ @sorryforcusses liked this ♥ @jdkrach liked this ♥ @Ary
♥ @kongtomorrow liked this ♥ @DocEon liked this ♥ @93418 liked this ♥ @glennewman liked this ♥ @martawess
@queefneyspearz liked this ♥ @sergiocalvet liked this ♥ @krispyfresh liked this ♥ @mentaldwarf liked this ♥ @Sam
♥ @IfSheBeWorthy liked this ♥ @JABSEN liked this ♥ @dinottosaur liked this ♥ @peterjkrause liked this ♥ @patrick
@xocleinad liked this ♥ @Kevin_Church liked this ♥ @LeahGolubchick liked this ♥ @AaronLosty liked this ♥ @Por
@leerinsocial liked this ♥ @YesThatKristian liked this ♥ @meckett liked this ♥ @charlie_en liked this ♥ @teaberryb
@fastchoker liked this ♥ @thepmann liked this ♥ @Starshapedgummy liked this ♥ @Leerhian2 liked this ♥ @latin4
this ♥ @Thebenweldon liked this ♥ @halciieon liked this ♥ @outriderc liked this ♥ @TrottersTens liked this ♥ @
@alwayscoffee liked this ♥ @DrNerdLove liked this ♥ @eighteentales liked this ♥ @qlcrises liked this ♥ @donnadan
♥ @malcolmmrjmcleod liked this ♥ @JillyPanilly liked this ♥ @RafaelRandi liked this ♥ @princehotbod69 liked this
@LordRetail liked this ♥ @lewstringer liked this ♥ @dosmas liked this ♥ @aaronivvy liked this ♥ @breadhiking liked
this ♥ @jp_jordan liked this ♥ @bigbrotherchan liked this ♥ @berntkat liked this ♥ @Benkeisermusic liked this ♥ @A
liked this ♥ @sir_flancelot liked this ♥ @krneely liked this ♥ @JayMo31415 liked this ♥ @gmcalpin liked this ♥ @w
liked this ♥ @IainNC72 liked this ♥ @SheedyGavin liked this ♥ @Zombustudio liked this ♥ @MikeyEddy liked this
this ♥ @DeanMcknight liked this ♥ @Grrrace liked this ♥ @insidejorb liked this ♥ @GoldKarmaDragon liked this ♥
♥ Amadeus_CV liked this ♥ @misskittyf liked this ♥ @Leask liked this ♥ @stareagle liked this ♥ @_Scyphozoa liked t
liked this ♥ @illustratoram7 liked this ♥ @mermaid_seph liked this ♥ @bigdoggles liked this ♥ @Xtine_Makepeace li
this ♥ @Kyven liked this ♥ @BenneCMO liked this ♥ @magencubed liked this ♥ @seaglasscritter liked this ♥ @ryar
@loudgayamerica liked this ♥ @turnintoabat liked this ♥ @chace_verity liked this ♥ @leekassen liked this ♥ @ONei
@jambonathanH liked this ♥ @jjakala liked this ♥ @millerunc liked this ♥ @LadyGreentea liked this ♥ @scmartel like
@_SassMenagerie liked this ♥ @denhoff25 liked this ♥ @John_Hartford liked this ♥ @NatalieEveComix liked this ♥
liked this ♥ @Heartsib liked this ♥ @KevinMcClean10 liked this ♥ @Hughes87n liked this ♥ @bobbytries liked this
liked this ♥ @drew_moss liked this ♥ @crashwong liked this ♥ @ComicBookHerald liked this ♥ @madaecnerwal liked t
liked this ♥ @MOfHealy liked this ♥ @ourladyofcoffee liked this ♥ @deezoid liked this ♥ @oddballuk liked this ♥
this ♥ @FishingWithJohn liked this ♥ @kennykeil liked this ♥ @Chojinlocke liked this ♥ @FizzVsTheWorld liked this
this ♥ @_maxbc liked this ♥ @davebrarian liked this ♥ @little_corvus liked this ♥ @jessnevins liked this ♥ @atoms
@andykhouri liked this ♥ @DrSkeletoid liked this ♥ @TEANTACLES liked this ♥ @AmosBurtonRisen liked this ♥ @th
♥ @midnight_peanut liked this ♥ @WaxBreath liked this ♥ @DigitalMeowMix liked this ♥ @JotredisHonored liked this
liked this ♥ @GriffinTalks liked this ♥ @Killian_Idiot liked this ♥ @deducinglyssy liked this ♥ @lorgchungo liked this
liked this ♥ @Kimota1977 liked this ♥ @jrome58 liked this ♥ @Fallentaco liked this ♥ @richjohnston liked this ♥ @
this ♥ @escapepodcomics liked this ♥ @tonyparkerart1 liked this ♥ @daijidoodles liked this ♥ @davedrawsgood
@monomizerart liked this ♥ @baphomouse liked this ♥ @the_rtg liked this ♥ @paolo.basurto liked this ♥ @gorbach
this ♥ @zcontrol_ liked this ♥ @movealongcoffee liked this ♥ @lizah_scienceart liked this ♥ @wild7studios liked th
liked this ♥ @meghan_harker liked this ♥ @downtown_kb liked this ♥ @book.nerd.noel liked this ♥ @scarlettburn l
@rsykes2000 liked this ♥ @eden161821 liked this ♥ @jon.schlaffman liked this ♥ @lelisor_dracusor liked this ♥ @j
liked this ♥ @emryse liked this ♥ @maxwellord liked this ♥ @myleswillsaveus liked this ♥ @ianisalways liked t
@angelprietomiguel liked this ♥ @vegrecorder liked this ♥ @lisaflanaganvoice liked this ♥ @captaindeathray liked this
liked this ♥ @ali_ross90 liked this ♥ @jlavochkin liked this ♥ @melamadorvaz liked this ♥ @fkalovehound liked this
♥ @brigidkeely liked this ♥ @thatdamnokie liked this ♥ @jelenedra liked this ♥ @rain7evergreens liked this ♥ @am
@seriouslydex liked this ♥ @naryathered liked this ♥ @auntiesuze liked this ♥ @theonewhoisntchosen liked this ♥ @
liked this ♥ @theresa-who liked this ♥ @bobbyskizza liked this ♥ @manicpixigirl liked this ♥ @thenthdimension liked t